Also by John A. Miller

Tropical Heat

Cutdown

Causes of Action

Jackson Street and Other Soldier Stories

COYOTE MOON

John A. Miller

A TOM DOHERTY ASSOCIATES BOOK

NEW YORK

COYOTE MOON

Book design by Michael Collica

A Forge Book
Published by Tom Doherty Associates, LLC
175 Fifth Avenue
New York, NY 10010

www.tor.com

Forge® is a registered trademark of Tom Doherty Associates, LLC.

Library of Congress Cataloging-in-Publication Data

Miller, John A.
    Coyote moon / John A. Miller.—1st ed.
        p.   cm.
    "A Forge book"—T.p. verso.
    ISBN 0-765-30627-1
    1. Oakland Athletics (Baseball team)—Fiction.   2. Heisenberg uncertainty
principle—Fiction.   3. Eccentrics and eccentricities—Fiction.   4. Needles
(Calif.)—Fiction.   5. Baseball players—Fiction.   6. Quantum theory—Fiction.
7. Trailer camps—Fiction.   8. Reincarnation—Fiction.   I. Title.

PS3563.I4132C69   2003
813'.54—dc21
                                                                      2003046850

First Edition: November 2003

Printed in the United States of America

0   9   8   7   6   5   4   3   2   1

For the Old Man—always a Soldier in my heart

ACKNOWLEDGMENTS

Although the writing of a novel would appear to be a uniquely solitary endeavor, in fact, it seldom is. This particular novel owes much to Harvey Klinger, literary agent nonpareil, and Bob Gleason, literary raconteur and executive editor at Tor/Forge.

ONE

★ ★ ★

Needles, California

Benny Rhodes loved his own bald head more than anything
else in the world he could think of. He loved to run his
hands over it, loved seeing its reflection in the shiny aluminum walls of his weary and somewhat out-at-elbow mobile home. It was the first thing he looked at in the morning
and last thing he considered at night. It, like the rest of him,
was tanned to a golden brown and, like the phrenologists of
old, he considered it the very mirror of his soul. He was
frankly and simply delighted with it. Some thought him eccentric.

"How about this new kid with the A's everybody's talking
about?" Benny's neighbor Al Bartholomeo asked.

Benny looked up from the two-day-old newspaper he was
reading. He was seated in a homemade Adirondack chair
under the aluminum awning that stretched across the front
of his rented house trailer. The awning, like the trailer to
which it was attached, had long since thrown in the towel
in its ill-fated struggle against the elements of the Mojave
Desert. Whatever paint or decals it had once proudly borne
were now no more than a vague memory, removed pigment
by pigment by sand, wind, and sun. It was nine-thirty in the
morning on the second day of April and the big Coors thermometer screwed onto the side of the trailer read 93 degrees

Fahrenheit. Benny wore a faded pair of cutoff blue jeans, huarache sandals, and nothing else. He shook his head in response to his neighbor's question.

"Every spring it's the same thing. I've seen a hundred just like this kid break hearts all over New England when the Red Sox tried to rush them into the lineup." Benny shook his head again, appalled at the very thought. "Wait'll June or July and if he's still on the roster, much less playing every day, well, that'll be something to talk about, believe me."

Benny knew whereof he spoke. For his entire life he had been a Red Sox fan and now, at the age of sixty-three, he knew in his heart of hearts that he would be long dead before they won a World Championship.

The neighbor, Al Bartholomeo, sat down next to Benny and waved a copy of the *Sporting News*. "This kid's different. He's batting almost .450 and holding base runners at first base, for God's sake." Al had to pause for a second to wipe the spittle from his lips. In his eagerness to share the news of the rookie they were calling the Soldier with Benny, he had rushed over without putting his teeth in and so tended to dribble a little when he spoke too quickly. "They say there's never been anyone like him."

Benny laughed. "Where's he from?"

"Some small town in North Carolina. The paper says he never played Organized Ball as a kid. Took it up in the army, if you can believe that."

"I can't." Like all New Englanders Benny, despite his many years of education and extraordinarily high IQ, harbored a deep-seated suspicion that anyone from the South was, by definition, a congenital liar and probable natural-born deviate. He wasn't necessarily proud of this belief, but neither could he entirely shake it. "If Oakland is counting on a rookie behind the plate you can be sure that every other team in the American League, particularly the Western division, is celebrating even as we speak."

A sudden zephyr from out of the desert rattled the sagging

awning and reminded Benny of how far from Boston he had
come in a very short time. He unconsciously ran a hand
over his slick brown head and smiled. Baldness was a relatively new phenomenon with Benny. Although sixty-three
years old he had, until just weeks earlier, sported a luxuri-
antly full head of hair. Snowy white hair, to be sure, but
nonetheless thick, and rich, and fine to look at, just what
one would expect to see adorning the head of a distinguished
professor at the Massachusetts Institute of Technology. Bernard Archibald Rhodes, Ph.D., LL.M., Litt.D., head of the
physics department, president of the faculty senate, husband,
father, mathematician, and scientist. Dr. Rhodes had testified
before committees of the United States Congress and had
dined on two separate occasions at the White House. *If they
could see me now,* he thought.

Death, of course, had changed everything. It wonderfully
focuses the mind, Dr. Rhodes realized, to watch a perfectly
delightful young man sicken and die within the space of
three months. Arthur Hodges, the decedent in question, was
just a few weeks short of his fortieth birthday when he
breathed his last in a hospice just off the MIT campus. Although separated in age by more than twenty years, Arthur
Hodges and Bernard Archibald Rhodes had been close intellectual companions who had spent countless afternoons
and evenings discussing questions of time and space, searching always for the arcane clues that might lead to the uni-
fication of Einstein's general theory of relativity with the
theory of quantum mechanics. Holder of an endowed chair
in mathematics at MIT, Arthur Hodges was frequently spoken of as the next logical candidate for the position of Lu-
casian Professor of Mathematics at Cambridge University, a
chair once held by Sir Isaac Newton himself. The only thing
the Drs. Rhodes and Hodges disagreed on was baseball. Bernard Archibald Rhodes loved it and Arthur Hodges did not,
for all intents and purposes, know it existed. Rhodes had
owned two season tickets to Fenway Park for the entire time

Arthur Hodges had been at MIT, first as Rhodes's student and then as a colleague and friend, and not once, not a single time, had he been able to lure Hodges to a game. Arthur Hodges was a creature of intellect, so completely so that he died a stone virgin and, what's more, had he thought about it, which of course he had not, he would not have considered for an instant that he had missed anything.

The death of Arthur Hodges was something of an epiphany for Bernard Archibald Rhodes. Shortly after the memorial ceremony (Hodges's remains were cremated and his ashes spread over the James River) Professor Rhodes drove into Boston and consulted an attorney. The morning following said consultation he smiled at his wife across the breakfast table and handed her a large manila envelope.

"What's this?" she asked, none too pleasantly. The daughter of a wealthy New England industrialist, she had never considered herself a morning person.

"That, my dear, is a legal document giving you ownership of all of our remaining joint assets, together with a quitclaim whereby I renounce any interest in the estate you inherited some years ago from your father. I say 'remaining joint assets' because yesterday I took the liberty of withdrawing the sum of six hundred thousand dollars from one of our money market funds, an amount which, together with my several pension funds, should be more than sufficient to support me for the rest of my life." He reached across the table and patted his wife's hand. "What with the two houses and the various other family investment funds I estimate that I'm leaving you with an estate well in excess of four million dollars."

"Leaving me?"

"I'm afraid so. At the memorial service for Art Hodges I realized that I could not for the life of me remember why on earth we got married forty years ago. I also realized that I'm tired of teaching and that the Red Sox are never, in my lifetime, going to win a World Series." He stood up from the table. "I've packed a few personal belongings. Everything else of mine you may either give to charity or have destroyed. Good-bye."

There was brief talk of a sanity hearing, but the parties advocating such a procedure were strongly advised against doing so by legal counsel and Dr. Rhodes left Boston, MIT, and his wife on a miserably cold and wet day in late November, bound for God only knew where.

Benny realized that Al had asked a question. "What's that?"

"I said, how about a cup of coffee?"

"Sure thing." Benny twisted in his chair so he could yell into the trailer's open door. "Hey, Becky, Al's here. Bring us out a cup of coffee, will you?"

Becky Morgan had just had her third abortion in eighteen months when she met Benny in the parking lot of a Super Saver drugstore on the outskirts of Norman, Oklahoma. Benny was slowly noodling his way across country, going nowhere in particular, and had stopped in Norman to visit an old colleague on the faculty of the University of Oklahoma. Becky was, at the age of thirty-one, a desperately unhappy albeit extraordinarily fecund elementary school teacher and three-time loser in love who had gotten to know the abortion clinic staff on a first name basis. She backed into Benny's car while leaving a parking space and the minor accident, on top of her already stretched thin nerves, had caused her to start crying. Benny calmed her down, bought her a nice lunch, and left the city of Norman that evening with a new friend and traveling companion.

"I'd say you're on a treadmill," Benny observed after hearing her story over lunch. He told her about the recent death of his friend Arthur Hodges and how it had opened a door in his life. "My advice is to do what I did: cut your losses and start over somewhere else."

Becky saw the wisdom of what Benny was saying and, although it wasn't exactly what he had had in mind, she asked if she could tag along with him. He thought about it for several seconds and concluded that he liked the idea. Some weeks after leaving Oklahoma they crossed the once mighty Colorado River at Needles, California, and paused for a time to ponder the mystery that was the Mojave Desert.

The kid at the radiator shop in downtown Needles where Benny had his engine's thermostat replaced was impressed to learn that they weren't on their way to any place in particular.

"Bitchin'," was all he said, but Becky knew that he would tell his friends about the old man (to the kid and his friends anyone over the age of forty was old) and the young woman with nothing but time on their hands. Thinking about it pleased her to no end.

Where you heading? the kid had asked when the job was done, wiping his hands on a green rag. He was a good-looking young man, eighteen or nineteen, all gonads and white teeth. *Los Angeles?*

Benny had smiled and said, *No, we're just on the road.*

The kid's eyebrows rose a fraction of an inch and he couldn't help looking at Becky and smiling. *Bitchin'.*

Benny decided he wanted to dip his feet in the Colorado River and the kid directed them to a dirt road north of town. Within sight of the river they came upon a weather-beaten, out-at-elbow trailer park and encountered an encampment of ancient Germans, their gleaming Airstream trailers circled like Conestoga wagons.

"I can see that you are an educated man," one of them said to Benny. "And that you are lost."

Benny smiled and nodded. "Aren't we all?"

"You are welcome to stay *und* have dinner *mit uns,*" the old German invited. A gibbous moon began to rise in the eastern sky and then seemed to stop, hunkering down over the *laagered* Airstreams and the muddy water of the Colorado River just beyond. "We," the old man swept his arm in an arc that encompassed his entire group, "believe that this place, this Needles, is a special place in the universe, *ja*?"

"How do you mean 'special'?" Benny asked.

"We believe that something is going to happen here. What will happen or when it will happen we do not yet know." The old German looked up at the moon and smiled. "Perhaps it is only that we will all die here in this place of extraordinary beauty."

They ate at three large picnic tables placed together to form a triangle. Leathery-skinned old women brought the food out of the Airstreams in large, steaming crocks. The two guests were given a place of honor next to the leader of the encampment, the man who had invited them to stay and eat. After dinner the Milky Way could be clearly seen pulsating in the relatively unpolluted night sky of the desert. Wrapped in a light cotton blanket Benny and Becky made love that night on top of one of the picnic tables. Before falling asleep Benny watched a scorpion attack and devour a large beetle that had blundered into its path. When he told the group the next morning at breakfast what he had seen they all nodded silently, as if one of their own had fallen during the night. *"Gut is gut und besser ist besser,"* one of them murmured enigmatically.

"This is the place," Benny said.

"Brigham Young," Becky responded.

"Brigham Young?"

"Although the story may be apocryphal, Brigham Young supposedly said, *This is the place,* when first he saw the Great Salt Lake."

"Only a fool would live in this miserable place that didn't have to," the proprietress of the trailer park informed them when Benny expressed just such an interest. "I don't know what these crazy goddamned Germans are thinking of," she waved an arm in the general direction of the polished Airstreams, "but their money's good and they mind their own business." A mule of a woman, Ruth Pierpont had run the marina and trailer park by herself since her husband died in 1978 and probably hadn't made a thousand dollars in net profit the entire time. She feared neither man nor beast and smoked a pack of Camels a day. "They've been here about three months now, waiting for the Apocalypse, or some such nonsense." She grunted derisively. "Assuming it doesn't materialize, I fully expect that come the end of July they'll all be dead or gone. Believe me when I tell you that neither you nor they know what heat is until you've spent a summer in the Mojave."

"I suspect that's the truth, but, to be honest, something here attracts me," Benny told her, running a hand through his hair.

Ruth nodded and lit a Camel with her Zippo, expertly clicking it shut and tucking it back into her overalls. "I probably shouldn't call you a fool since I'm still here myself, but I'll be damned if I know why. Morgan, my late husband, was too shiftless to work and too lazy to steal, so here I am. Besides, where the hell would I go?" She pointed with her cigarette toward an obviously vacant trailer. "Old man Robertson died in there two months ago and the county has taken it for back taxes. I'm guessing the county tax assessor would be tickled to death to deed it over to anyone willing to bring the taxes current." She paused and rather indelicately scratched her stomach. "The pad it's sitting on rents for a hundred dollars a month, not counting utilities."

"What did he die of?" Becky asked.

"Jesus Christ, the heat, what'd you think?" Ruth laughed, an odd, braying sound. "That and a good case of the DTs." The smile left her face. "Okay, down to business. I own this place lock, stock, and barrel, and I don't generally rent to transients or young people—it's been my experience that they're almost always more trouble than they're worth. I like the looks of you two, so you're welcome as long as you don't annoy me, your relatively few neighbors, or Jericho."

"Jericho?"

Ruth pointed to a large brown cat lounging in the shade of her trailer's patio awning. "Jericho."

Benny and Becky moved in the next day. One month later, on the first day of March, Benny, in an inspired moment, had Becky shave his head. The next day, the second day of March, she informed Benny that she was with child.

"I just put a fresh pot on," Becky called out of the trailer in response to Benny's call for a cup of coffee for their neighbor Al. Her voice was the happy, cheerful voice of a woman in love. "I'll bring it out as soon as it's ready."

Al put down his copy of the *Sporting News* with a sigh of envy. A postal clerk from the Bronx who had recently taken early retirement, he was the same age as Benny. His wife, Margaret, was a short, ill-tempered woman with porcine eyes and a quick New York tongue. He couldn't imagine asking her to get *him* a cup of coffee, much less a cup for a friend who had stopped by for a visit.

Benny gave him a sidelong glance and smiled. "Becky and I are giving a little get-together tonight," he said. "We'd like you and the ball-and-chain," as he referred to Al's missus, "to join us for a celebration."

"What are you celebrating?"

"Well, believe it or not, Becky's gravid."

"She's what?"

"She's pregnant. *Gravid* is a reproductive term normally reserved for the insect kingdom, but I happen to like the way it sounds. I find it far more euphonious than *pregnant*," Benny explained, laughing at Al's expression of astonishment. "I know it's hard to believe, but by God there's juice left in the old bull yet." Before he could say anything further Becky came out of the trailer with a pot of coffee and a plate of cinnamon toast. "Put that coffee down," Benny ordered good-naturedly, "and let Al feel your stomach."

Becky laughed. "Hush, you old fool; you're embarrassing him."

Indeed, Al looked thunderstruck.

"Besides," she continued, "I'm not even three months gone, so there's nothing to feel." She held up the plate she was carrying in her left hand. "Who wants cinnamon toast with their coffee?"

TWO

★ ✦ ★

Benny took to the Mojave Desert the way a pig takes to a cool mud puddle on a hot day: with great joy and exuberance. Although still only early spring, if the Coors thermometer outside the trailer wasn't registering at least in the low nineties when he and Becky rose on any given morning he was disappointed. Most days he took long hikes through the badlands of the Mojave, disappearing for anywhere from two hours to an entire day at a time. He took large quantities of water and a little food, and was literally astonished at the variety of things he saw as he learned to walk quietly among the dry washes, arroyos, honey mesquite, and Joshua trees.

"I saw a red-tailed hawk take a ground squirrel today," he told Becky one evening as they sat on the patio of their trailer, enjoying the warm evening, Benny with a gin-and-tonic, Becky with ice water. "It came down out of the sun," Benny swooped his right hand down onto the back of his left, "like this, and was airborne again before the squirrel even knew it was in danger. In the past three days I've seen hawks, owls, coyotes, and even two burros." He sighed and shook his head. "God alone knows where the burros came from, because they're certainly not native to the Mojave."

Becky smiled. Although she worried about his solo hikes she could see the obvious effect they were having on his physical and mental health. The incessant hiking, combined with the desiccating effect of the extreme low humidity, had quickly turned his body rock hard and nut-brown. They had made love before coming out onto the patio and she inhaled deeply, his taste still lingering sweetly on the back of her tongue. The sight of Benny moving about the trailer, his lean, muscular body glistening with perspiration, kept her in a blissful state of sexual stimulation. She looked up somewhat guiltily, realizing that Benny had said something.

"I'm sorry; my mind was wandering. What did you say?"

"I was just saying that I had the damnedest conversation with Gunter Schmidtbauer earlier this afternoon."

"How do you mean?"

Benny shrugged, somewhat at a loss for words. "It's hard to explain," he said, thinking back on the odd encounter.

"*Herr* Rhodes."

Benny was walking in from the desert when Gunter hailed him from one of the picnic tables in front of his Airstream.

"*Herr* Rhodes," Gunter said again when Benny got to the table and sat down.

"Please," Benny said as he removed his sombrero and wiped the perspiration from his head, "call me Benny."

"Thank you, Benny," Gunter acknowledged somewhat gravely, nodding his head. "And you may call me Gunter."

"Not exactly *Sagen wir du zu einander* but good enough for here and now," Benny added with a smile.

Gunter laughed delightedly. "I knew you were an educated man. Where did you learn German?"

"I'm afraid I'm not what you would call fluent by any means," Benny admitted. "What little I know I learned many years ago in college, back in the dark ages when all science majors were required to take a language course in what was then charmingly known as Scientific German."

Gunter handed Benny a bottle of beer. "Here," he said, "my latest batch. A wheat beer that goes very nicely with these radishes." He pointed to a bowl of bright red-and-white radishes on the table between them.

"Very good," Benny murmured, taking several sips. "You brew your own beer?"

Gunter nodded. "And Sophie," his wife, "grew these radishes." He took one and rather noisily bit into it. *"Lieber Gott,"* he said with another laugh, "she couldn't grow weeds back in Germany and here," he rolled his eyes in feigned astonishment, "in just three months she has her first crop of vegetables. Who can explain such a thing?"

Benny tilted his head back and drained half the beer in one long swallow. "Very nice flavor." He bit into one of the radishes and smiled as the pungent flavor spread across his tongue and up into his sinuses. "So, Gunter, what are you up to besides brewing beer and harvesting radishes?"

An enigmatic smile played across Gunter's face.

"Walk with me to the river," he said, gesturing toward the bank of the Colorado River a short distance away. "It is time we talked about what brought us, you and I, to this extraordinary place."

"Hitler himself pinned a medal to my tunic in 1942," Gunter told Benny as the two of them watched the Colorado River swirl past on its way to the Gulf of California. Gunter had shot down a prodigious number of aircraft, mostly Czech, Polish, and Russian, in the early stages of the war. "He was a madman, of course, and by 1942 we had already lost the war; we just hadn't realized it yet. In 1943 I was transferred back to France, and things became, how shall I put it, more difficult. The American and British pilots were much better trained, and their aircraft better designed and maintained. Still," Gunter shrugged and opened two more bottles of his home-brewed wheat beer, "we were young and so we did the best we could." He smiled and handed the beer and several radishes to Benny. "That is why politicians send young men off to war. They will almost always do the best they can. When the war goes badly older men—men in their thirties and forties—will begin to question things and will come home looking for answers, for someone to hold responsible, *ja*? On the other hand, young men are just happy to come home alive." He watched a large piece of driftwood caught in the river's swift current and unconsciously calculated the lead necessary to hit it with a bullet. "The last aircraft I shot down was an American bomber, a B-17. The war was by then clearly lost, but still we took off with whatever could be patched together well enough to fly to meet the bombers. I came up, so," he demonstrated, as fighter pilots of every nationality do, with two flattened hands, one held high, the other knifing up from below, "and triggered off a short burst. Almost immediately the bomber blew up in an enormous explosion. I remember being absolutely stunned, appalled, by the extraordinary violence of the explosion, the complete and instantaneous disintegration of the aircraft. Never had I seen anything like it and I had been shooting planes down for a number of years at that point. Ten young men gone in less than the blink of an eye. I landed my plane and never flew again." He shook his head. "It was a good thing the war was all but over or I would have been shot for refusing to fly. After the war I returned to my home in Oberkochen, in southern Germany, and worked for Carl Zeiss, as an optical engineer." He paused and looked carefully at Benny. "Do you remember me telling you, that first night when you slept on one of our picnic tables, why we," he waved his arm in the general direction of the Airstream *laager,* "the six of us, came to this place in the desert?"

"Actually, I do," Benny answered. "You mentioned that something drew you here. If memory serves, I believe you said that Needles was a special place, or words to that effect." He smiled, remembering Ruth Pierpoint's words. "Ruth thinks you've come here to wait for the Apocalypse."

Gunter chuckled. "Our landlady is an American original, *nicht wahr*? Sophie likes her a great deal, and so do I." He tapped the side of his head with his right forefinger. "And despite what she would have you believe, there is a very sharp mind lurking behind her rather rough exterior." He chuckled again, pleased in a perverse fashion at the fantastic notion of having traveled all the way to the Mojave Desert to await the end of the world. "No," he assured Benny, "we had no particular intention of staying here when we first arrived. Only after we had been here for a few days did I begin to sense that Needles was somehow special, that I, we, had been drawn here."

"Special in what way?"

Gunter shrugged. "I'm not sure. Not yet." He paused for a second. "Tell me, what brought you to Needles and the Mojave Desert?"

"Death."

Gunter nodded as if not in the least surprised by the terse answer. He did not respond, his silence an encouragement for Benny to continue.

"A young associate of mine, a brilliant physicist and mathematician, died last year. His death caused me to re-examine my own, um, priorities." Benny, never the most articulate of men, took a long swallow of beer. Suddenly, for the first time in many months, he recalled, with eidetic clarity, Arthur's passing.

Shortly before he died Arthur was moved from the university medical center to a small hospice in a quiet Boston neighborhood. He had a large private room with a comfortable bed and several easy chairs for visitors. For the first week he and Benny discussed matters of professional interest, articles in journals, papers given at prestigious meetings. The recent successful computing of the value of *pi* to over five billion decimal places in particular interested Arthur.

"Not long ago I would not have questioned the value of the time devoted to such a thing," he said to Benny. "But now, I must admit, I begin to wonder. So many numbers and still no pattern, still no order to be found."

"And none ever will be," Benny said, waving a hand dismissively. As a physicist he had never had much patience with the obsessive interest number theorists had always had with *pi*. As far as he was concerned it was simply a ratio, circumference to diameter, an irrational and transcendental number to which too many people, including an astonishing number of mathematicians, ascribed an almost mystical significance. "You are perfectly correct in questioning the waste of resources. Can you imagine the computing time wasted, logarithms churning into infinity?" He laughed. "What do the kids say these days? 'Get a life.' "

Arthur smiled. "You're a hard man."

"I'm a Red Sox fan," Benny said cynically. "I have to be hard." He brightened and pointed at Arthur. "And as soon as you get better I'm taking you to a ball game so you can see what you've missed all your life."

Arthur shook his head. "I think not." He sighed and looked out the window of his room. A gardener was mowing the lawn with an old-fashioned reel mower. "One of the nurses told me that the gardeners complain because the hospice won't let them use power mowers and trimmers." He looked back at Benny. "For the life of me I cannot begin to imagine what it would have been like to spend an afternoon watching other men throw a ball back and forth."

"You might have enjoyed it," Benny said lightly. "And you still could," he added, although both of them knew better. He had tried and failed numerous times to get Arthur to accompany him to a Red Sox game. "My guess is that you would have found it relaxing."

"I never felt the need to relax. My life has been entirely one of intellect, my joy derived from the contemplation of things not a hundred other men or women on the planet could even begin to understand or appreciate."

Arthur began to fail quickly after the first week in the

hospice. He stopped eating and, with his doctor's consent and Benny's approval, refused all medication other than painkillers. Benny had a cot moved into the room so he could spend twenty-four hours a day with his dying friend.

"I'm having the most vivid and affecting dreams," Arthur said. "I presumed it has to do with the cumulative effects of the morphine," he gestured weakly in the direction of the IV stand next to the bed, from which he received a continuous drip of the narcotic, "but they are nonetheless extraordinary."

"What kind of dreams?"

"Wonderful dreams," Arthur murmured. "Dreams I do not even have to be asleep to experience." He no longer had to close his eyes to see himself on a field of emerald green, precise geometric patterns delineated by thick, white lines. "Dreams so real that I can actually smell the grass."

Grass? "What do you see? Can you describe it for me?"

"An object curving through space." Arthur's voice fell off and he lay silently for some time, his eyes open, his breathing shallow and labored.

Benny pictured a grid representation of space, deformed by a planetary body's gravity, a photon of light curving as it passed through the gravitational deformity.

Suddenly Arthur's eyes focused again on Benny and he smiled. "It has spin," he said, "and I can see it as it approaches me."

Spin, Benny thought. *One of the fundamental characteristics of a subatomic particle.* He smiled, oddly comforted by the fact that even as he lay dying Arthur continued to struggle with the more abstruse concepts of particle physics. He realized that his friend was trying to say something else. "What?" he asked, bending down to place his ear closer to Arthur's mouth.

"I can see the seams as it spins, and I can actually predict the curvature based on perceived velocity."

Seams? Benny wondered. Before he could ask what his

friend meant by "seams" Arthur's hands twitched and his entire body suddenly jerked, but before Benny could become alarmed a smile spread slowly across his face.

"Can you see it?" Arthur asked, his voice barely audible. "Can you see the beauty of its flight?" Near death, he closed his eyes. His breathing stilled.

"Arthur?" Tears formed in Benny's eyes and began to course down his cheeks. "Arthur, I wish . . ." Benny sobbed, his mind so overwhelmed with grief he could not say the words he felt in his heart, "I wish . . ."

Arthur opened his eyes and, with some difficulty, focused a last time on Benny's face. "Patterns emerge," he whispered, joy evident in his barely audible words. "Patterns emerge."

Benny realized with a start that his mind had wandered and Gunter was waiting patiently. Suddenly embarrassed, he shrugged. "Anyway, here I, or rather, we," meaning Becky, "am." He smiled. "Or 'are.' " He smiled even more broadly. "But what are verbs among friends?"

"Just so. From what you tell me I think that from death you have found life. Doubly so, I think, given your . . ." Gunter paused, searching his English vocabulary for the proper word. He, as did everyone at the trailer park, knew that Benny and Becky weren't married but seldom had to face the issue directly with a descriptive noun or pronoun. He thought for a brief second and came at the problem from a slightly different angle. "Given the condition," meaning Becky's pregnancy, "of your young friend."

"I'd say that was a fair statement."

"So perhaps it is more accurate to say that *life* brought you to Needles rather than death, *ja*?"

"What are you getting at, Gunter?"

"I mentioned just a few minutes ago that I had not yet been able to understand why we have been brought here, to the desert. However, I believe that another piece of the puzzle, an important piece, has just been revealed to me."

Benny finished his beer and handed the empty bottle to Gunter. "And what piece might that be?"

Gunter took the bottle from Benny's hand. "You."

THREE

⋆ ⋆ ⋆

Scottsdale, Arizona

"What do you want?"

The young man stood quietly in front of the desk and nodded his head slightly as if the harsh, needlessly offensive manner in which the question was posed had been expected.

"My name is . . ." the young man paused for just the slightest of seconds, as if the name he was about to give was not quite familiar to him, "my name is Henry Spencer and Mr. Bishop told me to report to you."

Startled, Preacher Brown looked suspiciously at the young man standing almost at attention in front of him. Startled because the voice he heard was that of an older man, a much older man. The timbre, the maturity, the precise articulation, all bespoke a man with whom Preacher Brown was instinctively ill at ease. He narrowed his eyes and shifted his chew of tobacco from one cheek to the other.

"How old are you, boy?"

"Twenty-one."

Preacher didn't like the answer, didn't like it at all.

"You don't sound twenty-one, boy. You look it, but you don't sound it."

He wanted to pursue the issue but was stumped as to how to proceed. How, indeed, does one deal with a voice that clearly doesn't match a face, a body? It troubled him.

"Bishop tells me you're a catcher, is that right?"

"Yes, sir."

"And you just got out of the army?"

"Yes, sir."

"You're not much of a talker, are you?"

Henry shrugged. "What would you like to know?"

Preacher scooted aggressively forward to the edge of his chair. "I'd like to know why I never heard of you before; that's what I'd like to know. How is it that Bishop can tell me that you're . . ." Preacher stopped suddenly, not wanting to say that Willie Bishop, a retired career minor-league ballplayer who scouted for the organization in North and South Carolina, had told him that the young soldier he had seen catching for the 82d Airborne Division baseball team at Ft. Bragg, North Carolina, was the finest young prospect behind the plate he had ever seen. *The kid's ready for the bigs right this minute,* Willie had said, and Preacher knew that he was not a man given to superlatives when it came to discussing amateur talent. *I'll tell you what's the truth, Preacher,* Willie added. *You better give this kid a look before someone else does. Word's already starting to get around the Carolina League about him, and they ain't even seen him play yet.* Preacher decided to back up and come at it from another direction. "You ever play any Organized Ball?" he asked, his tone implying that he didn't believe the young man in front of him ever had. "I mean, other than *army* ball."

"No, sir."

"I didn't think so," Preacher snorted, "or I'd of heard of you." He shifted his gaze and spit in the general direction of the rusted metal trash can sitting next to his desk, missing badly. "Well, let me tell you something, soldier boy. There's a hell of a difference between the ball you been playing in the army and what you're going to see here in Scottsdale, you know what I'm saying?"

Henry assumed the question was rhetorical and remained silent.

"How long were you in the army?"

"Three years."

"Did you get all muscled up like that in the army?" And muscled up Henry was. Standing six feet, two inches tall in his stocking feet, he weighed slightly over 240 pounds, with a thirty-one inch waist. Even in pleated, loose-fitting cotton trousers the swell of his thighs was obvious, and although he wore a commodious long-sleeved linen shirt the muscularity underneath was more apparent than not. He was a big boy. Big. In response to Preacher's question he shrugged.

"I think I've always been stout," he said. "I worked out some in the army, but I guess my size just comes naturally to me."

"I don't like big, muscle-bound guys as ballplayers," Preacher informed the young man. "Never have. Say." A thought occurred to him and he narrowed his eyes in sudden suspicion. "You're not taking any of them drugs, are you? To make you big?"

Henry shook his head and did not smile. "No, sir."

"Well, you better not. I'd rather have a drunk on the team than someone taking pills," Preacher declared indignantly. He leaned over the trash can and spit out his chew, running a forefinger inside his cheek to clean out the last bits of tobacco. "I told Willie Bishop, *Mr.* Bishop to you, that I'd by-God give you a look-see, so I will. But I'll tell you right now you got no hope in hell of making the team. Or either the Triple-A team up in Tacoma. Maybe, just maybe, we can find you a spot in a rookie league somewheres, but don't count on it."

"Big sonofabitch, ain't he?"

Henry clearly heard the low-pitched voice behind him in the locker room, but he paid it no mind as he stood at the counter of the chicken wire enclosed equipment room. A well-groomed young man with short hair, pink cheeks, and white teeth dressed in a green-and-white knit golf shirt extended his hand across the counter.

"Hi, I'm Scotty Harrison, the assistant equipment manager. What can I do for you?"

"Henry Spencer. Mr. Brown told me to see you about getting organized with a practice uniform and whatnot."

"Well, let's see now." The young man picked up a clipboard with a computer printout and began running his finger down a list of names. "Spencer, Spencer, here we go." He looked up at Henry and smiled. "The B squad."

"B squad?"

"Yeah, we've got so many guys here at spring training that the team is divided into two squads, an A and a B. The A squad is comprised of the veterans from last year as well as a handful of marginal free agents with major-league experience who've been invited down for a tryout. Also a few minor leaguers, mostly from Triple-A Tacoma, who've been up and down or maybe led the West Coast League last season in ERA or batting average or ribbies. Like that."

"And the B squad?"

"Mostly nonroster invitees, career minor leaguers, and a sprinkling of high school and juco pheenoms."

"Juco?"

"Junior college. We've even got two industrial-league players here this spring. But hey, you never know, right? Better the B squad than punching a time clock somewhere. Where'd you play last year?"

"Army ball. Ft. Bragg."

"Oh, yeah? Pretty good ball?"

Henry shrugged and then shook his head. "Not really."

"Who'd you play?"

Another shrug. "Other army teams, navy teams, air force teams, community college teams, even some local high school teams. Anybody had a team, we'd play them."

"Win much?"

"Enough."

Scotty scratched his jaw. "You don't talk much, do you?" he said, unconsciously mimicking Preacher's words. "Well, whatever. As far as equipment goes, we supply everything except gloves and spikes. If you need shoes, the guys that have contracts with Nike and the other manufacturers get six or eight pair at a time. Find someone with the same shoe size and they'll generally sell you a pair of freebies." He leaned in over the counter toward Henry and lowered his voice. "The cheap fucks make millions and would have a hemorrhage if someone suggested they actually give a pair of freebies to a nonroster guy up for a tryout." He shook his head. "Welcome to the bigs."

"I've got everything I need."

"Good. The B squad will be working out at Simmons Field, about two miles from here. There's no clubhouse there, so you'll have to change at your motel. Which reminds me, if you haven't got a place to stay yet, most of the nonroster guys are putting up at a Motel 6 across the street from Simmons Field. I can probably get you partnered up with someone if you like. You know, help keep the expenses down."

"Thanks, but I'm all set."

"Well, if you don't mind my asking, where are you staying? Uh, sometimes Preacher or someone else on the staff will ask, you know?"

"Across town."

"Come again?" Scotty asked, confused.

"I'm staying across town," Henry responded. He put a big hand on the counter. "Do I pick up my stuff here or over at Simmons Field in the morning?"

"Who's Mr. America?"

Warren Mercer was a tall, thin sportswriter with wispy straw-colored hair and a red face. He was sixty years old and had been covering spring training camps for almost forty

34

years. His affectations included seersucker suits and straw hats, and he held firm to the belief that Judge Kenesaw Mountain Landis had single-handedly saved baseball. Warren had seen Henry Spencer talking to young Scotty Harrison and had immediately walked over to the equipment enclosure as Henry left the locker room.

"Name's Henry Spencer." Scotty, like almost everyone connected with the organization below the rank of general manager, absolutely loathed Warren Mercer. "He's a nonroster player."

"I *know* he's nonroster." Warren sighed. "Who is he? Where's he from? Who invited him for a tryout?"

"You'll have to ask Preacher or one of the other coaches," Scotty said, pleased to be able to give the impression that he actually knew something when in fact, of course, he did not. "I just handle the equipment."

"Understandably," Warren said *sotto voce* as he turned away, but loudly enough for Scotty to hear. He walked into Preacher Brown's office. "What's the story on Henry Spencer?"

Preacher was just lighting a cigarette. "Who?"

"The big . . ."

"Yeah, yeah," Preacher exclaimed, suddenly remembering the name, "I know who you mean." He took a drag on his cigarette, smacking his lips loudly. "There ain't no story. Willie Bishop saw him playing army ball down south and wanted me to take a look at him."

"You and Willie go back a long ways together. If Willie likes the way this kid looks . . ." Warren let his voice trail off.

"I don't care how good he looked playing for some jitney army team; he ain't never played no Organized Ball."

Warren nodded. Organized Ball. Mantra-like, the expression *Organized Ball* was repeated *ad nauseum* from Little League through high school, American Legion ball through the minors and on up to the Show, the term that separated *real* baseball from a kid's game played on sandlots and in the street. If you didn't play Organized Ball it didn't matter how good you were; you weren't a ballplayer.

"He's big, though," Warren observed.

"Yeah?" Preacher reached down and grabbed himself by the crotch. "So's my dick, but that don't mean it can hit a major-league slider."

Both men laughed.

"So what's the drill with the kid?" Warren persisted. He didn't know why he cared; there just seemed to be something more about Henry than met the eye. Maybe the way he walked, maybe just the way he stood at the counter when he was talking with Scotty. Goddamn it, he *looked* like a ballplayer.

"Couple of days with the B squad so I can tell Willie I gave the kid a look-see and then . . . " Preacher gestured with his thumb over his shoulder. "Sayo-fucking-nara." He smacked his lips again, the very picture of a ridiculous-looking old man sitting at a battered wooden desk in his underwear. "The last thing he'll hear in the major leagues will be 'don't let the doorknob hit you on the ass on the way out, kid.' "

"What if he's better than you think? What if Willie's right about him?"

"He won't be. He's not." Preacher looked up and squinted at the sportswriter. He had known Warren Mercer for many years and, at least as much as a ballplayer or manager *could* like a writer, he liked Warren. Or at least he didn't actively dislike him as he did most journalists. Flies, as they were known around the clubhouse, an appellation most hated. "Why the interest in a kid that's never even played Organized Ball? Take my word for it, he'll be history in just a couple of days."

"You know me, Preach." Warren reached up and rubbed his bulbous, pitted nose. "Maybe I just smell a story."

"What you smell is your breath blowing back into your face."

Warren gave an obligatory chuckle and got out his pen. "Where's the kid from?"

"Wait a minute." Preacher fumbled with a notebook on his desk. Marked NONROSTER, it contained biographical information compiled by the Director of Player Personnel's staff on each nonroster player invited to spring training. "Here it is. Kernersville, North Carolina. Born December 4, 1975, graduated from high school in 1993, spent three years in the army after that. I guess he just got out."

"Where was he stationed?"

"82d Airborne at Fort Bragg. Paratrooper."

Warren raised an eyebrow. "They're supposed to be pretty tough in that outfit."

"Yeah?" Preacher remained unimpressed. "Maybe he should have stayed in if he's so tough."

Warren laughed. "You don't like him, do you?"

"I don't care anything about him." Preacher pointed a finger at the writer. "Let me tell you something. I been around this game a long time. Maybe, as some of your friends in the press have been all too eager to point out, too long."

"Never me."

Preacher nodded. "You're right, never you. And that's one reason you're still welcome in my office. Anyway, like I was saying, I been around Organized Ball most of my life, and I ain't never seen too many surprises, like guys showing up out of the blue with major-league talent. It's like a dog laying an egg: it don't happen much."

"But when it does it makes a helluva story."

Preacher grunted in response.

"I got a feeling." Warren patted his hip pocket where his billfold nested. "I'll bet you twenty dollars here and now that the kid surprises you. I ain't saying he'll make the big team, not right away, but I'll bet he lasts through spring training and then goes up to Tacoma. What do you say?"

"Make it a hundred and you got a bet. And keep in mind that I'm the one who'll be sending him down the road."

Warren solemnly extended his hand. "If he's got the talent I'm guessing he's got, you won't cut him just to take a hundred dollars of my money."

"Don't count on it," Preacher said.

The two men shook hands.

Henry got out of the shower and stood, towel in one hand, before the full-length mirror in the garage apartment's bedroom. The image reflected transfixed him. It was of a young man, tallish, fair skinned, blond and blue-eyed. He was heavily muscled but not disproportionately so, the effect overall impressive and yet nonetheless aesthetically pleasing. Henry's gaze began at his reflected face and moved slowly downward, following the graceful flow of neck to trapezius to well-defined deltoids. The pectorals rose from the front of his shoulders, belling outward on either side of his sternum, cutting down abruptly to frame the upper abdomen. His stomach fell in a straight, ribbed line to his lower abdomen where a modest thatch of fine, soft, sandy-colored hair guarded his genitalia. His trunk was joined from below by impressively muscular thighs, the *vastus medialis* of the quadriceps bulging heavily like ripe pomegranates above dimpled knees. Henry took his penis into his right hand, and ran his forefinger up from the base of the shaft, amazed at the density of sensation in the flaccid organ. He held it up and sideways to better view his scrotum, his testicles hanging loosely after the hot shower. He stood there for several minutes, so taken was he with the image in front of him.

"Would you like some coffee?"

Startled, Henry looked up from his plate. After showering

and dressing he had driven out into the desert to a Mexican restaurant his landlady had told him about. "Excuse me?"

"Coffee," the young waitress repeated. Her name tag said RAMONA and her dark skin and jet-black hair identified her as Hispanic. She put one hand on her hip and with the other held up the coffeepot. "You're going to have to pay attention, because the questions only get harder."

"No, no thank you, I don't drink coffee. At least I don't think I do," Henry replied.

"Don't you know?"

Henry nodded, certain now. "I do know, and no, I don't drink coffee."

"How about dessert? Do you eat dessert?"

Henry laughed. "Frequently."

"Good." Ramona picked up his plate and utensils and left the table. At the waitress service station she nudged the restaurant's only other waitress, her sister. *"Beisbol,"* she said cryptically.

"Did he tell you that?"

Ramona shook her head. "He didn't have to. Tell Papa I'm taking the rest of the night off."

Her sister giggled. "You know he doesn't like you going out with customers, particularly *Anglos*."

"Just tell him, but not until I've left." She picked up a small bowl and a clean spoon and returned to Henry's table. "A flan," she explained, placing the bowl in front of Henry with a flourish. "I made it myself."

"What's a flan?"

"What's a flan?" Ramona repeated incredulously. She looked around and lowered her voice conspiratorially. "Don't ask too loudly," she advised. "My father already thinks *Anglos* are culturally deprived, but even he would be astonished to learn that there are some who don't know what a flan is."

"What's an *Anglo*?"

"Madre de Dios," Ramona muttered, crossing herself sar-

castically. Uninvited, she sat down at the table with Henry.
"Eat your flan," she ordered. "Where are you from?"

"North Carolina." He took a careful taste of the flan.
"This is just a custard."

"And I am just a Mexican," Ramona responded. She stood
up and took her apron off. "Hurry up."

"Where are we going?"

"You are going to drive me out to Carefree, where we
will listen to the coyotes laugh and you will explain to me
how it is that people from North Carolina are so provincial
that they think civilization ends at places like Nogales or
San Luis Río Colorado."

Henry's car was the only one in the restaurant's small
gravel parking lot.

"Looks like business is a little slow tonight," he observed
as he opened the passenger side door for Ramona.

"It's only Tuesday night. A small restaurant such as ours
profits only on Friday and Saturday nights. We get some
business on Sunday afternoon, but usually very little during
the week. What kind of car is this?"

"A 1982 Pontiac. I bought it from a buddy going overseas,
just like he bought it before me and countless owners before
him. The perfect army car, handed down from one PFC or
Spec. 4 to another."

"You were in the army? Turn here," she pointed to an
intersection they were approaching, "and then turn left at the
second light. That will put us on the road to Carefree."

Henry nodded in response to her question about his
having been in the army.

"And you grew up in North Carolina?"

Another nod.

"Most young men I know like to talk about themselves.
In fact, in my experience that's all they want to talk about."
She smiled. "Well, almost all."

They rode in silence for a time, both admiring the stark
beauty of the Sonoran Desert on either side of the two-lane

blacktop. A mile out of Carefree, Ramona directed Henry onto a dirt road. They parked at the base of a huge boulder between two giant saguaro cacti, two-thirds of a mile off the highway. He put the old Pontiac's top down and asked Rosa why she had invited him out for a drive.

"I don't know," she answered truthfully, suddenly not as confident as she had been. "I can assure you that my father will be quite angry with me."

"Do you work for him full-time?"

"No. I take classes at Arizona State and only help out at the restaurant between quarters."

"What are you studying?"

She laughed. "Who knows? For my father it is enough that I take classes. For myself, I have no idea what to do. I have been taking classes for five years and I'm no closer to knowing than when I started. And you. You're here to play baseball aren't you?"

"Yes." He told her of his invitation to a tryout at the A's spring training camp and his meeting that afternoon with Preacher Brown, the team's manager.

"Will you return to North Carolina after they, you know, they cut you?"

"They won't cut me."

"But you said that the manager told you you could not make the team."

"He hasn't seen me play yet."

"Are you so good?" Before he could answer she held up a hand. "Listen. Do you hear them?"

Out in the desert a group of coyotes began talking to each other, barking in a high-pitched call-and-response that did indeed sound eerily like laughter.

Ramona smiled. "They are laughing at us."

Henry shook his head. "I don't think so. More likely they're laughing because they can't think of anything they'd rather be than coyotes."

They listened quietly for several minutes to the night sounds. Finally Ramona broke the silence.

"You were going to tell me if you were good enough to make the team."

Henry nodded. "I think so. But more important, I don't think I would be here if I weren't going to make the team."

Ramona laughed. "Such confidence. Would you like to kiss me?"

Henry thought about it for a moment and then nodded.

"Most boys would not have waited for me to ask," she teased.

She leaned toward him and tilted her face upward, eyes closed. She waited expectantly for several seconds and when nothing happened she opened her eyes. Henry's face was inches from hers, his breath still wonderfully sweet from the flan he had eaten. Their eyes met and she caught her breath.

"Why are you waiting?" she asked, her voice suddenly low and husky.

"I'm afraid . . ." he started to say and then stopped, knowing he could not articulate the turmoil that was in his mind, could not tell her that he thought this might be his first kiss. Instead he bent down suddenly and placed his lips on hers. After a time he felt her lips part and, without consciously willing it, his own parted and the tips of their tongues touched. They separated and Henry was glad it was dark, for he was sure his face was scarlet with desire.

"Did you like that?" Ramona murmured, her face at his neck.

"I thought I might die," Henry said, his voice full of wonder. "Again."

F O U R

Needles, California

"I'm thinking I might have been wrong about your husband and that German crew," Ruth Pierpont informed Becky over coffee. She knew Becky and Benny weren't married, but her sense of propriety was such that she referred to them as husband and wife nonetheless, particularly now that Becky was beginning to show her pregnancy. "We're building up to full summer heat and all the signs point to them having the constitutions of lizards."

The two women, with over thirty years separating them and ostensibly nothing in common, had taken quite a liking to each other.

"How about you?" Ruth nodded in the direction of Becky's pleasantly rounded stomach. "How are you going to be feeling about carrying that baby when it gets up to 105 degrees and climbing?"

Becky smiled. Although without question the heat could be somewhat oppressive, her love for Benny was such that if living in the Mojave Desert was what he wanted, then she was more than willing to adapt as best she could. On the plus side, one of the truly extraordinary things about the often intense heat in the trailer was that it freed them from the necessity of wearing any clothing, and she found their perspiring bodies erotic beyond description.

"Are you kidding?" she said in reply to Ruth's question. "Six months ago I was lost and crying in a strip mall parking lot in Norman, Oklahoma, thinking suicide was an attractive alternative to what had become an unbearably miserable existence. I had had a serious of self-destructive affairs with married men on the faculty of the University of Oklahoma who wouldn't even accompany me to the abortion clinic for fear of being seen by family, friends, or colleagues. Now I'm in love with a man who thinks the world of me, is ecstatic that he has impregnated me, and is intent on living the rest of his life with me. After all that, do you honestly think that a little heat is going to be a problem?" She laughed with delight and shook her head. "No way, José."

Ruth sighed and lit a cigarette, Becky's words reminding her of her late husband, Morgan. Born and raised in San Luis Obispo, California, the only child of devout fundamentalist Baptist parents, Ruth was an eighteen-year-old virgin when Morgan Pierpont drifted into town. An itinerant carpenter, the child of Dust Bowl refugees so poor they were actually grateful for a California life of stoop labor with short-handled hoes in the artichoke fields, he had grown up with a sweet and gentle disposition in Salinas, just over the hill from Monterey and Carmel. In 1955, long before anyone thought to coin the word *hippie,* Morgan arrived in San Luis Obispo with a blond ponytail, broad shoulders, and a 28-inch waist. Ruth's father had hired him to rebuild the stairs off the back of their house, and she walked around their detached garage the morning he started work to find him urinating into her mother's rosebushes. He smiled at her, completely uninhibited and unabashed, and carefully shook a drop of urine off the head of his penis before putting it back into his trousers. It was the first adult male organ she had ever seen and, as is not infrequently the case, it changed her life.

"I'm Morgan," he said, offering her the same hand that mere seconds earlier had so casually held the most fascinating and compelling object she had yet beheld. "Morgan Pierpont. You've got the prettiest red hair I believe I've ever seen. What's your name?"

Ruth thought she might faint, so strongly was the blood rushing through her ears. She lightly touched the young man's extended hand with her own, wanting secretly to bring her fingers to her lips and nose to see if they would smell and taste of his manhood.

"My name's Ruth," she heard herself say, as if from a distance, "and those are my momma's roses."

Morgan laughed, a young man's careless laugh, and Ruth felt a bolt of electricity surge up her legs at the sound.

"You've also got the greenest eyes," he noted, ignoring her comment about the roses. "Come with me tonight and we'll go dancing at this little place I know up toward Santa Margarita."

His invitation would have seemed no more remarkable had he asked her to fly to the moon with him, and that evening, after washing the supper dishes, she simply walked out the front door of her parents' modest frame house, knowing as she did that she would never return. She and Morgan drank beer and danced until the roadhouse closed and then joyously coupled and coupled again on a horse blanket in the bed of his pickup truck as the sun was rising over a golden field of California poppies.

Over the next three years they drifted as only young people can happily do, certain of their immortality, intoxicated with love and each other's body, and looking for nothing in particular. They worked when they needed money and traveled on a whim when they didn't. They got as far north as Vancouver and as far south as Oaxaca, in Mexico, as careless of the miles as the broken odometer on Morgan's 1938 Ford. On an early spring morning, in the shadow of El Capitan in Yosemite, Morgan asked Ruth to marry him, and they exchanged vows a week later before a Superior Court judge in San Francisco.

Ruth looked up from her coffee, her reverie broken by a comment from Becky. "I'm sorry; what did you say?"

Becky smiled, knowing that Ruth had been daydreaming for a second or two. "I said Benny's building me a mister outside the trailer today. He drove into Needles this morning for the parts he needs."

"What the hell's a mister?"

Becky shrugged. "It's some sort of shower thing, where the water is atomized into the finest mist you can imagine. Benny says the idea is that whenever you get too hot you just walk into the mist and it evaporates before it even hits your skin."

"Sounds queer to me," Ruth shifted her body in Benny's homemade Adirondack chair, "but I'd have to say that that old man of yours is a handy sumbitch to have around." She patted the broad arms of the chair with her hands. "I never had me a chair to fit my butt the way this one does. Tell him I'll give him twenty dollars if he'll build one of these for me."

"I'd hate to think he'd charge a friend for building her a chair," Becky replied. "I'll ask him to start on it as soon as he finishes the mister. And listen." She winked at her new friend. "One night soon when the moon comes up full we'll drink a few beers, take all our clothes off, and run in and out of the mister."

Ruth threw her head back and brayed like a Missouri mule. Jericho looked up with obvious disapproval on his face.

"By God, that'll be a sight to set the coyotes to howling, Ruth Pierpont dancing buck naked under the stars." She flicked the butt of her Camel out into the desert. "You tell that old man of yours to get that whatchamacallit up and running and we'll see what we see. But tell him to build my chair before we do any dancing—the sight of me without any clothes on might just kill him."

*   *   *

"How's the Jeep running?" Al Bartholomeo asked.

He had seen Benny messing around with the vehicle and had wandered over for some company. Some weeks earlier Benny had sold his Volvo sedan and purchased a battered Jeep Wrangler from Mark Little at the radiator shop in downtown Needles. Rigged out for desert use, it had a padded roll bar, fat off-road tires, two radiators, an oil-cooling system, and a rhino guard welded to the front bumper. A mottled green and brown in color, it had neither doors nor top, and Al, himself the owner of a meticulously maintained and polished five-year-old Buick station wagon, couldn't keep his eyes off it.

"Running great," Benny assured him. "I was just about to drive into Needles to pick up some plumbing hardware. Want to ride along?"

"You bet," Al said, pleased to be asked. He liked Benny a great deal and was eager to get to know him better. He also liked Gunter and the Germans but worried that they, perhaps, thought little of him. At the insistence of Margaret, his wife, he had recently purchased a television satellite dish for the top of his trailer. While he was in the process of installing it Gunter Schmidtbauer had walked up.

"Was haben wir hier?" he had asked. Seeing Al's puzzlement he repeated the question in English. "What do we have here?"

"It's a satellite," Al had answered, rather unnecessarily. "For the television."

Gunter had nodded politely and walked off. Al felt certain that the Germans looked down on him because of the television, but he didn't know what to do about it. He climbed into the Jeep with Benny. "What kind of plumbing repairs are you doing?" he asked. As a home owner in the Bronx he had done a fair number of plumbing repairs himself over the years and thought to offer his expertise, such as it might be.

"Actually, I'm building a mister outside the trailer."

"A mister?"

Benny explained the essentials. "The cooling occurs as the result of the dramatic temperature differential between the area in which the atomized water is rapidly evaporating and the surrounding environment. An individual walking into what you might call the cooling zone feels the temperature difference but does not get wet because the water, already almost a vapor when it is expelled from the heads, evaporates almost instantaneously." He eased the Jeep into first gear and headed out of the trailer park, driving slowly in an effort to keep from stirring up any additional dust. As soon as they were away from the trailers he shifted into second and accelerated. When they got into Needles Benny pulled into the radiator shop's driveway.

"Whoa, Doc." Mark Little walked out to greet them, obviously pleased to see Benny. He put a hand on the side of the Jeep. "How's she running?"

"Great," Benny assured him as he and Al got out.

"Done any off-roading yet?"

Benny smiled and shook his head. "Not yet. I think I prefer to see the desert mostly on foot."

"It's getting too damned hot for that, Doc. Hey, how about a beer?"

"Sounds good. Say, you know Al Bartholomeo, don't you?"

"Sure," Mark said, extending a hand to Al as the three of them walked into the shop's small office. "We've never met, but I've seen you around town." He took a ring of keys off his belt loop and unlocked the Coca-Cola machine. Seeing Al's questioning stare he laughed. "Shoot, every filling station in America keeps the beer in the Coke machine." He winked at Benny as he handed the two older men cold bottles of beer. "Ain't that right, Doc?"

Benny tapped the long neck of his bottle against Al's and Mark's. "Long life," he toasted, tipping the bottle back and taking a long drink. "If I was back in Boston I'd be having this beer out at the ballpark, watching the Red Sox."

"Speaking of baseball, Doc, they say this rookie with the A's is going to set the league on fire this year," Mark said. Although he wasn't much of a fan, it was hard to ignore the media attention young Henry Spencer was already receiving.

"Not you, too," Benny groaned, feigning consternation. "That kid's all Al here talks about." He waved a dismissive hand. "Forget him. Rookies will break your heart quicker than a good-looking woman, believe me." He took a sip of beer and wiped the sweating bottle across his brow. "Have you started on the reading list I gave you?" He had grown fond of the young man and, ever the teacher, had been gently but firmly guiding him toward a more reasoned understanding of the physical world in which he lived.

"Yeah, Doc, I picked a couple of the books up at the library. That was pretty neat, going in there and getting a card and all." Like the vast majority of his contemporaries, Mark had graduated from high school and in the process had never read a complete book, cover to cover, whether for recreation or school, in his life. "I haven't had a chance to get started yet, but I will soon. That one on the atomic bomb looks real interesting."

"You'll enjoy it," Benny promised. "Much of it you won't understand, but we'll talk about those parts after you've worked your way through it."

"Cool," Mark said. He looked at Al. "Are you a scientist, too, Mr. Bartholomeo?"

Embarrassed, Al shook his head. "No, I'm retired," he mumbled. "From the post office."

Benny, sensing Al's discomfort, cleared his throat. "I almost forgot why I came into town," he said to Mark. "I know you're not in the plumbing supply business, but I thought you could help me find some of these things." He gave Mark a hand-written list of items.

"You doing some plumbing for Miz Pierpont out at the trailer park?"

"Well, in a broad sense I guess you could say that I am," Benny responded. "In an even broader sense I'm going to be taking advantage of some of the physical laws of nature that we've been talking about the last month or so to make life in the desert a little more joyful."

"Whatever." Mark studied the list for a second. "Listen, why don't you let me phone this list over to Mr. Grieves at the hardware store. I get off here in about an hour and I could pick it up at the store and run it out to the trailer park for you then."

"I hate to inconvenience you like that," Benny said.

"It's no inconvenience," Mark assured him. "Besides, Miz Pierpont's been wanting me to check out the water pump on her pickup and I can do that at the same time."

Back in the Jeep, Benny asked Al if he needed anything while they were in town.

"Can't think of a thing," Al said as Benny eased into the light traffic.

As they got out into the desert and Benny slowed down to negotiate the gravel road out to the trailer park, Al started fidgeting in his seat.

"What's on your mind?" Benny asked.

"Well, I was wondering." Al paused, clearly not sure how best to proceed. "That reading list you and Mark were talking about? Well, I go to the library quite a lot, mostly looking at magazines and stuff, and was thinking, maybe you could . . ." Al's voice petered out as they neared the trailers.

"I'd be happy to," Benny said, knowing what Al was trying to get at. "I'll write down a couple of titles that should get you started."

FIVE

⋆ ✦ ⋆

Henry was the first player to arrive at Simmons Field, before even the municipal employee whose task it was to unlock the gates and lay out the bases. He sat in the Pontiac and yawned and watched the rising sun turn the Maricopa Mountains from red to ochre to sandy brown. He had gotten up early, before dawn, to take Ramona back to the apartment she shared with two other ASU students. When the first of the players staying at the Motel 6 across the street from the ballpark began straggling over, Henry opened the car door and swung his stocking feet out. He put on his spikes and stood up, leaning backward to stretch his spinal erector muscles. The size XXXL practice uniform he had gotten from Scotty Harrison fit snugly across his broad shoulders but ballooned absurdly at his small waist. Ramona had laughed when he put it on for the first time that morning.

"It looks as if Omar made it," she teased.

"Omar?"

"The tentmaker," she replied, exasperated at his failure to comprehend even the simplest of jokes. "Bring it with you when you come for dinner tonight. My mother will take it in so that it looks like it was tailored for you."

"Your mother?" he asked, pleased that she had assumed he would want to dine with her that night.

"*Sí.* Of course. Mexican women can do anything. Tailor

clothes, cook, work the fields, have babies." She snorted. "They have to."

"I will be at the restaurant by six," he told her when he dropped her off.

"Don't forget to bring that jersey," she reminded him, playfully pulling the commodious shirttail out of his pants. "Tomorrow you will look like a major leaguer."

He leaned against the front fender of the Pontiac and watched the first dozen or so young men from the motel walk toward him.

"Hi, I'm Buddy McNerney," the first to reach him said, extending a hand to be shaken. He didn't look like he could possibly be more than eighteen or nineteen. "Welcome to the leper colony."

Henry smiled and took his hand. "Henry Spencer," he responded, nodding at the entire group.

"Where you from?" one of them asked.

"North Carolina."

"The Carolina League?"

Henry shook his head. "No, I just got out of the army."

"No shit," one of them murmured, vaguely impressed. In the almost thirty years since the end of the Vietnam era it had become something of an oddity for a young man to run into a veteran his own age. "You played ball in the army?"

Henry nodded. He looked at Buddy. "The leper colony?"

The youngster laughed. "You bet. The nonroster gang." He jerked a thumb in a generally easterly direction. "Spring training for the big boys is over at the Cactus League complex. Air-conditioned clubhouse, fully equipped training facility, equipment manufacturing reps hanging around like flies, giving out free gear, the whole nine yards." He turned and pointed to a low, scrofulous concrete block structure at one end of the parking lot. Signs at each end indicated separate entrances for MEN and WOMEN. "The clubhouse for the leper colony," he explained.

Before Henry could respond a nondescript rental van pulled into the lot.

"Okay, guys, give us a hand here," Scotty Harrison called out from the driver's seat. In the back of the van were bats, balls, and all the detritus associated with Organized Baseball. Spring training had begun.

"How did it go?"

Henry shrugged. Ramona had just served him a large plate of food, most of it unfamiliar to him. "Smells great. What is it?" he asked.

"*Chiles rellenos,* an avocado taco, chicken *enchiladas* with green chile sauce, and a beef tortilla." She sat down across from him. "And of course *refritos* and rice. How did the practice go?"

He dug into the food with gusto. "Pretty much what I expected. Mostly calisthenics, stretching, throwing the ball back and forth, hitting fungos, stuff like that. The first couple of days'll be spent getting organized, setting up pitching and catching rotations for batting practice and whatnot. Letting the coaches get to know the players. By next week we'll start scrimmaging."

"Are they very good?"

"Who?"

"The other players."

Henry shook his head. "Not really. Keep in mind that none of the kids on the B squad will make the big club. Oh, I suppose that one of the pitchers could possibly turn into a spring pheenom and get the call, but not likely. Most are trying desperately to win a spot on the Triple-A team up in Tacoma. Some will; most won't. But almost certainly none will make the roster of the Oakland club."

"Except you."

Henry smiled as he watched Ramona expertly roll him a

corn tortilla with refried beans and rice. "Except me," he confirmed.

Out of the corner of his eye he saw a large-bellied man with an enormous Pancho Villa mustache glaring at him from the entry to the kitchen. "If looks could kill I'd be a dead man right now," he said, winking at Ramona.

She turned to look and spoke to her father in a flood of rapid Spanish. He took off his apron and walked to the table.

"Father," she said, "I'd like you to meet Henry Spencer. Henry, this is my father, Señor Fuentes."

Henry quickly rose to his feet. "I am pleased to meet you, sir," he said formally, extending his right hand. "Your daughter has been most kind to me."

The older man nodded and shook Henry's hand. "I understand you are a baseball player," he said, his English clear and almost without accent.

"Yes, sir, I am."

"Ramona thinks, based upon exactly what criteria I do not know, that you are an exceptionally talented player."

"I am," Henry said without a trace of humor.

"Good. Please," he indicated that Henry should sit down, "enjoy your meal." He turned and left the table.

"Do you know the German word for 'mustache'?" Henry asked Ramona as soon as her father disappeared into the kitchen.

"Do I know what?"

"The German word for 'mustache.' Your father's mustache just reminded me."

She shook her head. "I don't know any German."

"It's *Schnurrbart*. It's a contraction of the verb *schnurren*, which is the sound a cat makes as it purrs, and the noun *Bart*, which means whiskers. So the word for 'mustache' comes from the sound of a purring cat and the word for whiskers."

Ramona laughed. "Where did you learn to speak German?"

"I'm not sure I can. It just came to me when I saw your father's mustache."

"It just came to you?"

Henry nodded. "Yes." He put his fork down and stared intently at the plate of food in front of him. "I get the feeling from time to time that all manner of wonderful things, memories, are hovering just out of reach in the back of my mind. For example, at today's practice we were going over the signs to be used between pitcher and catcher, you know, to call the pitch. Anyway, Bill Watson, a pitching coach in the A's minor-league organization, was talking about the importance of varying the sequence of pitches during the course of a game so the other team couldn't pick up a pattern. Out of the blue, without even thinking about it, I said that it seemed to me that given the number of pitches available to any given pitcher at the major-league level, assuming the pitcher wasn't just a knuckleballer and the catcher a moron, although in fact such a combination is far from inconceivable, the operation of the Heisenberg Uncertainty Principle would make looking for a pattern in the pitches called problematic at best. The very act of looking for a pattern, knowing that the other team knows that you are looking for one, changes it." Henry smiled and looked up at Ramona. "Bill Watson said he wouldn't put too much store by anything Heisenberg said. He claimed he had played against Heisenberg back when they were both rookies in the old Iowa Instructional League. Said Heisenberg was a real flake and never even came close to making it to the Show."

"Was he?"

"Was he what?"

"A flake."

Henry shook his head. "Actually, Werner Heisenberg was a German physicist who hit his stride, intellectually speaking, in the 1920s and 30s and his Uncertainty Principle strictly speaking has to do with events occurring at the sub-

atomic level. Nonetheless I thought it instructive to the point
Watson was trying to make."

Ramona didn't know what to say.

It didn't take Henry long to get to know the kid from the
Scottsdale Park and Rec Department who unlocked the gates
at Simmons Field every morning. His name was Julio
Blanco and he was a junior at a local high school, a pitcher
for his school team in Tempe. Although practice didn't of-
ficially begin until 9:00 A.M., Henry, still on army time, was
usually sitting in the parking lot not later than 7:30, the time
Julio was supposed to open the gates to the field. After opening the gates and putting out the bases on the diamond Julio
and Henry would play catch, throwing a baseball back and
forth until Julio's arm was properly warmed up. Henry
would then let him take the mound and pitch to him, limiting
the youngster to fastballs and change-ups.

"Let me show you my slider," Julio would always ask.
"Tell me what you think of it."

"No, no breaking stuff. Stay with the fastball and change.
Better yet," Henry would say, walking out to the mound,
signaling that the morning's workout was over, "forget about
baseball altogether and spend the summer in the library."

Julio would laugh at the ridiculousness of Henry's suggestion as he put his glove away and began the rest of the
morning's chores at the park. He had to sweep the stands,
empty the garbage cans into the Dumpster in the parking lot,
and, twice a week, mow the outfield, all before the other
players and the coaching staff showed up at 9:00. Because
the park was just across the street from the motel where most
of the nonroster players were staying, Henry's early arrivals
were soon noticed. The first couple of days the players were
scornful, attributing his behavior to a deplorable, misguided
effort to impress the organization's staff. Then, one by one,
as his undeniable athletic prowess began to be noted, they,

too, began to drift across the street earlier and earlier, until by the end of the second week of spring training most of the nonroster players were on the field by 8:00 at the latest, playing catch, hitting fungos, or just standing around talking and spitting.

"Hey, Soldier, you *sure* you ain't never played no Organized Ball?"

Buddy McNerney, a catcher himself, voiced the generally held suspicion shared by most of them, the coaching staff included, that Henry must indeed have played a great deal more ball than he admitted to, given his impressive skills as a catcher. One of the boys, in honor of Henry's status as an ex–military man, had started calling him Soldier, a nickname that immediately stuck.

Buddy's question, asked after practice one day as the boys lounged in the shade of Simmons Field's wooden stands drinking beer and spitting tobacco juice at grasshoppers, elicited only a smile from Henry.

"I mean," Buddy continued, "that pickoff move to first base today was about the most radical thing I've seen in person, you know what I'm saying?"

"Fuckin' A," one of the boys murmured in agreement, sharing a knowing nod with the others.

The move spoken of had occurred during a scrimmage that afternoon. With a man on first base Henry had taken the pitch and without shifting his body, still in a forward-leaning catcher's crouch, had whipped a strike to the first baseman, catching the base runner completely off balance for a perfect pickoff.

"That was a yellow hammer for sure, Soldier," the kid who had been picked off agreed, referring to Henry's throw. "I never seen the ball until I heard it hit Bobby's," the first baseman's, "glove."

Henry shrugged. "Baseball's really quite simple," he assured the boys in a kindly fashion. "It's a game, nothing more and nothing less. People that talk about how hard it is to play are simply saying that they themselves can't play it. At its highest level it is simply an exhibition of extraordinary athleticism by a group of genetic freaks."

"Freaks?" one of the boys repeated, unsure that he had heard correctly.

"Freaks," Henry confirmed. "I don't mean that necessarily in a pejorative sense, rather that whenever the ability to do a certain thing is limited to a hundredth or a thousandth of one percent of the general population then by definition those with such an ability are freaks."

"You sure do talk funny, Soldier," Buddy said with a laugh. "But you've got yourself a big-league cocksucker of a pickoff move; there ain't no doubt about that."

None of the boys disagreed with Buddy's assessment.

"What do you mean he's got them out there an hour before practice?" Preacher Brown looked suspiciously at Bill Watson, the minor-league pitching coach he had designated to run the early nonroster workouts.

"Just what I said," Watson answered. "Apparently he gets to the park about seven-thirty every morning to start warming up. I guess one by one the rest of the kids seen him over there and started drifting over to be with him." He paused and helped himself to a chew from a pouch of Red Man on Preacher's desk. "Damnedest thing I ever saw. I guess he's sort of like a natural leader."

Preacher snorted derisively. "Those dumb fucks would follow a goat if they thought it would help their chances to move up in the organization."

Bill Watson shrugged. "I wouldn't sell him short. I'll tell you what's the truth: he's got the best arm I ever seen." He told Preacher about the pickoff throw to first base Henry had made the day before. "When he did it you could have heard a grasshopper fart, that's how impressed everyone was. I'll tell you something else: No way Bobo could've have made that throw."

Watson was talking about Roberto Martinez, the team's All Star catcher. Nicknamed Bobo because of an almost simian intellect, Roberto had been with the club for five years and had caught almost every single game for the past three. Elected by the fans to the All Star game the past two years, he caught a good, workmanlike game, consistently batted between .260 and .270, and could be counted on to drive in 75 to 80 runs a year. Also known to his teammates, in private, as Hook in honor of his tendency to fondle women in hotel elevators, Bobo kept an extensive collection of child pornography in his Oakland condominium.

"That ain't sayin' much," Preacher responded, alluding to Bobo's notoriously weak throwing arm. In fact, with a runner on first he was loath to call anything but fastballs, a tendency that did nothing to endear him to the pitching staff.

"He's hitting, too, driving a ton of balls out of the park."

"He's hitting Single- and Double-A pitching, is what you mean," Preacher pointed out, "and not even in competitive situations. Nobody's throwing hard yet and sure as hell no breaking stuff." Preacher shook his head, indicating that the morning briefing was over. "We got a catcher," he said, meaning Bobo Martinez, "and two good prospects at Tacoma. The only thing that soldier boy is gonna be hitting," Preacher chuckled and unconsciously grabbed his crotch, pleased with his ability to come up with the *bon mot,* "is the road."

Bill Watson didn't need a weatherman to know when someone was pissing in his face. He knew exactly what Preacher's problem with Henry Spencer was: he had not come up the ladder of Organized Baseball. The fact of the matter was that the Preacher, like most of the men associated with major-league baseball, could not intellectually accept the notion that anomalies existed, athletes of such exceptional ability that the normal rules did not, or at least should not, apply. As a minor-league coach trying to make the Show himself, Bill Watson accepted the chain of command like Oral Roberts accepts the Gospel, and that usually meant that if Preacher Brown didn't like a particular prospect, even if Bill thought him wrong, that was the end of the matter. However, he also liked to think of himself as a company man first and foremost, with allegiance to the Organization rather than to a single individual such as the Preacher. In just a few days he had seen enough to know that the Soldier, as his teammates were calling him, was special, and that it was his, Bill Watson's, duty to see that he was signed, sealed, and delivered, Preacher Brown's provincialism notwithstanding. Leaving Preacher's office he spotted Warren Mercer talking to one of the players.

"Hey, Warren, got a minute?" he asked, keeping his voice low. He nodded toward the clubhouse's exit door. "How about meeting me for a drink later this afternoon. On the QT, you know what I'm saying?"

S I X

★ ⋆ ★ ⋆

"I'd like to see how he does in a game situation with the A squad."

Preacher Brown nodded in response to Robert Edgerton's comment. Edgerton, the organization's managing general partner, always showed up at spring training when the exhibition games between the other major-league teams in the so-called Cactus League began. Although he gave free rein to the Preacher in the day-to-day running of the club during the season, he liked to think of himself as very much a hands-on managing general partner, particularly in matters regarding player personnel. In the two weeks since the opening of spring training a couple of articles had appeared in the Bay Area newspapers about young Henry Spencer, the nonroster invitee with the cannon arm and power reminiscent of Jose Canseco in his first couple of years with Oakland. His teammates had nicknamed him *Soldier* and his image excited not a few of the fans, male and female, in the City.

"I know you're concerned about his lack of experience in Organized Ball," Robert said, dismissing the Preacher's misgivings with the wave of a hand, "but the media have picked up on him and he's become a story. We need to get him off the B squad for a couple of games just to show that we've given him a good look."

Preacher nodded again. He was mad, big-time mad, but

he knew that what Edgerton was saying was true.

"I never said I wasn't planning on giving him a good look," Preacher declaimed, actually believing it himself. He affected an injured yet nonetheless dignified air. "Me and Willie Bishop go back a ways in baseball," *a hell of a lot further than you do, you sonofabitch,* he thought venomously but did not say, "and if Willie thought he had potential, well, then, that was good enough for me. It's just that I hate to rush a kid along, you know, put him up against big-league talent too quick. My thinking was, if he had a good spring maybe start him off in Rookie League or either A ball one and let him work his way up." *The way God intended.* "Particularly with the way Martinez has been playing the last couple of years."

Edgerton frowned at the mention of Bobo Martinez. The organization had had to pay $5,000 to a woman in Kansas City last September to hush up an incident in which the catcher had exposed himself to the woman and her two young daughters in the ladies' room of a restaurant frequented by the team. It hadn't been the first such incident involving Martinez and his perverse compulsions, although it had been the first time the organization had actually had to pay money. In all the other cases (there had been four others) the team had successfully discouraged the complainants with the heavy-handed threat of countercharges of enticement and loose behavior, and had seen to it that nothing reached the media. Then there was the matter of Martinez's extensive collection of child pornography, the mention of which Edgerton forbade in his presence. Before turning a deaf ear on the matter, just after Martinez's second consecutive election to the American League All Star team, Edgerton had learned that the catcher went so far as to maintain a traveling collection of photos that he took on the road with him and shared with a network of baseball-loving pedophiles in most of the American League cities. *My God,* Edgerton's informant had told him, *they've even got them printed up like baseball cards that they trade back and forth.*

Edgerton occasionally wondered why the team had never had a problem getting someone to room with Martinez on the road. *Still,* Edgerton had to admit, *the man did drive in 78 runs last year while batting .267 and catching 137 games, statistics which could not simply be ignored.* Toward the end of the season Edgerton had had a psychologist who specialized in treating deviant behavior talk to Martinez, with an eye toward establishing a relationship that could lead to regular counseling. The therapist had been shocked almost speechless by the brief encounter.

"What's that you were saying about Martinez?" Edgerton asked, realizing that he had lost the thread of the conversation he had been having with his manager.

"Just that it would be a mistake to rush this kid along when we've got Martinez playing so well and Sanders and Dean at Tacoma both almost ready to come up."

"We're not rushing him along; we're merely giving our fans a look at him before the press makes him out to be the reincarnation of Thurman Munson, or whoever."

In his first Cactus League game, against the Seattle Mariners, Henry Spencer went four for four with three solo home runs and a double, and picked two Seattle base runners off first base. Oakland lost 5 to 3. After the game Richie Sanders and Billy Dean, catchers at Oakland's Triple-A club in Tacoma, called their agents and told them to seek an immediate trade. Dean's agent, a corpulent tax attorney in Minneapolis, couldn't believe his ears.

"Edgerton told me not two weeks ago that you were slated to move into the number two position behind Roberto Martinez this season," he said.

"That don't mean jack shit now," Dean assured him. "You didn't see the game tonight. Take my word for it, this new guy, the one they're calling Soldier, is going to be the number one catcher and the only thing Martinez'll be catching this season is flies on the bench."

The two Triple-A catchers, Sanders and Dean, weren't the only ones impressed by Henry's debut. The Bay Area press contingent, led by Warren Mercer, knew they had seen something extraordinary, even though it was just a spring training game.

"I've been around major-league baseball damned near forty years now," Warren patronizingly informed Marybeth Fisher, a so-called sports journalism intern with the *San Jose Mercury News,* "and darling, I have never, ever seen an arm like that. He made both those pickoff throws to first base without so much as rising out of his catcher's crouch. That's why the runners were caught so flat-footed. Usually when a catcher makes a throw to first, and believe me, there aren't many who even try to actually make such a play, he has to rise up while he's cocking his arm back, particularly a right-hander like this kid. That gives the runner a chance to get back and unless he's fallen asleep out there, in which case it's the first base coach's fault for not keeping him on his toes, it's usually not even close. Which is why most catchers don't even try. But, Jesus, this kid, a flick of the arm and the runner hasn't even started back to the bag."

And on the bus taking the Mariners back to their own spring clubhouse, the Seattle players, too, were impressed. Not so much by the hitting, which, they all knew, meant little until the season started and rookie hitters had to contend with big-league breaking shit and 90+ mile per hour fastballs that hop around on their way to the plate like a bug on a hot skillet. *Lots of kids can throw fastballs that don't do anything, one pitching coach was fond of telling listeners. Fastballs that don't do anything on their way to the plate in the major leagues generally get planted well back into the outfield bleachers and the kids who throw them end up cooking chicken-fried steaks for a living in places like Topeka, Kansas.* Besides, the veterans on the Seattle bus had been around the game awhile and had seen the Cansecos, the McGuires, the Griffeys, *et al.*, and would need to see a great deal more from the rookie called Soldier before they would be impressed with his long-ball abilities. But the arm. Motherfucker. That was big-league already and no one who had seen the two throws to first base could doubt it.

"I'm standing there practically with my dick in my hand," Jimmy Carson, one of the two runners picked off by Henry, laughed. "I mean, who in the fuck ever saw anybody could throw like that?" He laughed again, not the least embarrassed that he had been thrown out. "There won't be any lollygagging back to first after the pitch when word of this kid gets around the league."

"Hey, Dusty," one of the players called from the back of the bus, "why can't you throw like that to first?"

Wayne "Dusty" Rhodes, the Mariners' starting catcher, had been in the big leagues for nine years and had been stunned by the power and accuracy of the rookie's throws to first base.

"Fuck you," he growled in response to the question.

Everyone laughed, particularly those who were not catchers.

In the Oakland clubhouse, after the game, the Bay Area media were frustrated by the fact that they could not find Henry Spencer's locker, and, therefore, could not find him. In fact, as a nonroster player working out with the B squad over at Simmons Field, Henry had no locker and had, as usual, put on his uniform in his garage apartment before leaving for the game. Neither Preacher Brown nor any other member of the coaching staff had thought to tell him to stick around and therefore, with no reason to go into the clubhouse after the game, he immediately left the park in his Pontiac.

"Where's he staying?" one of the print reporters asked

Scotty Harrison, the assistant equipment manager.

"Most of the nonroster invitees, the B squad guys, are staying at the Motel Six across from Simmons Field," Scotty answered, not quite successfully hiding a smile.

Of all the reporters listening, only Warren Mercer guessed the significance of Scotty's bemused expression. After the gathered press left, en masse, to confront Henry at the Motel 6, Warren sidled up to Scotty.

"Are you going over to Sammy's tonight?"

"Why do you ask?" Scotty responded.

Warren shrugged. "I'd like to buy you a drink is all. Maybe ask a question or two about the team." He paused for a second. "I figure a kid like you might know a thing or two."

"You know the Preacher's rule about the staff not talking about team matters."

"No, no," Warren soothed, "I wouldn't do anything to get you in trouble with the Preacher. No, I was sort of thinking about doing a story, or even a series of stories, on the unsung people behind the scenes. People without whom the team couldn't take the field. Someone like you, for instance."

Scotty looked at Warren for a moment and then smiled. "Quit blowing smoke up my ass, Warren. I don't know where he's staying."

Warren chuckled, pleased in some small way that Scotty wasn't quite as stupid as he had thought. "Maybe you do; maybe you don't. What the hell, I'll buy you a drink anyway."

Scotty nodded and returned to separating sweaty uniforms, jockstraps, and socks into different piles for the laundry. "I'll be over at Sammy's a little later, when I finish up here," he said over his shoulder.

"Did you play well?"

Ramona picked up the empty plate from Henry's table.

Although it was late, after eleven o'clock, the restaurant was bustling with a good Friday night crowd. Ramona and her sister were busy shuttling between the kitchen and the tables. She paused in front of Henry and pushed a strand of jet-black hair from her face. Of all the people in the small dining room only she and Henry were speaking English.

"Well enough," Henry answered, the barest hint of a smile playing with the corners of his mouth. He had taken a quick shower at his apartment before changing clothes and driving out to the restaurant and his hair was still wet. He cast his eyes about the room. "It looks as if you'll be busy for some time yet."

"I'm afraid so." Looking down at his lap Ramona could clearly see the outline of the head of his penis through the thin cotton trousers he was wearing. He obviously had on no undershorts, and it was all she could do to keep her hands to herself. She turned and in rapid Spanish irritably ac-knowledged a call from the kitchen to pick up an order. "At least two more hours."

"I don't mind waiting."

Ramona shook her head. "Go home and go to bed." She smiled, thinking about the key Henry had given her. "If you stay here I'll never get anything done."

"I know it's late, but listen, there's a hell of a story here; I can feel it." What Warren Mercer could feel was the jolt of the two double scotches he had just belted down on an empty stomach. He was on the pay phone at Sammy's Deli, an after-game hangout in Tempe popular with the Oakland coaching staff. Sammy's consisted of a long bar fronting a filthy kitchen, which specialized in aged stuffed cabbage and greasy corned beef sandwiches that no one in their right mind would order. "I want you to get out to Kernersville, wherever the hell that is, and get me everything you can on a kid named Henry Spencer. What's that? Goddamn it, I don't care what time it is, you hear me? This is a *story* I'm talking about. Maybe *the* story of spring training." Warren looked at his watch. If it was 11:00 P.M. in Arizona what the hell time was it on the East Coast? The two double scotches made such calculations difficult, particularly in the noisy atmosphere of Sammy's. "No, no, no." Warren shook his head as if the party on the other end, a reporter who worked the city desk for the Raleigh *News & Observer,* could see him. "Spencer, Henry Spencer. He grew up in Kernersville, North Carolina, graduated from high school in 1993. That's right, 1993. You got that? Yeah, then he went into the army, served as a paratrooper with the 82d Airborne at Ft. Bragg. Which reminds me, it would help to get someone checking him out over there as well. Whatever you can find. You know, kids he grew up with, his parents, teachers, the coach on his army baseball team. Shotgun it. Yeah, I know, I'm sorry I woke you up, but it couldn't wait. This kid's the most exciting thing I've seen in a hell of a long time and no one, I mean no one, ever heard of him before. There should be plenty here for both of us, you know what I'm saying? Good. I'll call you tomorrow." Warren hung up and walked back to the bar. He motioned to the bartender for another scotch and put his hand on Scotty Harrison's shoulder. "What're you having?" he asked.

"I still don't know where he lives," Scotty answered, "but as long as you're buying I'll have another margarita. No salt."

Waves of heat rolled over Ramona and Henry, intense caloric radiation from their bodies reflected back upon them by the thin walls of the un-air-conditioned garage apartment. At one point, in an instant of almost insane lucidity, as Ramona crouched on top of him, plunging herself frenziedly up and down, Henry watched an errant drop of perspiration roll down the side of one of her swaying breasts, gathering mass and momentum until finally, inexorably, it reached her nipple and slowly, almost regretfully, fell onto his torso. *Force,* he thought, *equals the product of an object's mass and its momentum.* Of an instant he wanted to stop, to somehow gather up the errant drop of perspiration, to taste it on his tongue, to savor and explore whatever complexity of sodium and phosphorous and electrolytes made up the chemistry of her sweat. Then, in an epiphanous revelation amidst Ramona's cries and gasping exhalations, the image of Sir Isaac Newton came to Henry, and he knew that the insignificant droplet of perspiration that had so fascinated him was governed by the same laws of motion that governed the heavenly bodies themselves. He knew that given sufficient information such as, for example, its mass, acceleration, the friction coefficient of the skin of Ramona's breast, anyone, even a baseball player, could accurately predict its movement, even as far as knowing the force with which it must impact on his own body. It took him a second to realize that both he and Ramona had reached orgasm together and, more important, that his recognition of the application of Newtonian physics to the movement of the drop of her perspiration had coincided with his own ejaculation. Ramona lay atop him, her body racked with sobs of spent passion.

"My God," he whispered, his voice full of awe at the wonder of it all.

Ramona lifted her head from his chest and smiled, thinking his invocation of the Lord's name had to do with the intensity of their lovemaking. *"Sí,"* she murmured, sinking back down onto Henry's body, "it was wonderful for me, too, my love."

"Philosophiae Naturalis Principia Mathematica."

"What's that?" Ramona looked back up. Raised, of course, in the Catholic Church, she, while not able to understand Latin, could certainly recognize it when she heard it.

"Philosophiae Naturalis Principia Mathematica," Henry

repeated. "It's the name of a book written by Sir Isaac New-ton."

"A book?" Ramona nested herself against Henry's body and inhaled deeply, nearly undone by the overwhelming bouquet of sweat, semen, and feminine lubricant. She ran her tongue over one of his nipples. "I never heard of it."

Henry sighed. "Remarkably enough, until just now neither had I. It was written in the late 1600s and it governs and binds our lives today no less effectively than when it was written."

Ramona slid down his torso until she was at eye level with his still slightly tumescent penis. A small droplet of semen clung to its tip, pearl-like and luminescent in the low light of the room. "Such beauty," she whispered, more to herself than to Henry. She took him into her mouth and began nursing gently.

Henry lifted his head from the pillow, tilting it forward, and admired the swell of Ramona's buttocks. She lay partially on top of him and had thrown one leg over his. He could just see a hint of her thick, black pubic hair peeking out between her legs.

"I'm sure I've read it, although how and when and under what circumstances remains unclear," he said, putting his head back down on the pillow and closing his eyes, concentrating for a moment on the remarkable sensations coming from his rapidly hardening member. "There is," he continued quietly, "you will admit, a certain incongruity in a young, little-educated baseball player professing to a more than passing familiarity with a centuries old treatise on the physical laws that govern all movement in the universe. You need not answer," he reassured her, knowing that her attention was focused elsewhere. "The question was rhetorical."

"You're done here, Soldier." Bill Watson squinted into the newly risen sun coming up over Henry Spencer's right shoulder. The rest of the B squad boys stood bunched a few feet away, not unlike a group of range cattle contemplating the intrusion of a cowboy on their otherwise tranquil plain. "Preacher Brown told me to tell you."

"Done?" Henry asked. He yawned. He had lain awake for most of the night, arcane formulae from Isaac Newton's book running rampant through his consciousness. "What do you mean?"

Coach Watson smiled. "I'm not boring you here, am I? What I mean is that you're promoted up to the A squad for the rest of spring training. This is your big chance, Soldier. You'll be reporting over to the Tempe facility starting this morning."

Henry nodded in a somewhat absentminded fashion. He looked at the boys standing around hanging on every word. "Am I the only one?"

"You're it," Watson replied shortly. "Listen, damned few players ever get the opportunity to go from the B squad to the Show." He was beginning to get a little annoyed at Henry's lack of enthusiasm. After all, it was he, Watson, who had gone out on a limb in the first place to get him noticed. 'You don't seem overly pleased."

"I don't know what you mean. I came here, as a baseball player, with certain athletic skills. Those skills either are or are not of use to this organization. I have no control over that decision. If my skills prove useful, then presumably I'll be offered a contract. If not, I'll do something else to make a living. In either case the organization, presuming it to be managed by reasonably intelligent and competent individuals, will act solely in its own self-interest. Why I should be pleased, and, if so, demonstrate it, escapes me."

Watson didn't know what to say. Young Buddy McNerney laughed out loud and spoke for all of them, coach and aspirants alike. "I'll tell you what's the truth, Soldier: you can say the goddamnedest things."

In the clubhouse at Tempe all the players noticed Henry's

quiet, unobtrusive arrival while studiously pretending to ignore him. No one knew him, which, in the formalized, lock-step system of Organized Baseball, was in itself a pronounced oddity, and everyone in spring training, particularly the veterans, viewed unknown entities with a suspicion bordering on outright paranoia. He reported to Scotty Harrison, the assistant equipment manager.

"Hey, Soldier," Scotty quipped, a smile of genuine welcome on his face, "welcome to the A squad." He leaned across the counter separating the equipment room from the rest of the locker room and lowered his voice somewhat. "Man, what a game you had last night. Everybody's talking about it."

"Thanks. Do I get a regular locker, or what?"

"The works. Your own locker and a new workout uniform to go with it." He held up a clean white jersey and turned it around to show Henry the large roster number stitched on the back. "How does number 19 sound to you?"

Henry shrugged. "I suppose one number is as good as another." He thought for a second. "Nineteen is a prime number, for whatever that may be worth."

"A prime number?" Scotty asked, thinking the term a Southern colloquialism.

"Prime," Henry confirmed, nodding. "Any number having no factor except itself and one."

"Factor?" Scotty felt the sense of the conversation gradually slipping away from him.

"That's correct. Put another way, a prime number is not evenly divisible by any number except itself and one. There are countless interesting things about prime numbers. For example, any whole number can be shown to be comprised of factors of prime numbers, but in only one way."

"Is that a fact?" Scotty was certain his leg was being pulled. After all, he, Scotty, had been to college and he couldn't remember, in the entire course of his liberal arts education, coming into contact with anything called prime numbers.

"Indeed it is a fact. Prime numbers have fascinated all manner of men and women since long before Euclid's time."

"Hey, Spencer."

A voice boomed across the locker room. Both Scotty and Henry turned to see Preacher Brown beckoning from the door of his office.

"I want to see you in my office. Now."

"Like I said," Scotty quipped as Henry started to leave the equipment counter, "welcome to the A squad."

"I'm not going to lie to you, Spencer," the Preacher assured Henry as soon as he entered his office. "We liked what we saw last night. Liked it a lot. We've decided to keep you here in Scottsdale for a while, let you see some big-league pitching, get a feel for the competition. You'll be sharing most of the catching with Bobo Martinez, our regular catcher, and Richie Sanders, a kid we like a lot from Triple-A. Billy Dean, our other Triple-A prospect, got traded this morning to Kansas City for a couple of pitching prospects. But," the Preacher pointed a gnarled forefinger at Henry, "don't be thinking that this means you've got a shot at making the big club, because you ain't. Based on what we saw last night I'm thinking now that it looks like you can start off the season in A or either Double-A ball and maybe, if you work your tits off, we can get you up to the Triple-A club in Tacoma for a couple of games late in the season, you know what I'm saying?"

Henry nodded but said nothing.

"You sure you ain't never played no Organized Ball?" Preacher Brown found himself unable not to ask again and, in so asking, confirm how much Henry's play had impressed him.

Henry smiled and shook his head. Again he said nothing.

The Preacher nodded. "You don't have much to say, but

I'll tell you what, I like that in a rookie. Too many of these goddamned kids today don't know when to shut up." Preacher stared at the wall behind Henry and his eyes seemed to lose their focus. "When I was playing ball if a rookie so much as opened his mouth in the clubhouse one of the veterans would put a foot up his ass." He looked back at Henry. "What the fuck are you doing still here?"

The Oaklands played the San Diego Padres in an interleague exhibition that afternoon. Bobo Martinez started the game and played the first three innings. Henry replaced him in the bottom of the fourth and in the remaining six innings went three for three with two home runs and a frozen rope line drive that got to the right fielder so fast Henry was held to a single. He also threw out four base runners, three trying to steal second and a pickoff at first. The Oaklands shut out the Padres 4 to nothing. Robert Edgerton, the managing general partner, left the stands before the start of the ninth inning. In the dressing room after the game three reporters gathered around Henry's locker. Mickey Oswald, one of the team's veterans, observing the scene, walked over to Bobo Martinez's locker.

"Hey, Bobo," Mickey said, "the guys think maybe we should start calling you Wally."

"What the fuck are you talking about?" Bobo asked suspiciously.

"Wally. As in Wally Pipp."

"Hey, man, I don't know nothing about no Wally Pipp," Bobo responded. He looked over to where Henry was surrounded by the reporters. "Fuck that Wally Pipp, whoever he is."

"What?" Preacher Brown almost swallowed his chew, so astonished was he by what he heard. "Are you out of your fucking mind?"

Robert Edgerton assumed that Preacher's second question

was rhetorical in nature and chose not to address it. Instead, he reiterated his intention to trade Bobo Martinez to the New York Mets.

"I said I just got off the phone with the Mets organization and they have expressed an interest in obtaining Bobo Martinez."

"Jesus H. Christ," Preacher exploded, "every fucking team in all the major fucking leagues would have an interest in obtaining Bobo Martinez. In case you forgot, he's an All Star catcher in a business where competent catchers ain't exactly coming out of the woodwork."

"He's also a pederast and a pornographer."

Preacher narrowed his eyes suspiciously. "What's a pederast?" he asked.

Edgerton sighed. "Listen. You know as well as I do that Martinez is an out-of-control pervert. He'll fit right in with the Mets. Besides, I've got a feeling that this Spencer kid is the real McCoy. As far as I'm concerned he's ready to take over the starting catcher's job right now."

"You're not the team manager." Preacher thrust his chin forward aggressively. "I am. And I say there's no way we're trading Martinez."

Edgerton looked down and examined his fingernails carefully before answering. "It would be a mistake for you to take an unalterable position on this matter." Although softly articulated, Edgerton's words seemed to fill the Preacher's small office. "I don't believe you fully appreciate the depth of my concern about Martinez's moral turpitude and the negative financial effect it could have on this organization."

"It hasn't bothered you a great deal in the past," Preacher observed.

"We haven't had the, um, options we now have available."

"If you're talking about the Spencer kid, forget it. I been around this game too long to be impressed by some kid having a good spring. Particularly a catcher. It takes years to develop a good catcher. Chrissakes, he's never even played Organized Ball before."

"I don't care." Edgerton was adamant. "Spencer's going to start for us, we're going to bring Richie Sanders up from Triple-A to back him up, and Martinez is history."

"Who're the Mets offering for Martinez?" Preacher Brown heard the finality in his boss's voice. He didn't like it, but he heard it and, as he had just pointed out, he had been around baseball a long time, certainly long enough to know that the least secure job on any club was the manager's.

"Schneider, Gomez, and Clarke."

Herman (the German) Schneider was an aging short relief pitcher known throughout the National League for his willingness to come inside with heat, or at least with what had been heat earlier in his career. With his fastball down to the low eighties he now relied more and more on questionable breaking balls, an increasingly higher percentage of which, in not breaking very radically, found their way to the stands. Julio Gomez, a young left-handed Puerto Rican, was still considered a pitching prospect although he had not risen above Double-A ball in three years in the Mets organization. Bobby Clarke, a utility/role player from Bethune, South Carolina, had played for Pittsburgh and Philadelphia in the National League and Kansas City in the American before joining the Mets. A workmanlike if unimaginative relief catcher and first baseman, he played with a total disregard for his own body and typically worked his way through two entire pouches of Red Man chewing tobacco in the course of a nine-inning game, whether on the bench or in the field. Depending on which position he played, opposing catchers or first basemen would spend several minutes at each change-over covering with infield dirt the large puddles of brown saliva left at home plate or first base. In short, Bobby Clarke was a player whose capacity for expectoration, in a business where big-time spitters were a dime a dozen, was legend.

"Not much for an All Star catcher," Preacher muttered.

"Martinez's perversions have become well enough known throughout the league, throughout *both* leagues, so as to materially degrade his marketability, his catching skills notwithstanding." Edgerton looked pointedly at Preacher. "We're just lucky that Willie Bishop found this kid Spencer when he did."

Preacher grunted a sour response, remembering how hard he had had to fight with Edgerton over the past winter to keep his old friend Willie Bishop on the organization's payroll, even as a part-time scout.

"In any event," Edgerton continued, "Spencer's our man, for better or worse."

SEVEN

★ ✦ ★

"Hey, Bell, come here." Preacher Brown waved to Billy (Dickhead) Bell, his starting pitcher for the afternoon's exhibition game against the Seattles. Bell had been warming up in the bullpen and was ready to take the field with the rest of the squad. Preacher waved everyone else out to the field and took Bell's elbow in his right hand. "Listen, I want you to do something out there," he said, his voice low. He nodded in the general direction of home plate where Henry Spencer stood waiting. "When the rookie," he nodded again toward Henry, "calls for a fastball I want you to throw a slider. When he wants a slider, throw the change. Everything he calls, you throw something different, you know what I'm saying?"

Billy Bell, nicknamed Dickhead by his teammates because of premature balding and an odd egg-shaped head, hadn't the vaguest idea what his manager was talking about. Nature had graciously compensated Billy, dull-witted almost beyond belief, for his gross stupidity by providing him with a seemingly bionic right arm, not only one capable of throwing a lively fastball in excess of 95 miles an hour but also one possessed of a hard overhand slider that broke just in front of the plate like it was rolling off the edge of a table. The illegitimate issue of a filling station attendant and an unemployed waitress from Bettendorf, Iowa, Billy had never in his life heard anything so queer as a manager wanting a pitcher to intentionally ignore signs from a catcher.

"But aren't you calling the pitches, Skip?"

Billy was referring to the fact that Preacher, as had become the general custom, called every pitch. Whoever was catching was expected to look to the dugout between pitches to pick up Preacher's signs and then relay the same to the pitcher. Why he, Billy, would be asked by the very man calling the pitches to ignore the same was incomprehensible.

"Look, Billy," Preacher glared at his confused pitcher, "just do what I tell you, okay?"

Billy took the mound and threw his allotted number of warm-up pitches. Diego Martinez, the first batter for the Seattles, occupied himself for several seconds obliterating the precisely laid out chalk lines that defined the boundaries of the batter's box. He then carefully dug a small depression at the very rear of the box with his right foot and took several preliminary swings, all the while expectorating through the gap in his front teeth in a strange, amphibian-like fashion. When satisfied with his pre-swing ritual, he stepped out of the batter's box, unconsciously adjusted the fit of his protective cup, and crossed himself with his right hand while silently invoking the intercession of the blessed Virgin in the upcoming confrontation with the opposing pitcher. During the entire procedure Henry waited patiently in his catcher's crouch, conscious of the umpire's fetid breath wafting over his right shoulder. As soon as Diego reentered the batter's box and took his stance, Henry glanced toward the dugout where Preacher signaled for a fastball. Henry relayed the sign to Billy Bell and awaited the pitch. Billy immediately went into his windup and threw a heater right down the middle. Diego, loath to swing on the first pitch, a tendency known throughout the league, muttered a Spanish expletive when the umpire signaled a strike. Diego's expletive was repeated, albeit in English, by Preacher Brown, who bounded out of the dugout and walked to the mound.

"What the fuck did I just tell you?" he demanded as soon as he got to the now nervous pitcher.

"Jeez, Skip, I forgot."

"Forgot? How in the fuck can you forget? I told you not two or three minutes ago." He turned to wave Henry back to home plate. "That's all right," he called out, accompanying his words with shooing motions. "I'm just having a word with Billy. Don't come out." He turned back to the pitcher. "Now what the fuck are you supposed to do?"

"Whatever he calls for, throw him something different?" Billy answered hopefully.

"Exactly. Do you think you can do that?"

"If you say so, Skip." Billy nodded his head energetically, doing his utmost to convey sincerity.

"Thank you," Preacher said, his tone implying no such feeling of gratitude. "Don't make me come out here again."

As soon as Preacher reached the dugout Billy clenched his jaw and looked toward home plate for the sign. Another fastball. *Fast ball, fastball,* he told himself, his mind working feverishly. *What'll I throw, what'll I throw?* Well into his windup he realized that he had not settled on a specific pitch and he panicked, sending the pitch several feet over Diego Martinez's head. Henry didn't even come out of his crouch to try to catch it.

Ball one.

Shitfuck, shitfuck, an agitated Billy mouthed, glaring in at Henry as if it were his fault.

"*Madre de Dios*," Diego muttered as he stepped out of the batter's box to cross himself once again.

Henry looked toward the dugout and relayed Preacher's call, yet another fastball, out to the mound. This time Billy made up his mind well before going into his windup. *Slider, slider,* he told himself as he whipped the ball past his right ear, breaking his right hand and wrist sharply as he released the pitch. Henry set himself to receive the pitch and adjusted the position of his catcher's mitt as the ball sped toward him.

Just before the ball's rotation caused it to dive down and away from the hitter Henry visually picked up the spin and with a snap of his wrist dropped his mitt, anticipating where the ball was likely to go. At the same instant Diego swung his bat. To the careful observer the swing of the bat and the flick of Henry's mitt were simultaneous motions such that no one could have known that Henry had not been expecting a breaking ball. Diego missed and Henry, never breaking his crouch, picked the ball cleanly off the dirt just to the left of home plate.

Strike two.

Henry, knowing that he had called for a fastball and that Billy had thrown a slider, thought momentarily about going out to the mound to go over the signals. He decided not to do so, reasoning that with someone like Billy Bell almost any explanation for the mix-up was likely to be nonsensical. He had had only one brief conversation with the young pitcher, but it had been enough to alert him to Billy's status as a borderline moron. He glanced toward the dugout for Preacher's signal. Slow curve. He relayed it out to Billy and settled into his crouch, prepared to catch an off-speed break-ing ball. Billy went into his motion and snapped off a hum-mer that whistled over the inside of the plate in excess of 96 miles per hour, catching both Henry and Diego Martinez, who had guessed that with two strikes Billy would nibble around the corners with slow shit, off guard. Henry flinched at the speed of the pitch but managed to catch it, while Diego jumped back from the plate as if avoiding a snake.

Strike three.

Diego muttered florid Spanish imprecations as he headed back toward his own dugout.

"Time," Henry said over his shoulder to the umpire as he stood up and started toward the mound.

"I think we've got our signals crossed," he said to Billy. He dropped the ball into the pitcher's glove. "You've missed the last two pitches I called for." Henry paused for a second to give Billy a chance to respond. "Actually you missed the last three," he amended when no response from the pitcher was immediately forthcoming, "if you count the pitch that went over everyone's head. I'm not sure exactly what you were trying to throw on that pitch, but I'd called for a fast-ball."

Billy didn't know what to say. He didn't want to look Henry in the eyes, so he stared down at the rubber. "Hell, Soldier," he mumbled, using the nickname that had followed Henry over from the B squad, "Preacher tol' me to."

As Henry had expected, Billy's response made no sense. Or did it? "What do you mean he told you to? Told you to what?"

"You know," Billy said, scuffing the rubber with the toe of his right shoe, wondering the while how he could explain something he himself didn't understand. The need to think was making him more and more nervous. "He tol' me to."

Henry put his right hand on Billy's shoulder, a gesture calculated to calm the agitated pitcher. "That's okay, Billy," he said in a soothing voice. "If he told you to do it, there's nothing to worry about. Just tell me, what did he tell you to do?"

Maury Nance, the third baseman, started edging toward the mound. "Is everything okay, Billy?" he called out. He was not used to seeing a pitcher-catcher conference take place after just one hitter in a game. "You okay, Soldier?"

The shortstop and first baseman, seeing Maury Nance approach the mound, decided to join the conference themselves. Just then the umpire, an obese young man in his middle thirties sporting a fifty-four-inch waist, began waddling toward the mound.

"What the hell's going on here?" he groused. "Are we playing a ball game today, or what?"

Henry glanced around at the growing crowd and realized he would never get anything intelligible out of Billy with so many onlookers. "Never mind," he said, smiling at the pitcher. "Good strikeout," referring to Diego Martinez.

"Play ball for chrissakes," the ump admonished, asserting his authority on the long walk back to home plate.

"It looked like you and Bell were having some difficulty getting together on the signs," Warren Mercer observed. He was leaning against Henry Spencer's locker, a small hand-held recorder in his right hand.

Henry, sitting in a canvas director's chair, shook his head. "Not really," he answered noncommittally. "Did it look that way?"

"That's what I said. I just thought, you know, first start with the big club and all, maybe you were a little nervous."

"I'm curious." Henry looked directly at the reporter. "Where did you go to school?"

Nonplussed, Warren raised his eyebrows. "School?" he asked, unused to questions from the ballplayers, most of whom assiduously avoided all contact beyond the absolutely necessary with reporters, either print or television. "Why, San Francisco State College." He smiled. "Of course, it was a state *college* when I went there, but they've come up in the world since. Why do you ask?"

"No particular reason. I guess I was just curious as to the process by which someone decides to become a sportswriter."

Warren narrowed his eyes, unsure whether or not Henry was slyly framing an insult in the form of what appeared to be an innocuous question. He had been around ballplayers long enough to know that, quite like policemen, they almost universally regarded everyone outside their own insular world with ill-disguised contempt. He decided to give Henry the benefit of the doubt and assume that his question was no more than it appeared to be.

"Well, you know what they say," he responded, taking a humorous tack. "Those that can, do; those that can't, write about it. Or something like that." He affected a rueful, self-deprecating smile. "I've always loved baseball and, not being talented enough to play it, I long ago decided that writing about it was the next best thing."

"I don't understand how someone can profess to 'love' baseball," Henry said, bending down in his chair to untie the baseball shoes he had purchased the day before from Marty Simpson, the team's starting right fielder. Marty had an endorsement contract with a shoe manufacturer that provided him with, among other things, an almost unlimited supply of free athletic equipment, most of which he promptly sold to less fortunate teammates like Henry. "I mean, it's just a game, an athletic activity." Henry straightened up and began to unbutton his uniform. "I suppose I can understand how people, non athletes such as yourself, might enjoy watching a game from time to time, but *love*?" Henry shook his head. "Why did you think I was having difficulty with regard to the pitches today?"

It took Warren a second to realize that Henry had shifted back to the subject that they had originally been discussing.

"Well, maybe *difficulty* was too strong a word," Warren allowed. "It just appeared in the first inning or two that you were surprised by some of the pitches Bell was throwing."

"I don't think so," Henry said, pulling his jersey over his head. He smiled. In fact, on the way back to the plate after his short-lived conversation at the mound with the intellectually challenged pitcher he realized that Preacher Brown must have ordered Bell to ignore the signs given. The only logical explanation was that Brown must have wanted to see how he, Henry, would react to the unexpected in a game situation. Or, there was also the possibility that the manager wanted to make Henry look bad, for whatever reason. In any event, it took Henry only a minute or two to figure out that Bell's extraordinarily limited imagination was such that for each sign given he would throw only one wrong pitch—that is to say, if Henry called for a fastball, Bell would always throw a slow, breaking pitch. A call for a slider would always result in a fastball, and so on. Once understood, it required no thinking on Henry's part and the game proceeded as if nothing untoward were taking place.

"Umhmm." Warren gradually became aware that most of the conversation in the locker had halted when Henry took his shirt off. Although weight training had become popular among many ballplayers in the past decade, few men of Henry's size and muscular definition were seen even among football players.

"That's a stone buffed motherfucker," one of the players murmured, expressing everyone's sentiment. They all looked and, although many were frankly ill at ease at the thought of finding pleasure in the sight of another man's naked body, they all admired.

"Well," Warren persisted, determined to draw Henry into a conversation, "you certainly had no problem at the plate today."

Indeed he hadn't. Henry had gone three for four, with a home run, a double, and a single. The one out had been a fly ball caught at the warning track in dead center.

Warren looked at his notes. "Seven at-bats with the big boys so far and, let's see, what have we got here, three home runs, a double, and two singles." He smiled. "Were you a little disappointed with that fly ball that was caught today?"

"Actually I got under that ball just a little." Henry was quite serious. "It was a breaking ball that didn't really drop like I thought it would and so I was just a touch under it."

"You knew it was a breaking ball?"

Henry nodded. "Sure. I picked up the rotation of the ball as soon as it left the pitcher's hand. Too, based on his pattern I knew that he was going to throw a breaking ball on that particular pitch."

"You detected a *pattern* in the pitches he was throwing?" Warren knew that all clubs worked very hard to avoid patterns of any kind that opposing teams and hitters might pick up. He had trouble believing that a rookie like Henry could so easily detect something that experienced baseball men like the Preacher (and yes, he himself) had missed.

"There are patterns in everything. It is simply a question of looking for them, being able to discern, to separate, to understand. Compared to, say, solving nonlinear equations, baseball is a very simple game. Finding a pattern in a given sequence of pitches merely requires the ability to concentrate. Given that baseball is a childlike game, one must presume that a child could, if properly motivated, do it. As to the breaking ball in question, the pitcher just didn't quite snap it off like he wanted and so it didn't break as much as it otherwise might have." Henry looked at the reporter and smiled. "Midway to the plate I knew it wasn't going to move as much as I had anticipated and I started to adjust my swing, but there wasn't quite enough time."

Warren shook his head, scarcely able to credit what he was hearing. "Do you realize that Ted Williams himself said that the most difficult thing in all of sports was hitting a pitched ball with a bat?"

"One should always keep in mind that merely saying a thing is difficult does not necessarily make it so. I suspect that you would seldom be wrong if you inferred that a person making such a statement does so in an attempt to explain, or excuse, their own shortcomings." Henry stood up and slipped on a pair of rubber shower sandals. "Who's Ted Williams?"

"He told you that? Told you that he saw that the pitch wasn't breaking as much as he thought it would and tried to adjust his swing with the ball almost to the plate?"

Warren nodded. He was sitting in Preacher Brown's office. "That's what he said."

Preacher laughed and broke wind loudly. "That boy's as

full of shit as a Christmas turkey. And I'll bet you believed him."

"I didn't say that. I'm just repeating what he told me. But I'll tell you what I do believe." Warren leaned forward and put both hands on Preacher's desk for emphasis. "I believe that boy is something special."

"Yeah?" The Preacher stood and grabbed his crotch. "So's my dick." He laughed at what he considered to be an exceptionally clever witticism and sat back down. "You've been to college. What the fuck's a non-whatchamacallit equation?"

"Nonlinear, and damned if I know. It obviously has something to do with math. He just said it was harder than picking up patterns from opposing pitchers."

"Now how the fuck would a kid born and raised in the South, just out of the army, no college or anything, know something like that? You've just had smoke blown up your ass and you don't even know it." Preacher jerked a thumb toward his office door. "Get the fuck out of here," he growled, not unkindly. "We're taking this ball club north in a couple of weeks and I've still got a shit load of work to do."

In the locker room Henry was toweling off after his shower when he was approached diffidently by Richie Sanders, the young Triple-A catcher promoted to the big club with the trade of Bobo Martinez to the Mets.

"Hey, Soldier, that was a hell of game you caught today," Richie said shyly. "Say, you don't mind the guys calling you Soldier, do you?"

Henry shook his head. "Not really, although you should keep in mind that this almost compulsive adolescent use of nicknames by ballplayers, and all professional athletes for that matter, plays directly into management's efforts to trivialize the individual, thus providing the owners with what I consider to be a distinct advantage in all labor-management negotiations." Henry pulled on his trousers, *sans* underpants. "I think you'll find that few chief executive officers of Fortune 500 corporations are referred to as *Soldier,* or *Bobo,* or *Preacher,* or *Nails,* whether among their peers or in the press. While the nicknames lend perhaps a colorful air to the overall ambiance of the game, the players should be aware that there is a price for everything, in this case a subtle and yet nonetheless very real one."

"Huh?"

"I wonder how many people have noted the correlation between the fact that Jimmy Carter failed in his bid for reelection after one term as President and his insistence that he be referred to always as *Jimmy* as opposed to the more adult *James.*"

Richie had been warned by Buddy McNerney of the B squad that Henry was given to saying unintelligible things. He was, nonetheless, a hell of a ballplayer.

"Uh, yeah, I see what you mean, but, like, you don't mind if the guys call you Soldier, do you?"

"Call me what you like," Henry answered agreeably.

"Yeah, well, anyway, like I was saying, you caught a hell of a game out there today, Soldier." Richie moved a step closer to Henry and lowered his voice. "Dickhead Bell told a couple of us what the Preacher made him do in the game today and we wanted you to know we thought it was horseshit, trying to show you up and all."

"I wouldn't spend a great deal of time worrying about it." Henry slipped his bare feet into a pair of buttery-soft deerskin huarache moccasins Ramona had given him the day before. *Only crazy Anglos wear those hard leather shoes,* she told him. *Mexicans know that happiness travels up from the feet.* "Preacher was merely trying to express his irrational displeasure at the fact that notwithstanding my lack of credentials I've done so well this spring. He finds it most disquieting that I have not come up through the system of

Organized Baseball. You might go so far as to say that my presence on this team deeply disturbs his *wa*."

"His what?"

"His *wa*. It's an Eastern concept having to do with tranquility and harmony."

Richie nodded sagely. "You mean eastern like back in North Carolina, right?" All the boys knew that Henry came from the Tarheel State. Richie himself was from Blackstone, Virginia, and felt a warm glow of comradely affection for a fellow Southerner, particularly one with an arm like Henry's. He assumed that this *wa* was some sort of colloquialism peculiar to whatever rural county the Soldier had grown up in. In fact, now that he thought about it he recollected hearing as how it was definitely a North Carolina thing. He had an uncle who had gotten a dose of the clap from a mill worker down in Durham when Richie was still a teenager playing American Legion ball and he remembered him, his uncle, allowing as how North Carolinians had some mighty queer habits. He thought they were a little on the dirty side, not quite reaching a level of personal fastidiousness that, say, a man from Virginia was used to in folks. Richie, although impressed at the time, now discounted such a notion as likely influenced by his uncle's unfortunate bout with gonorrhea. On the other hand, Richie knew for a fact that North Carolinians did have certain habits peculiar to themselves, such as, for instance, always slamming doors when going into or out of a house. He nodded again, more to himself than to Henry, knowing that *wa* was something a Yankee would never understand. He quickly gave a silent word of thanks that he'd been born a Virginian and a Southerner.

"Something like that." Henry, dressing completed, closed the door to his locker. "In any event, I appreciate your comments regarding the game."

"Most of us are going out for a couple of beers before dinner. Want to join us?"

"Perhaps another time," Henry said. "I have a previous engagement."

"What are you going to do when spring training ends and he follows the team back to Oakland?"

Ramona and her sister Rosa were sitting at one of the tables in their father's restaurant, drinking *sangria* and resting their feet. It had been a busy evening and in a few moments Ramona would leave to drive over to the garage apartment where she now spent her nights. Rosa's question was spoken in a low voice so as not to reach the ears of their father, who was in the kitchen cleaning up. Ramona shrugged.

"Has he said anything about that?"

Ramona shook her head.

"He is like all *beisbol* players." Rosa snorted and poured them each a fresh glass of sangria. "Here today, and gone tomorrow. Papa is right."

Ramona stood up, anxious to feel the weight of Henry's body on top of hers. "You talk too much," she said, not unkindly. Both sisters laughed, sharing the joy of youth, the certainty that they would always feel this way. "And Papa is old."

"We called you in to tell you that we've decided to put you on the big-league club roster and take you back to Oakland for the start of the season."

Henry sat at a large table in a hotel suite in downtown Phoenix. Seated across the table from Henry was the team's manager, Preacher Brown, and the managing general partner, Robert Edgerton. Also present was Sarah Gill, the partnership's general counsel. He nodded in response to Preacher's opening statement but said nothing. Of course, with the Bobo Martinez trade and the way he had torn up the Cactus League with his bat and his throwing arm, he and nearly everyone else on the club with even half a brain (which excluded approximately one-half to two-thirds of the players and clubhouse staff) had known that he would make the trip to Oakland for Opening Day.

"I won't lie to you," the Preacher continued. "We've been pleased with the way you've played. The plan is for you to back up Richie Sanders."

The statement was absurd on its face inasmuch as Richie had not caught so much as an inning of a single exhibition game since Henry had been brought over from the nonroster group.

"If he gets injured or needs a break you'll be there to help out."

Again, Henry said nothing.

Robert Edgerton mistook his silence for a bargaining ploy. "You're a very lucky young man to be given an opportunity like this," he interjected. "Not many organizations, regardless of how you've played in spring training, would be willing to take such a huge risk. I hope you realize that." He waited for a response. When none was forthcoming he spoke again, irritation evident in his voice. "Do you understand what I'm trying to say?"

"I do. My skills are such that you felt you could dispense with the services of Mr. Martinez for the coming season. Given his major-league record it must be clear to even the dullest mind that there were other considerations to which I am not privy which figured into your decision to trade him, but that is neither here nor there. Suffice it to say that you, all of you, believe that I can perform satisfactorily as the team's starting catcher. Clearly, this," Henry smiled and indicated the instant gathering with a small gesture, "is an effort to induce me to become contractually obligated to the team for the least amount of money possible."

The lawyer, Sarah Gill, who had never before met or even seen Henry, was visibly startled. The voice emanating from the young athlete across the table was, she told herself, all wrong. Everything about it, timbre, pitch, inflection, intonation, bespoke a worldliness, a maturity, that did not comport with her considerable experience in dealing with baseball players, even older ones at the end of their careers. She looked closely at Henry and blinked several times, as if so doing would somehow clear her vision, would bring what she saw more into focus with what she heard.

"Have you got an agent?" Edgerton asked suspiciously.

Henry shook his head.

"Good." Ms. Gill laid an official Major League Player's Contract in front of Henry. "That is to say, I, we, think you'll find that in dealing with this organization there will be no need to rely on outsiders for advice. Rest assured that I will fairly answer any questions you might have as regards the nature of this contract and your rights and obligations thereunder. You will note that despite your inexperience as a ballplayer the team agrees hereby to pay you the annual sum of $300,000. On top of that, just for signing the contract today, the team will pay you a generous cash bonus of $25,000, payable in equal monthly installments over the next three years." She turned to the contract's last page and indicated the line on which Henry was to sign his name. "You may use my pen," she added, handing Henry a Mont Blanc fountain pen.

Henry took the pen and slowly unscrewed the cap. He held the pen up to his eyes and carefully examined the scrollwork on the bright silver-and-gold nib. "I understand, you realize, that $300,000 is the Major League minimum which a team, under the agreement with the Players Association, can pay an active player on its roster."

"Well, technically, that's . . ." Edgerton started to respond.

"I didn't say it was unacceptable," Henry said, holding up his hand to interrupt the managing general partner. "I was merely pointing out that I understand what the number represents. As to the signing bonus," Henry smiled at Preacher Brown, Edgerton, and Sarah Gill in turn, "it would be less than gracious of me to quibble over such a generous gesture on the team's part." He signed the contract and returned the pen to Ms. Gill.

Edgerton smiled and reached across the table to shake Henry's hand. "Congratulations. And as you'll soon find out, your salary is not the only benefit you will derive from being a member of the Oakland A's. We've taken the liberty of opening an account in your name at the East Oakland Savings and Loan. In addition to a checking account into which all sums due you from the team will be automatically deposited, as a member of the team you are automatically entitled to a MasterCard account with a $25,000 credit limit." Edgerton neglected to add that he was a director and majority shareholder of the aforesaid savings and loan, and that the MasterCard account granted to all A's ballplayers carried a 24% annual interest rate, the highest legally allowable rate in effect in the entire state of California. "My secretary will provide you with all the details. Lastly, the team has designated a condominium for your residence during the season. It's located in Hayward, a mere fifteen minutes from the Alameda County Coliseum. And you'll be pleased to hear that several of your teammates will be staying in the same complex." Again, Edgerton neglected to inform Henry that he, Edgerton, indirectly owned the condominium complex in question through a real estate development and management company that he owned. He handed Henry a set of keys together with a map showing the unit's location. "A representative from the company that owns and manages the condo will get in touch with you regarding the rental agreement." He reached across the table and patted the back of Henry's hand. "Don't worry about the rent. I've already looked at it and made sure it's fair." In fact, the rental amount he intended to charge Henry, and the amount he charged all of the Oakland players he was able to wheedle into one of his many units, was approximately 25% above the fair market rate for comparable units.

"Thanks, but that won't be necessary." Henry rose and pushed the keys back across the table. "I'm not sure yet what I'm going to do, so I'll find a place on my own."

"What?" Edgerton wasn't sure he had heard correctly.

"Oh, and I won't be needing the bank account either," Henry added. "I'd prefer to be paid in cash." He turned and left the suite, closing the door softly behind him.

"I don't like it," Preacher said as soon as Henry was out of the room. "No sir, I don't like it one little bit." He looked at Edgerton. "That boy knows we lowballed him on the contract and he didn't do or say anything about it. That ain't natural, not these days." He pointed at the managing general partner. "Something's wrong with that boy and we're going to be sorry we traded Bobo Martinez before this whole thing is over."

"Nonsense." Edgerton spoke with authority. "He's right out of the army, a young hick barely out of North Carolina. He knows nothing, *nada, niente.* As far as the bank thing and the condo goes, he's just trying to show some independence. Don't worry." Edgerton nodded to add emphasis to his words. He looked over at his lawyer. "What do you think?"

If Sarah Gill knew anything, she knew who the boss was. In addition to being the team's general counsel she was a partner in a San Francisco law firm that relied on Robert Edgerton's varied business interests to the tune of high six-figure billings each and every year. She, like Preacher Brown, was troubled by the young man who had just left the suite, although for quite a different reason. Not a particularly religious woman, she nonetheless worried when voices didn't match bodies. On the other hand, she knew that Robert Edgerton wanted to be reassured that everything had gone well in the just completed negotiation and contract

signing. She smiled. "I think you made a hell of a deal."
She rose from the table and pointed at the newly signed
contract for emphasis. "And, whatever else happens, you
have the comfort of knowing that he won't be playing baseball for anyone else for quite a long time."

Preacher Brown grunted and looked with ill-concealed
distaste at the team's general counsel. He hated lawyers almost as much as he hated the agents who had become as
ubiquitous as the cockroaches that thrived in minor-league
(and not a few major-league) clubhouses. *Fuck you, sweetheart,* he thought, knowing full well that when things turned
to shit, as he without a doubt expected them to, he, Preacher
Brown, would be held solely accountable. *And the horse you
rode in on.*

"If you knew that the amount they offered you was inadequate why did you sign?"

Henry stood in front of the bathroom mirror, gazing intently at his face. He ran the fingers of his right hand across
his forehead and down his nose. From there he trailed his
fingers across his lips and over his strong chin, looking for
all the world like a blind man exploring another man's face
for a sign of recognition. He heard Ramona's voice but not
her question. "I'm sorry; I didn't hear what you asked."

Ramona appeared at the bathroom's door, barely visible
in the mirror behind Henry's broad back. "You didn't hear
because you didn't listen. You are always looking at yourself
in that mirror. One who didn't know you would say that you
are vain."

"But you know better."

It was a statement, not a question.

"*Sí,* I know better. With all your looking, has the face
become finally familiar?"

"No." Henry turned from the mirror with a smile. "Now,
what did you ask me a second ago?"

"I asked why you signed the contract if you knew the amount they were offering was inadequate."

"The amount per se was not important. I was prepared to sign for whatever they offered. What was important was how they conducted themselves, whether or not they would be willing to abuse what is essentially a grossly skewed balance of power between team and player. The salary offered by a team is but one facet of the equation, albeit certainly an important one for most players."

"But not for you."

"Not for me." He paused for a moment, thinking how best to articulate the inarticulable. "Something is going to happen in Oakland, something of importance to me."

"What?"

Henry shook his head. "I don't know."

"Something to do with the team?"

"No." Another shake of the head. "Something to do with me." He looked at Ramona and found himself stirred anew at the sight of her full, heavy breasts, and the sweep of her belly from her navel down to the confluence of her thighs. "Will you come with me?" His voice was almost a whisper. "To Oakland?"

EIGHT

★ ⭑ ★

Berkeley, California

Two enormous blue gum eucalyptus trees framed the entrance to the cottage Henry and Ramona rented in the Berkeley hills, hard by the Lawrence Hall of Science. The impressive but trashy blue gums, with assistance from the grove of redwood trees that completed the encirclement of the tiny cottage, kept the air redolent with the scent of pitch and resin. At night, when the hot, still air sixty miles away in the Sacramento Valley sucked the fog in through the Golden Gate and over the East Bay hills, the trees soughed quietly, as if grateful for the moisture that condensed on their limbs and dripped to the ground. Across Grizzly Peak Boulevard from the cottage a large regional park provided a daytime home and trysting ground for a host of quadrupeds that swarmed out of the park every night in search of easy pickings. Raccoons, deer, coyotes, the occasional fox, and feral cats worked the Berkeley hill neighborhoods with an insouciance bordering on outright insolence. The nighttime din of mammalian mastication was frequently augmented with exuberant noise from the University of California fraternity and sorority houses on the campus below, strangely reassuring sounds connoting the inevitable triumph of hormones over intellect.

Henry and Ramona had three days to furnish the cottage

before Henry and the team left for its season-opening road trip, a seven-day swing through Seattle and Anaheim. They bought a futon, a kitchen table, and two wooden chairs to sit on while they ate.

"Only two?" the furniture store salesman asked when Henry told him how many they wanted. "What about when you have friends over for dinner?" He smiled somewhat nervously. Although he fancied himself a stand-up comic of some talent, he had no wish to antagonize the extremely large young man in front of him. "Wouldn't you want them to sit, too?"

Henry shook his head solemnly and the salesman wisely decided not to press the issue.

For three days Henry practiced with the team at the Alameda County Coliseum and, with Ramona, pounded the new futon into submission at night. A home delivery service run by Cal students delivered to their front door complete meals prepared by the finest restaurants in Berkeley's famed gourmet ghetto. Other than to attend practice and to purchase the furniture, they left the cottage only once, to purchase Henry a jacket and tie. At a team meeting just before the end of spring training Preacher Brown had reminded everyone that club rules required the players to wear a sport coat and tie when traveling with the team. Since Henry's wardrobe consisted entirely of casual wear, he sought Ramona's assistance in the purchase of the requisite items. In downtown Berkeley, on their way to a clothing store they chanced upon a secondhand shop, which, as luck would have it, had just purchased the clothing estate of a recently deceased gentleman of obese proportions. Among the articles presented for resale was a dark blue pinstriped suit, the coat of which fit Henry's massive shoulders quite nicely.

"His wife told us that he choked to death on a piece of beef," the salesperson, an anorexic young woman with red-rimmed eyes and a large safety pin piercing her right nostril, informed them. "In a restaurant in Stockton," she added with a sniff of disdain, her tone implying that anyone so foolish as to dine in Stockton, particularly on the flesh of a dead animal, deserved exactly what he or she got.

To complete the ensemble Henry purchased, also from the decedent's estate, a size 22 white dress shirt with short sleeves and a silk tie that would have stopped conversation in a bowling alley, featuring, as it did, a hand-painted topless hula girl rampant on a background field of electric blue. The entire outfit, coat, shirt, and tie, cost $35.00.

At a notions store Ramona bought a packet of single-edged razor blades, and a needle and thread with which to alter and take in the coat's voluminous waist. The suit pants were discarded as soon as they got home.

"I told you all Mexican women could sew," she proudly reminded Henry as he modeled her handiwork back at the cottage.

Although puckered in one or two places, the new seams she had cut and sewn were by and large respectably done, certainly to Henry's uncritical eye. To be sure, the coat hung a little unevenly, the result of one seam being a quarter of an inch longer than the other, but for the most part the result was not displeasing. And even if it could be said that he looked more upholstered than dressed, when the coat was worn with the Hawaiian-motif tie few observers would notice the fit at all.

On the morning the team was to depart on its season-opening road trip Ramona dropped Henry off in the Coliseum parking lot near the entrance to the clubhouse.

"Have you got enough money for your ticket?" he asked before getting out of the car. Ramona had decided to fly back to Phoenix while Henry was away.

"More than enough," she reassured him. "You look very handsome."

"Here." He thrust a wad of bills, several hundred dollars,

into her hand. "Buy something nice for the house." He hesitated for a second. "I hope your father isn't going to be too put out with you."

Ramona shrugged and then smiled. "I'll see you in a week."

After watching her drive from the lot Henry picked up his small flight bag and entered the long, dark concrete tunnel leading to the clubhouse. Inside the clubhouse a large crowd, at least a hundred men and women, was milling about. Several long tables had been set with an elegant buffet and two bars were tended by tuxedoed bartenders.

"Henry! Henry Spencer!" Robert Edgerton's voice rang out over the noise of fifty different conversations. "Come over here." He waved his arm from across the room. "I'd like you to meet some people."

Richie Sanders was standing off to one side like a poor relation in cowboy boots invited to a black-tie function, physically and psychically apart from the celebration taking place. Ignoring Edgerton, Henry turned to Sanders and asked, "What's going on?"

"Bo Siefert," a veteran utility infielder, "told me that the team does this every year. A big party to kick off the season." Richie looked around nervously, as if afraid a guard might ask him to leave at any moment. "I'll tell you the truth, Soldier, I never seen nothing like it in the minors." He giggled, his eyes wide. "I guess this is all part of being in the Show."

"Who are all these people?"

"Damned if I know, but Bo said a lot of them were going to be flying with us up to Seattle. On the team charter." Richie could scarcely credit such an extravagant expenditure of money after spending a number of years in the minor leagues, where the organization was so loath to part with a dollar that baseballs were used until the horsehide was almost black with oil and dirt and the ball itself was literally as hard as a rock. The new balls they practiced with in Oakland seemed almost soft by comparison. He shook his head. "Have you got words?"

"I haven't. When do we leave for the airport?"

Before Richie could answer, several of their teammates walked over from one of the buffet tables and joined them.

"Soldier!" Dickhead Bell looked at him admiringly. "Where in the fuck did you ever get that tie?" Bell, generally thought to be the absolute worst dresser on the team, a not insignificant feat given the presence of teammates with less than rocket scientist intellects and, for all intents and purposes, almost unlimited financial resources, knew fine art when he saw it. "I ain't never seen tits like that on a tie."

Bell's loud comments drew a small crowd of onlookers, a number of whom noticed that, in addition to the topless hula girl tie, Henry was wearing an un-ironed white shirt, the dark blue pinstriped suit jacket he and Ramona had purchased in the secondhand store, a pair of tan cotton trousers, and the deerskin huarache moccasins Ramona had given him in Phoenix. Several of the invited guests sniggered.

"Goddamn it, I got to have me that tie." Dickhead had arrived early for the party and was several drinks ahead of most of his teammates. He stared intently at the object of his desire. "I'll give you a hundred dollars for it," he declared.

He, like everyone on the team, had heard through the grapevine that the Soldier had been signed for $300,000, the major-league minimum. He himself, after last season's record of 15 wins and 5 losses with a 2.44 ERA, had signed a new three-year contract worth a total of $4.5 million. A hundred dollars for the tie was a lot for the rookie, but he, Dickhead, felt that he could afford to be a little generous.

"Cash fucking money," he added, to buttress the offer.

Henry just smiled, assuming that the pitcher, obviously somewhat inebriated, was teasing him.

"A hundred dollars?" Theo Carter, the team's starting left fielder and stolen base record holder, spoke up, his voice incredulous. An African-American from Cincinnati, Ohio, Theo was finishing up the last year of a contract that was paying him $3.5 million that season. He was looking forward to testing the free-agent market at the conclusion of the year, certain that he would be able to obtain a contract that paid him *real* money. He knew that Dickhead Bell, not unlike many of his white teammates, did not particularly care for any of the brothers on the team and he saw an opportunity to jab him a little. "For *that* tie?" He shook his head in mock disgust at Dickhead's penuriousness. "Man, that's chump change." He turned toward Soldier. "I'll give you *five* hundred dollars." He reached into his pocket and pulled out a thick roll of bills. "Money talks; bullshit walks," he added in the hope of further annoying Dickhead.

A soft *ooh* went through the onlookers and the conversation level throughout the room dropped as more people realized that an event of some importance was taking place in the corner.

"Goddamn it, goddamn it," Dickhead responded, his brain vapor locked at the sudden offer made by his teammate, his *black* teammate. His eyes bulged from his face, adding to the already curious appearance of his oddly misshapen head. He was determined not to be shown up in front of everyone, especially not by a black man. "I seen it first," he grated to Theo, his pitted brown teeth exposed between grimaced lips. He turned back to Henry. "I'll give you, I'll give you . . ." Dickhead's voice dropped as he feverishly tried to come up with a number, "I'll give you a *thousand* goddamn dollars." He said the last with a flourish, spittle flying from his lips, looking not at Henry but at Theo.

The offer hovered over the clubhouse, the enormity and ridiculousness of it silencing everyone. Finally, unable to bear the tension, first one ballplayer, then another, began laughing. As each man joined in, *seriatim,* Dickhead's face grew redder and redder as he realized that they were laughing at him. He looked at Theo with raw, undistilled hatred in his eyes and clenched and unclenched his fists. For a brief moment several players closest to the two men thought there might be a fight.

Henry quickly unknotted the tie and handed it over to the distraught pitcher. "Here," he said quietly, drawing Dickhead's attention away from the object of his fury. "I want you to have it. As a gift."

"By God, I offered you a thousand dollars and that's what I'm going to pay," Dickhead sputtered, his honor at stake.

"No." Henry's voice now carried an edge that cut through Dickhead's anger. "I'm giving it to you as a gift." He paused for a second and held the dim-witted pitcher's eyes firmly with his own. "Do you understand what I'm saying to you?"

"Yeah, sure, I guess so." Dickhead looked desperately about, trying to ascertain whether or not he could accept the gift and still retain his dignity and honor. He realized he had no choice. "Yeah, I understand." He took the tie from Henry. "Thanks, Soldier. I appreciate it; I surely do."

Theo Carter turned away with a broad smile on his face, his goal of making Dickhead Bell look the fool accomplished. Across the room Robert Edgerton renewed his call for Henry.

"What was that all about?" he asked when Henry joined him, although in point of fact he didn't really want to know. The relationship among ballplayers on the team, on any team in the league, was a delicate matter at best, and he, Edgerton, was just as happy that a *de facto* segregation existed between black and white players. The less racial interaction the better, he instinctively felt, an opinion obviously shared by the players themselves.

"What was what all about?" Henry responded impassively.

"Never mind. I have some people here I want you to meet." He turned to a handsome middle-aged couple standing next to him. "Howard, Ellen, I'd like you to meet Henry Spencer, the team's new catcher. Henry, this is Mr. and Mrs.

Stanhope. Mr. Stanhope is an investment banker in the City."

Henry nodded and accepted Stanhope's right hand in his own. The banker's small, soft hand, somewhat to Mrs. Stanhope's dismay, quite disappeared as Henry's fingers closed gently around it. She unconsciously held her breath until it reappeared, apparently none the worse for wear, at the end of the handshake. Also distracting her was the obvious fact that Henry wore no underclothing beneath his thin cotton slacks. She nodded at Henry when he looked at her and carefully kept her hands to herself.

"Congratulations on making the team," she said. "I'm sure your parents must be quite proud of you."

Henry smiled. "Do you have children?"

"Why, yes, we have two boys, twelve and fourteen." She smiled instinctively at her husband, proud of the accomplishment of having two fine young sons to carry on the family name. Both boys attended an exclusive boarding school in Carmel.

"Are you hoping that they grow up to play professional baseball?" Henry asked.

"Why, er, no. I mean, they're both excellent students." Puzzled, Ellen Stanhope looked at her husband for moral support. She turned back to Henry, unable to resist a furtive glance at his crotch. She quickly looked up with a nervous smile "Are you a parent?"

Henry shook his head. "I don't believe so, although, to be honest with you, there seem to be large portions of my life that are less than clear to me."

"Oh, my." Mrs. Stanhope now really was confused. "I'm not sure . . ." her voice trailed off.

"Yes, well, thank you, Henry." Robert Edgerton leaped into the breach. "I'm sure Mr. and Mrs. Stanhope will be following your progress this season with great interest."

"What an *odd* young man," Mrs. Stanhope observed after Henry had, in the firm grasp of Edgerton, walked away.

"What do you suppose he meant about parts of his life not being clear to him?"

"He's clearly a mental defective," her husband replied. "As would be anyone who spent their life in a gymnasium as he obviously has."

The beneficiary of an Ivy League education, Mr. Stanhope had little regard for anyone below his own station in life, and in fact considered most of the world's population to be little more than a natural resource best utilized by men like himself. He had accepted Edgerton's invitation to attend the team's season-opening reception only because he thought his wife might be amused by the sight of the players, much as one might be amused by the animals at a zoo or a circus. He had not anticipated actually having to speak with one, and the experience merely confirmed his previously held opinion of all professional athletes.

"And that remark about not believing he was a parent," Mrs. Stanhope continued, exasperation evident in her voice. "How can one not know whether or not one is a parent?"

"Does King know whether or not he has offspring?" Mr. Stanhope asked rhetorically. King was the family's golden retriever. "For that matter, does James?" James was the gardener, handyman, and resident caretaker at the family country estate in Sonoma County. When the family spent weekends at the estate James was required to wear long-sleeve shirts because of tattoos on both arms, which, although not of a risqué nature, were nonetheless considered inappropriate viewing for the Stanhope children.

"Oh, Howard." Ellen Stanhope gave her husband a look of mock reproval. "You shouldn't say things like that." Still, she had to admit, her husband had a point.

Robert Edgerton guided Henry into Preacher Brown's office off the main clubhouse floor. "Henry, I hope you're not going to make me regret my decision to bring you onto the team."

Henry assumed that the managing general partner's statement did not require a response and so he stood silent.

"Part of being a major leaguer," Edgerton continued, "an important part, is dealing with the public, and dealing with the public means telling them what they expect to hear and nothing more. As far as the public is concerned you had a perfectly normal childhood with perfectly normal parents who are as proud as punch that their son is a major-league ballplayer. Do you understand?"

"I can't imagine why my possession of a certain degree of athletic ability would impress anyone one way or another. I mean, it's not exactly akin to finding a cure for cancer, is it?"

"That's not the point." Edgerton looked closely at Henry. "The public doesn't give a damn about curing cancer, at least not while they're out at the ballpark. What they care about is the game, and its immutability. It's a straight, clean game, played by straight, clean men."

"Men like Bobo Martinez?"

Edgerton's eyes narrowed at the mention of the recently traded catcher's name. "What do you know about Martinez?"

Henry shrugged. "Enough to know that he would hardly fit anyone's description of a straight, clean man."

"Martinez was, is, an aberration. The instant I found out about his perversion I got rid of him," Edgerton lied. "Forget about Martinez." Edgerton paused for a second, trying to figure out a different tack. "You know, Soldier, you don't mind if I call you Soldier, do you, even though you didn't come up through the system, that is, even though you've never before played Organized Ball, you must nevertheless appreciate the wonderful history of baseball in this country, the tradition of the game. Young boys daydreaming of putting on the pinstripes and playing at Yankee Stadium."

"They'd be better advised spending their time at the library," Henry interrupted.

Shocked, Edgerton completely lost his train of thought.

"Aren't you the least bit proud to be a major-league ball-player?"

"I hadn't really thought about it, to tell you the truth. But if I did think about it I guess I'd have to say that I'm not, at least not particularly. I have certain abilities which you and Preacher Brown have determined are useful to the club. You and I have agreed upon a salary and here I am." He turned to leave the office. "By the way, you mentioned my parents being proud of my status as a major-league ball-player. My parents are dead." He paused for a second. "At least I think they are."

In the four games at Seattle to open the season Henry, batting sixth in the lineup, went ten for sixteen at the plate, threw out three runners trying to steal second, one trying to steal third, and picked two men off first base. The pickoffs at first occurred during the first game and thereafter few base runners were willing to risk much of a lead off the bag, thus contributing to Henry's success at throwing out subsequent base stealers. Oakland won three of the four games. In Modesto, Buddy McNerney read of Henry's performance in a day old copy of the green sports section of the *San Francisco Chronicle*. Like all minor leaguers Buddy kept a single-minded focus on what was going on with regard to player developments at his position in the bigs. While pleased that the young man he had nicknamed Soldier was doing so well right from the get-go, he also knew what such success meant to every catcher up and down the line in the A's minor-league organizations. And if he didn't, his team-mates were more than willing to clue him in.

"McNerney," one of them called out after reading the same sports section, "you better find you something to do in the Real World, 'cause it looks like the Soldier is gonna be lighting fires in Oakland for more years than you've got left."

On the team charter from Seattle to Anaheim, Warren Mercer cornered Henry in the rear of the plane.

"Nice series in Seattle."

Henry nodded an acknowledgment but did not reply.

"You're seeing the ball particularly well for this early in the season," Warren persisted.

Henry shrugged. "Their pitchers were throwing strikes."

"Isn't that what opposing pitchers are supposed to throw?"

"Not to someone hitting as well as I do, particularly when the seventh, eighth, and ninth hitters in the batting order are coming up behind me. After my first two at-bats in the first game their manager should have pitched around me. That he failed to do so does not speak well of his intellectual capabilities."

"Do you really think he should have ordered his pitchers to pitch around a rookie batting in the sixth position, regardless of how well he was swinging the bat?"

"What would you have done?"

Warren considered himself an old-time baseball man, one to whom the concept of giving in to anyone, particularly a rookie playing in his very first big-league game, was anathema. *In my day,* he thought but did not say, *when real men played the game, the pitcher would have knocked you on your ass after that second hit.* "I guess I'd have pitched to you just like the Seattles did."

"Then I guess you would have been wrong." Henry's gaze was uncomfortably direct. "On the other hand, baseball, as is every other field of human endeavor, is marked more by timidity than boldness. Only after a particular strategy has been proven wrong on countless occasions will someone feel that the risk of changing that strategy has become less than the risk of sticking with it. In other words, even if doing something a certain way is demonstrably wrong, provided the doing has been sanctioned as correct over a sufficiently long period of time, then managers will stay with it until literally forced to do otherwise, and even then will try something new only after assuring themselves that the threat of so doing has been reduced to an acceptable level."

The A's played three games in Anaheim and won all three. Henry went seven for twelve with two home runs, a double, and a triple. As he had in Seattle, he picked two men off first and threw out one runner at second. He would have foiled two other steal attempts but for the fact that Scooter Riggs, the A's second baseman, dropped two perfect throws for errors. Word of Henry's start was beginning to seep around the league as managers and players read the line scores of each game. As impressive as the numbers were, most everyone dismissed them to one degree or another, based on the twin facts that Henry was a rookie and that, because he had never played Organized Ball, no one had ever heard of him before. Even Preacher Brown, Henry's manager, downplayed his stats at every opportunity.

"Have you ever seen anyone start off this fast?"

Preacher lit a cigarette and let his irritation at Warren Mercer's question show in his jerky motions. The two men were sitting in the manager's office in the visiting team clubhouse after the A's last game with the Angels.

"Goddamn it, Warren, you know we've only played seven games for chrissakes. The pitchers aren't even loosened up yet. They're just grooving balls down the middle to him."

Warren, knowing Preacher's volatile temper, chose not to point out the fact that nobody else on the team was hitting even close to the Soldier's mark. "How about his arm?" he asked, taking a different tack.

"It's a hell of an arm; I'll give you that." Preacher paused and studied the tip of his cigarette. "He's young and strong and can throw the piss out of a baseball." In spite of his annoyance at having to talk about the rookie he still felt had been forced on him by Robert Edgerton, he smiled. "By God there won't be too many teams anxious to run against that arm when word gets around."

"Word's already getting around," Warren observed.

"But he's raw," Preacher continued, ignoring Warren's comment. "You know yourself you just can't rush a kid into catching. It's the most demanding position on the field. He's making mistakes."

"Like what?"

Preacher shook his head. "Lots of little things. For instance, tonight, when Bradley came home on Jackson's single to right field. Soldier saw that Marty's," the A's right fielder's, "throw in wouldn't make it in time for a close play at home and so he didn't try to block the plate. I told him after the inning that he's got to block the plate anyway on a play like that. Make the runner either knock him over or force a hook slide. As big as the Soldier is, most runners are going to go for the hook slide and a certain percentage will miss the plate, giving him a chance for a late tag and an out he otherwise wouldn't have. Shit like that." He gave Warren the look of a man who knows what he's talking about. "You can't take a kid right off the farm . . ."

"You mean right out of the army," Warren corrected.

"Whatever. All I'm saying is you can't take a raw kid, one that's never played no Organized Ball, and expect him to know things like how to force a hook slide. Important things."

"But he can learn."

"Sure he can learn, but in the meantime, arm or no arm, he ain't the catcher Bobo Martinez is and I'm thinking we'll lose a game now and again because of it." Preacher pointed his finger at Warren. "The big leagues ain't no place to learn how to catch."

"You going to move him up in the batting order?"

"No." Preacher stubbed out his cigarette on the concrete

clubhouse floor and stood up, preparing to undress and head for the showers. "Experience tells me that rookies don't belong in the first four or five slots in the batting order."

Warren thought about the conversation he'd had with Henry on the flight from Seattle to Anaheim. "He'd be driving in a lot more runs if he were hitting third or fourth."

"In case you hadn't noticed, we've won six out of our first seven games. I'd say I'm doing things just about right, wouldn't you?"

Warren watched Preacher peel his uniform pants off and noticed that the old man was wearing a cup. *Why in the hell is he bothering to wear a protective cup?* he wondered. "You know," he said casually, reaching over and taking a cigarette from Preacher's open pack, "I asked a friend of mine back in North Carolina to check around on the kid, find out a little information on him."

"You sportswriters are all alike," the Preacher snorted. "Always sticking your noses up someone's butt, sniffing around where you don't belong. What'd did you find out?"

"Not much." *Not much,* Warren thought, was a goddamned understatement. *What do you mean nobody in his own hometown knows him?* he had asked incredulously when given that information.

"That's not what I said," Bernard Johnson, the Raleigh *News & Observer* reporter had replied somewhat irritably over the telephone. "I said that the people in Kernersville that I talked to seemed to know of him while not exactly knowing him. Or his family."

"What the hell does that mean?"

"It's hard to explain," Bernard replied.

And it *was* hard to explain.

Oh, yeah, I been knowing young Henry Spencer for years, someone would say. *My sister's boy went to school with him. Didn't he join the army or something?* And when people were asked about the Spencer family the responses grew even more vague. *They weren't from around here, not orig-*

inally. I believe I heard that Henry's mother's people was from up around Asheville. I don't recollect where his father was from. I believe they're both dead now, but don't hold me to that. I kind of lost track of them after young Henry moved away. Baseball? No, I don't believe I ever heard of Henry playing any ball around here. Maybe someone over at the high school would know.

But nobody did. "Some of the teachers claim they remember him," Bernard told Warren, "but I can't seem to pin them down on anything specific. His grades were good enough to pass but not good enough to attract attention. He didn't play on the school baseball team and damned if he wasn't absent the one day pictures were taken for the yearbook."

"Doesn't that seem strange to you? I mean, coming from a small town and all, shouldn't people know him and his family better?"

"Not really. Thanks mainly to Hollywood, small town life is generally thought to be a great deal more communal than is actually the case. Think about it. The vast majority of people on this planet are so unremarkable that they go through life without raising any sort of a stir. Other people meet them, go to school with them, work with them, hell, live next door to them, and in fact never really know much if anything about them or their families. Most people, whether small town or big city, have too many worries of their own to spend time wondering about so-and-so's boy who they haven't seen or heard about for years." The *News & Observer* reporter paused and chuckled. "Of course, if young Henry Spencer turns out to be a famous big-league ballplayer, there will be no end of people throughout the county who will claim intimate knowledge of him and his family."

NINE

⋆ ✦ ⋆

As April ripened into May and May into June, Henry set
the American League West on fire with his bat and arm.
After a six-game home stand (three against the Tigers and
three against the Blue Jays, all six of which the Oaklands
won) and a foray into both the American League Central
and Eastern divisions, his stats were being trumpeted
throughout the land and tickets for Oakland away games
became a hot item among those with a speculative approach
to life. Henry appeared on the cover of *Sports Illustrated*
and, although a few senior sports beat writers around the
country grumped biliously about all the attention being paid
to a mere rookie, sports fans and prepubescent autograph
speculators sat up and looked about not at all unlike the
residents of a prosperous prairie dog village.

"I'm pregnant."

Henry nodded solemnly in response to Ramona's quietly
spoken pronouncement.

"I went to see a midwife last week and she confirmed it."
Ramona sighed. She and Henry, having just made love, were
lounging on the futon. "I knew it before seeing her, of
course." She looked up at Henry from the vantage point of
his chest, on which she had been reclining. His eyes were
closed and he had a beatific smile on his calm, relaxed face.
She, too, smiled, confident from the expression on his face
that her words had pleased him.

In fact, his smile was the result of an image of stunning beauty that had appeared, completely unbidden, in his mind, the mathematical formula illustrating the relationship between integral and differential calculus:

$$\int f'(t)dt = f(b) - f(a)$$

The formula, arrived at in the late seventeenth century by both Sir Isaac Newton in England and the German mathematician Gottfried Wilhelm Leibniz, represented a spectacular achievement of intellect, and could fairly be said to be the very foundation upon which rests all of modern science. Coincidentally, it had manifested itself in Henry's consciousness at the precise instant of his ejaculation while making love to Ramona. Although he had never seen the formula before, its significance blossomed in his mind with all of the beauty of a rosebud opening for the first time, droplets of dew on the petals refracting the early morning sunshine. By the time his *vas deferens* had ceased its shuddering contractions Henry understood the formula's meaning. He sat up, dislodging Ramona from her position of repose, and reached for the yellow tablet and pencil he had begun keeping next to the futon. He wrote out the formula and wordlessly showed it to Ramona. She shook her head, indicating a lack of comprehension. He thought for a moment and then quickly wrote out two additional formulae:

$$\int f(t)dt$$

$$f'(x)$$

"This one," Henry pointed with his pencil to the first of the two additional formulae, "is the basic formula on which integral calculus is based. The long $\int$ figure at the beginning is called an integral sign and with the formula one can determine such things as the area of an object with curved sides or borders." He pointed to the second of the two additional formulae. "This is the basis of differential calculus, with which one can obtain such information as the instantaneous velocity of an object at any given point in time. The first formula I showed you represents the integration of these two different paths of the calculus, demonstrating, in essence, that each is the reciprocal of the other." He paused and smiled at the wonder of it all. "Have you got words?"

Ramona hadn't. Later, after they had risen and showered together, she once again told Henry that she was pregnant.

"I know," Henry replied. He inhaled deeply, savoring the complex aroma of the dark roasted Mexican coffee that Ramona had taught him to love. They were standing on the back deck of their rented cottage looking down on the eucalyptus and redwood trees that lined the hillside all the way down to the campus of the University of California. "I sensed the life within you several weeks ago. The child is a girl and she will be as beautiful as her mother."

"Have you ever considered the likely effect all that tobacco juice is having on your mouth and throat?"

Henry was sitting next to Bobby Clarke in the visiting team's dugout in Tiger Stadium. It was the top of the fourth inning and Bobby was in the process of stuffing the better part of an entire pouch of Red Man chewing tobacco into his mouth. The worn-out chew it was replacing was sitting on the grass immediately in front of the dugout. A small lake of brown saliva puddled at Bobby's feet on the concrete dugout floor.

"Mmnthfuck." Ordinarily Bobby, a multiyear major-league veteran, wouldn't have deigned to reply to a mere rookie, but Henry's extraordinary talent made a response, even an unintelligible one, somewhat mandatory. "Mmmnscthpt," he added, his jaw, teeth, and tongue working in frantic unison to mold the fresh tobacco into a manageable wad. He let fly an amber stream of liquid that splattered off the dugout floor.

Although Henry had no idea what Bobby had just said, he was nonetheless fascinated by the huge bulge the tobacco made in Bobby's cheek.

"Come on, Soldier. Chrissakes, you're on deck."

Preacher's whining voice brought Henry out of his fantasy of seeing Bobby's cheek spontaneously explode under the pressure of the tobacco he was attempting to chew. He caught Bobby's eye as he stood to move over to the bat rack.

"My guess is that mouth and throat cancer would be a particularly unpleasant way to die," he advised the utility player. "Especially given that it is so easily avoided."

"Mmmnthfuck," Bobby replied not unpleasantly, accentuating his response with a loud breaking of wind as Henry left the dugout.

Theo Carter, batting ahead of Henry, fouled off three pitches in a row before taking ball four and trotting down to first base, where he spent several seconds adjusting his protective cup and massaging his hamstrings for the benefit and entertainment of the spectators along the first base line. The crowd grew silent with anticipation as Henry walked toward home plate from the on-deck circle.

"I wouldn't dig in too deeply if I was you, rook," the Detroit catcher kindly informed Henry as he settled in at the plate for his second at-bat of the game. He lifted his catcher's mask away from his face to spit. "Mumbles"—the Detroit pitcher was nicknamed Mumbles by his teammates because of a pronounced speech impediment—"ain't too happy about that foul pole."

Henry smiled but said nothing. In his first at-bat he had reached out for a breaking ball clearly out of the strike zone and muscled it off the right field foul pole for a home run.

He settled into the batter's box and indicated his readiness for the first pitch with a curt nod of his head. Mumbles the pitcher paid absolutely no attention to the signs his catcher was flashing, concentrating instead on the back of Henry's head where he intended to plant a major-league fastball. The frequent butt of his teammates' childish clubhouse humor, Mumbles could throw big-league heat and intensely hated seeing his pitches leave the ballpark. He took an exaggerated windup and launched a 93 mile per hour bullet straight at Henry's neck. The windup, as it was intended to, made it difficult for Henry to pick up the ball's rotation as it left Mumbles's hand, and by the time he realized it was a straight fastball he knew he would not be able to duck out of the box in time to avoid being hit. He tensed his upper body, turning slightly away from the pitch and turtling his head, intending to take the ball off his deltoid muscle. The ball's velocity caused it to rise several inches over the last ten or twelve feet of its flight path and it struck Henry just behind his left ear, sending his batting helmet flying and dropping Henry immediately to his knees.

"Fuck!" Bobby Clarke had just gotten his new chew comfortably situated in his cheek when he saw the beanball pitch and his teammate go to the ground. His stumpy legs propelled him out of the dugout and across the first base line like a crab scuttling to avoid a hungry seagull. Mumbles saw him coming and his smirk of pleasure from seeing Henry on his knees turned to concern as he realized that the Oakland player who had rocketed out of the dugout would be on him before one of his own teammates could intercede and protect him. Bobby Clarke drove his shoulder into Mumbles's ribs and knocked him off the pitcher's mound, getting in three swift punches to the Detroit pitcher's face before both men were covered by ballplayers from both teams.

*   *   *

"What is your name?" The doctor in the emergency room shone his pencil light into Henry's left eye, trying to ascertain the speed with which the pupil contracted in response. "Can you tell me your name?" he repeated.

"Arthur?" Henry's voice had a dreamy quality about it, as if it were working its way out of a thick fog. "Does Arthur sound familiar?" he asked.

The doctor chuckled and winked at the attending nurse. "You're asking me? Don't you know what your name is?"

Henry nodded, his mind suddenly clearing. "Actually, it's Henry, Henry Spencer. Or at least that's what everybody calls me."

"What do you mean, that's what everybody calls you?" The doctor smiled and held up a piece of paper. "It says here that Henry Spencer is your name."

"I know, but somehow it doesn't seem right. Frankly, I've often been puzzled by that fact."

"What fact?"

"The fact that although Henry Spencer is my name somehow it doesn't seem right. Then, just a second ago, when you first asked me if I knew my name, the name Arthur came to mind, and it seemed correct."

"Well, I wouldn't worry about it if I were you," the doctor said, his thoughts already elsewhere. "You've got a pretty good concussion and I don't want you thinking about anything in particular for the next twenty-four to forty-eight hours. We're going to keep you overnight for observation and take good care of you whatever your name is."

Observation is right, the ER nurse thought as she admired the bulge of Henry's privates beneath the thin cotton sheet covering him. A supervising nurse with an advanced degree from Duke University she was, although by no means a fan of the national pastime, nobody's fool—as soon as Henry had been brought unconscious into the examining room she had quickly raised the side of the sheet for a firsthand view. *"Whoa,"* she murmured, dropping the sheet reluctantly. She knew as surely as she knew her own name that this was one patient who wouldn't lack for attention from the nurses on the floor.

Outside the ER examining area Bobby Clarke stood waiting, still in his Oakland road uniform. Both Bobby and the uniform were somewhat the worse for wear from the brawl that had erupted after Henry's beaning. At the bottom of a large pile of players, his hands tightly locked around Mumbles's throat, Bobby had been spiked by one of the combatants, from which team it would never be determined, and had taken twelve stitches just below his left eye. The eye was swollen shut and the area around it had already begun turning black and magenta. He was tossed out of the game and had accompanied Henry in the ambulance from the ballpark.

"How's Soldier doing?" he politely asked as the doctor and nurse emerged from the treatment area.

"What in the world is wrong with your cheek?" the doctor responded sharply, ignoring Bobby's question.

"My cheek?" Bobby thought for a second. "Oh, I've got a chew going." He smiled as much as the immense wad of tobacco in his mouth would allow. A small drop of amber saliva leaked from one corner.

"You can't chew that in here," the doctor said, indignation palpable in his voice. "This is a hospital."

Properly chastised, Bobby disgorged his tobacco into his right palm. "Sorry, Doc, I wasn't thinking." He looked around for a place to put the partially masticated mass and, failing to spot an appropriate receptacle, placed it in his uniform hip pocket. The nurse went slightly pale. "Anyway," Bobby continued, wiping his palm on the front of his uniform, "how's Soldier doing?"

"Soldier?"

"Yeah, you know." Bobby nodded toward the examining room the doctor and nurse had just exited. "Soldier. Henry."

Comprehension dawned on doctor and nurse simultaneously. "He's doing just fine," the doctor said brusquely, wanting to end the conversation as quickly as possible. "He's had a concussion and we're going to keep him here overnight as a precaution. Now if you'll excuse me . . ."

"Jesus, Soldier, you missed a helluva fight."

Several of his teammates were gathered around Henry's bed in his hospital room.

"Quick as you was beaned, Bobby here," Bo Siefert, the speaker, draped an affectionate arm around Bobby Clarke's shoulders, "was out of the dugout and on that asshole like ugly on an ape."

A proud Bobby Clarke beamed. He knew that just such an incident had been needed to make him a real member of the team. "I nailed that ratfuck a couple a good licks, too," he informed Henry.

"Fuckin' A," Bo confirmed. "The sonofabitch'll think twice about throwing at an Oakland player the next time."

Henry smiled. "It really wasn't necessary."

"Not necessary?" Bobby, as were his teammates, was shocked at Henry's words. "Jesus, Soldier, you can't let a guy throw at you and just stand there."

He shook his head. He knew that Henry was eccentric, but such an attitude was beyond eccentricity. It was potentially suicidal, especially for a man with a heavy bat like Henry's. If it became known throughout the league that Henry wouldn't protect himself, pitchers on every team would naturally protect their ERAs by throwing at him. And if a player was hit and couldn't immediately take up his own defense, his teammates were expected to do it for him. Why else be on a team?

"No fucking way," Bobby added. He dismissed Henry's comment as coming from one who had had his bell rung and therefore wasn't in full command of his faculties.

"You should have seen that sumbitch when they finally

pulled me off him." Bobby threw his shoulders back and thrust his chest forward in manly pride. "I fucked up his day big-time."

And indeed he had. Mumbles was near unconsciousness from a lack of oxygen when Bobby's fingers had been finally pried from his neck, and his face was bleeding badly from the blows Bobby had managed to land before they were inundated by ballplayers.

"Hey, Benny, come in here and look at this." Al Bartholomeo waved at Benny from the door of his trailer. "ESPN's doing an interview with that big rookie on the A's. Henry Spencer."

Benny smiled and turned his head toward his neighbor's trailer. He had been down at the river, dangling his feet in the muddy water and tickling his brain thinking about unsolvable nonlinear equations. He and young Arthur Hodges had frequently played games with such equations, trying to construct partial solutions that would fool the other into following the same down dead-end roads. For some reason, he found himself thinking about Arthur a great deal while watching the Colorado River swirl past the trailer park and its odd collection of inhabitants. Perhaps, he told himself, it was a natural result of the strange, almost unintelligible conversation he had had with Gunter Schmidtbauer.

"Hurry up," Al urged, nodding toward the small television. "They're getting ready to interview him right now. Chris Berman," the ESPN commentator, "said nobody knows much of anything about him, you know, his personal life and like that. Come on in and close the door."

Al's trailer was the only one in the park that was air-conditioned (Al was also the only one with a television). Although Benny could certainly have afforded to purchase an air-conditioning unit, he and Becky preferred the heat and the freedom of wearing little (or, in the privacy of their

trailer, no) clothing. For their part, the Germans, after a lifetime of the cold and the damp of Northern Europe, seemed
happy only when the temperature climbed well above 100
degrees and were openly contemptuous of Al's need to chill
the air of his trailer. Al knew that they laughed at him and
he would have liked to have shown them that he, too, could
do happily without air-conditioning, but he feared his wife
a great deal more than he did being thought too pampered
to take a little desert heat.

"I can't stop in just now," Benny said. He really didn't
want to go into the air-conditioned trailer, for the clammy
coldness reminded him too much of Boston and all he had
gladly left behind. More surprising, given his lifelong love
of the Boston Red Sox, he found that since he and Becky
had settled down in the desert he really found it difficult to
sustain any interest in baseball, Al's constant entreaties to
watch games on his television notwithstanding. "Maybe
later," he called over his shoulder as he quickened his pace
past Al's trailer. "I'll catch a game with you later this week."

"Jeez, you ought to see him," Al said, his voice trailing
off as he contemplated Benny's retreating back. "He's a big
kid. And tough," he continued even as he moved back into
the trailer. "He got beaned the other day in Detroit and didn't
even miss a game."

"Who are you talking to?" his wife Margaret demanded,
her eyes narrowed in suspicion. "You didn't invite that nasty
Benny in here to watch television, did you? I hope for your
sake you didn't." She put both hands on her hips and thrust
her lower jaw toward her thoroughly cowed husband. "It's
disgraceful, the two of them living together, her young
enough to be his daughter, and now pregnant and walking
around with hardly any clothes on. You can see her stomach
and everything." She looked closely at Al. "Are you listening to me?"

The thought of Benny and Becky was especially galling

to her since she had tried just the other day to advise Ruth
Pierpont about the moral dangers inherent in allowing unwed
couples in the trailer park.

Blow it out your ass, had been Ruth's pithy response.

"Henry, or may I call you Soldier since that's the nickname
your teammates seem to have given you, that was quite a
hit you took on the noggin in Detroit." Chris Berman, the
ESPN interviewer, chuckled for the benefit of his viewers,
letting even the more dull-witted among them know that he
intended to have some fun with this interview. "I understand
that you had some difficulty remembering your name in the
hospital."

The young ballplayer nodded solemnly. "That's true; I
was somewhat confused when I first regained consciousness.
However, in all honesty I must say that I have always been
rather in some doubt as regards my sense of identity."

Berman laughed and looked directly into the camera.
"Haven't we all, Soldier? Haven't we all? Now, tell me, what
does it feel like to be leading the league, as a rookie, in just
about every statistic you can name: batting average, slugging
percentage, on base average, doubles, triples, home runs.
Wow!" Berman feigned a look of astonishment for his viewers. Without waiting for an answer to his question Berman
plunged on. "Which ballplayer, or players, did you look up
to as an example of how you wanted to play when you were
growing up in," Berman paused to consult his notes, "here
we go, when you were growing up in Kernersville, North
Carolina."

"Frankly, I don't remember much about growing up, but
someone I've been thinking of a great deal lately is Max
Planck."

"Max Planck," Berman repeated, desperately searching
his mind for a clue as to which team Max Planck might have

played for, and when. "I'm sorry, Soldier, but you've stumped me on this one. Wait a minute—wasn't he a catcher with the old Philadelphia Athletics?"

"No," Henry replied in a kindly fashion, as if talking to a child, "he was a German physicist and is generally regarded as the father of quantum mechanics. It is probably impossible to overstate the importance, the truly revolutionary nature, of his original theory of quanta. Additionally, he was the discoverer, or formulator if you will, of what came to be called Planck's Constant, the formula for which is, if you're interested, h = 6.63 × 10 to the minus 27th power erg-seconds." Henry paused for a second and then, in an effort to be helpful, added, "It, Planck's Constant, is a very small number which ultimately helped lead Albert Einstein to several conclusions, including that light travels not necessarily in waves but also in discrete bundles which we now know as photons." Henry smiled into the camera, warming to the subject. "As another example of its extraordinary importance in the development of our understanding of matters in the subatomic realm, I don't believe it would be an overstatement to say that Werner Heisenberg would never have been able to propound his Uncertainty Principle without prior knowledge of Planck's Constant. I could give further examples of the significance of Planck's work, but you and your viewers who have not yet done so might first wish to read *Neue Bahnen der physikalischen Erkenntnis,* Planck's original paper on the hypothesis of quanta."

Chris Berman had been in the business long enough to know when a ballplayer was blowing smoke up his ass. When the feed had gone back to ESPN headquarters (and he was sure that Henry Spencer was well out of earshot) he turned to his cameraman. "Max Planck my ass," he said angrily, shaking his head. "Does he think I'm some kind of moron, or what?"

*　　*　　*

"Max Planck?"

Benny scratched his head quizzically and looked with disbelief at Gunter Schmidtbauer. The two of them had been sitting outside Benny's trailer in the gathering dark drinking Gunter's home-brewed wheat beer and eating radishes and corn chips when Al wandered over.

"Have a beer," Gunter invited, handing one to Al.

"Thanks." Al waved a piece of scrap paper in Benny's direction. "Max Planck," he said, repeating the name. "I wrote it down. The ballplayer, Henry Spencer, said he was some sort of German," Al cut his eyes nervously in Gunter's direction, "a, um, physicalist, or . . ."

"Physicist," Benny said, "he was a German physicist, and I can't imagine a young ballplayer . . ."

"Here it is," Al interjected, suddenly worried that Benny might not believe him, waving the paper on which he written Planck's name. "It's right here in black and white. I wrote it down."

Gunter took the paper from Al's hand and held it up to the shaft of light coming from the open door of Benny's trailer. *"Es ist wirklich,"* he said, nodding at Al. "He even wrote down the formula for Planck's Constant." He handed the paper to Benny.

"Yeah, I was going to ask you about that," Al said, pleased that he had thought to write down the information. "What is it?"

Benny shook his head and smiled as if he were about to address a nervous simpleton. "It is very difficult to explain if you don't have the necessary foundation in mathematics and the physical sciences. Suffice it to say that broadly speaking, it has to do with the measurement of radiation from vibrating particles. And," he looked once again at Gunter, shaking his head, "in any event, I doubt seriously that this young ballplayer knows anything whatever about Max Planck and his work. I suspect that someone put him up to it, gave him the name to use in the interview as a prank."

"I don't know," Al said doubtfully. "He sounded awfully sure of himself. And some people are saying that he's the greatest rookie of all time, maybe even the greatest ballplayer."

Benny smiled. "Hope springs eternal," he said, thinking suddenly of his late friend Arthur Hodges and wondering what he might have made of a baseball player conversant in Planck's Constant. *Not likely,* Benny thought, taking another bite of one of Gunter's pungent radishes, *not very likely at all.*

TEN

★ ✦ ★

July rolled around as predictably as a midlife crisis, and about as welcomed by all who worked outdoors for a living. The Oaklands played a six-game home stretch to open the month and then went on the road for eleven days, their second trip back through the fecund ranks of the American League East.

"Hey, Soldier, did I ever show you how a one-armed Polack counts his change?"

Henry looked up at Bobby Clarke from the laptop computer Ramona had purchased for him as a surprise gift before the road trip. The team was milling about the Oakland airport waiting to board their charter flight for Boston. As is generally the case with professional athletes not actually engaged in a team-directed activity, they were, for the most part, at a loss for what to do, and consequently many just wandered aimlessly about the concourse looking for attractive women to show off for.

"I'm not sure I understand," Henry said, smiling at Bobby and setting aside the laptop. Since Henry's beaning a couple of weeks earlier he and Bobby Clarke had become quite friendly, an odd couple of the first order.

"Shit," Bobby liked to tell their teammates, usually within Henry's hearing, "this boy's a goddamned genius, but I got to get him some common sense, if you know what I'm saying."

Perhaps not surprisingly, most did.

"A one-armed Polack," Bobby repeated, feigning aggravation for the benefit of several onlooking players. "You know, how does a one-armed Polack count his change?"

"What's a Polack?" Henry asked.

"Goddamn it, Soldier, it doesn't matter what a Polack is, okay?" Bobby, beginning to lose patience, no longer had to merely feign aggravation. "It's just some dumb sumbitch, okay?"

"I understand," Henry said, wanting to mollify his new friend. "How does a one-armed . . ." he paused dramatically, ". . . Polack count his change?"

Bobby smiled broadly and, reaching into his pants pocket with his left hand, took out a handful of loose change. He turned his back to Henry, unzipped his fly, and inserted his right arm inside his trousers at the belt line. He turned back to Henry and, extending his right index finger through the open fly, he began sorting through the coins in his left palm. The watching players roared with laughter and even Henry smiled in amusement. Several passersby looked over at the commotion and just as quickly looked away.

"I understand," Henry reassured Bobby. "Your finger is supposed to represent the one-armed man's penis, correct?"

"Son," Bobby rolled his eyes dolefully, "if I didn't know for a fact that you was from North Carolina I'd have to say that you recently arrived here from Mars."

Henry smiled. "I may have." He reopened the laptop computer. "But nonetheless," he looked back up at Bobby, "I did like your joke."

"No kidding?" Bobby looked skeptical.

"No kidding."

Bobby sat down next to Henry and nodded at the laptop. "What're you doing with that thing?"

Henry angled the computer so Bobby could see the screen. "I'm seeing how quickly the mathematics program I wrote for it can solve a nonlinear differential equation and display a two-dimensional plot of the solution." He made a number of keystrokes, waited a few seconds, and watched as the solution and its complex plot came up on the screen.

Bobby scratched his head. "I got to tell you, Soldier, it's Greek to me. Tell me something—how's being able to do something like that going to help you get through life?"

Henry, not wanting to run the laptop's battery down, turned it off. "Think of it as a tool, Bobby, nothing else. It's merely a kind of shovel, or wheelbarrow, or a baseball bat, nothing more."

"That's not what I meant, Soldier. See, while you're staring at that damned computer you're not seeing what's going on around you, you know what I mean?"

"No."

"Well, dern." Bobby looked around for an example to illustrate his point. He spotted Theo Carter talking to the young woman working at the counter of the concourse newsstand. "Look yonder." He pointed at their teammate. "What's Theo up to?"

Theo was leaning on the counter, his head inclined toward the young woman, his voice low so she had to move closer to him to hear what he was saying. "He's . . ." Henry paused, suddenly remembering an expression Bobby and the other players frequently used. "He's promoting some pussy."

"No, he's not. They're just flirting, playing around. See how he looks up at her and then down at his hands, then back to her, then maybe down the concourse. He's giving her a chance to look at him without having to meet his eyes. By doing that he's respecting her, telling her everything's okay, that they're just going to have some fun, do a little flirting without either one disrespecting the other. That's important, because he initiated the situation with her, not the other way around."

"I don't understand."

"Well, look. You know all those women that follow ballplayers around the hotel lobbies, come up to us in bars, restaurants, give us their phone numbers, try to come up to the room, shit like that?"

Henry nodded.

"See, a man can't respect a woman that comes on to him like that. If that girl over there behind the counter had done that, called Theo over or flashed her tits at him, or like that, he'd be over there talking trash to her, grabbing his crotch, dissing her big-time. Instead, they're smiling, teasing, what the guys call just goofing."

Henry smiled. "Perhaps he is telling her about Professor Schrödinger's cat."

Bobby groaned and covered his ears. "Come on, Soldier, you're not going to start on that damned cat again, are you?"

The day before, in the Oakland clubhouse, during one of his infrequent game strategy talks, Preacher Brown had used the homespun expression *more than one way to skin a cat.* Henry, who normally paid scant attention to his manager's typically nonsensical, profanity-strewn speeches, had been idly bringing up iterations of random trigonometric mappings on his laptop computer screen when the word *cat* triggered a reflexive verbal response.

"Schrödinger's cat."

"What?" Preacher's question had more than a little groan in it, as he knew that Henry seldom said anything that made any sense whatever to anyone in the clubhouse.

"Your colorful expression brought to mind the conundrum posed by Professor Schrödinger's cat."

"Does this have anything to do with baseball?" Preacher's tone of voice conveyed both weary skepticism and annoyance. He hadn't the vaguest idea what a *conundrum* was and suspected he wouldn't like it if he did know.

"Yes, it does, in the sense that baseball, much as Schrödinger's fictional cat, can be thought of as a metaphor for the difficult, perhaps ultimately impossible, task of integrating quantum physics with classical physics. Professor Schrödinger hypothesized a cat in a sealed box, a canister of poison gas, and a trigger initiated by a random event at the subatomic level. According to classical physicists the random event either occurred or it didn't, and the cat is therefor either dead or alive—one merely need look into the box. For the quantum physicists, however, the answer is not so easy. Using waveform analysis, the two possible outcomes can be neither known nor predicted, and the very act of looking into the box has the potential of changing the outcome. Indeed, some have said that *both* outcomes are possible at the same time in an infinite number of different, albeit very real, worlds."

Bobby White, who had struck out three times in his last game and was still considerably annoyed by the excessively large strike zone allowed by the umpire, spoke up. "Man, that's bullshit, killing a cat like that," he said heatedly, surprising those sitting closest to him. While waiting for a teammate to finish with the sports page the week before he had actually looked at the front-page section of the *San Francisco Chronicle* and had seen a photograph of a demonstration against the University of California staged by an animal rights group to protest the use of laboratory animals in experiments. Although Bobby was unimpressed at the time, Henry's words brought the image back to his mind. "My girlfriend's got a cat," he added to buttress his position of moral authority.

"I'll bet that professor's cat wouldn't have stood there looking at all those called strikes like you did," Wally Barnes needled.

"Hey, fuck you, man," Bobby responded with a surprising degree of animation. "We're trying to have a serious conversation here. About cruelty to animals, in case you haven't been listening."

"I agree with Bobby," another teammate said. "All this experimenting with animals is wrong."

"Professor Schrödinger's cat, strictly speaking, was metaphorical," Henry pointed out.

"I don't care what kind of cat it was, Soldier," Bobby said, shaking his head, "it was wrong to kill it like that. I'm not criticizing you," he added hastily. "I mean, I know you didn't have anything to do with it personally; I'm just saying that these professors need to understand that cats are like people, you understand what I'm saying? You can't just be killing them to prove a point."

"Yeah," Dickhead Bell interjected, pleased that the conversation had finally taken a turn he could understand. "If they had to kill something why didn't they use a fucking rat, or something like that that no one gives a shit about." He personally didn't care all that much for cats but felt confident that no one would object to the killing of rodents, whether for scientific purposes or not. "I hate a fucking rat," he added for good measure.

"He hasn't accepted Christ into his life."

Preacher Brown looked up from his desk, an annoyed expression on his face. He was filling out the post-game report that Robert Edgerton required after every game, a task that under the best of circumstances he found demeaning. In the old days, he liked to think, you managed a game and then, win or lose, went out and sucked down a few beers. The way God intended. The good news tonight was that they had won, beating the Cleveland Indians in the first game of a three-game series. Henry Spencer had gone two for two, with a home run, a double, and three walks. "What the fuck are you talking about?"

Lyle Roberts stared back, fundamentalist religious fervor providing amply sufficient courage to ignore the anger in his manager's red face. "I said that Soldier hasn't accepted Christ into his life."

Lyle Roberts was the self-appointed Oakland team representative of the Washed in the Blood of the Lamb Church of Born Again Christian Athletes, an organization that operated on the lunatic fringe of the athletic evangelical movement. A rather dull-witted Georgian by birth, he was, by major-league standards, an exceptionally mediocre shortstop with a notoriously light bat. That he was on the team at all was attributed by most observers to the fact that Preacher Brown generally liked to have at least one witnessing Christian on his teams. He thought it contributed to a moral atmosphere, which, in turn, led to hard work and ultimately a more favorable win-loss ratio. The African-Americans on the team, tending perhaps to a somewhat higher degree of cynicism on such matters, thought it more than a little significant that Roberts was as white as a man can get and still not qualify legally as an albino.

Shit, Theo Carter had once said, *you don't see no .117-batting, slow-footed brother carrying no motherfucking Bible around this locker room, do you?*

"Watch it, boy," Preacher warned, his annoyance with Lyle increasing. "You're swimming on thin ice here. I've told you before that you got no bidness trying to convert anybody on this team. If somebody wants to pray with you, well, that's fine with me. But we ain't running no tent show here, no revival meeting. You hear what I'm saying?"

Lyle crossed his arms and stared back at his manager, his prominent Adam's apple as noticeable as a flag at half-mast. "People are starting to talk, Skipper, and not just in Oakland."

And they were. Henry's prodigious statistics were beginning to trouble some of the more superstitious ballplayers in American League cities. It was only the first of July and he was on a pace to hit well over eighty home runs in the course of the season, a feat known instinctively to be humanly impossible by all who considered it. He was also batting in the neighborhood of .450, and that only because he was now the victim of frequent intentional walks. His reputation behind the plate was such that no one even attempted to steal against him, and leadoffs at first were so short that the Oaklands led the league in double plays. "It ain't natural," was heard increasingly throughout the league. While of course none of the players on any of the American League teams against which the Oaklands played had ever heard of *Dr. Faustus,* more than a few began, in the small hours of the night when ignorant men and women worry about the principalities of the air and turn to the Old Testament for comfort, to wonder about the source of the Soldier's great and heretofore unknown talent. His own teammates had begun to cast quizzical, almost fearful sidelong glances at him in the dugout, and had become a great deal more restrained in their congratulations when he hit a home run or made an exceptional fielding play behind the plate. Two or three of them, for whatever protection such talismanic symbols might bring, were even keeping Gideon Bibles they had stolen from hotel rooms in their lockers. *My thinkin' is that it can't do no harm,* was Dickhead Bell's rather Aristotelian reasoning when the presence of the Bible in his locker was noted. *Besides,* the millionaire pitcher noted with no small satisfaction, *it didn't cost me nothin'.*

Even Ramona noticed the change. Although Ramona was not a Player's Wife, Henry's extraordinary talent was such that she was somewhat grudgingly allowed to view games at the Oakland Coliseum from the Wives' Section. (In the rigid extended family hierarchy of Organized Ball the Players, of course, came first, followed immediately by their Wives. After the Players' Wives there came an extended moral free fall, which ended with the Players' Girlfriends, regarded for the most part as little more than whores by the Wives.) By early June she could see that the Players' Wives, at the few games she attended, were even more distant than had been the case earlier in the season.

"It's not you," Henry assured her one night after they had made love and she mentioned the wives' standoffishness. "They're becoming increasingly afraid of me. The players.

And they share their fears with their wives, who in turn fear you."

"Why are they afraid of you?"

"Because of what I do on the field." He raised himself up on one elbow and looked down on Ramona. "Because I just appeared one morning at their spring training camp, an unknown and unsuspected prodigy. And mostly because they are finally starting to believe that I have no past, no life before Arizona and Oakland." He smiled shyly. "To be honest, it would frighten anybody, me as well as the next man."

Ramona, looking up at Henry, thought her heart would burst with the love she felt. "I love you," she whispered.

Henry nodded. *You were given to me,* he thought but did not say. *You were given to me for some purpose or reason I cannot understand.*

A tear gathered in the corner of one of his eyes and Ramona, seeing it, reached and gathered it up with the tip of her finger. She brought it to her lips and tongue and pulled him down on top of her, putting her tongue on his lips when their faces came together. He felt the now familiar wonderful stirrings in his testicles and penis and closed his eyes, letting the erotic sensations wash over him. After some time he shifted his position, kneeling between her legs and taking her pelvis in both of his large, powerful hands, gently but firmly pulling her onto himself. She moaned as he entered her and he closed his eyes, catching his breath as her wetness and warmth enfolded his member and drew him deeper. She cried out his name as she arched her back to meet his thrusts, *"Henry,"* she cried, *"Henry,"* but the name he heard in his mind's ear was *Arthur,* and in the end, shuddering as he ejaculated, he collapsed on top of her and whispered not *I love you* but *"Thank you."* Later, as they lay at the very edge of sleep, he looked up, his eye caught by a movement above them.

"Look." He pointed at a tiny mouse moving carefully

along one of the exposed rafters over their futon. "We are, all of us, in many ways, like that mouse, alone in the universe and afraid of everything that is not mouse-like." A ray of moonlight, filtered through the eucalyptus trees that surrounded the cottage, fell across the futon and illuminated his face as his voice dropped to a whisper. "And I fear that for reasons I do not yet understand, I am most un-mouse-like."

"I asked him about it," Lyle continued, thrilled that his God had given him the strength to approach his teammate, a man who could very well be the Antichrist, come to destroy the world. "I comed right out and asked what was the source of his great strength and ball-playing ability. I did. I asked him had he accepted Jesus Christ as his personal Savior."

Preacher Brown didn't particularly want to ask but felt compelled to do so. "What did he say?"

"He laughed at me."

Henry smiled. "I'm not sure your question's not based upon a *non sequitur*," he said in a not unkindly fashion in response to Lyle's questions. "I mean, I don't exactly see how athletic ability is connected to or follows logically from a fundamentalist belief in Christian dogma." He paused for a moment. "I will say, however, that I do not disbelieve the notion of the ubiquity of some sort of divine presence pervading the universe. Obviously such a concept or notion cannot be demonstrably proven one way or the other. However, on the plus, or positive, side are many factors which argue strongly for some unifying principle of divine oversight. Take, for example, the four fundamental forces which appear to bind the universe: the strong, or nuclear, force, electromagnetic force, the weak force, and gravity. Of course, you are probably aware that a number of physicists have come to regard the weak and electromagnetic forces as essentially one and the same, differing only in the realms in which they operate. And since so little as regards the weak force has been empirically demonstrated it is difficult to do more than engage in informed speculation. In any event, as regards my original point, many would say that the existence of a God is proven by the simple elegance of the forces by which He or She controls His or Her creation. Personally, I would tend not to aggressively discount such thinking, particularly to the degree that it satisfies an inchoate need at the individual level for the comfort of knowing that someone, or something, is listening. Beyond that," Henry bent down to tie the laces of his spikes, "I'm not sure it's possible, or even desirable, to go."

Lyle felt as if Henry were speaking to him from underwater. He wasn't exactly sure what his large teammate had meant by what he had just said, but Lyle was fairly certain that it was a negative response to his original question. While he was trying to puzzle his way through the maze he felt Henry had intentionally led him into, young Richie Sanders, the team's backup catcher who had yet to catch a single inning, much less start a game, walked up with Bo Siefert.

"Hey, Soldier, me and Bo was wondering could you tell us again about rational numbers?"

Henry smiled. During yesterday's rain delay several of the boys had gotten into a poker game in the clubhouse. After listening for a short time to a nonsensical discussion about the laws of probability he had drawn a limited version of Pascal's Triangle on the dugout blackboard and had shown how the rows of numbers on the triangle could, among other things, provide exact answers to an almost infinite variety of questions about how numbers can combine.

"For example," Henry had told the poker players, "if I completed this triangle down to fifty-two rows, the sixth number over in that row will tell us precisely how many different five-card poker hands are possible using a deck of fifty-two cards." He thought for a moment. "I don't have the number precisely at hand, but I believe that it is well in excess of two-and-a-half million."

$$1 \quad 1$$
$$1 \quad 2 \quad 1$$
$$1 \quad 3 \quad 3 \quad 1$$
$$1 \quad 4 \quad 6 \quad 4 \quad 1$$
$$1 \quad 5 \quad 10 \quad 10 \quad 5 \quad 1$$
$$1 \quad 6 \quad 15 \quad 20 \quad 15 \quad 6 \quad 1$$
$$1 \quad 7 \quad 21 \quad 35 \quad 35 \quad 21 \quad 7 \quad 1$$

PACSAL'S TRIANGLE

"There are also some extremely interesting patterns to be found within the triangle," Henry continued, warming to the subject. "One in particular is that the Fibonacci series, two, three, five, eight, thirteen, twenty-one, thirty-four, et cetera, is derived by adding the numbers in the upward diagonals."

A further description of how the rows of numbers worked had led naturally enough to a more generalized conversation on the very nature of numbers themselves.

"Just think of rational numbers as fractions," Henry reassured Richie and Bo. "Ratios of two integers. Remember that it all starts with the natural numbers, one, two, three, four, five, and so on. The integers are merely the natural numbers to which have been added negative numbers and the concept of zero. Having natural numbers and integers, we need the ability to create fractions or ratios of integers, and so the rational numbers came into being as a concept. For example, if you divide two into one you get one-half, a rational number. If we didn't have rational numbers we wouldn't have batting averages or on-base percentages or earned run averages."

Lyle felt the flow of the conversation leaving him behind. He held up his Bible. "The only numbers that matter are the ones contained in the Good Book," he intoned sententiously.

Both Richie and Bo burst into laughter at his patently ridiculous words.

"Yeah, right," Bo said, shaking his head. "Tell that to the club when your contract comes up for renewal after this season." He looked at the shortstop with thinly veiled contempt. "My guess is you'll be cooking chicken-fried steaks for a living somewhere below the gnat line in south Georgia this time next year."

"Actually," Henry interjected, "Lyle may have something of a point, although I would put it differently. God," he smiled at the would-be evangelist, "however you define Him or Her, is indeed in the numbers." Henry held up a single finger. "An illustrative example comes immediately to mind, namely, the relationship between the Fibonacci series derived from Pascal's Triangle and the sunflower seeds that are consumed in an almost astonishing quantity by baseball players throughout the nation. A physical examination of the flower itself reveals that the left- and right-hand spirals of the blossom typically are represented by adjacent numbers in the Fibonacci series."

Preacher had heard more than enough. "Leave him alone, goddamn it. That kid's playing a ton of ball for us and I don't want anybody, particularly a Jesus shouter, fucking with him, you understand me?"

Lyle was unfazed by his manager's profane outburst. "Evil must be rooted out wherever it occurs," he intoned, holding up his Bible. "It is possible that he has made a pact with the devil. If so, not just our mortal souls are in danger but all of Organized Baseball."

Preacher looked at Lyle and saw his chances for an American League championship fading in the heat of the fanaticism that radiated from the slightly built shortstop. "You're history," he said, the words surprising him almost as much as they surprised Lyle Roberts. He pointed at his door and on beyond to the locker room. "Clean your locker out and hit the fucking road."

"What?" Lyle's face had gone ashen. Although he believed passionately in the divinity of Jesus Christ, he also knew that no other team above the Double-A level would ever offer him a contract based on his athletic ability.

Preacher snatched up the telephone on his desk and punched in a three-digit number. "Harrison," the assistant equipment manager, "Roberts has just been unconditionally released. Get over to his locker and pick up his uniforms and anything else that belongs to the club. Got that?" Without waiting for an answer Preacher slammed the phone down and looked at the stunned ex-shortstop. "What the fuck are you still doing here?"

ELEVEN

By the first of July the Mojave Desert had pretty much driven underground, driven out, or killed all sentient life within its confines. Those creatures remaining, including the few human beings who existed on the periphery, were a tough and wily lot, committed by nature or personal perversity to living in an environment scarcely less inhospitable than the dark side of the moon. Four of Gunter's small band of six gave up and fled during the latter part of June, dismayed at, among other things, the astonishing volume of water sucked from their bodies on a daily basis. Two of them, Herman and Anna, took their Airstream and lit out for the northern rain forests of Vancouver Island. The other couple gave Gunter a power of attorney to sell the third Airstream and boarded a Greyhound in Needles, vowing to catch the first available flight from Los Angeles to Germany. There was sadness in their leaving, but Gunter took their loss philosophically.

"Many are called; few are chosen," he opined while drinking beer two evenings later. He and *Frau* Sophie Schmidt-bauer, who said little and missed less, were enjoying a lingering sunset with Benny, Becky, and Ruth Pierpont. "A concept the Lord went to some length to impress on Gideon. And in an environment not very much different from this one." He smiled and pointed his bottle in the direction of Al's trailer, where a small air-conditioning compressor could be heard laboring day and night. "Not a few of us thought *they* would have left by now, *nein*?"

Ruth laughed. "He'll by-God leave when she," meaning Al's shrewish wife, "tells him to, and not one minute before."

"I wouldn't be too sure of anything as regards Mr. Bartholomeo anymore," Becky interjected. "He's clearly undergone something of a sea change the past month."

"True enough," Benny agreed thoughtfully.

Ruth accepted another bottle of Gunter's homebrew from Sophie. "I won't argue with you that he's been acting mighty queer lately, but I'm thinking his missus still wears the pants in that trailer." She wiped the cool bottle of beer across her sweating brow. "I'm glad it's your turn to cook dinner tonight," she said with a sigh to Benny. "Lord, there's not even a hint of a breeze out here."

The big Coors thermometer on Benny's trailer hadn't budged an inch from 122 degrees Fahrenheit since the sun had gone down. On the other side of the trailer, mesquite charcoal was glowing in the fifty-five-gallon steel drum Benny had converted to a barbecue.

"We could turn the fan on," Becky pointed to the large industrial pedestal fan Benny had purchased in Needles and kept on the patio outside their trailer, "but it would just blow hot air."

Benny shook his head. "After dinner I'll turn on the mister. That should cool us down." He winked at Ruth. "Unless you want to take a turn first."

Everyone smiled, for Ruth's newfound, and surprising, enthusiasm for *au naturel* romps through the atomized water was no secret among the small group of friends. *I expect Morgan,* her late husband, *is spinning in his grave,* she informed the four of them, Benny, Becky, Gunter, and Sophie, the first night they all took off what little they were wearing to dance, hand-in-hand, through the mist of cooling water.

Although somewhat lubricated, to be sure, by three bottles of beer and two tequila shooters, Ruth found herself that first time to be not the least inhibited by the lack of clothes both while dancing through the water and afterward, sitting in one of Benny's Adirondack chairs. *The only problem with being naked,* she told Becky after having thought about it, *is that there's no place to put my smokes.*

"Oh, by the way," Benny said to Ruth, "before I forget it, I saw a family of wild pigs on my walk today."

Ruth nodded. "Morgan used to shoot one every now and then," she informed them, "for the fresh pork."

"I mentioned it because according to my reading there aren't supposed to be native swine, or peccary, in the Mojave. In the Sonoran Desert, yes, but not the Mojave."

Ruth bellowed with laughter. "Not supposed to be here? Tell that to the pigs." She shook her head, amused at Benny's reliance on a printed field guide to tell him what to expect in the desert. "I've eaten a few and I can assure you they tasted just fine, wherever their license plates might have said."

Benny chuckled and looked up at the heavens. The desert sky was so clear and unpolluted that the Milky Way was visible in all its pulsing, writhing beauty. After a lifetime in Boston, where only a few of the brightest stars were visible on any given night, it was a sight that never failed to move him.

"Benny wrote a wonderful poem today," Becky said, a smile on her face.

"A poem?" Ruth asked. "Uh-oh." She rolled her eyes at Sophie Schmidtbauer. "What in the hell about?"

"About nothing in particular," Benny answered. He pointed his finger at Becky. "I told you not to tell anyone," he remonstrated good-naturedly. They had made love that afternoon, and afterward he told her that he had dreamed about Arthur Hodges for six nights in a row. Even more surprisingly, for he had always considered himself to be a most private man, he told her that he had mentioned his dreams to Gunter earlier that day.

"I suppose it's because he died so young, so . . ." Benny paused, searching for the right word, "so *unfulfilled.*" He shrugged. "As foolish as it may sound, I think the unfairness of his death is what troubles me so."

"Perhaps," the German had responded, clearly unimpressed with Benny's reasoning. "Or, perhaps . . ." Gunter's voice petered out.

"Perhaps what?"

"Men like you and I, men of a certain age and with a technical or scientific background, tend not to be *spiritual* in our thinking, *ja*? When confronted with something new we tend towards explanations based upon empirical, rather than intuitive, evidence."

"Meaning?"

"I told you shortly after you arrived that it was my dreams, my inchoate dreams, that drew my companions and I here to Needles, to the desert. For what purpose, of course, I do not yet know. Only a few years earlier such a thing simply would not have happened. I was an engineer, a man trained in science and technology, not a philosopher. But I came to realize as I grew older that much of what I yearned for, what we as human beings yearn for, cannot be quantified, cannot be solved like a quadratic equation. You yourself left Boston for much the same reason, no?"

"Not exactly. I left Boston because, well, because I realized that I no longer wanted to maintain the life I had there. I certainly had no sense that I was setting off into the sunset in search of spiritual things." Benny's voice unconsciously dropped when he pronounced the word *spiritual,* as if he were embarrassed even having it in his vocabulary.

"And yet here you are. You will recall that shortly after

you arrived I told you that you were, somehow, another piece of the puzzle that brought us all here. *Und jetzt,* just as I had back in Germany, you are having prophetic dreams." Gunter raised his hand as Benny started to protest his use of the word *prophetic.* "It is not a coincidence that you are having these dreams. I believe that the spirit of your friend is trying to tell you something. Something important."

Benny laughed but spent the rest of the day thinking about what Gunter had said and, after making love with Becky, told her of the conversation.

"I know this will sound a little too *New Age* for you," she had said, "but I think you should keep a journal." Benny snorted with derision, but Becky just shook her head and continued. "No, I mean it; I think you should write about your dreams and what they may mean as regards your feelings for Arthur."

Late that afternoon he rather shyly showed her the poem he had written.

"It's a wonderful poem," Becky assured the small gathering. She looked at Benny. "Read it aloud for everyone."

Benny ran a hand over his bald head and began to speak.

"It doesn't pay to assume
that old friends will die first.
Imagining one's sadness at funerals
is an exercise best left to the young.

"And yet worry nonetheless nags
like the most persistent of auditors,
despite the fact that all accounts
perforce will reconcile soon or late.

"Credit today,
debit tomorrow.

"The bottom lines will indeed converge,
for the tears shed at old friends' funerals
may yet participate in unions
a thousand years hence."

"That's nice," Ruth said with exaggerated politeness, "but it doesn't rhyme."

"Poetry doesn't have to rhyme," Becky assured her.

"I don't know," Ruth continued doubtfully. "Call me old-fashioned, but I like it better when it does. Anyway, what's it called?"

" 'A Message from the Bank,' " Benny answered.

Ruth laughed. "Whenever I get a message from the bank it generally costs me something."

"It is about your friend, no?" Gunter asked. He turned to his wife Sophie. "The young mathematician who died last year," he explained.

"Partly." Benny was not surprised that Gunter had intuitively gone to the heart of the poem. "But more than that it's a statement about the absurdity of life itself. We live our lives as if we were the focal point of the universe when in fact we are nothing more than an accident of planetary evolution, a mote of dust in a far-flung arm of a minor galaxy in a universe of inconceivable proportions."

"You got that right," Ruth asserted, lighting another Camel and taking a swig of her beer. "Why do you think I smoke these ankle breakers?" She snorted, exhaling smoke through her nose. "Here today, gone tomorrow, that's my motto. *Carpe* that old *diem* is what my old man Morgan used to say," she nodded at Benny, "or would have if he hadn't been too busy having a good time."

Gunter's wife, Sophie, ignoring Ruth's hyperbole, clucked in gentle disagreement with Benny's sentiment. "I think we are far more than an accident, much more than, how did you put it, a mote of dust."

Gunter smiled in the darkness. Sophie was a woman of quiet, yet powerful, intellect.

"Perhaps," she continued, "your friend might have thought so, too."

Benny shook his head. "No, he didn't. Arthur was, like most mathematicians, indeed most scientists I've known, a committed atheist. He believed that life ended with death, period."

"Whoa," Ruth interjected somewhat disjointedly, "I didn't say I didn't believe in God." She finished her beer with a long pull and shook her head emphatically. "No way, José. Morgan may be dead, but he was still my husband."

Sophie looked at Gunter questioningly. *"Ich verstehe nicht,"* she said softly.

Before Gunter could answer, a shaft of yellow light flashed across the darkened trailer park as the door to Al's trailer opened. His wife's voice followed less than a nano-second later, the sound not unlike a power saw blade hitting a nail. *"Shut the door, you moron,"* she screeched. *"You're letting all the cold air out."*

Benny, taking advantage of the opportunity to gracefully bow out of a conversation he felt had gotten far too personal, not to mention practically unintelligible, got up from his homemade Adirondack chair. "I think it's time to put the *shish kebab* on the grill." In the darkness he could see Al walking toward their group and he sat back down with a distinct sigh, not wishing to be rude by leaving in the face of a visitor.

"Guten Abend, Herr Bartholomeo," Gunter called out as the retired mailman entered the wan cone of light thrown through the window and open door of Benny's trailer. *"Wie geht's?"*

"Danke, gut." To everyone's literal astonishment, in the past three or four weeks Al had developed an interest in, and shown an undeniable affinity for, the German language,

going so far as to purchase a vocabulary and phrase book and several audio instruction cassettes from a bookstore in Needles. His wife, offended at the thought of anything foreign, would not let him practice his pronunciation in their trailer, so he was often seen down by the river, sweating copiously while laboriously working on his vocabulary. Perhaps as he had intended, Gunter and Sophie took a keen interest in this new and decidedly unexpected development and tried to help him with his grammar whenever possible. Al pointed to an empty stool. *"Darf ich hin sitzen?"* he inquired.

"Bitte," Gunter replied, charitably deciding not to correct Al in front of the others. "Your accent is improving almost every day," he added in English.

Al, not a man used to compliments of any sort, beamed unabashedly. *"Vielen dank',"* he said, meaning it. He held up a small piece of paper. "Do you know what this is?" he asked. On one side of the paper was a hand-drawn symbol.

$$\Phi$$

Gunter took the paper from Al's fingers and examined it in the scant light. He shrugged and handed it to Benny. "It is the Greek letter *phi,* is it not?"

"Yes," Al replied, obviously pleased with himself. "But do you know what it stands for?"

Benny groaned, guessing where the conversation was leading and wishing he had gone ahead with his intention to put their dinner on the grill. At the sound of his groan Al turned in his direction, a smile on his face.

"Don't tell him," Al urged. He turned back to Gunter. "I *knew* he would know."

"And you thought I would not?" Gunter affected an air of hurt feelings. "Keep in mind I am an engineer, while *he,*" gesturing toward Benny, "was . . ."

"Is," Benny interjected, "not *was.*"

"While he *is* only a physicist," Gunter continued, taking the piece of paper back from Benny. "I presume you," pointing toward Al, "are, how do you say it, getting at the fact that *phi* is the symbol used by mathematicians to represent the Golden Section, correct?"

Al smiled, pleased but not the least surprised that the two men he had come to admire most in all the world had both been familiar with the mathematical significance of the Greek letter *phi.* "I got a book from the Needles library," he said by way of explanation. "Did you know that *phi* plus one equals *phi* squared?"

"I almost surely knew it at one time," Gunter gravely assured Al, "but I must admit frankly that it had slipped from my consciousness at some point in the past several decades."

"Not exactly," Benny said, getting up from his chair.

"Not exactly, what?" Al asked.

"*Phi* plus one doesn't exactly equal *phi* squared. The numbers are very close, but not exactly the same. Close enough for Plato, and, in fact," he winked at Gunter, "close enough for most thumbnail engineers as well."

"*Lieber Gott,*" Gunter exclaimed in mock surprise. "How do you know so much?"

Benny smiled. "Your initial point, that a mere physicist wouldn't normally care, if he or she even knew, a great deal about a rather mundane mathematical concept like *phi* and the so-called Golden Section, was well taken. However, as brilliant a mathematician as my colleague Arthur Hodges was, he was nonetheless fascinated by, and declaimed endlessly on, believe it or not, this very subject." Benny shook his head and turned toward his trailer. "While I go put dinner on the grill, I'm sure Al, here, can regale everyone with tales of Platonic ecstasy arising out of nothing more than simple, if not simpleminded, ratios."

Behind Benny's trailer, sparks rose from the mesquite-fired grill like a cloud of fireflies competing with the panoply of stars overhead. Benny tended skewers of sweet lamb marinated in garlic and olive oil, golden and green peppers, and mushrooms. He looked up from the grill as Gunter came around the corner of the trailer.

"What happened to Al?"

"We finally had to give him a beer together with radishes and corn chips to shut him up." Gunter shook his head at the wonder of it all. "Can you imagine, a man like Al lecturing us on the geometry of the pyramids and the Fibonacci additive number series."

"He's discovered Fibonacci, has he?"

"And worse, he wanted to explain how Leonardo da Vinci's painting *The Last Supper* was composed using the Golden Section."

"Actually, he's right about all of that."

"He is?" Gunter sounded doubtful.

Benny nodded. "Leonardo da Vinci, Raphael, Michelangelo, all of the great artists from the Renaissance forward were familiar with the Golden Section. Fibonacci comes into it because one is rather easily led to the additive series he supposedly discovered by some rather obvious and elementary manipulations of *phi*." Benny paused to turn the skewers on the grill. "I say *supposedly* because Chinese mathematicians had been playing around with the same additive series at least a couple of centuries before Fibonacci was born. As to the Golden Section, da Vinci even illustrated a book devoted to the subject. It had an outright mystical status from the time of Plato through most if not all of the Middle Ages. Fortunately, these days about the only people who get excited about the notion that there exists some sort of hermetic significance to *phi* and the Golden Section are undergraduate students, most of whom are liberal arts majors who discover them while taking a required bonehead math course. Which reminds me." Benny tilted his head as if trying to look around the corner of his trailer. "What the hell do you suppose got Al started on all of this?"

"That baseball player everyone seems to be talking about."

"You're kidding."

Gunter shook his head. "He said that the young man was talking about the Egyptian pyramids and the Golden Section during a recent interview on television. Afterwards, Al went into Needles and picked up some books on the subject at the public library." Gunter paused for a second, making sure he had the words he wanted to say lined up correctly. "Don't you think that all of this . . ."

"No."

Gunter smiled. "You know what I was going to say." It was a statement, not a question.

"Of course. You were going to try and draw some sort of connection between Al's sudden interest in things mathematical and Arthur Hodges." Benny paused, and began taking the skewers off the grill. "Believe me, strange coincidences can be found in damned near everything under the sun. They're what fuel screwball conspiracy theorists from the Kennedy assassination to the Roswell Incident to the question of who built the pyramids. Entire industries exist devoted exclusively to separating the gullible from their money with *proof* that one coincidence or another, take your pick, is evidence of something far larger, and generally far more sinister, than meets the eye." He shook his head. "Ignorance and superstition, not to mention cheap labor, built the pyramids, not aliens from another galaxy, and the fact that some ditzy ballplayer from North Carolina appears out of the blue spouting mathematical and physical concepts that he can't possibly understand in no way vitiates the fact that my good friend Arthur Hodges is dead and gone."

Although he had already eaten dinner, Al allowed himself to be talked into just a taste of Sophie Schmidtbauer's *Kartoffeln Salat*. While the others murmured over the delicate mesquite flavor of the tender lamb skewers he entertained them with tales of the Brooklyn post office, occasionally lapsing into German when he came across a word or phrase that happened to be in his growing vocabulary. The overall effect, while decidedly out of the ordinary, was oddly appealing, particularly to Ruth. She thought of her late husband, Morgan, and a familiar heat began rising between her legs.

Since Morgan's death Ruth had enjoyed the pleasures of sexual congress but seldom, and in fact, in the last four or five years, had pretty much given it up entirely as a wish not likely to be satisfactorily fulfilled. She had lain, mostly without a great deal of joy, and not for a number of years, with the occasional transient resident of her trailer park, but had given it up as a bad idea when the last one she slept with implied that he should receive free rent for his services. He became something of a pest, going so far as to think he might intimidate her with a show of aggression, but he badly misjudged her character. The first and only time he slapped her across the face, ostensibly to teach her a lesson in humility and submissiveness, she put a .38 caliber hollow-point bullet into his right leg and then had him arrested and prosecuted for assault when he got out of the hospital five weeks later.

The deputy sheriff who handled the case, Hector Gonzalez, became a good friend, dropping by regularly when off duty for a cold beer and a meal. He was married and had eight children and loved the peace and quiet of Ruth's patio and trailer. While Ruth wouldn't rule out entirely the possibility of sex with a married man, it was a sufficient disincentive that she and Hector remained, for the most part, friends rather than lovers. She enjoyed his company and even became friendly with Tranquilina, his wife.

"If you were Mormon instead of Catholic," she occasionally teased Hector, "who knows what might happen."

Over the years the lack of attention had an irresistibly negative effect and she gradually went from blouses and skirts to bib overalls. Her libido remained strong, however, and many nights before sleep she transported herself to a golden field of California poppies where a handsome young carpenter always waited and never failed to make her feel young and desirable again.

By God, she thought, much to her own surprise as she considered Al Bartholomeo, *if it weren't for that shrew of a wife of his, I might take an interest in the little bugger.* She was, admittedly, somewhat in her cups by the end of the evening when the thought first came to her, and she was by no means the kind of woman who would ordinarily encourage someone already spoken for, but once there the thought took hold and she couldn't not think about it, or him. She kept glancing at him and thinking that perhaps, as Becky had implied earlier, she had been hasty in her initial judgment of the retired mailman.

Becky noticed Ruth's surreptitious glances in Al's direction, and she smiled as a thought occurred to her.

TWELVE

★ ✦ ★

The salesman at the computer store in Las Vegas, a blow-dried hustler who had cut his teeth as a youngster in Cleveland going door-to-door with brooms, lightbulbs, industrial-strength toxic home cleaning supplies, and Mexican vitamins, knew right away that this was going to be about as easy a sale as he was likely to encounter in this lifetime.

"Gentlemen," he said smoothly as he came around the counter and shook hands with Benny, Gunter, and Al, "Floyd Harper's the name, and we're talking laptops here, am I right?"

Without waiting for an answer he powered up the top-of-the-line IBM, loaded with RAM and featuring the fastest processor available. He immediately marked Al as the already sold buyer and Benny and Gunter as tagalong tire kickers, to at least one of whom, he made a quick mental wager with himself, he would also sell a computer that day.

Al had had no trouble talking Gunter into accompanying him to Las Vegas to buy a laptop computer, but Benny had taken some effort.

"Come along," Gunter had insisted. "You know far more about computers than I and someone has to advise our friend Al on how he should spend his money."

"Not many years ago you would have needed an entire room full of processors to come close to equaling the power of this laptop, am I right?" Floyd watched the three men as he spoke and quickly focused in on Benny as the challenge, the one to whom he really wanted to sell an expensive computer. "You're an academic, a teacher, am I right?" he said to Benny, already working with the intuitive skill of a cutting horse separating one cow from the herd. Floyd nodded, more to himself than the three men, as he brought up on the screen a sophisticated math software program the distributor had loaded on the demo model specifically for such customers. *You just have to know what to look for,* he told himself. *In this case the bald head is a dead giveaway.* "I'll ask it to factor a polynomial equation and then simplify the answer." He had absolutely no idea what a polynomial equation was, but all he had to do was enter the few keystrokes the software distributor had had him memorize. He turned the laptop towards Benny as numbers and arcane mathematical symbols scrolled impressively across the screen.

"I used to teach math and science at a community college in Southern California," Floyd lied, "but with all these Republican tax cuts now the order of the day I'm afraid," he lifted his hands, palms up, and rolled his eyes towards the ceiling, "we're entering a rather dark time, intellectually speaking."

In fact, Floyd dropped out of school after the ninth grade and had most recently spent eighteen months on a minimum-security prison farm in Southern California for operating a decidedly low-tech telephone boiler room from which he defrauded retired military and civil service personnel through the sale of nonexistent Medicare supplemental insurance. A fellow prisoner, a young California Institute of Technology graduate, sentenced to three years for electronically transferring bank balances that did not belong to him, had advised Floyd to get into computer sales when he was released from incarceration. *It's like money from heaven,* the felonious computer scientist assured him. *America is literally teeming with barely literate simpletons eager to buy expen-*

sive hardware with which they can do nothing but play mo-ronic games.

Benny watched the procession of numbers flowing across the screen for several seconds with growing impatience. Finally he muttered something to himself and, placing his hands on the keyboard, quickly and expertly entered a complicated set of instructions. The screen went blank and the computer's processor could be heard chirping and whirring.

"You need to be careful about what you enter into a computer as powerful as this," Floyd said apprehensively, worried that perhaps Benny might somehow gum up the program and crash the operating system. If so, Floyd knew that God alone, and perhaps the IBM field sales rep, would know how to restart it.

Benny held up a hand. "Just wait a minute," he counseled brusquely.

After what seemed like a long time a series of incredibly beautiful, full color, three-dimensional geometric shapes began to appear, resolving themselves out of nothingness and then dissolving as the next iteration took shape. Even Floyd, ostensibly the expert, could scarcely believe his eyes.

"A succession of stellations and truncations of geometric forms," Benny explained to Gunter and Al. "Unfortunately, as I'm sure our new friend Floyd here would agree," he added sarcastically, nodding in Floyd's direction, "of extremely limited real-world usefulness, beyond the purely esthetic." He smiled at Gunter. "I've had any number of students who got caught up in the esoterica possible with this particular program." With several keystrokes he changed the program back to the one Floyd had brought up and looked at the salesman. "Frankly, I'd be astonished if you get much call here for either software *or* hardware capable of factoring polynomial equations. In fact," he continued, clearly annoyed at Floyd's obvious assumption that the three of them were so simple as to be impressed by the mere scrolling of unintelligible numbers and symbols across the screen, "excepting those few remaining academics in the physical sciences, I'd be willing to wager that there aren't 100 people in the entire state of Nevada who could tell me with any authority what a polynomial equation is, much less what it means to factor one."

"Well," Floyd answered, feeling a sale slipping away, "I merely use it to demonstrate the range of possibilities of this particular laptop, principally to customers such as yourself who can appreciate the usefulness of raw computing power."

Benny jerked a thumb in Al's direction. "He's the one looking for a laptop and what he needs is no more than 32 megabytes of RAM and a processor no faster than 160 megahertz."

"How much did that cost?"

Margaret Bartholomeo's voice sounded precisely like a high-speed saw blade hitting a nail. Possessed of an ill disposition at the best of times, she had watched with growing dismay and outright annoyance her husband's newly discovered interest in the German language and all things scientific. Al scarcely looked up from the new laptop computer he was unpacking.

"The amount isn't important," he murmured. "What's important is what I can learn with this computer."

Margaret flushed with sudden anger and her neck wattles puffed up like a horned lizard. She darted forward and snatched the invoice off the small galley table Al was working on. When she saw the total amount billed to their credit card her eyes widened and then narrowed into slits as she looked from the invoice to her husband. When she spoke, her voice quivered with rage. "Three thousand . . ."

Al raised a hand. "Stop."

More than the command, the look in her husband's eyes

silenced Margaret. She had never seen such a look of determination before and, at least for the moment, it confused
her.

"I *told* you that the amount isn't important. What's important is that I wanted it and I bought it." Gathering up the
computer and packing materials, Al rose. "I'll be over at
Gunter's for the rest of the afternoon," he informed her as
he left the trailer.

"If you're looking for Gunter, he and Benny took a hike out
into the desert," Ruth Pierpont called out.

Al stopped in his tracks and then walked over to where
Ruth and Becky sat shelling field peas.

"Get out of that sun and take a load off," Ruth advised,
nodding towards one of Benny's Adirondack chairs. "I expect they'll be back before too long." She finished the last
of the field peas and stood up. "How about a cold beer?"
Before Al could respond she looked at Becky. "How about
you? Want some ice water or some juice?"

"No, thanks," Becky answered, pushing herself up from
her chair. "I think I'll take a shower and lay down for a
while before dinner."

Ruth grunted and went inside her trailer for the beer.
Becky smiled at Al.

"Benny said you bought a computer today."

Al nodded happily. "A laptop." He proudly held up the
packaging for Becky's approval. "I also bought a couple of
software programs to help me with my math and language
studies."

"Good for you."

Becky turned and started walking across the dusty park
to her trailer.

"Here." Ruth banged out of her trailer and handed Al a
bottle of beer. She had quickly changed out of her bib over-

alls into a sleeveless white cotton blouse and brightly colored print skirt. They sat down and each took a long drink. "Ah, that's good," Ruth said, wiping her lips with the back of her hand. She shook a Camel out of a crumpled pack and lit it, inhaling deeply. "Lord, I can't remember the last time I shelled peas for dinner."

"From Sophie Schmidtbauer's garden?"

Ruth nodded. "Anything that old woman touches turns green," she said admiringly. "Christ, I wouldn't have thought you could grow much of anything other than mesquite and weeds in this godforsaken desert, but damned if she doesn't have a fresh crop of one vegetable or another ready to pick just about every week." She sighed and took another long drink of beer. "I'll tell you what's the truth, life has sure enough gotten better, or at least a hell of a lot more interesting, since all you crazy people moved into the neighborhood. Used to be all I had for sober, reasonably intelligent company out here was the occasional visit by Deputy Sheriff Hector Gonzalez, serving a warrant on one or the other of my ne'er-do-well tenants."

They sat quietly for several moments, watching the heat devils dance across the barren landscape.

"I, um, I like your skirt," Al said finally, meaning it.

He had never before seen her in anything other than her bib overalls, and he literally couldn't remember when last he had complimented a woman, any woman, on what she was wearing. It shocked him that he was able to do so now.

Ruth's blush was barely noticeable under her permanent tan. "What'd you get in Las Vegas?" she asked, changing the subject quickly. "One of them computers?"

"Yes," Al said, taking the laptop from its carton. "And some educational software. I was going to get Gunter to help me set it up." He fumbled with the small computer and its various manuals, wishing he knew how to say what he really wanted to say to her. "Would you like to help me?"

"Oh, Lord," she said, unconsciously putting a hand to her hair, wishing she had shampooed it that morning, "I don't know a thing about computers."

"It's easy," Al assured her. "You read the 'Getting Started' directions from the manual to me and I'll do the work." He smiled at her. "It'll be fun."

"What are you looking at?"

Benny came into the trailer and found Becky standing staring out the window. Since leaving Ruth with Al she had showered and taken a short nap.

"Look." She motioned him over and pointed toward Ruth's trailer.

"Who's that in the print skirt?" he asked.

Becky giggled. "It's Ruth."

"Ruth Pierpont?" Benny's voice betrayed his disbelief. "*Our* Ruth Pierpont? I can't picture her in anything but those bib overalls she's always wearing. In fact, I never thought of her as a *woman,* at least not in a sexual sense."

"Think again," Becky advised. "All she needed, all *any-one* ever needs, is for someone to notice."

"Who's that with her?" Benny squinted as he tried to bring the somewhat distant image into clear focus. "Is that Al? Wait a minute." Benny looked skeptically at the love of his life. "Don't tell me that Ruth . . ."

"Yes," Becky confirmed, "Ruth and Al are becoming an item."

"What about Al's ball-and-chain, the evil-tempered Mrs. Bartholomeo? Christ Almighty, she'll cut his unit off with a butcher knife if she finds out." Benny shivered at the very thought and unconsciously put a protective hand down to his crotch. "Mine, too, if she thinks I, or you for that matter, had anything to do with it." He looked suspiciously at Becky. "You didn't have anything to do with it, did you?"

"Not exactly, no."

"What precisely do you mean by 'not exactly'?"

"I encouraged Ruth to start wearing something a little more feminine is all."

"Said the spider to the fly," Benny responded, exasperated. "I can't believe it. How could Ruth be attracted to Al? He's got false teeth, for God's sake."

Becky laughed. "What's that got to do with anything? You sound like a little boy who's just found out what his mother and father have been doing behind closed doors," she teased. "Honestly, haven't you seen the way they've been looking at each other the past couple of weeks?"

"No."

"And as for the ball-and-chain, as you call her, my guess would be that she's about to become history."

Benny looked back out the window and shook his head.

"What do you see?"

"They're going into Ruth's trailer." He looked at Becky, shocked. "They've actually gone into her trailer, in broad daylight."

"Yes!" Becky exclaimed, thrusting a triumphant fist into the air. She pulled Benny from the window and took his hands into hers. "Make love to me," she whispered huskily, placing his hands on her full breasts. She quickly undid the waistband of his cutoff shorts, the only thing he was wearing. "Make love to me like the very first time on the picnic table outside Gunter's trailer."

"I'm not exactly much to look at," Ruth said quietly, suddenly shy as they walked down the trailer's narrow hallway to her bedroom. "I'm afraid I've let myself get a little sloppy around the edges the past few years."

"I think you're beautiful." Al took her face into his hands and kissed her.

"Heavens," Ruth said quietly as Al withdrew his lips from hers. She sat down heavily on her bed. "I don't know if I've ever felt anything so . . ." She paused to look up at Al and was startled to see him heading for the door. "What's wrong?"

He barely hesitated as he opened the door and stepped out. "I'll be right back," he called over his shoulder.

Benny caught a flash of light in the corner of his eye. He glanced quickly out the window. "Wait a minute; he's leaving."

"What?" Becky disengaged herself and stood up to look over Benny's shoulder. "Dammit, he was only in there for a minute or two."

"Maybe Al's a premature ejaculator."

Benny could tell from Becky's look that his lame attempt at humor had fallen flat. They watched as Al strode briskly by their trailer, a look of determination on his face. He saw the two of them looking out at him and he nodded as he passed by. He didn't seem to notice that neither had any clothes on and that Benny was still more than a little erect.

"He's heading straight for the ball-and-chain," Benny observed in a worried tone of voice. "This doesn't look good at all."

Becky stood with her hands on her hips, the very image of a perplexed, pregnant Venus. "What do you suppose could have gone wrong?" she mused, more to herself than to Benny.

Benny sighed, guessing that it would be some time before Becky was back in the mood for lovemaking. He walked over to the trailer's small refrigerator and took out a beer. "I could have told you it wouldn't work," he said in a quite self-satisfied tone of voice, opening his beer and settling down on the sofa. "Al has never struck me as the sort of man who could stand up to a strong woman."

Becky stood silently at the window, her arms crossed over

her breasts, her right foot tapping an annoyed rhythm on the linoleum floor.

"Hush," she said gently. "I'm trying to think what could have gone wrong. Besides," she turned and wagged a finger at Benny, "Ruth might be over there crying right now, and she's been a very good friend to both of us." She walked over and sat on the arm of the sofa. "I wonder if I should put something on and go over and see if she's okay?" she said, running an affectionate hand across Benny's bald head.

A broad smile played across Benny's face. "I don't think you need to worry about it."

"How can you say that? I told you . . ."

"Look," Benny said, pointing out the window in front of the sofa. Al could be seen hurrying toward Ruth's trailer. Benny gently slid Becky off the sofa's arm and onto his lap. "Now, where were we?"

For two days no one saw any sign of either Al or Ruth. Lights could be seen in Ruth's trailer at night, and two silhouettes were seen to move from time to time as if dancing behind an opaque curtain. The faint sound of laughter was occasionally to be heard, but no hard, physical evidence of the lovers themselves presented itself.

On the morning after the first night, Al's wife unceremoniously dumped his clothing and a few of his personal belongings out onto the cement patio, hitched up their trailer to the station wagon, and left the trailer park without a word to anyone. Margaret Bartholomeo's departure didn't particularly register on any of the neighbors until Gunter's wife Sophie noticed a coyote carrying a pair of Al's trousers out into the desert, for what purpose no one ever determined.

"Well, I think it's very romantic," Becky said.

She and Benny and the Schmidtbauers were enjoying the

late sunset on the evening of the second day. It had been a brutally hot afternoon and all four of them were looking forward to the dying of the light so they could take off their clothes and stroll through Benny's water mister. Out of her line of sight Benny rolled his eyes at Gunter and moved his right hand back and forth in a masturbatory motion.

"Ich auch," Sophie Schmidtbauer sighed. She had wrapped several ice cubes in a handkerchief and was holding it against the back of her neck. In her mind's ear she could still hear the wet sounds of Gunter's belly on hers as they made love that afternoon in their steaming Airstream, and it pleased her to no end as the ice melted and cold water ran down her back. She had no idea why, but since coming to the desert she and Gunter couldn't seem to get enough of each other.

"Romantic or not, they must be about out of food and beer," Benny observed. "Maybe we should leave a CARE package of some sort at the door to her trailer."

Gunter laughed, tickled by the image. "I haven't heard the expression 'CARE package' since after the war, in Europe." He shook his head, as memories of bitterly cold winters with no heat to speak of and little enough food came flooding back. "CARE packages saved many lives in Europe between 1945 and 1950. *Und jetzt,* we find it may be possible to save two American lives with just such a package in 2003."

"What goes around, comes around," Benny said dryly. "And, speak of the devil . . ." He nodded toward Ruth's trailer, from which Ruth and Al were even then emerging.

The two lovers stood on the trailer's patio for a minute or two, looking about and blinking their eyes as if they had just arrived unexpectedly in an alien land.

"Ruth!" Becky yelled and waved. "Come on over."

"Howdy," Ruth said sheepishly as she and Al came up to the patio. She wiped a thin bead of perspiration off her upper lip. "Thought we'd get out for a breath of fresh air. Plus, we're damned near out of beer."

Al nodded happily and looked at Benny. "Polynomial equations," he said cryptically.

Benny looked puzzled for a second and then smiled as he remembered. "Oh, yes, the slick salesman in Vegas. Floyd."

"We worked our way through the algebra tutorial I bought with the laptop," Al explained. "We had to go over the part dealing with polynomial equations several times."

"We?" Benny wondered if, in his new iteration, Al had taken to using an imperial *we*.

Al smiled giddily. "Turns out that Ruth has a natural affinity for numbers."

Ruth rolled her eyes dramatically and threw her hands in the air. "Christ Almighty, we been staring at that damned computer most of our waking hours." She started to laugh but cut it short when she suddenly noticed that Al's trailer was gone from its pad.

Al followed her glance and saw, too, for the first time that his wife had hitched up the trailer and left. He shrugged. "Can't say as I'm surprised," he said, more to himself than anyone else. He looked at Ruth. "Since we're going into Needles tomorrow to pick up some new software, I suppose I should see a lawyer about getting things started on the legal end of things."

"There's not but three lawyers in Needles," Ruth replied, "and two of them are drunkards." She laughed. "One of them actually lived out here for a year or two until I ran his ass off for not paying his rent. I've been knowing the third, Betty Jean Carlson, for damned near forty years. She helped me get Morgan buried back in '78, and what's more, helped me keep this place out of the hands of those bastards down at the bank while she was at it. She's done all my legal work, what there's been of it, ever since. I expect she can handle a divorce without too much trouble."

"Und jetzt," Gunter said, adroitly changing the subject, "tell us about this software the two of you are shopping for."

"Don't get him started," Ruth said, rolling her eyes. "For the past two days this man has dragged me kicking and screaming from the stone age to the digital age and tonight I'm returning the favor."

"What do you mean?" Sophie asked. She had, over a period of some months, been gradually shedding garments in response to both the Mojave's otherworldly heat and her own shrinking inhibitions. For the first time in her life since she was thirteen years old, she wore no brassiere, and her thin cotton blouses struggled mightily to contain her large, heavy breasts. With her support undergarments went her European reserve, and she displayed an earthy sense of humor theretofore unsuspected by all but Gunter.

Ruth accepted a cold bottle of Corona from Benny and took a long pull. "For reasons we're all aware of, Al has not yet been able to shed his clothes and dance through the mister with everyone else. Tonight, when the sun goes down, that's going to change."

"Lieber Gott," Sophie declared, getting up from her chair, "why wait until then? Who's going to see us?" Her breasts fairly burst forth as she quickly unbuttoned her blouse and slid out of her skirt and panties.

Gunter laughed delightedly and turned on the mister at the hose bib next to Benny's trailer. Becky jumped up and, quickly stripping, joined Sophie.

"Al, you see what you've let yourself in for?" Benny asked in a tone of mock reproof. "Complete and wanton licentiousness."

Al looked at Ruth, his eyes wide.

"Go to it, sweetheart," Ruth said to him. "You don't need my permission. I'll join you after I finish my beer."

"Who would have guessed such a change was possible?" Benny asked quietly, speaking of Al. "In such a short time."

It was late in the evening and Ruth and Al had said good

night and returned to her trailer. Sophie had made and brought over a fresh pot of strong Sulawesi coffee and Benny and Gunter were sampling the fruit of Gunter's latest labors, a small pot still he had constructed in a shed he built behind the Airstream.

"Potent," was Benny's pronouncement when he first tasted the colorless, odorless liquid. "I don't know if I'd call it good yet, but it is without question potent."

"But we see it all the time, don't we?" Becky shifted in her chair to ease the pressure of her pregnancy against her bladder. "Usually without even being conscious of it we fall into patterns, ways of doing things. Take books, for example. Why would Al ever have considered reading a book? I suspect he grew up in an environment that, if anything, ridiculed higher education, or at best considered it a luxury too dear for the likes of the Als of this world. It makes absolutely no difference that he always had the intellectual capability, the capacity, to reach much higher; he lacked the motivation, the incentive, to stand out, to break away from the environment in which he lived all his life."

Benny shook his head. "I don't buy it. People pull themselves up by their bootstraps all the time."

"Nein." Gunter leaned forward and jabbed a finger in Benny's direction. "Almost never. We almost always stay in the social class to which we are born."

"Maybe in Europe . . ." Benny began.

"No," Becky interrupted fervently, "Gunter's right. Our class structure in America is every bit as rigid as anywhere else in the world; we just don't like to admit it. And the so-called Horatio Alger myth is just that, a myth. The children of poor and working-class Americans by and large stay right where they started—poor and working-class. Exceptions are so few and far between as to be virtually nonexistent."

"I thought you said we see such changes as we're seeing in Al all the time," Benny reminded her.

"And we do," Becky agreed. "Assuming the capacity or

capability is there, if the person is suddenly removed from the environment that theretofore held them back, then they can, and often do, blossom. What almost never happens is the removal of the person from the environment in the first place. In Al's case, he retires and he and his wife come out here to the desert. A good start, but not in and of itself enough."

"The ball-and-chain has to leave?" Benny ventured.

"Her leaving was the last important element in Al's transformation," Becky continued. "The initiating factor was the presence of you and Gunter."

Benny smiled indulgently and shook his head.

"It is true," Sophie murmured. "We saw it from the very beginning."

"We?" Benny asked.

"Gunter and I first," Sophie answered. "*Und* then Becky. Before the two of you arrived here Al wanted to be friends with Gunter but was afraid. Then, when you showed up he found a, how would you call it, a commonality in this baseball thing, a way to get around the fact that you were a smart, educated man and he was only a retired postal worker. Al looked up to you and Gunter, saw that to be smart, to be educated, was a good thing, a thing to be admired."

"Exactly," Becky concurred. "So he turned off the television, or at least stopped watching it, and began to think. From that instant it was a foregone conclusion that his wife, the remaining link to his old world, one he no longer identified with, would have to go." She smiled in the darkness, remembering the serendipity of her first meeting with Benny. "And just when she needed to be, there was Ruth."

"Lift that section for me, *bitte*," Gunter said, indicating a section of PVC piping to Al.

The two men were finishing the last run of an irrigation system Gunter was installing for Sophie's newly enlarged truck garden. Word of her fresh vegetables, their size, color, and exceptional flavor, had percolated into the surrounding community, and the owner of Needles's only health food restaurant had starting coming out to the trailer park twice a week to buy whatever was ready to harvest. Sophie, who never before had grown so much as a daisy, now yearned to turn the desert green. Gunter had rented a small tractor and tilled more land than could be watered from the Airstream, which led naturally to the irrigation system, which would pull as much water as they needed, albeit illegally, from the Colorado River. Sophie needed help with the extra land and hired one of Hector Gonzalez's nephews three afternoons a week. Gunter also constructed an efficient composting shed and he now recycled their organic waste, including the sour mash from his small still operation, into the garden.

When the last section of pipe was glued the two men retired to the shaded patio in front of Gunter's Airstream for cool wheat beers, radishes, and parched corn.

"Sound engineering, *nicht wahr?*" Gunter asked proudly, nodding toward the exposed portions of the new irrigation system.

"Sound indeed," Al agreed, wiping the cool beer bottle across his sweating brow. "Maybe not 'thousand years' sound, but *gut genug.*"

Gunter smiled. It pleased him that Al had grown comfortable enough to engage in a degree of banter with him. Al was still a little reserved, a little tentative, with Benny, but that was understandable. "So, what's on your mind today?"

"May I be candid?"

"Aber natürlich."

"Has it ever occurred to you that there is something . . ." Al paused a second to consider his words, "something *odd* here."

Gunter thought he knew what Al was getting at but kept

his counsel, wanting his friend to find a way to be more specific.

"I mean," Al continued when he realized that Gunter wasn't yet going to respond, "isn't it odd that the six of us, us *particularly*, ended up here together in this godforsaken, or at least what used to be a godforsaken, trailer park on the edge of the Mojave Desert?" He took a drink of his beer and held up one of Sophie's extremely pungent bright red radishes. "I used to hate radishes," he added, "and now I eat them, and other things I never used to eat, had never *heard* of, like this parched corn, all the time."

"It is odd," Gunter agreed, "and in some ways you are the oddest element in the mixture." He sighed. "At first, frankly, I gave you no consideration. When Benny and Becky arrived I thought, 'This is it; now we will see what we will see,' but I was clearly wrong." He shook his head, amused at his oversight. "I should have known that in such matters nothing is left to chance, that loose ends aren't permitted to just flap in the breeze."

"What are you talking about?"

"I never told you because, as I just said, I didn't see that you were somehow involved."

"Involved in what?"

"Whatever is going to happen here. Whatever brought all of us together here. I told Benny shortly after he arrived that I thought he and Becky and Sophie and I were brought here for some specific reason—precisely what reason I did not then, nor do I yet, know. Something. But clearly you, too, were drawn here and are as much a part of whatever is going to happen as the rest of us. What threw me off, misled me as to the significance of your presence here, was your wife." Gunter paused and pointed out toward the land he had recently tilled. Sophie could be seen on her hands and knees, working compost into the light, sandy soil. "Who could have known? All her life she had no interest, no aptitude for green things, but here she barely looks at something and it grows."

He laughed. "I'll never get her out of the desert now. We're here forever."

"How did my wife confuse things for you?" Al asked.

Gunter thought for a moment. "Are you familiar with the Chinese philosophy or practice of *feng shui*?"

"No, I'm not."

"You should be, and conceptually it's very easy to understand. Many Chinese believe that the way a building is oriented on a piece of land, indeed the very design of the building itself, operates to focus either good or bad spirits, *feng shui*, on the building and its occupants. Bad *feng shui* inevitably results in misfortune, ill will, and poor health. It is an ancient philosophy and not without a great deal of validity, I think. Even today many Chinese companies and individuals would find it inconceivable that a structure, either a home or an office building, would be designed without the active participation and approval of a *feng shui* priest. I believe that people, too, can exert the equivalent of either good or bad *feng shui* on their surrounding environment. You, no less than I or Benny, were drawn here to Needles for some reason. Your wife, who accompanied you, was a source of extremely bad *feng shui*, effectively blocking you, and the rest of us, from the very thing that brought us together." Gunter shrugged, "Perhaps she was the reason my comrades lost faith and left. *Feng shui*, good or bad, can be extremely powerful. Who knows how far such a thing can reach?" Gunter paused for a second and bit into a large radish, taking obvious delight in the crisp texture and sharp, pungent flavor. "On the other hand, something," he added while still chewing vigorously, "something very strong, enabled you to break through the evil force your wife represented. And," Gunter swallowed the last of the radish and looked carefully at Al, "I believe we both know what it was."

"We do?"

Gunter nodded. "The baseball player."

THIRTEEN

★ ✦ ★

A pearlescent light coursed through the trailer park like water flowing downhill as the red rim of the sun struggled over the eastern horizon. A great horned owl swept noiselessly above the *laagered* Airstreams, climbing effortlessly to her home in the hills overlooking the Colorado River. A timer switch mechanically noted the hour and opened a relay, which in turn activated an electric pump immersed in the river. Seconds later muddy water began to bubble into the shallow irrigation trenches that ran parallel to the planting beds in Sophie's garden. A pair of gaudily colored Western Tanagers swooped down to bathe and drink, as did several desert swallowtail butterflies. A gray fox, sitting on its haunches in the long morning shadows cast by one of the Airstreams, cocked its head, inexpressibly pleased at the happy sound the gurgling water made as it worked its way slowly and resolutely through the garden.

Sophie Schmidtbauer rose quietly and sat on the edge of the bed, offering a silent prayer of gratitude that she had lived to celebrate another sunrise. She then brushed her teeth and combed out her thick, iron gray hair, letting it hang freely to her shoulders as she slipped on a bright cotton shift and leather sandals. In the kitchen she took down the wooden coffee grinder she had inherited from her mother and, placing it between her knees, ground enough beans for a large pot of coffee. When the coffee was finished brewing she poured most of it from the brewing pot into a large, stainless steel thermos. She walked back to the bedroom and leaned over the sleeping form of her husband, Gunter. *"Morgenfrüh, du, Liebchen,"* she whispered, a smile playing across her lips.

Gunter stirred and opened one eye. *"Schon so spät?"* he teased as she walked back to the front of the Airstream.

"Kaffee is doch fertig," Sophie called over her shoulder as, taking the thermos with her, she left the trailer. On the patio a hooded oriole waited impatiently for her, turning his bright orange head and black face from side to side as she stepped from the trailer. Sophie reached into the pocket of her shift and took out a peanut, which she offered to the bird. He hopped along the top of the picnic table on the patio and fearlessly took the peanut from her fingers. *"Du Vielfrass,"* she chided gently, turning away to stroll over to Ruth's patio.

"Is the fence working?" Ruth asked as she stepped from her trailer with a coffee cup and a pack of Camels.

Sophie nodded and poured both Ruth and herself a cup from the steel thermos. As her garden grew it attracted legions of rabbits from the desert and she had had to surround it with a rabbit-proof fence. "One or two rabbits get in each night, but I catch them as soon as I go into the garden."

"I presume they'll start showing up on the supper table," Ruth said as Becky walked up, a coffee cup in one hand and a glass of ice water in the other. "In a nice red wine sauce."

Sophie laughed and shook her head. "I turn them loose outside the fence."

"Good for you," Becky said as she joined them, her cup held out for coffee. She was limiting herself to half a cup per day during the pregnancy, an additional reason, as if she needed one, she would celebrate when the baby was born. "Lord," she sighed, sipping the strong, aromatic coffee, "it's going to be wonderful to be an adult again, able to drink all the coffee I want."

"Not to mention a cold beer every now and then," Ruth interjected dryly. She lit a cigarette, careful to sit downwind of the two nonsmokers. "Now," she continued, turning her attention back to Sophie, "about those rabbits you catch every morning."

The three women had, almost without thinking about it, become close friends. None of the three could explain how or even exactly when the early morning coffee klatches had started—it just seemed now to be something they had always done. The first hour after dawn was a time when the desert was at its most benign, before the sun's hammer struck the earth's anvil, before the three men, Benny, Gunter, and Al, rose and added their masculine energy to the mix.

"We will eat no meat from my garden," Sophie said firmly, refilling her and Ruth's coffee cups. As her garden had grown and diversified Sophie ate less and less meat of any sort until, finally, without having made a conscious decision to do so, she became a vegetarian. When she put the thermos down, a house finch flew up and landed on her shoulder, twisting its head so it could look at her face. As she had done with the oriole, Sophie gave it one of her peanuts, and it flew off. Ruth and Becky, indeed all of them, at first astonished, had grown accustomed to Sophie's expanding retinue of birds and small mammals that she fed and occasionally sheltered in homes that Gunter built out of scrap lumber.

"How's Al coming along on the swimming pool?" Becky asked Ruth, adroitly changing the subject.

"Christ Almighty, don't get me started," Ruth answered, shaking her head. "Ever since he helped Gunter on Sophie's garden irrigation project, he's been driving me crazy with the pool thing." She rolled her eyes dramatically and chuckled. "Although, God knows, he's a hardworking little spud."

"I'll say," Becky agreed. Since Al and Gunter had completed the irrigation project Al had, almost single-handedly, rebuilt the park's freshwater delivery system, installing new PVC piping and valves. "I can't get over how much he's accomplished in just a week."

"Gunter has been spending a lot of time with him in the evenings, helping him with the computer," Sophie noted. "They've used it to do the engineering calculations and design the swimming pool Al wants to build."

"Benny calls them the odd couple," Becky laughed. "He says the best part is never knowing when he starts one of his walkabouts what he'll find when he gets back."

Ruth nodded and held her cup out to Sophie. "Just a warm-up," she cautioned. "And speaking of hard work, how is Hector Gonzalez's nephew José working out in the garden?"

"Very well. He's doing more and more for me every day. Plus, he's helping me with my Spanish vocabulary as we work."

"I'm not surprised," Ruth said. "José and his brother have done the occasional odd job around here and neither of them ever gave me the impression of being slow. My guess is that you'd have a hard time finding dust on any of the Gonzalez clan." She stood up and lazily stretched her arms over her head. "And as far as that pool is concerned, I wouldn't send away for a designer swimsuit just yet. Al's going into Needles later this morning to get a quote on his materials list and my guess is he's going to find that the mister we all run through at night is as close to a swimming pool as this old trailer park is likely to get in the foreseeable future."

Gunter was snoring in the shade of his patio awning when Al walked up with two cold, sweating bottles of Corona. He opened his eyes and accepted the proffered bottle of beer. *"Lieber Gott,"* he murmured after taking a large sip, "that tastes good." He looked at his watch. "Two o'clock," he informed Al, "and everybody is taking a siesta."

"Not everybody," Al observed, tilting his bottle neck in the direction of Sophie's garden.

Gunter laughed. "That old woman never gets tired," he said affectionately. "One of the deputy's nephews was not enough; she has now hired a second." Indeed, they could see Sophie on her hands and knees preparing a new section of raised planting beds with two of Hector's nephews. "Plus, she's got them teaching her Spanish as they work." He sighed. "I'm going to have to get a larger immersion pump for the irrigation system when I install the piping for the new section. Speaking of which, did you get the estimate for building your pool?"

Al nodded. "I must have been crazy to have come up with that idea. A pool of the size I had in mind would cost a fortune for materials alone." He smiled ruefully. "I don't know what I was thinking. It must have been the heat."

"I wouldn't give up the idea just yet," Gunter advised. "Perhaps you could approach it on a long-term basis. You know, rent a backhoe and dig the hole, then some months later do the plumbing, then later still lay the rebar and pour the concrete, *und so weiter.* Get it done over a period of a year or two as funds become available."

"We'll see," Al said, doubting that Ruth would go for such a plan. He sipped his beer. "Oh, by the way, not to change the subject but that kid up in Oakland, the ballplayer, is still going strong. I saw a sports page in Needles this morning that said he's on a pace to break Barry Bonds's home run record by the end of August if he stays healthy."

Gunter sat up straighter in his chair. "Ah, yes," he murmured, "the enigmatic young baseball player/physicist. Have you been giving him some thought since our conversation last week?"

"I guess I have," Al said noncommittally. "Although to be honest, since my, um, circumstances have changed I haven't been as interested in baseball as I was before."

"I understand." Gunter paused for several seconds, enjoying a sudden breeze that stirred across the patio. "I think a great deal these days about mortality." He smiled. "Particularly my own. And, as you know, I have come to consider the possibility that this young man is somehow tied into whatever it is that brought all of us together here in the desert."

"Benny thinks you believe that . . ."

Gunter waved a hand dismissively. "You should not be influenced by Benny in this matter. Like all scientists he thinks in a linear fashion, and cannot free his mind to consider possibilities outside the realm of his own experience. He will tell you quite honestly, for example, that he does not believe in God, or a Supreme Being of any sort."

Al shifted in his chair, uncomfortable with the notion of a theological discussion with another man.

Gunter, seeing his discomfort, laughed. "Do not worry, my friend; I have not become a, what is it called, a Born Again Christian. But I will tell you this: I have felt the hand of God in my life—I know He exists."

Al could not resist. "How?"

"You have heard of the Battle of Stalingrad, no? During the Second World War?"

"Of course."

"The German Sixth Army was sacrificed at Stalingrad. That madman, Hitler, refused to allow them to be withdrawn in the face of the first large-scale Soviet offensive. By the end of January 1943, when the survivors finally surrendered, over two hundred thousand German soldiers had been lost."

"Sounds bad."

Gunter looked away from Al, and his eyes lost their focus. "Believe me when I tell you that you are incapable of imagining how bad it was. The city was under twenty-four-hour bombardment by Soviet heavy artillery, the temperature remained at the twenty-below-zero level for weeks at a time, and rations were so scarce that by the middle of January the commanding general, Field Marshal Paulus, stopped feeding the wounded in order to preserve the strength of the remaining soldiers capable of fighting. Thousands of men went stark raving mad, countless more literally froze to death, and an untold number died with no wounds whatever—they simply accepted death and gave up." Gunter sighed and looked back at Al. "My fighter was disabled by ground fire and I had to make an emergency landing at Stalingrad. There was no hope of evacuation, and I, like every German trapped in the city, simply assumed that I was going to die there, whether by artillery, starvation, or freezing to death. Then, a miracle. On January 26, a mere five days before Paulus surrendered, a Luftwaffe pilot, badly wounded while attempting to airdrop supplies, managed to land his plane inside the German perimeter. And not just inside the perimeter, but practically in front of me. Before the Soviets could react with mortars or artillery we pulled the dying pilot from the plane, I got into the cockpit, and . . ." Gunter sailed a hand upward, imitating a plane taking flight. "When I landed, my squadron comrades didn't know what to make of me— everyone had assumed that I was either already dead or, like everyone else at Stalingrad, as good as dead in any event. My commander, given the completely improbable nature of my escape from certain death, suggested, only half-jokingly, that I had made a Faustian bargain with the devil."

"Had you?" Al asked in a teasing manner. He had no idea what a Faustian bargain might have been but suspected that the suggestion wasn't entirely complimentary.

"Gott in Himmel," Gunter laughed, "no, but I suspect anyone trapped at Stalingrad might well have done so had the devil indicated he was open to offers."

"What was his point?" Benny asked quietly. He and Al were sipping brandy and watching the last of a small meteor shower race across the night sky. It was a little after 1:00 A.M.

and everyone else had long since gone to bed. "I mean, many men in combat survived specific incidents that, at the time, seemed overwhelming."

"He thinks that God gave him back his life for some specific purpose."

"And what do you think?"

Al really didn't want to answer Benny's question. He doubted that anything he could possibly say would impress Benny and he badly did not want to be thought a fool. On the other hand, as smart as Benny was, neither could the strength of Gunter's intellect be denied. Furthermore, Al felt strongly that the old German's life experiences, particularly his remarkable survival of a war that neither he, Al, nor Benny had fought in, counted for much. "I don't know." He shrugged. "Listening to Gunter, it's easy to believe that our coming together here in Needles, you and Gunter and I, as fantastic as it is given our background and the timing of our arrivals, has to be more than mere coincidence."

"No, it isn't easy to believe," Benny countered gently. "There is a well known rule in science and philosophy called Ockham's Razor. Basically it states that given a choice of theories to explain an unknown or puzzling phenomenon, one should always choose the simplest one. A corollary rule is that the unknown phenomenon should always be explained in terms of what is already known. So, applying Ockham's Razor to both our little desert community on the banks of the scenic Colorado River and the, as Gunter is wont to call him, enigmatic baseball player, we have to conclude that there is nothing mysterious or occult about either one. The best explanation for our all being here together at the same time is that we *are*. In other words, in a society as mobile as ours there is simply nothing whatever remarkable about any given random combination of subsets of a population for any give time at any given location."

"And the baseball player?"

Benny shook his head. "Again, the simple explanation

would seem to me to be the best. He's simply a talented young athlete. As far as his obvious interest in the physical sciences . . ." Benny paused and shrugged. "Even baseball players can read." He drank the last of his brandy and smiled in the darkness. "You won't go far wrong if you keep in mind that, at least in this country, if you hear the sound of galloping hooves you will always be well advised to think *horses* rather than *zebras,* at least until you actually see the animals. Since there is little likelihood that we'll ever see or talk to the young man in question, I think it would be best if we think of him as just a baseball player, and not some sort of arcane clue in Gunter's cosmic puzzle." Benny stood up and yawned. "Time for bed. Oh, by the way, I saw a badger on my walk today." He shook his head, still impressed. "Imagine that."

FOURTEEN

"Well, Soldier, the good news is that the finger's not broken." Thornton Wills, M.D., the Oakland team physician, looked at Henry with a cheery smile on his florid face. Soundly despised by all the players as nothing more than the managing general partner's medical mouthpiece, Thornton was no stranger to distilled spirits. "But the nail's history. We could wait and let it fall off on its own, but like most competent physicians I've always preferred to take the initiative rather than just let nature run its course." His voice dropped in tone as he continued in what he assumed was a reassuring bedside manner. "Don't worry, I'll have it off before you can say *Bob's your uncle*."

Henry sat on the trainer's table, his right hand in the grip of the slightly inebriated team doctor. He had gone two for four in that afternoon's game against the Tigers and had been nailed on the pinky finger of his catching hand by a foul tip off one of Dickhead Bell's 93 mile per hour hummers in the top half of the seventh inning. The injury was exacerbated by the fact that Henry had long since removed most of the padding from his mitt, preferring the feel of a much lighter and therefore more mobile glove. His finger was now swollen like a Vienna sausage and the tip was frothy red from the blood seeping steadily out around the nail bed.

"I think not," he said in response to the proposed course of treatment as he carefully withdrew his hand from the doctor's grasp. He was well aware of Thornton's medical short-comings and had no intention of following any advice he might offer, certainly not without seeking a second opinion. In the instant matter he knew that Ramona would be able to make up an herbal poultice from ingredients readily obtainable at any health food store in Berkeley, and that such a poultice would be far more likely to be of benefit than anything the doctor might recommend.

"Are you aware," he asked in all seriousness, getting up from the table, "that one of your pupils, the left one to be precise, is considerably more dilated than the other?"

The sudden change in subject confused the doctor, and before he could answer, Rafael Castillo, a reserve shortstop from the Dominican Republic, walked into the room. He smiled when he saw Henry standing there and broke into a flood of rapid Spanish.

"What's he saying?" Thornton asked, his annoyance evident in his tone of voice. Although as team doctor his practice included a good many Hispanic players whose knowledge of English, not including profanity, was often challenged at best, Thornton would have been astonished had anyone suggested he learn even a modicum of Spanish.

Henry turned from his teammate to the doctor. "He says he's having trouble urinating."

"Who isn't?" the doctor said sarcastically, laughing at what he took to be a clever rejoinder. "All right," he said with a great deal of resignation while pointedly looking at his watch, "let's take a look at it. Probably," he said as an aside to Henry while motioning for Rafael to drop his drawers and expose himself, "nothing more than a dose of the clap." He shook his head in feigned wonder. "What is it about these people that makes them constitutionally unable to unroll a condom is beyond me." He looked again at his watch and grimaced. "Whatever this is better not take long," he muttered as he grasped Rafael's penis gingerly between his right forefinger and thumb, "or I'm going to be late getting back over to the City for cocktails and dinner."

Henry left the trainer's room as Thornton began his examination. The clubhouse was almost empty when Henry entered the large locker room.

"How's the finger?" Bobby Clarke, one of the few remaining players, called out.

"It's fine." Henry walked over to where Bobby was dressing and held it up for his inspection. "I declined to let Doctor Thornton take the nail off."

"Shit." Bobby shook his head in disgust as he bent over to tie his shoelaces. "I wouldn't let that asshole near me if I was practically bleeding to death. Besides, everything he sees goes straight upstairs to the suits." He laughed, a short, bitter exhalation of tension. Bobby had not been getting a great deal of playing time with the A's and, now a member of his fifth major-league team, saw the end of his career in the not-too-distant future. "You know something, Soldier? I been traded four times in my career and not once, not one fucking time, has anyone from management told me, *We appreciate what you done for us, Bobby,* or, *Good luck with your new team.* Nothing. See, whenever management does something it's business, you know what I mean? But goin' in the other direction, whoa, that's a different story. Everyone from the suits upstairs to the gomers in the stands talks about loyalty to the team, sacrifice, play hurt, whatever it takes, but let some teenager from Guate-fucking-mala come along with a little more zip on his throw-in from right field and it's 'don't let the doorknob hit you in the ass on the way out.' And every time I left a team they had the equipment manager standing right there when I packed my shit to make sure I didn't steal a goddamned T-shirt or something." He laughed once more, the tension suddenly gone from his voice. "Listen at me. I sound like a man with one foot in the grave and the other on a banana peel. Let me see that finger." He quickly examined Henry's injured finger, turning the hand over to inspect it from all angles. "Shit, leave it alone. If the nail wants to come off it'll come off on its own. You let that goddamned drunk Thornton fuck with it and you're apt to lose the whole finger."

A sudden thought entered Henry's mind as he stood watching Bobby finish dressing. "Would you like to have dinner tonight?" he asked somewhat awkwardly.

"You bet, Soldier." Bobby stood up and rolled his shoulders. "What have you got in mind?"

One of the clubhouse boys, actually an African-American gentleman in his mid-sixties who had worked in a number of menial positions for the team through four changes of ownership, eight league championships, and four World Series championships, and had never made more than $11,000 in a single year (*I think we should just fire the old son of a bitch*, one of the team's internal auditors remarked, only half-jokingly, during the most recent annual staff salary review process, *given the fact that he's already been fully depreciated*), stopped Henry and Bobby as they were leaving the clubhouse.

"Mail," he mumbled, indicating the canvas mail sack he had dragged over from the team's administrative offices on the other side of the Oakland-Alameda Coliseum.

Henry received by far the most fan mail of any member of the club. At first, when the mail was little more than a trickle, he and Ramona read every letter and in fact answered all but the most unintelligible. Now that the trickle had become a thundering cataract, they seldom even read the letters, having discovered that most were pleas for autographs (to be held as little more than an investment by adolescent speculators) or, in an astonishing variety of forms, appeals for money, most of the correspondents apparently of the mistaken belief that Henry was being paid untold millions of dollars.

Henry nodded a *thank you* as he hoisted the heavy bag. Some weeks ago he had, in an effort to save the old man, known only as "Blue" (in fact, on the entire professional and administrative staff of the club only the payroll clerk knew the old man's actual name), the effort of hauling his mail from the club office suite to the clubhouse, not an inconsiderable distance, directed that it be held for him in the mail room. Shortly thereafter Scotty Harrison, the team's young assistant equipment manager, approached Henry at his locker.

"Blue thinks you don't like him."

Henry looked up, puzzled.

"What I mean is, Blue thinks you told the mail clerk to hold your mail because you don't like him and you want to get him fired."

"How could anyone think such a patently ridiculous thing?" Astonished, Henry shook his head. "I did it as a favor, to spare him the burden of carrying it all the way over here."

"I understand and I assumed that's what it was. But, see, if Blue doesn't do things like that, then, believe me, the club will start wondering why he's on the payroll at all. Bizarre as it may seem to you or I, or any rational person for that matter, his fear is not entirely unfounded." Embarrassed, Scotty laughed nervously. "It isn't exactly like it's much of a job, but it's the only one old Blue has. Hell, everybody's got to have a rice bowl, you know what I'm saying?"

Ramona was preparing corn tortillas for a late supper when Henry and Bobby arrived. It had been an unusually warm day in the Bay Area and the tiny redwood bungalow was filled with the sweet redolence of the blue gum eucalyptus trees that surrounded it.

"Although we haven't met before now, Henry has spoken often of you," she told Bobby graciously after Henry introduced them.

"Is that a fact?" Bobby answered, smiling broadly, obviously pleased. "Well, me and Soldier do spend a lot of time together, particularly on the road." Bobby hitched up his trousers and winked at Henry in a proprietary fashion. "I been sort of schooling him on life in the majors." He looked around the tiny cottage. "This is a nice place you've got here," he said, while thinking, *Where the hell's the furniture?* He wondered if everything had been repossessed. "What kind of trees are those?" He pointed towards the open doors leading to the deck and the trees just beyond.

"Eucalyptus," Ramona answered. "Can you smell them?"

"Yeah, I can. Reminds me when I was a kid, the smell of pine trees." He laughed. "My old man worked in a sawmill up in northern Minnesota in the summers. When he was sober. We lived in a trailer and my brothers and I used to hang around this lake and get into fights with the Indian kids."

"Fights?"

"Yeah, the whites and Indians up there didn't much care for each other." He laughed again. "Probably still don't. Eucalyptus, huh? I don't think they had any of them in Minnesota."

"I doubt they did," Henry said. "They were brought to the Bay Area from Australia, another example of environmental ignorance. Would you like something to drink?"

Ramona laughed. "Why not just ask him if he'd like a beer?" She turned to Bobby. "Henry has become a home brew enthusiast and would be heartbroken if you did not sample one of his latest batch."

"No kidding, Soldier, you make your own beer?"

"I do," Henry confirmed. "The entire fermentation process is a fascinating one, don't you think?"

"Well, to tell you the truth, I never thought much . . ."

Before Bobby could finish his answer he was startled by the sight of a dense white cloud of fog that rolled out of the bottom of the refrigerator when Henry opened the door to get their beer. It settled and spread along the floor of the cottage, dissipating and quickly disappearing when it reached the open doors leading to the deck.

"Jesus Christ, what the hell is that?" he asked, unconsciously taking one step backwards as the floor-clinging fog approached his feet like something out of a grade-B horror movie.

Henry handed him an amber bottle of beer. "Carbon dioxide," he said dismissively. "From the dry ice I've got stored in the refrigerator." He paused and took a sip of his beer. "Honey wheat," he said with a sigh of pleasure.

"Honey what?"

"Wheat. The beer's an unfiltered honey wheat summer brew, my latest recipe." He handed Bobby a wedge of lemon. "Here, try some lemon with it. How do you like it?"

"Fine, fine," Bobby said after quickly tasting it. "Look, what the hell's the deal with the dry ice? Isn't that stuff dangerous to be keeping around the house like that? I mean, in the refrigerator with all the food and everything?"

"Not now, Henry," Ramona interrupted from the kitchen. "No starting with the cloud chamber until after we eat." She sounded, she suddenly realized, like a mother telling a son he couldn't play with his toys until after supper, and the thought amused her greatly.

"I can't really show him until after it gets completely dark anyway," Henry reassured her. "What are we having for dinner?"

"Black beans and rice." She looked out and caught Bobby's eye. "Does that sound good to you?"

Black beans and rice? Bobby wasn't sure if he had heard correctly. *What the fuck kind of dinner is that?* "Sounds great," he responded, not sure what else he could say. "With beef, or what?"

Ramona smiled. "For the past month Henry and I have been experimenting with a pretty much vegetarian diet," she explained. "I serve the beans and rice with corn tortillas and a fresh guacamole salsa made with onion, tomatoes, toma-tillas, avocado, and lime. Very healthy, very good, very Mexican." She paused as she put the steaming black beans into a plain unglazed serving bowl. "Henry, where should we serve dinner?"

"We only have two chairs for the table," Henry explained to Bobby. He looked at Ramona. "Why don't we just all sit on the floor? We can put the bowls and plates and everything in the middle and everyone help themselves."

"Like the Romans," Bobby said, feeling that he should say something to make his hosts feel more comfortable with the fact that, odd as it may be, they had no furniture to speak of. *Jesus,* he thought, *I know Soldier's only making the major-league minimum, but you'd think he could afford a couple more chairs, or whatever.*

"The Romans?"

"Yeah, sure, like Ben-Hur or Moses or whatever. I re-member seeing them in the movies, you know? They ate on the floor, too. Or on couches or something." He nodded, certain now of the memory of Saturday matinees past. "Be-cause they didn't have chairs either. Or the Indians for that matter, although I sure as hell never ate with any in Min-nesota."

Because Ramona was not spending her days in the com-pany of professional athletes it took several seconds of con-centrated effort to be able to understand what Bobby was trying to say. She and Henry began placing their supper on the floor near the open door leading to the deck.

Bobby, lost momentarily in the Minnesota of his youth, shook his head at the thought of the Indians he and his brothers had grown up fighting. "I doubt those sorry fucks even had this much furniture," he said quietly, forgetting for a second that he was a guest in Henry and Ramona's home. He looked at Ramona. "I'm sorry; what did you say?"

She smiled and indicated that he should seat himself on the floor. "Dinner is served."

*   *   *

"Lord, that was good."

Bobby couldn't remember when he had enjoyed a meal as much. "I mean, when you said we were having black beans and rice I never had no idea it could taste so good. And all that stuff in the salsa." He shook his head in apparent disbelief that a meal without meat could be so satisfying. "Still," he added quickly, lest Henry or Ramona think he was likely to become a vegetarian in the near future, "a little beef or chicken never hurt anybody, if you know what I mean." He put both hands on his distended stomach. "Whoa. I hope Preacher isn't going to be expecting me to run out any bunt singles tomorrow, if you know what I'm saying. I'm as full as a tick." He sat up, suddenly remembering something. "Wait a minute." He pointed at Henry. "You were going to tell me what you keep dry ice in the refrigerator for."

"A cloud chamber."

"A what?"

Henry smiled. "I'll show you." He went into the bedroom and brought out a large 20-gallon capacity cylindrical glass container.

"In case you were wondering," Ramona said to Bobby, "I had to go all the way down to San Jose, to a chemical supply house, to find just the right container. While you guys were in Seattle." She shook her head. "And believe me, it wasn't inexpensive."

"But it was worth it," Henry interjected. He put the cylinder on the floor and gingerly inserted a thick section of dry ice. He next soaked a thick cotton pad with alcohol, placed it on an open shelf suspended from beneath the container's glass top, and put the top onto the container. "What's going to happen in the next several minutes is quite interesting apart from the ultimate purpose of the chamber itself. Watch carefully."

Bobby edged closer to the container, not at all certain that what Henry was doing was entirely safe. He remembered from junior high school that a chemistry teacher had inadvertently blown something up in the school lab, losing several fingers in the process.

"A dramatic ambient temperature difference now exists in the relatively short distance between the top and the bottom of the chamber," Henry explained. "At the top, alcohol vapor is mixing with the warmer air. As that mixture expands downwards it cools and the air becomes supersaturated, forming a dense mist, or cloud."

Indeed, even as Henry was speaking, a cloud began to form and diffuse throughout the chamber. The quiet beauty of the air-alcohol vapor reaching the supersaturation point and turning into a visible, gently moving cloud was such that all three of them, even Henry and Ramona, who had seen it several times in the past two or three days, found themselves scarcely breathing. Henry turned off the overhead light and backlit the chamber with a small gooseneck lamp Ramona had found at a thrift shop in Berkeley.

"What the . . ." Bobby's startled voice was little more than a whisper. He pointed, rather unnecessarily, at a line that appeared, seemingly out of thin air, and lanced through the cloud like a tracer round, quickly fading to nothingness.

"One of the building blocks of the universe," Henry explained, his finger caressing the thick glass side of the chamber as he simulated the path taken through the cloud. "An elementary particle, made visible in the most mundane of fashions."

Bobby looked at his teammate and noticed that his eyes were glowing in the light reflecting off the sides of the chamber.

"You cannot imagine the things the invention of this simple device in 1900 made possible." Henry seemed to be speaking more to himself than to Bobby. "We take for granted the notion that the laws of energy and momentum conservation apply to individual interactions between elementary particles, but in fact actual proof of that concept was not obtained until the mid-1920s, and it could not have been demonstrated then without the use of the cloud chamber." Henry looked at Bobby as if suddenly remembering that he was there. "The visible tracks you see in the cloud are actually liquid droplets from the supersaturated vapor condensing around the ionizing radiation passing through it."

Bobby was perplexed. "Jesus, Soldier, I don't know what to say. I mean, I never saw anything like this before."

Henry smiled.

"How is the finger?" Ramona asked. She and Henry had made love and were lying naked and uncovered on the futon. A sliver of moonlight, filtered through the redwoods and eucalyptus, fell across and softly illuminated their bodies.

"It's fine." Henry held the bandaged finger up into the moonlight. Their lovemaking had set it to throbbing, but the discomfort was minimal and more than offset by the pleasurable sensation of a cool East Bay breeze ruffling the fine hair on his chest and lower abdomen. "I think Bobby enjoyed coming over for dinner."

Ramona smiled. "Once he got over the shock of a vegetarian meal and eating on the floor, yes, I think he did."

They lay quietly for several minutes, both unable to sleep. Finally, Ramona rolled to her side and got up off the futon.

"I'll make some hot chocolate," she said, padding into the kitchen.

Henry, too, got up, turning on the small gooseneck lamp that sat on the floor next to the futon. He dragged the mail sack he had brought from the clubhouse over to the futon and lay back down.

"So many unhappy people," Ramona said, returning with two mugs of hot chocolate and seeing Henry sorting through the fan mail. "So many lives lived through the accomplishments of others." She sat cross-legged on the futon and accepted a handful of letters. "Albuquerque, Trenton, Atlanta, Mobile, New York," she intoned, reading the postmarks. She had taken to reading only letters from little-heard-of, interesting-sounding communities, towns like Zelienople, Sunflower, Copperopolis, Turtle Island, Truth or Consequences, and Indian Wells. "Here's one," she announced, pleased she had found a letter from a town she had not heard of before. "Needles, California."

Henry looked up from a letter pleading for financial help to send what was described as a mixed-gender, multiracial, multiethnic children's slow-pitch softball team in San Francisco to a tournament in Japan. To further, the letter went on to assure Henry, world peace through noncompetitive athletic encounters. The writer explained that in order to create and maintain a spirit of noncompetitiveness during games, scores and statistics were not kept and the children were counseled whenever it appeared that they were trying too hard. Henry decided to post the letter on the bulletin board in Oakland's locker room. "Needles," he murmured, taking a sip of his chocolate. "Why does that sound familiar?"

"I don't know," Ramona answered. "It's probably just another ten-year-old begging for an autograph." She tore open the envelope and began reading.

FIFTEEN

"I told you I smelled a rat about this whole deal right from the get-go."

Preacher Brown leaned over Robert Edgerton's desk. He had come so quickly from the clubhouse to the executive suite that he had neglected to remove a huge wad of chewing tobacco from his mouth. He hammered his fist down on the gleaming wooden surface of Edgerton's desk for emphasis.

"Goddammit, I told you something was queer about that boy before we ever traded Bobo Martinez."

Edgerton looked up at his team's manager in astonishment and no small amount of fear. Preacher's face was a scarlet red and the prominent veins in his neck throbbed obscenely. Several flecks of chewing tobacco hung to the corners of his mouth and he looked more than a little deranged. *Has he lost his mind?* Edgerton wondered as he held both hands up, palms outward, placatingly. "Calm down, Preacher; calm down. What are you talking about?"

"What am I talking about? What am I talking about?" The question seemed only to further enrage Preacher. "You sonofabitch, we've gone and traded Martinez and here it is only the middle of July and we got no goddamn catcher. What the fuck do you think I'm talking about?"

"I don't know." Edgerton had a sudden, heart-stopping thought. "Christ, don't tell me Spencer's been injured." *Lord, don't let it be that,* he thought.

"Even better," Preacher answered sarcastically. *And I'm almost glad, too, you miserable cocksucker.* "He's quit."

"Quit?" Edgerton's voice rose ridiculously, his one-word rejoinder little more than a bleat. "He can't do that." His face hardened. "This is about money, isn't it?"

Preacher sighed, the fight suddenly gone out of him. He sat down and ran a gnarled, arthritic hand over his face. "You know, when I was a ballplayer, we played purely and simply for the love of the game. Money never meant a goddamn thing." He looked at Edgerton. "That boy ain't a ballplayer, never *was* a ballplayer, never gonna *be* a ballplayer. Not a for-real one. All he ever was was a goddamn freak, someone who came along out of no-goddamn-where who could throw better and hit better than anyone else. He never had the game in his heart." Preacher shook his head, appalled that such a thing could be. "I never trusted him, not for a minute. I told you, time and again back in Arizona this spring, someone like that, someone like him, is bound to break your heart, bound to let you down."

"Wait, wait, wait." Edgerton waved his arms, once again in control, his mind racing to consider all the possibilities. *An agent,* he thought. *I'll bet a goddamned agent has gotten his meat hooks into Henry Spencer.* He snatched up the telephone on his desk and buzzed his secretary. "Get Sarah Gill on the phone and tell her to get her ass over here right away. And tell her to bring a copy of Henry Spencer's contract." He slammed the receiver down without waiting for an acknowledgment and pointed at Preacher. "Now, tell me from the beginning, word for word, exactly what transpired."

"What the fuck are you talking about?" Preacher looked up from his plain, metal desk, not yet truly annoyed but moving clearly and inexorably in that direction. Henry Spencer stood in front of him dressed, not in his practice uniform as he should have been, but in blue jeans, a rather poorly tailored linen shirt, and huarache sandals. "Why aren't you out taking batting practice with the rest of the team?"

"I'm leaving," Henry repeated.

"What the fuck are you talking about?" Preacher repeated, still not connecting the meaning of Henry's words with the reality standing in front of him. "Leaving where?"

Henry reached over and placed his catcher's mitt on Preacher's desk, a gesture of closure so obvious that Preacher knew immediately what Henry meant.

"That's it?" Edgerton's tone of voice bespoke his skepticism. "Nothing more?"

Preacher shook his head.

"You mean you didn't ask him for an explanation?"

Before Preacher could respond, Sarah Gill, the team's general counsel, hurried in.

"Henry Spencer has left the team," Edgerton explained. "Did you bring his contract with you?"

"Yes." She opened her briefcase and took it out. "Do we know why he left?"

"No." Edgerton shot an annoyed glance toward Preacher. "But I suspect he's gotten himself an agent and is planning to hold out for more money."

Sarah sat down and primly crossed her legs, revealing a flash of white inner thigh that was missed by neither Preacher nor Edgerton. "Well," she said in a self-satisfied tone, holding up Henry's contract, "whatever else he's after, we know for certain that he can't play for any other team without our consent."

Preacher shook his head and sighed, a doleful sound. "It's not about money," he said, his voice barely above a whisper.

"It's not?" Sarah Gill looked from Preacher to Edgerton, confusion on her face. "But I thought . . ."

Edgerton dismissed Preacher's comment with a peremptory wave of his hand. "Believe me, it's about money." He snorted derisively. "It's always about money. We should be hearing from his new agent any time now." He paused and thought for a second. "The first thing we do is prepare a press release to the effect that Henry has requested a couple of days personal time off, which we've granted. That should give everyone a little breathing space, a little cooling-off time. Then, if they, meaning Henry and his agent, want to hold some kind of press conference to tell the world that he's left the team as a ploy to force us to renegotiate an otherwise valid contract, they'll look like the bad guys, not us."

Sarah nodded her approval. "Excellent tactic."

"Next," Edgerton continued, "I want you," he pointed to Sarah, "to research and prepare a no-holds-barred lawsuit, charging whoever Spencer's agent turns out to be with tortious interference with a contractual relationship."

The pupils of Sarah's eyes dilated in an autonomic response to the pleasure that Edgerton's words sent coursing through her body. "I don't think anyone's tried that before," she murmured huskily, more to herself than to Edgerton. Endorphins cascaded over, under, and around the myriad folds of her brain as the thought of thousands, perhaps tens of thousands of billable hours ran through her mind. It was the kind of lawsuit that lawyers dream about post-coitally, legal research and trials and appeals running almost to infinity. The kind of lawsuit that put 7-series Beemers into the garage and the kids into Stanford.

"Well, it's about goddamn time someone did," Edgerton rumbled, unconsciously grabbing at his crotch in a gesture of testosterone-fueled aggressiveness. "That boy signed a contract and by God this team's not about to roll over and take it up the ass, pardon my French, just because some fast-talking agent caught his ear." He turned toward Preacher. "Richie Sanders can catch until we get this whole mess straightened out; and believe me, it's not going to take a lot of time. Or at least it better not." His words clearly implied that he was going to hold Preacher responsible for the entire affair, win, lose, or draw. "Bobby Clarke can back him up if he needs any help. Plus," he added, suddenly remembering the schedule, "we've got the All Star break coming up. That gives us a little more time."

Preacher got up and left the room without a word.

"He doesn't seem very . . ." Sarah paused, searching for the right word. "Very motivated."

"Preacher's getting to be a pain in the ass," Edgerton said. He shrugged. "He's old. And, just between you and me, this is his last season with Oakland. In fact, now that I'm thinking about it I want you to check his contract and make sure we won't owe him severance pay or any other benefits when I decide to fire him."

"They're gone, Skipper, lock, stock, and barrel."

Bobby Clarke sat in Preacher's office, the adjoining locker room darkened and empty. It was almost 9:00 P.M.

Preacher nodded, his worst suspicions confirmed. That afternoon, after practice, he had told the team that Henry had been granted a couple of days personal time off. "You'll catch the three games remaining until the All Star break," he informed young Richie Sanders, who, having never yet caught a major-league game, promptly got a major-league stomachache. His obvious discomfort at the sudden and wholly unexpected elevation to starting catcher transmitted itself almost instantly to the pitching staff, obsessively attuned as they were to the mental stability of the team's catchers, or, more properly, the team's *catcher,* since no one, least of all Richie Sanders, thought that the Soldier would ever *not* catch a game. *"Fuck me,"* one of the starters murmured to his mates, knowing that he was scheduled in the rotation to pitch the second of Richie's three games, and knowing further that his ERA was already the highest among the starting battery. Randy, hearing the *sotto voce* comment, felt suddenly worse.

As the players began to drift out after showering and changing, Preacher brought Bobby Clarke into his office and closed the door.

"You're a friend of the Soldier's, aren't you?" he asked.

"Well," Bobby hemmed, always on guard and uncomfortable when a manager asked a question, any question, "I don't know if you could call us friends exactly, but, yeah, we're sort of like friends, if you know what I mean."

Preacher hadn't the faintest idea what Bobby meant, although he had been around Organized Baseball long enough to know that a player, given an opportunity, would always lie to his manager rather than tell the truth. "I want you to go by his house over in Berkeley and see how he's doing. And listen." Preacher stabbed a blunt finger toward Bobby's chest and his voice dropped menacingly. "I want this on the QT. Whatever you see, whatever he says to you, you bring back to me, tonight, and no one else, you understand?"

"Yeah, sure, Skipper, you know me." Bobby thought for a moment. "Listen, Skip, you want me to ask him anything in particular?"

"No. Just see how he's doing, if he needs anything. And then come right back here."

Bobby knew that the little redwood bungalow was deserted even before he got out of his car. Although the front door was locked he was able to peer through a couple of windows and see that even the laughably meager amount of furniture owned by the Soldier and Ramona was gone.

"They're gone, Skipper, lock, stock, and barrel."

Preacher did not appear to have moved an inch in the

hour that Bobby had been gone. A half-full bottle of Jack Daniel's sat on his desk next to an empty glass. He nodded almost absentmindedly in response to Bobby's statement, his eyes fixed on the whiskey bottle in front of him.

"Soldier never said nothing to me about moving when I had dinner with him the other night," Bobby offered. "I guess he must have found another place or something kind of unexpectedly, huh? Say." Bobby suddenly thought of something. "You don't think he got evicted or anything, do you?"

Preacher leaned back in his chair and stretched. He had known, in his heart, that Henry had meant it when he had said that he was quitting the team, so he was not surprised to hear that he had so suddenly left town. *That boy was odd from the start,* he thought, running a hand over the few remaining bristles on top of his head, *sort of like a dog laying an egg.* He poured three fingers of whiskey into the glass and took a drink.

"When's the Soldier due back?"

Bobby ordinarily wouldn't have asked his manager such a thing, but he felt that his running out to check on Soldier had made him and the Preacher co-conspirators in the question of Henry's whereabouts. That Preacher hadn't offered him a drink wasn't a particularly good sign, but, Bobby reasoned, he had never been known as the kind of manager who liked to fraternize with his players.

"He's not." Preacher reached a sudden decision and finished off the remaining whiskey in his glass with a quick drink.

"What?" Bobby was sure he hadn't heard correctly, or that his manager hadn't misinterpreted his question. "I mean, when's the Soldier coming back to the team?" He and everyone else in the locker room had seen the press release Scotty Harrison passed out after practice, the one that said Henry had asked for and received several days of personal time off.

"Goddamn it, didn't I just say he's not coming back?"

"Yeah, Skip, but I thought . . ."

"You don't get paid to think, you got that? I don't give a shit what the goddamned front office thinks; I got a team to run here, you hear me?"

Bobby started backing slowly out of Preacher's office. He heard what his manager was saying, but he could make neither heads nor tails of it, and experience told him that when a team's manager starts talking or acting irrationally, it behooves his players to be elsewhere.

"Yeah, sure, Skip, sure, whatever you say." He was at the threshold and almost away. "You know me, Skip; I'm a company man all the way."

Preacher ignored Bobby and snatched up the telephone on his desk, quickly punching in seven digits. "I been in this game too long to be anybody's patsy, especially . . ." He paused as a voice came on the other end of the line. "Yeah, Warren, it's me, Preacher Brown. Yeah, yeah. Listen, that press release you birds got today about Henry Spencer taking a few days off? Well, if you want the real story I suggest you get your ass over here. What?" Preacher cradled the telephone between his ear and shoulder and poured himself another drink. "What the fuck do I care what time it is? Listen, if you can't make it I'll give it to that bitch over at the *Examiner.* The one that's always screaming about access to the locker room after games, for chrissakes. She thinks you and me been around too goddamn long, gettin' by on our reputations. Maybe she's right. What? Yeah, I'll have Blue, the clubhouse boy, wait by the clubhouse door to let you in." Preacher hung up without saying good-bye. "Fuck that Edgerton," he mumbled, taking another drink. "I got a goddamn team to run here in case he didn't notice."

SIXTEEN

✦

Needles, California

Henry left baseball and the Oakland A's with no more thought than a man gives a soiled shirt taken off and thrown into the hamper. He and Ramona departed Berkeley with $2362.00 in cash, two ceramic jugs of spring water, four bean burritos rolled in aluminum foil, and all of their furniture tied to the top of Henry's 1982 Pontiac. They padded the top of the car with a blanket, then positioned their small kitchen table upside down. Between the table legs they laid the futon, rolled tightly and covered with the rest of their bedding. On the ends of the futon they tied their two chairs. The backseat was filled with their clothing, kitchen utensils, and the other detritus of their small household, including, carefully padded with their two pillows, the glass container with which Henry constructed his cloud chamber. The few items they decided to leave behind they left in their driveway with a note to passersby indicating that it was free for the taking.

They camped the first night on the shore of Mono Lake, thirty miles or so to the east of the hordes of tourists clogging the Yosemite Valley floor. Henry woke during the night to the snuffling sound of a large gray coyote cautiously exploring the ground around where he and Ramona lay wrapped in a light cotton blanket. The coyote saw that Henry was awake and the two of them stared at each other for what seemed like many minutes, both able to see quite clearly the shimmering starlight reflected in the dilated pupils of the other.

"Henry?" Ramona stirred from a light sleep. "Is something wrong?"

At the sound of her voice the coyote whirled from their small campsite and was gone, his passage so swift and silent as to raise doubt that he had ever been there at all.

"He winked at me," Henry noted with wonder, more to himself than to Ramona. He sat up, pulling the blanket that covered them with him.

"Who did?" Ramona quickly pulled the light blanket back over her bare breasts. "Is somebody here?"

"Only a coyote, and he is gone now."

"Then who winked at you?"

"The coyote. We were looking at each other and at the sound of your voice, just as he was leaving, he winked at me."

Ramona laughed and sat up next to Henry. "The Navajo believe that the coyote spirit is that of a prankster, or practical joker." She yawned and caressed her growing abdomen. "My breasts hurt."

Henry got up and rummaged through one of their bags. He found a jar of cocoa butter and sat down again.

"I felt as if the coyote knew me, or knew of me," Henry said as he began to gently massage the cocoa butter into Ramona's aching breasts. "The wink was to tell me that he knows of our journey."

"Perhaps it was a *she*," Ramona teased. "Perhaps instead she was trying to tell you that your daughter will grow into a fine, intelligent, independent young woman."

"Like her mother."

"Exactly." Ramona closed her eyes and leaned into Henry's strong and tender hands. "Or, she may have been wondering whether or not we finished all of the bean burritos we had for dinner. The trouble with coyotes is that it's hard to know precisely *what* they're thinking."

"This coyote was a *he,* and he was definitely trying to tell me something. Lay down and I'll massage your tummy with cocoa butter."

"Mmm," Ramona murmured as she sank back onto the blanket. "What do you think he was trying to tell you?"

"I don't know, not exactly, but I'm sure he knew me and would have communicated had I been able to understand."

A wonderful lassitude settled over Ramona as Henry's hands gently caressed her swollen abdomen. She unconsciously opened her legs as his hands moved slowly from her lower abdomen to the inside of her thighs. So light was his touch that at first she did not realize that he had begun to make sweet love to her. Her breath quickened as he gently covered her, taking care not to put any of his weight on the child. As a powerful orgasm swept over Ramona she cried out, her guttural passion carried on a night breeze to all the creatures of the high desert.

Almost three-quarters of a mile away two coyotes, a female and the large, powerful Alpha male that had looked into Henry's soul earlier, heard the cry even as their olfactory senses detected the pheromones Henry and Ramona had unconsciously broadcast during their arousal. The male threw back his head and answered with a cry that was at once laughter and heartbreak, a sound that reached Henry's ears even as he was ejaculating. *Yes,* he wanted to answer, *yes, I hear you and I know we are brothers, seekers after something we can never hope to find in a universe whose boundaries are forever beyond our vision.*

For the next three days Henry and Ramona worked their way almost aimlessly east and south, staying on secondary roads and buying food and bottled water at small grocery stores in towns shown only on the most detailed of maps.

As they meandered through the badlands on both sides of the California–Nevada border the heat rose dramatically as the altitude and humidity plummeted. For three nights in a row they made love and slept on the ground next to the car, under a spectacular sky vaulted with the myriad stars of the Milky Way. They drank immense amounts of water and ate little food as their bodies reacted to the stunning heat and the almost complete absence of humidity by concentrating urine and copiously perspiring. By the third day they and all their belongings were so covered with dust that an idle glance no longer revealed the true paint color of Henry's Pontiac.

"Whoa, dude."

Mark Little, at the radiator shop in downtown Needles, was clearly impressed with Henry's bulk. A high school weight lifter himself, he knew Grade-A beef when he saw it.

"Far out," he added, giving Henry raised eyebrows, a nod of his head in the direction of the dust-covered Pontiac with the furniture piled on top, and a thumbs-up sign of admiration and approval.

The large Proctaid Hemorrhoid Cream thermometer out by the gas pumps indicated a brutal 121 degrees Fahrenheit at 11:22 in the A.M. The eighteen-wheelers roaring by out on Interstate 40 seemed to undulate through the thick, distorting ribbons of heat rising from the roadbed.

"Man, you guys look like road warriors, for sure. Where you comin' from?"

Henry, of course, had no idea what a road warrior was. He waved his right arm in a generally northerly direction. "We camped up in Death Valley last night."

"Whoa." Mark was big-time impressed now. "You just drove down from Death Valley?" He looked somewhat skeptically at the old Pontiac. "How'd you come down?"

Henry shrugged. "It took some doing," he admitted. "We thought we were lost at one point and ended up over in Nevada, place called Searchlight. An old gentleman there told us that there weren't enough roads in this part of the country for a fellow to get lost on."

Mark laughed. "I heard that." He nodded again in the direction of the Pontiac. "You must have one hell of a radiator in that bad boy. What is that, an '85?"

"It's a 1982."

"So, like, where you heading?"

"Right here, Needles." Henry showed the kid the return address on an envelope he took out of his hip pocket. "I wonder if you could tell me how to find this address?"

Mark looked and laughed again. "Hey, you bet. That's old Miz Pierpont's trailer park, down by the river." He wiped the perspiration off his forehead with a green shop rag, leaving a thin diagonal trail of grease slashing across his left eyebrow. "There's some strange shit goes on out there." He held up a hand to let Henry know that, despite his words, he was not being judgmental. "Used to be just a bunch of losers lived out there, winos, folks dodging process servers, shit like that. Now she's got, like, these old dudes from the Third Reich, or whatever, and this old professor, a real Einstein but a nice guy, if you know what I mean. Hey, I was the first one he talked to when he got to Needles." Mark nodded his head affirmatively. "Yeah, he comes by here all the time to give me books to read, and like that. The way I understand it is, he was involved with the atom bomb or something, and couldn't take it anymore so he dropped out. And get this; he just shows up out of the blue and settles in out at Miz Pierpont's with this dudette who's now out to, like, here." He held his hands in front of his belly, simulating a pregnancy, and shook his head admiringly. "And another old dude who's from back east, New York I think, his wife blasted out of there a month or so ago. Hooked up the trailer, took the car, and, get this, left his ass flat on the lot." He paused and bent down to get a better look at Ramona in the Pontiac. Even though abused by the heat and clearly in need of a bath and a shampoo, she was a young woman well worth a second look. "Howdy, ma'am. Would you like to use the rest room?"

Ramona, silently amused at the impertinence of the question, shook her head.

Mark straightened up, tilted his head towards Henry's, and lowered his voice out of respect for Ramona's delicate gender. Clearly his next words were meant solely for masculine ears. "Check it out, word here in Needles is, his wife caught him, the old dude from New York, not the professor, laying pipe with Miz Pierpont, if you can believe that." The kid's tone of voice indicated without doubt that he, personally, couldn't. "And now he's, like, moved in with her in her trailer. I mean, don't get me wrong, I like Miz Pierpont, I've known her all my life and all, but, whoa, she must be close to, like . . ." the kid paused momentarily, trying to imagine an age so advanced as to suitably impress Henry, "like, sixty years old." He paused again, stunned by the overwhelming magnitude of the number. "Maybe older." Despite the heat, the kid shivered at the imagined sight of so much wrinkled skin. "Whoa, and I almost forgot, some nights, when the moon is, like, full, they all dance around naked doing some kind of voodoo shit or something. Course, I personally can't say for sure, but, man, who would have guessed a bunch of old dudes like that, frolicking around and all." He shook his head again, confounded by the very thought. "It bugs some people here in town, but me, hey, whatever gets you through the night, you know what I'm saying?" He suddenly thought of something else. "Whoa, they're not like friends of yours, are they? I mean, I don't want you thinking I'm dissing them out there, or anything like that."

"Not to worry," Henry reassured the kid. "We've never met." He pointed to the envelope, hoping to get the one-sided, seemingly nonsensical conversation back on track. "I was hoping you could give me directions on how to find the address."

"Hey, no problem." He gave Henry quick directions. "You can't miss it."

He watched for a minute as Henry and Ramona drove away, thinking he couldn't wait to tell his friends about the big white dude and the Mexican woman who looked like they just wandered in out of the desert like Moses or some-goddamn-thing. *And get this,* he could hardly wait to see their faces when he got to the punch line. *They wanted directions out to Miz Pierpont's place. Whoa!*

"Excuse me."

Ruth Pierpont looked up from the passed around, dog-eared issue of *Scientific American* she was reading and cast a hard look in the direction of the dust-covered Pontiac and the large young man who stood beside it. The article she had been reading had to do with an arcane interpretation of string theory and was, for all intents and purposes, gibberish to her. She was wearing a thin cotton skirt, a bright blue silk blouse, and a polka-dot kerchief tied around her hair. She nodded in response to Henry's question.

"What can I do for you?" She couldn't imagine that anyone would be looking for a trailer to rent, not in July with the heat above 120 degrees, but experience told her that couples who hauled their furniture around on the tops of their automobiles were frequently looking for just that.

"I wonder if you could direct me to a gentleman by the name of Gunter Schmidtbauer," Henry said. "I believe he lives here."

"Are you the baseball player he wrote the letter to?"

"I am."

"I figured you were. Nobody's stupid enough to just wander in here in the middle of July looking for a place to rent." Ruth bent down to scratch an ankle and get a better look at

Ramona, who remained seated in the car. "I would say," she said, straightening up and nodding at the top of the Pontiac, "that you two came prepared to stay awhile."

Before Henry could respond, Al emerged from Ruth's trailer carrying a cup of coffee and a German-American dictionary.

"I can't make heads or tails of this goddamn article," Ruth told him, handing the *Scientific American* she had been reading. "I think an idiot wrote it." She jerked a thumb in Henry's direction. "And Gunter's ballplayer's shown up."

Al broke into a broad smile and extended his right hand. "I don't know what to say. When Gunter told us he had written to invite you here none of us were sure you would even answer his letter, much less actually show up. Lord," he said, turning back to Ruth, "this is actually him, Ruth; this is Henry Spencer, the one Gunter wrote the letter to."

"In the flesh," Ruth snorted. "Listen, Al, you know I'm crazy about you, but it's too hot to be standing out here in the sun socializing like a bunch of damned fools. Why don't you and Henry mosey on over to Gunter's trailer or someplace and get acquainted while I and . . ." she bent down and gestured toward Ramona, ". . . what's your name, sweetheart?"

"Ramona."

"I like that name," Ruth said. "I like it a lot. I'll be honest with you, Ramona—you look like you and your young man here have done some hard riding in the last few days. You smell like it, too. How would you like a hot shower and a chance to get into some fresh clothes?"

Ramona smiled and nodded.

"I thought you would." Ruth straightened up and spoke once more to Al. "Take a hike, big boy. Me and Ramona here will see you two in a couple of hours."

"What's she like?"

Ruth and Becky were sitting on the patio of Ruth's trailer

sipping iced coffee. Ramona, having showered and changed clothes, was napping on Ruth's bed.

Ruth lit a Camel and looked guilty doing it. "Al's been on my case to quit smoking," she explained, taking a quick drag. She nodded towards the trailer. "In regards to your question about Miss Ramona, she's dead tired and I'm thinking about four or five months or so gone."

"Gone? You mean . . ."

"You got it. Pregnant." Ruth laughed. "Lord, when this trailer park used to be populated with mostly winos and low-life drifters a gal could enjoy a cigarette without feeling like she was being antisocial. Now, with nothing but rocket scientists and pregnant women on the horizon, I'm having to sneak around for a smoke like a schoolgirl."

"Ramona's a pretty name," Becky said.

Like everyone else she had laughed good-naturedly when Gunter told them he had written the young baseball player and invited him to come to Needles. Now that the young man had actually shown up, however, she found herself vaguely troubled by what it might mean. On the other hand, Ramona's presence, and her pregnancy, was oddly comforting.

"She's a pretty girl," Ruth responded. "Mexican, and with a bit of spunk to her if I'm not mistaken. She told me she met her young man when he was in Scottsdale for spring training. Said that when the team moved north to Oakland she went along, and if I haven't forgotten how to count she must have been pregnant when they left Arizona." Ruth laughed. "I'd say he's lucky her old man didn't follow them up there with a shotgun. Mexican's don't usually put up with shit like that, leastwise not the ones around here." Ruth pointed towards Becky's trailer with her cigarette. "What's your old man think of these two showing up out of the blue like this?"

"I think he's mostly amused. Al brought Henry around to meet us even before he took him over to Gunter's. Benny was getting ready to take his daily walkabout, so we didn't have time to say much more than 'hello.' " Becky took a sip of her iced coffee. "What do you think about them?"

"Honey, I been seeing pilgrims move through here for more years than Carter's got pills, and most all of them had one thing in common: they was trying to get away from someplace else, or maybe trying to be someone they hadn't been before. Gunter and his Germans, you and that old man of yours, Al," Ruth cast a rueful eye at the empty pad from which Al's trailer had recently departed, "and his missus, you're all cut from the same cloth." Ruth leaned over and put an affectionate hand on her young friend's arm. "Although Lord knows, no one before you folks had ever gotten Ruth Pierpont to thinking about taking off her clothes and dancing naked under the stars."

"I hadn't thought of our, Benny and my, coming here in quite that way, but it's true."

"Course it is. And I'll tell you something else: there's nothing wrong with it. A lot of the folks who've drifted in here over the years to catch their breath, work the kinks out, try on a new suit of clothes, so to speak, have left the better for it." She shrugged. "Not all, but I'm thinking a lot more have than haven't."

"Do you think Benny and I will be the better for it?"

Ruth shook her head. "You two already knew who you were when you got here. You just needed a change of scenery." She thought for a second. "Same for Gunter and his Germans."

"How about Al?" Becky teased.

Ruth snorted. "Now that he's shed of his missus, Al is definitely, what do they call it these days, reinventing himself. Big-time. And I don't mind telling you," Ruth blushed in spite of herself, "the new Al is putting a sparkle in these old eyes."

"Has watching all the pilgrims, as you call us, passing

through here over the years ever made you want to think about reinventing yourself?"

"Oh, hell yes, I've thought about it, and I'd have probably given it a try years ago if it weren't for the fact that I don't know who the hell I'd be if I wasn't who I am." She shrugged. "After I buried Morgan and got used to not having him around I guess I started thinking that being plain old Ruth wasn't such a bad thing."

"Do you mind if I ask what Morgan died of?"

Ruth shook her head. "Not at all. The sonofabitch died of bad feet." Ruth laughed, a bitter, humorless sound. "Bad feet and stupidity. As he got older his feet were always bothering him, so he never wore regular shoes or boots. All he could tolerate was buckskin moccasins, and like that. So, one day, working around here, he stepped on a rusty nail, wouldn't go see a doctor or anything, and ten days later developed tetanus. He went to see a doctor then, but . . ." Her voice trailed off and she stared out towards the desert as if looking for something, or someone. "I'll tell you what: there's a whole lot more comfortable ways to die than from tetanus." She sat alone with her memories for several seconds and then looked back at Becky. "Lord, I thought that man hung the moon." She chuckled. "Remind me to tell you how he swept me off my feet when I was just eighteen years old. Can you believe that? Anyway, me and Morgan, after we finally settled down, were always, I don't know how to say it, I guess *satisfied* is as good a word as any, we were always plain and simply satisfied living out here in the Mojave. Folks tend to leave you alone, let you be who you want to be."

"Who do you think," Becky nodded towards the trailer where Ramona lay napping, "Ramona and Henry want to be?"

"Good question." Ruth reached down and chucked Jericho under the chin. "Damned good question."

*   *   *

Benny squatted quietly on his haunches on the edge of a shallow dry wash and watched a dusty Mojave rattlesnake slowly swallow a ground squirrel. He was mildly troubled by the young ballplayer Al had introduced to him earlier that morning. When the young man spoke his voice, the sound, the timbre, Benny wasn't sure exactly what, had triggered an almost eidetic recall of a conversation he, Benny, had had with his protégé and friend Arthur Hodges a year or so before Arthur had died. They were relaxing in Benny's office when a graduate student had stopped by to tell them a joke. *How does a one-armed Polack count his change?* the student had asked. Benny, who had heard or, more accurately, seen the old burlesque routine joke several times in the past, smiled. *What's a Polack?* Arthur asked. Benny remembered quite clearly the graduate student's fading smile as he realized that Arthur's question was a serious one.

Turning his attention back to the tableau being acted out below him in the wash, Benny realized that if one was ever interested in closely observing a rattlesnake in the wild with anything approaching impunity, a good time would be while its mouth was otherwise occupied with a large rodent. Deciding to test this hypothesis, he scrambled down the side of the wash and cautiously approached the snake. Quickly sensing his presence, the snake tried to coil, but even this rudimentary defensive maneuver was hampered by the fact that the partially consumed squirrel acted as a quite effective counterweight to everything the snake tried to do. Frustrated, it finally decided to disgorge its recently acquired meal, but even this tactic was clearly going to require more time than it had were Benny of a mind to do more than merely get close to it.

In all of his life, all of his many years as a man of science, a teacher and molder of mind and intellect, nothing had prepared Benny for the raw malevolence in the rattlesnake's foreboding, lidless eyes. Transfixed, Benny squatted down in front of the snake and watched as it successfully, and more quickly than he would have thought possible when first it occurred to him to approach it, unburdened itself of the partially swallowed squirrel. He knew he was in danger, that he should be moving to safety, out of the enraged reptile's range, yet he felt, rather than fear, a growing sense of excitement, of recklessness.

What would it be like, he asked himself, shocked by the thought even as it roared into his consciousness, *to be struck by a poisonous snake?*

On a higher plane of reasoning Benny had no trouble instantly concluding that no sane man would voluntarily allow himself to be bitten by a rattlesnake. Notwithstanding, however, his intellectual ability to dismiss what he was clearly thinking of doing as utter foolhardiness, the realization that on a much deeper, more primitive level the pros and cons were not so starkly defined came as a revelation.

As Benny considered the implications of the act he was contemplating, the snake completed the regurgitation of the squirrel. Although his heart was pounding in his chest a wonderful lassitude came over him as he watched the snake coil itself not three feet from where he squatted. He knew, as he watched its head dart from side to side, that it was using heat sensors far more than vision to focus its strike zone, and that it was going to strike in a very few seconds.

"Here," he said quietly, holding his right hand at the snake's eye level. He began to weep as a rapture unlike anything he had ever imagined filled his heart. "Here," he whispered, remembering the words from a childhood catechism class as he moved his hand closer to the snake. "I am the body, the . . ."

Benny heard his own words as though from a great distance, and the snake's head, when it finally struck, seemed to move in a terrible slow motion. He felt the surprisingly heavy impact of the snake's head and a dull, insistent pain from the two fangs it thrust into his hand. The snake spastically shook its fangs free and withdrew immediately into another coil, its rattles setting up a constant, angry buzzing. Benny knew that the snake was preparing itself to strike again and yet he found himself strangely unable to move, as if the snake's spirit was somehow reaching into his nervous system and interfering with or blocking the synapses between brain and muscle. With startling clarity he knew precisely what the squirrel had experienced in its last few seconds of life.

A flash of light caught Benny's eye and he looked up. Above him, kneeling quietly on the bank overlooking the dry wash, as he himself had kneeled when first he spotted the snake, was the apparition of a man. The brilliant afternoon sun was directly behind the man, and an aura of shimmering golden light and heat danced about his head and shoulders. The liquid, golden light was the most beautiful thing Benny thought he had ever seen and he cried out in spontaneous joy, suddenly wanting very much to live. Before he could move, however, the snake drew back its head to strike again and Benny knew he was lost, knew that he would not survive another attack.

"No!" he yelled, as if the force of his words alone would register on the snake, turn it away. Then, in a motion too fast to immediately register on Benny's confused mind, the apparition jumped from the bank in a shower of pebbles and sand and thrust its own hand in the path of the striking snake.

SEVENTEEN

★ ⁺ ★

Benny had only the vaguest recollection of being picked up and carried back to the trailer park. From that point he was aware of activity around him, mainly Ruth's commanding voice, but it was all seemingly at a great distance, much like an observation made from the wrong end of a powerful pair of binoculars. He heard the wail of the fire department rescue vehicle's siren, and felt the acceleration and sway as he was transported to the county hospital, but could summon forth no personal sense of urgency. By the time he reached the hospital, Benny sensed a quieting of the voices and frenzied activity taking place around him. Drifting in and out of consciousness, he realized that one of the higher functions of his brain, the one controlling pain and fear, had been compromised, effectively switched off, by a constituent biochemical in the snake's venom. *What a pleasant way to die,* he thought, mildly curious as to who, or what, might greet him as his life ended. For a fleeting second he wished he could comfort Becky and the others, but he knew he could not and the impulse passed almost as quickly as it had arisen. The image of a young man materialized in front of him, and with a start Benny realized that it was Arthur Hodges, his departed friend and colleague. Benny smiled and tried to speak but could form no words, tried to raise his hand in greeting but could not move. Arthur waved and the image began to recede, dissolving into nothingness as Benny struggled to cry out.

"I'll be honest with you," the doctor said to the small gaggle of people standing in the emergency room. In addition to Becky, Ruth, Al, Gunter and Sophie Schmidtbauer, and Henry and Ramona, there was an EMT, two nurses, a physician's assistant, and an Alzheimer's patient who was wandering aimlessly through the facility and stopped to see what all the commotion was about. "I wouldn't have believed it possible that two men could contrive to get themselves bitten, one right after the other, on the same day, by the same snake." A young African-American woman from San Francisco, she was finishing up a residency program at UCLA that rotated her through a number of rural county emergency rooms such as the one in Needles. She had never before seen a snakebite case and, inasmuch as she planned to return to an inner-city pediatric practice in the Bay Area upon the completion of her residency, frankly doubted she would get another such opportunity. Much less two. She turned to Henry. "The good news is that given the absence of symptoms it's clear that Mr. Rhodes got all of the snake's venom and you got none. If I had to guess I'd say that either the rattlesnake used up his supply in striking him or, as the EMT here just now told me, this was one of the not infrequent times where a snake bites but does not inject venom." She really was quite pleased to see an actual snakebite case before going off this rotation. She nodded toward the EMT. "Didn't you say that no venom is injected in something like 25 percent of the cases on record?"

"Yes, ma'am," he answered. "We get one or two rattlesnake bites in here every year, and I'd say, on the whole, about a quarter of them don't involve venom."

Henry nodded agreement. "I told the EMT on the way here that I didn't think the snake had injected any venom."

"*Lieber Gott,* how would you know such a thing?" Gunter asked. He and Sophie stood behind Al and Ruth and Becky.

"I didn't feel anything other than the bite itself. I think I would have felt something else, a burning or something, if venom had been introduced."

The doctor looked skeptical. "I don't know about that. I think the shock, both physical and emotional, of the strike itself would tend to mask any discrete sensation of venom being injected."

"Did you give them both antivenin shots?" Al asked. "Is it hard to get?" Al, as was the young physician, was extremely interested in the whole notion of snake-bites-man. A lifelong resident of Brooklyn, he had never in his life seen an actual snake, whether deadly or benign, outside the confines of a zoo. He wondered what a shot of antivenin might cost, and, more to the point, what a death caused by rattlesnake venom might look like. Or feel like. "Would most people die without it?"

The doctor smiled at Al's questions. "Given the likely absence of venom, I doubt it was needed by Mr. Spencer, but yes, we administered antivenin to both of your friends. As well as a tetanus booster and broad-spectrum antibiotic. Although they're not particularly common, snakebites aren't exactly unheard of in the Southwest, so most emergency rooms keep a supply of antivenin on hand. As to whether or not someone who *was* injected with venom would die without it," she shrugged, "who knows. The literature seems to indicate that most healthy, young adults could expect to survive without treatment, but I don't think I'd personally want to test that hypothesis. Too many variables. How much venom injected, the site of the injection, underlying known or unknown health problems, all kinds of things. And even if you survived the venom, there are a host of other problems to contend with, many of them not the most pleasant things in the world."

"Like what?" Al could sense that Ruth was starting to

lose patience with his questions, but he found the subject was too compelling to leave without taking advantage of the presence of a medical expert.

"Well, just off the top of my head, there's a tendency for severe tissue degeneration to develop around the site of many snakebite wounds—the complex proteins in snake venom do exceedingly nasty things to living flesh. Also, lots of ground rodents in California carry plague, and frankly, I'm not sure that that wouldn't be a potential problem if you were bitten by a snake that had recently bitten an infected rodent." She smiled. "I tell kids that the easiest way to quit smoking cigarettes is not to start. The same might be said about surviving snakebites—take a few reasonable precautions and don't get bitten in the first place."

Ruth snorted in agreement. She had warned Benny any number of times about being careful on his walkabouts, and was not the least astonished that he had somehow contrived to get himself bitten by a rattlesnake. Once you got ten feet into the desert the damned things were practically underfoot wherever you stepped.

"Well," the doctor continued, checking Henry's blood pressure one last time, "I'd say you could leave the emergency room any time you want."

"I'm going to stay here tonight with Benny," Becky informed everyone. Benny had already been transported from the emergency room to a private room in the small hospital.

"You're welcome to, but it's really not necessary," the doctor said, hanging her stethoscope around her neck. "I'm only keeping him overnight as a precaution." She smiled. "I just hope I'm in as good a shape as he is when I'm his age." And she meant it. She was more than a little impressed with Benny's overall condition, the hardness of his muscles, the lack of body fat. She had no way of knowing without testing, but she was willing to bet that his cholesterol levels were well below average as well. She had no trouble understanding Becky's obvious pregnancy. *Girl,* she thought, glancing at Becky out of the corner of her eye, *you hit the jackpot with this man.* There was clearly something about an older man, particularly one as hard and fit as this one, that attracted a lot of younger women. Herself included. She was less pleased, given the compelling melanoma statistics when viewing a population of Caucasian desert dwellers, with the deep, nut-brown tan that covered 90 percent of Benny's body. She put a hand on Becky's arm. "I want Mr. Rhodes to start wearing sunscreen. Lots of it. Believe me when I tell you that you're never too old for skin cancer. And next time, have him do us all a favor and carry a big stick when he goes walking around out in the desert, okay?" She turned from Becky and, winking at Ramona, motioned with her thumb toward Henry. "And the same goes for Hulk Hogan, here."

A major-league hunk, she thought as she left the treatment area, *but I'd take the older one any day.*

"This is the *Tribune* city desk, Ron Millard speaking."

"Mr. Millard? This is Tammi Daves calling, from Needles."

"Yeah? What can I do for you, Ms. Daves?"

"Well, you probably don't remember me, but I'm the admitting clerk at the Needles Community Hospital emergency room. You were passing through here several months ago on your way back to Los Angeles and stopped by the hospital and gave me your card. You said that if something interesting came up, if somebody famous should come into the hospital, I should call you. You said it would be worth something to me."

"Yeah, right, Ms. Daves, I remember; we had a cup of coffee together." In fact he didn't remember this particular woman, but he always made it a point whenever possible to stop at out-of-the way, jerkwater hospitals and clinics, buy a cup of coffee, and pay a little attention to whichever plain

Jane admitting or records clerk happened to catch his eye. It was a neat little trick he picked up from an old tabloid stringer on his first newspaper job, back in Trenton, New Jersey. Nothing much ever came from it, but you never know. Only a year ago he paid twenty dollars to a medical records clerk for a tip about a prominent Los Angeles politician, married, of course, who was getting treated under a false name for a persistent case of gonorrhea at a little clinic outside Bakersfield. The clerk, who had been passed over for a raise right after the clinic's doctor bought a new Mercedes-Benz, even faxed him a photocopy of the patient treatment record. He used the information, which he agreed never to make public, to gain access to the politician he otherwise would never have enjoyed, and thereby moved up a couple of rungs in the newspaper's city room pecking order. All for twenty bucks. "What have you got for me, sweetheart?"

"Well, um, how much money . . ."

"Just for making the call you get twenty dollars," he said smoothly. "I can go up from there depending on what you have for me."

"Two men were admitted to the emergency room this afternoon for a rattlesnake bite."

"Jesus." Ron winced, hoping this wasn't just about a couple of John Does getting bitten by a snake. Still, on second thought, perhaps he could do something with it, juice it up a little here and there, come up with a story that might go out over the wire, particularly if one or both of the bozos died. *Creative journalism,* he chuckled to himself, *where would America be without it?* "Was it anybody we might know?" he asked hopefully.

"Well, one of them . . ."

Starlight shimmered faintly off the silvery sides of the two Airstream trailers, sparkling points of light that seemed almost to wash down the polished aluminum surface like rainwater. So striking was the image that Henry placed his palm against the trailer, wondering for a brief instant if he could feel the wetness his eyes suggested was there. Feeling nothing, he smiled and entered the trailer as quietly as he could. Gunter had offered Henry and Ramona the use of the empty Airstream left behind by his departed colleagues.

"Who knows," he had said only half-jokingly when he gave them the key, "you will probably decide to stay here and will want to purchase it."

Not wishing to turn on a light, and being unfamiliar with the layout, Henry groped his way back to the bedroom, guided the last few steps to the bed by the sound of Ramona's breathing. He slid off his shirt and pants and let them drop to the floor.

"How are you feeling?"

"I'm sorry I woke you," he whispered as he slid into the left side of the bed and gathered Ramona into his left side. She turned onto her right side and threw her left leg on his thighs, her left arm across his chest. He held his bandaged right hand up and tried unsuccessfully to see it in the darkness. "My hand is swollen and hurts a little but not too much." He leaned his head down and kissed her, playing the tip of his tongue along the bottom of her upper lip. Reclining his head back against his pillow, he asked her, "What do you think about this?"

"About what?"

"About staying in this trailer."

Ramona chuckled, a warm and loving sound that Henry knew he would never tire of hearing. It was the sound he associated with their first meeting, in her father's restaurant, when she laughed at him for not knowing what a flan was.

You are going to drive me out to Carefree where we will listen to the coyotes laugh and you will explain to me how it is that people from North Carolina are so provincial that they think civilization ends at places like Nogales or San Luis Río Colorado.

Her gentle laugh was a sound that lay upon his heart like a feather comforter.

"And now," Henry whispered, "we're on the *Río Colorado.*"

"What did you say?"

"Nothing. You were going to tell me what you think about being here."

"Ever since I was a little girl I wanted to live in one of these shiny trailers."

Henry knew a smile was playing across her face even if he couldn't see it.

"My father, of course, was shocked and scandalized by such a notion, but I, I always dreamed of life in a ship of the desert."

"A what?"

"In pioneer days people would occasionally put sails on the big Conestoga wagons. They called them ships of the desert, and I always dreamed of a life in one."

"Tomorrow we'll buy it from Gunter."

"El Jefe!"

Earl Hutchins was drinking beer in the parking lot outside the Needles Mini Mart with three friends when Hector Gonzalez, the San Bernardino County deputy sheriff, pulled in for a cup of coffee. It was ten o'clock and Hector was working the three-to-midnight shift.

"*Jefe* my ass," Hector shot back. "If I was the *jefe* I'd be at home in bed right now. Which reminds me—what are you guys doing out here this time of night?"

"A better question would be, what the hell's going on out there at Ruth Pierpont's place?" Earl asked, ignoring Hector's question. He had heard about the snakebites from his main squeeze, a part-time secretary at the hospital. He winked at his buddies. "I hear they've gone from dancing naked outdoors to snake handling."

Hector shook his head as he sipped his coffee. The incident had been reported to the sheriff's office by the county EMT. "There's a whole lot of things illegal in California, but stupidity ain't one of 'em." He pointed his coffee cup at Earl. "If it was, you guys would be in a lot of trouble. And furthermore, you don't know shit about anybody dancing naked out there or anywhere else." He shifted his heavy gun belt under his considerable gut with a sigh. He had foolishly eaten more than a handful of fiery hot jalapeños with dinner the night before and they had hit his lower intestines this morning like a stick of dynamite. He had gone through the better part of a bottle of Pepto-Bismol earlier in his shift before throwing in the towel and switching to coffee.

"You been hitting the 'pink lady' again?" one of Earl's friends asked, noting a touch of color at one corner of Hector's mouth. His sensitive stomach was notorious throughout eastern San Bernardino County.

The deputy nodded and belched, a deep *basso profundo* sound. "Whoever heard of a Mexican can't eat jalapeños?" he asked, more to himself than to Earl and his friends.

Earl caught a whiff of Hector's stomach gases and quickly backed away, waving his hand in front of his face. "Jesus Christ, Hector, that breath of yours would take the paint off aluminum siding. I'm thinking you better see a doctor or something. PD-goddamn-Q." He thought of something else. "Listen. I also heard that one of the two guys that was bit was that ballplayer from Oakland everybody was so hot about. The one that disappeared off his team a week or two ago."

Hector shook his head and feigned annoyance. "Don't you guys have anything better to do than stand around out here worrying about other people's business?" He took another sip of his coffee and mopped his perspiring brow with an already wet handkerchief. "It must be at least 110 degrees."

Earl was unimpressed. "Shoot. You're just upset because that New York guy whose wife left him is beating your time with the widow Pierpont."

Hector started to say something but stopped and held up his hand. "Wait a minute." He put his head inside his patrol car to listen to the radio. "Shit. The Highway Patrol wants help working a big wreck out on the Interstate." He pointed to Earl. "One of the things that *is* illegal in California is drinking beer out in a parking lot like this. Why don't you guys take it home and get inside where it's cool?" *Still,* he thought as he turned on his flashing lights and pulled into traffic, *maybe I should take a ride out there tomorrow or the next day and see how Ruth's doing.* He had been doubling up on shifts, covering vacation absences all over the county, and hadn't been out to the trailer park in a couple of weeks. The sheriff's office had heard, too, again from the EMT, that one of the snakebite victims was the Oakland baseball player Henry Spencer. *It never hurts to know what's going on in your own backyard.*

EIGHTEEN

⋆ ⋆ ⋆

Oakland, California

"I take it you haven't seen this yet."

Warren Mercer dropped the morning edition of the *Los Angeles Tribune* on Preacher Brown's desk in the clubhouse.

"Seen what?" Preacher asked, eyeing the folded newspaper with distrust. He knew instinctively that he wasn't going to like whatever it was Warren had come across.

The headline said it all: BASEBALL ROOKIE PHENOM JOINS DESERT SNAKE HANDLING CULT.

"Looks like they found your missing boy," Warren said needlessly.

Preacher snatched up the front-page section and began laboriously reading the article Warren had helpfully highlighted. "Where the hell is Needles?" He held up his hand while continuing to read, indicating that he really didn't care.

Warren anxiously watched Preacher work his way through the article, suddenly wondering what on earth had made him think it would be a good idea to bring this kind of news to Preacher's attention. He thought about slipping quietly from the office while Preacher was occupied with the article but thought better of it. He started slightly when Preached finished the article and abruptly looked up.

"Fuck it," he said quietly, with a tone of finality.

That's it? Warren wondered. *He loses the greatest chance he'll ever have to win a pennant and probably the World Series and all he can say is* fuck it*?*

"That boy was as queer as . . ." Preacher paused, searching for the right words, and, not finding them, shrugged. "Fuck it," he repeated.

"What do you think Edgerton will say?" Warren knew that the organization's managing general partner had been telling everyone around the league and in the media that Henry's absence was only temporary.

"What the hell can he say? This is going to make him look like an idiot, which is what I been telling you and everybody else who'd listen from day one. The long and short of it is that we got rid of Bobo Martinez, an All Star catcher, just to make room for some kid out of no-fucking-where who'd never played a game of Organized Ball in his life, a flake who sat around the clubhouse talking about things nobody ever heard of before." Preacher paused as the phone on his desk started ringing. He jerked a thumb toward it for Warren's benefit. "What do you want to bet that's Edgerton right now? Somebody's probably told him about the article and he's finally realized that he fucked up big-time." Preacher laughed, a bitter, hollow sound devoid of humor. "I'm history." After the eighth ring the phone stopped ringing. "And you can bet the official word will be that *I'm* the one who talked *him* into trading Martinez and keeping Spencer. When this all shakes out I'll be lucky to get a job as a Little League first base coach in Davenport, Iowa."

"Hard to argue with that," Warren said, trying to make a joke of it.

Preacher Brown didn't bother to smile.

Needles, California

Ruth and Al were enjoying a midmorning cup of aromatic Guatemalan coffee on the patio of her trailer when Hector Gonzalez drove up.

"Take a load off," Ruth invited, nodding toward one of Benny's now ubiquitous Adirondack chairs. "Have you two formally met?"

Hector sat down with a sigh and gratefully accepted a cup of coffee from Al. "Thanks. Not exactly," he added in response to Ruth's question, extending his right hand to Al. "We've seen each other around town, but we've never been introduced. I'm Hector Gonzalez."

"Pleased to finally meet you," Al responded, returning the hearty handshake. "Ruth's told me a lot about you."

"I told him you eat like a horse and are getting as fat as a pig," Ruth interjected deadpan.

Hector sighed and shook his head for Al's benefit. "Everyone in town thinks we," nodding towards Ruth, "are lovers. They don't believe me when I tell them that Tranquilina, my wife, sends me out here for secondhand domestic abuse when she's tired of giving it to me herself."

"I know whereof you speak," Al said with a smile.

"Spare me the male angst, for Christ's sake," Ruth said. "I'm fresh out of crocodile tears." She took a Camel from a pack lying on the large wooden cable drum that served handily as a patio table.

"I like the new look," Hector said, indicating Ruth's cotton blouse and long skirt. He smiled at Al. "I tried for years to get her out of those damned bib overalls." He suddenly realized that what he said could be taken two ways and hurried to add, "You know what I mean. Now if you can only get her to quit smoking."

"He's got me down from a pack to five smokes a day,"

Ruth informed him smugly. "In a month or two I'll quit altogether." She sat back with her coffee and cigarette and put her sandaled feet up on the cable drum. "You drive out here just to socialize or is there something on your mind?"

"Both." Hector, too, sat back and enjoyed the small breeze coming through the patio.

In the middle distance they could see Sophie Schmidtbauer hard at work in her rapidly expanding garden.

"It's a good thing the French and Spanish beat the Germans to Mexico," Hector said, meaning it.

"If they hadn't there'd sure as hell've been no *mañana* in the Mexican version of the Spanish language," Ruth observed caustically.

"José," his nephew who now worked for Sophie two afternoons a week, "told me that her husband has built an irrigation system."

Ruth snorted, knowing that it was illegal to draw water from the Colorado River for irrigation without a permit. "You out here to roust him for *that*?"

"I've got more to worry about than the goddamned Colorado River. I told José to tell him to be sure and bury his pipes so the *federales* can't see anything from the air." Hector shook his head with disgust and shrugged for Al's benefit. "Your tax dollars at work protecting the interests of big agribusiness." He paused for a heartbeat. "You saw the story in the Los Angeles paper?"

"The little weasel that wrote it came sneaking around here a day or two ago," Ruth said, grinding out her cigarette. "Pissed me off big-time. The sonofabitch offered me twenty dollars to tell him about the snake handling cult we're supposed to be running out here."

Hector smiled. "I know. He came back into town and wanted me to come out here and arrest you for assaulting him."

"They must be getting pretty soft over there in Los Angeles if they call a little feminine slap across the face an assault," Ruth sniffed. "You going to arrest me?"

"I laughed at him and told him you were a vengeful woman and that if he really annoyed you he might find one of those rattlesnakes you people are supposed to be worshipping in his room over at the Holiday Inn." Hector finished his coffee. "On the other hand, you bloused his lip pretty good, so I doubt it was just a 'little feminine slap.' Still, I wouldn't worry about him filing charges if I were you."

"I'm not," Ruth assured him.

"The ballplayer and his wife . . ." Hector hesitated for a second, not wanting Ruth or Al to misinterpret his question, "are they planning on staying here awhile?"

"Oh, they're not . . ." Al started to say, meaning to tell Hector that Henry and Ramona weren't married, when Ruth briskly interrupted him.

"They didn't say and I haven't asked," Ruth answered. "Whose business is it but theirs?"

"Now, Ruth, goddammit, don't get on your high horse with me. I'm just trying to help out."

"How do you mean?"

"For a while, at least, my guess is that they're going to attract a fair amount of interest. And, since they're living here, so will you and everyone else out here, especially with that idiot reporter from Los Angeles writing tabloid stories."

"You're not saying they should leave, are you?"

Hector shook his head. "You know me better than that, Ruth. I'm just saying that until this whole thing blows over I'd use a little discretion, socially speaking, if you know what I'm saying."

Ruth jutted her jaw forward truculently. "No, I don't."

Hector sighed in defeat and stood up. "I've got to be going. Thanks for the coffee. Al, it's good to meet you. And listen." He pointed a friendly finger at Ruth. "I'm serious now—don't be beating up any more reporters just because they happen to annoy you."

*   *   *

"What did Hector want?"

Becky and Ramona walked up, each sipping a glass of ice water. Becky wore a loosely fitting white cotton caftan that billowed about her legs as she walked, giving an impression of grace and lightness that belied her heavy, late-term pregnancy. Ramona, three months behind her in gestation, wore cutoff shorts and a T-shirt.

"Nothing in particular," Ruth answered airily, giving Al a cautionary look. "Just dropped by to say hi and meet Al. What are you ladies up to?"

"We thought we might go into town and pick up some groceries, a few items for Ramona's kitchen," Becky said. "Did you know that Ramona's father runs a restaurant in Scottsdale?"

"Can't say as we did," Ruth answered. She looked up at Ramona. "What's he cook?"

"Mexican."

"That settles it," Ruth said, getting up from her chair. "I'll go into Needles with you and we'll get everything we need for a big Mexican dinner tonight. You'll supervise," she said to Ramona. "Al's been trying hard to develop his touch in the kitchen and I think a little ethnic variety's just the thing he needs. Besides," she winked at Becky, "some jalapeños might liven things up around here."

Benny put a finger to his lips and, with his other hand, pointed out the small family of wild pigs that was dozing in the sparse shade of a large creosote bush some forty yards from where he and Henry stood watching. They had hiked three hours north and west of the trailer park, into the badlands of the southern Mojave and the foothills of the Sacramento Mountains.

"Not much moves aboveground in the heat of the day around here," Benny whispered. "Only the things that are too big to get underground," he added with a smile, "and they generally try to stay as quiet as possible until it gets dark. Creosote, by the way," Benny couldn't resist passing on a little arcane knowledge, "is an exceptionally long-lived plant. Many botanists now think that some examples are older even than the bristlecone pines. The resin exuded by the leaves not only protects it from heat, ultraviolet light, and moisture loss, but also tastes terrible, so almost nothing eats it."

They continued their walk, giving the pigs a wide berth. Benny frequently stopped to point out subtle nuances and shades of the sounds and colors that most would have missed. Though the heat was fierce and unyielding, Benny seemed not to mind. He led Henry to a large outcropping of crumbling rock that threw a broad band of shade. They had gained perhaps fifteen hundred feet in altitude and could see, to the south and the east, the meandering Colorado River.

"We'll stop here for lunch." Benny pointed to the rocks. "All of this was formed by sedimentation at the bottom of the sea that covered this entire part of the country half a billion years ago. Under intense pressure and heat the sediment formed marble, schist, and quartzite. These," he waved his arm to encompass the entire hillside, "were ultimately pushed up by younger, granitic rock."

"It's all quite beautiful, isn't it?" Henry said as Benny kneeled and unpacked lunch from their rucksacks.

Benny looked up. "Yes, it is. Interestingly enough, some people would argue that the Mojave is not in fact a stand-alone geologic or geographic phenomenon at all, but rather is more properly viewed as a transitional zone between the Sonoran Desert to the south and east and the Great Basin Desert north of us. An interface, if you will, between north and south. I'm not sure what significance such an argument has in the overall scheme of things, but," he smiled, "you never know, do you? All we can count on here and now is the beauty of the view."

Henry nodded and pointed towards the river below them. "Were you aware that the ratio of a river's length as measured by the actual distance it covers versus the straight-line distance between its source and its terminus is always roughly 3.14, the value of *pi*?"

"So?" Benny took a long drink of water and passed the plastic bottle to Henry. "Assuming the validity of that statement, which I wouldn't necessarily do out of hand, what is the significance of it? What exact point are you trying to make?"

Henry had been looking forward to engaging Benny in just such a conversation, hoping to use it as means of getting to know him. "That numbers, mathematics, control every aspect of the physical world."

Benny shook his head. "You haven't really answered my question. Even if the ratio of a river's physical length to the straight-line distance between origin and terminus is always roughly *pi,* so what? Who cares? What does it matter?" Benny paused and took a bite out of a carrot that had been harvested from Sophie's garden. "And by the way, who got to decide how 'roughly' is close enough to *pi* to justify ascribing some sort of arcane significance to it?" He munched happily for several seconds. "God, these carrots are sweet."

"But . . ."

"Don't worry," Benny interrupted. "There's no answer. Sit down and have something to eat." He handed Henry a carrot. "You've fallen prey to a sickness that I think of as the 'rapture of science.' Our whole society has, even those poor benighted souls who wouldn't know *pi* if it walked up and bit them on the ass. Did you ever stop to think that perhaps, just perhaps, this wonderful ratio you describe involving rivers is no more that out-and-out coincidence? That it has absolutely no meaning whatsoever?"

Henry smiled. "Didn't Einstein say that 'God does not play dice with the universe'?"

Benny snorted with derision. "Just because Albert Einstein chose to believe such a thing doesn't make it so. In fact, I happen to think that God does play dice with the universe. Why wouldn't She? I think She has a wonderful sense of humor—She gave us Einstein, didn't She?" Benny wagged his carrot at Henry. "Listen to me. Albert Einstein was a scientist, not a philosopher, more's the pity. The minute he gets away from physics, or I guess I should say 'got away,' the minute any scientist gets away from pure science, warning bells should go off. In fact, any time a scientist says *anything* warning bells should go off."

"Why?"

"Because their lofty pronouncements, whether scientific or social, arise from a position of assumed high intelligence and education, and therefore take on a veneer of authority which in many, if not most, cases is completely unwarranted. If you look at any period of history you will find that men and women of science are far more often than not completely wrong in both their scientific and their social thinking." Benny finished his carrot and in short order ate a handful of radishes and an apple while drinking the better part of a quart of bottled spring water. "Never *ever* let anyone do your thinking for you," he advised. "Question everything, particularly the authority of anyone who undertakes to tell you what is right or wrong." Benny settled into a reclining position against the rock. "Why did you follow me out into the desert last week?"

"I don't know." Henry slowly shook his head. "I wanted to talk to you, but I suppose I could have just as easily waited until you got back from your walk. I asked Gunter and he told me he didn't think you would mind if I caught up with you."

"How in the world did you find me?"

"I almost didn't. In fact, I was ready to turn back when I heard the snake's rattles down in that gully."

"Did you . . ." Benny paused for several seconds before continuing, "see the first strike?"

Henry nodded but did not speak.

"So you knew that I allowed the snake to bite me."

Again a nod, but no words.

"Why did you jump into the dry wash and prevent the snake from striking me a second time?"

"It was clear that you did not wish to be bitten again. There was no time to think, so I acted. Preacher Brown, my manager in Oakland, would have been proud. He was always telling me that I think too much, that I should rely more on instinct." Henry smiled. "He was wrong most of the time about most things, but on that occasion he would have been right."

"Do the Red Sox have a chance at the pennant this year?"

If the sudden change in subject surprised Henry he did not show it. "No."

"A division championship?"

"No."

"How about Oakland?"

"Not without me," Henry answered, no hint of boastfulness in his voice.

"Are you going back? To Oakland?"

Henry shook his head. "I don't think so. I think we, Ramona and I, will stay here for some time."

Benny yawned. "I've found that a little nap after lunch is one of the more intelligent things a man can do for himself, although out here, as you have already seen, one needs to be prepared for close encounters with the local fauna. Last week I woke up on this very spot to find a rather largish hairy spider, probably a tarantula although it could have been a large wolf spider, carefully exploring my abdomen. It seemed to sense that I had awakened, probably because of a change in the rhythm of my heartbeat, because it deliberately walked up my chest and stopped on my breastbone, watching me for what seemed like quite a long time before rather delicately descending to the ground and going on about its business. I doubt seriously it had ever seen, or even imagined, a human being before." He closed his eyes but opened them after only a second. "Oh, by the way, if you decide against taking a nap, I would strongly advise you not to wander off very far while I'm snoozing—it's a good deal easier to get lost out here than you might think, and the environment is, to say the least, unforgiving." He closed his eyes and was soon snoring.

"Whoa!"

Mark Little could scarcely believe his eyes when the fire engine red Lamborghini Testarossa pulled into the radiator shop in downtown Needles. The gull-wing door on the driver's side opened with a quiet hiss and a short, portly, middle-aged man awkwardly disentangled himself from the seat and got out. There was a very young, very attractive woman in the passenger seat, wearing a miniskirt so short that Mark could see the shiny white crotch of her panties. The man quickly looked down to make sure he wasn't standing in grease or oil and then pointed directly, if rudely, at Mark.

"Are you Mark Little?" he barked as he reached into the Lamborghini and took a leather cigar case off the dash. He was wearing cream-colored pleated silk trousers with mauve silk suspenders and a hand-tailored, undyed linen shirt.

"Yes, sir," Mark answered. He normally wouldn't have added the *sir,* but something about the little dude seemed to indicate it was warranted.

"Kid, I'm not going to stand around here and pull your dick, you understand what I'm saying?"

"Yes, sir." Mark unconsciously straightened up, assuming a rough approximation of the military position of attention. He badly wanted to look again at the crotch of the young woman in the car but felt compelled to keep his eyes on the man.

"It's too goddamned hot to be fucking around; I can tell

you that right now." Dark perspiration marks were already starting to show around his suspenders. He extracted a thick, blunt Cuban cigar from the leather case and began the elaborate ritual of preparing it for smoking. "I knew all I needed to know about you before I ever left Beverly Hills."

"You did?"

"What do you think a car like this costs?"

Mark was having a hard time keeping up with the rapid-fire nature of the conversation. He shook his head in response to the question. "A lot?"

The man grunted as he lit the cigar. "Two hundred and fifty thousand dollars. That's one quarter of a million dollars, big boy, and I can assure you that I don't make that kind of money coming out to the boondocks without doing my homework." He paused and looked closely at Mark. "Do you understand what I'm telling you?"

"Yes, sir." In fact, he had no idea what the man was talking about, but thought it prudent not to admit it.

"Good. The report that was prepared for me, at no small expense I might add, indicated that you had some brains." Actually the report hadn't indicated any such thing, but it didn't cost anything to flatter the kid a little. "Here's the pitch. I want to get a message out to Henry Spencer, out at the Pierpont Trailer Park."

"A message? I can tell you how to get out there."

The man shook his head. "Listen to me. I didn't say I wanted to see him; I said I wanted to get a message to him." He repeated the words very slowly, as if talking to a simpleton. "A message." The man paused again to examine the newly formed ash on his cigar. "And of all the people in Needles I'm told, believe it or not, that you're the best man to get the job done." He reached back into the Lamborghini and took a business card and a fat Mont Blanc fountain pen out of a small leather purse the woman handed him.

"Turn around," he ordered. When Mark complied he

placed the card against his back and wrote two words on one side of the card. "Here." When Mark turned back around, the man handed him the card. "Give this to him, personally. Today. Do you understand?"

"Yes, sir."

"Give it to him personally," the man reiterated. "I don't want to find out later that you gave it to someone to give to someone else out there to give to him. This card goes directly from *your* hand to *his* hand, or it goes nowhere. In which case you call me. If I don't hear from you by tomorrow morning I'm going to assume that you delivered the card. Got that?"

"Yes, sir." Mark didn't think he had said "sir" so many times in one conversation in his entire life.

"Good." The man reached into his silk trousers and took out a roll of bills held together with a gold money clip. He peeled one off and gave it to Mark. It was a 100-dollar bill. "Take your girl out to dinner." He paused for a second and looked at Mark almost as if seeing him for the first time. "You do have a girl, don't you?"

"Oh, yes, sir."

"Good. Take her dinner, but *after* you deliver the card to Henry Spencer. Personally."

Mark started to say *yes, sir* again, but the man was already getting back into the Lamborghini. Mark quickly ducked his head to check out the young woman and was rewarded with another glimpse of her panties before the gull-wing hissed closed. As soon as the Lamborghini was gone Mark examined the card the man left. It was heavy, with cotton fibers visible in the finely textured paper. A name, Irving LeClair, was engraved in black ink on one side, together with an 800 number. There was no address and no title to indicate who or what Mr. LeClair was. On the reverse Irving had written two words in a broad, cursive stroke: *Call me.*

*   *   *

"Now let me get this straight." Benny looked at Ramona with mock severity and disbelief. "Are you telling me that Al, here, cooked this entire meal?"

A brilliant red corona pulsing electromagnetically over the low peaks of the Sacramento Mountains barely illuminated the four couples and one cat sprawled in satiety about the patio of Ruth's trailer. The two Airstreams in the near distance reflected the colors of the setting sun like twin billets of newly cast aluminum, going from white to red to black as if heat were radiating from some place deep inside them.

"Yes," Ramona affirmed. "I helped a little here and there, but Al has a definite flair for Mexican cuisine. Oh," she suddenly remembered, "and Sophie made the *salsa de chiltepin,* the guacamole, and the *pico de gallo* with fresh vegetables and peppers from her garden."

"And you're sure Al did everything else?" Benny still sounded skeptical. "Keeping in mind that, although we've come to love and cherish Al, he has not yet traveled extensively and has had few, if any, truly multicultural experiences that would prepare him for such a cuisine."

"Al did everything else," Ramona assured him. "I may have advised and helped a little in the prep work, but he did the *carnitas* enchiladas, the Doña Ana *gorditas,* and the chimichangas *con carne seca."*

"This was the first real cooking I've ever done," Al admitted, a hint of amazement in his voice. "I had no idea it could be so, so *exciting.*"

"I've always believed there was a strong correlation between food and sex," Becky interjected. "Show me a man or a woman that loves to cook and my guess is that he or she will be a good bet to tickle more than your palate."

As the laughter swirled around him Al was grateful that it had gotten too dark for anyone to see him blush.

"Tomorrow I'm going into Needles to buy a cast-iron kettle and skillet and a good set of knives."

"Good luck," Ruth said, stifling a belch. "In case you hadn't noticed, Needles ain't exactly the capital of gourmet cookery. If you want anything beyond what the dime store sells you're either going to have to drive up to Vegas again or else get it out of a mail-order catalog." She winked at Benny. "When I saw how naturally he took to cooking I told him to throw that goddamned computer away and buy some cookbooks."

"I'll drink to that," Benny said. "It is a sign of a dying civilization when scientists are valued far above good cooks."

"You are becoming a Luddite," Gunter observed wryly.

"Perhaps I am," Benny admitted happily. "But can you think of anyone better qualified than I to reject science and technology in favor of the simple life?"

"I'm with Benny," Ruth announced, as she carefully lit the second of her self-imposed daily ration of two Camels. "I'm sixty years old and I've always made it a point never to own anything I couldn't fix myself. It's one reason I stopped buying automobiles in 1967—they got too complicated." She nodded in the direction of her '67 Ford pickup truck.

"You are an exception," Benny assured her. "One we should all emulate. Most people have long since been seduced by technology and science, and have happily bought into the false premise that personal computers, digital cell phones, E-mail, and god-knows what else, will make their lives better."

"Everyone longs for a back-to-nature existence until they get a stomachache," Gunter argued dryly. "Then they want immediate access to an emergency room with the best doctors money can buy, all of which is provided by the advancement of science."

Benny shook his head. "In which case they, whoever they are, are in for an unpleasant surprise. We spend an almost unimaginable amount of money on health care in America and the rest of the industrialized world and we're sicker than ever. All we've been able to accomplish is a slight shift of mortality from acute disease to chronic disease, and we may actually be seeing the beginnings of a movement back in favor of acute disease with the rapidly growing development of antibiotic-resistant microorganisms. No," he shook his head again, "I think it's abundantly clear that, taken as a whole, science and technology, particularly in the latter half of this century, has utterly failed of its promise to mankind."

Two coyotes, no doubt smelling the remains of their sybaritic feast, began to chuckle and sing on the periphery of the trailer park. Despite a pale, lingering glow over the Sacramentos, several planets were now visible in the sky and the Dipper ostentatiously pointed the way to the North Star.

Two headlight beams and the characteristic sound of tires crunching on gravel announced the arrival of an automobile. It parked behind Ruth's trailer and one car door could be heard opening and closing. The figure of a man could be seen walking around the trailer to the group gathered on the patio, but no one could make out who it was.

"Hey, Miz Pierpont, Doc, it's me, Mark Little from down at the radiator shop in town."

"Mark," Benny responded with some surprise, "what brings you out here—don't tell me a question regarding something you've been reading."

"Nah," Mark assured him, "nothing like that. Hey, I heard about that snake thing last week. Whoa." He shook his head, impressed, as many others in town had been, that Benny and Henry had managed to get themselves bitten by the same snake. "Heavy shit," he added respectfully. He would have liked to have said something complimentary to Ruth Pierpont about her slugging the reporter from Los Angeles but wasn't sure how it would be taken. Most everyone in town already knew she was not a woman to be trifled with, and her run-in with the reporter had only confirmed it. He peered around the group and identified Henry not so much by being able to see his face as by the sheer bulk of him. "Hey, big dude," he said, giving a thumbs-up sign that was mostly lost in the darkness.

"I didn't know you two knew each other," Benny said.

"Oh, sure," Mark said nonchalantly. "We met when he first come to town."

" 'Came,' " Becky corrected automatically. She put a hand to her mouth when she realized that she might have embarrassed the young man by correcting him in front of the others. "When he first 'came' to town," she added quietly.

"Yeah, that's what I meant," Mark said, unruffled by his grammatical shortcomings. "Anyway, it's the big guy I come, I mean, came, out to see tonight."

"Me?" Henry asked.

"Yeah. A seriously strange little dude came into the shop this afternoon and wanted me to give you this card." Mark handed Irving LeClair's business card to Henry. "You should have seen the bitchin' car he was driving—a Lamborghini Testarossa. And the babe he had with him. Whoa!" He shook his head, knowing it would be some time before he forgot those white panties. "Anyway, he wanted me to bring you that card." He debated with himself for a second on whether or not to reveal that the man had also given him a hundred dollars, and quickly decided against full disclosure.

Henry took the card and placed it in his pants pocket without so much as glancing at it. "Thank you," he said.

"Hey, no *problemo*." Mark was a little disappointed that Henry hadn't examined the card or said more. "I'm outta here."

For several minutes after Mark's departure the group sat silently, all wondering idly who the seriously strange little dude might have been. *"Probably a reporter or some sort,"* Benny told Becky later, as they got into bed.

Sophie had been yawning for at least half an hour before young Mark arrived and, as soon as he left, felt she should cut to the chase so that she and Gunter could go to bed. "What are you going to cook tomorrow night?" she asked Al.

"If it was somebody from television or a newspaper wouldn't the card have said so?" Ramona asked.

She and Henry lay naked on top of their bed, a ceiling-hung mosquito net billowing gently in the slight breeze coming through the window above them. She lazily ran a hand across his chest, brushing her fingertips over the kid-soft skin of his nipples.

Henry nodded but did not speak.

"Are you going to call him?"

"I don't know." The hint of a smile tugged at the corners of his mouth. "Whoever he is, he certainly impressed Mark Little." Henry turned on his side to face Ramona. "I'm glad we came here."

She smiled in the darkness, his sweet breath warm on her lips and face. "What did you and Benny talk about on your hike today?"

"He told me about a large spider, a tarantula, that crawled up on him while he was napping last week."

"You're teasing me."

"No," Henry said seriously, "I'm not. At first I wondered if it were some sort of parable." He smiled, suddenly remembering the story about Werner Heisenberg's Uncertainty Principle he had related to Bill Watson in spring training. "But then I realized he was only telling me about a spider, nothing more."

"Did it bite him?" Ramona wondered if Benny was somehow unfortunately prone to puncture wounds.

"I don't think so."

Through the open window they could hear the sweet and tender sounds of lovemaking coming from Gunter and Sophie's trailer. Ramona sighed, pleased at the thought of making love with Henry when they were as old as the Schmidtbauers. Before she came to Needles the only older people she had known were her own parents and grandparents, and it was not possible to think of them as sexual beings. "Perhaps Gunter is right," she murmured.

"About what?"

"About this being a special place." She pointed out the window, vaguely in the direction of the Schmidtbauers' moon-washed Airstream. "That's what he told you, isn't it?"

Henry nodded. "Yes, but I couldn't tell if he meant special in and of itself or special because of the people gathered here. To be honest, I don't understand much of what he has said to me."

Ramona suppressed a smile, remembering the ongoing and genuine confusion Henry had caused his teammates in Oakland. "I think it's the people," she assured him. "Benny and Becky, Al and Ruth, Sophie and Gunter. They seem genuinely pleased that we've decided to stay, at least for the time being."

"I'm not so sure Benny is all that pleased. He clearly does not agree with Gunter, at least on philosophical matters, and I'm afraid that he sees me somehow as . . ." Henry paused, not sure how to articulate what he felt. "I don't know, I'm just afraid he isn't happy that we've come here."

Ramona shook her head. "Trust me on this. He may not agree with whatever Gunter thinks, but it's clear, at least to me, that he's already quite fond of you." She snuggled close to Henry and yawned. "And not just because of the rattlesnake."

NINETEEN

★ ✦ ★

Beverly Hills, California

"Irving, Henry Spencer is here to see you."

"Thank you, Fredrica." Irving LeClair rose from behind a gleaming redwood burl desk. He wore mocha-colored trousers woven of linen and silk, brown silk suspenders, and a crisply ironed robin's egg blue Egyptian cotton shirt with a white collar. His two-office suite occupied the entire third floor of a small three-story building in Beverly Hills, and looked down on an exquisitely designed Japanese rock garden in the building's rear courtyard. In addition to Irving's desk there was a single grouping of furniture—a black leather love seat and two matching club chairs. The floor was an exotic red-hued hardwood, flawlessly finished and strikingly attractive. Several antique rugs were placed about the room, as were three or four *objets d'art.*

"Henry." Irving took Henry's right hand in his own and grasped it with a surprisingly strong grip. "Please," he swept him toward the love seat, "sit down. I trust," he said when they were seated, Henry on the love seat, Irving on a facing club chair, "that you had no trouble finding my office."

Almost a week had passed since Irving had traveled to Needles to leave his card with Mark Little. Henry, somewhat reluctantly, had called him two days later.

"Henry," Irving had confidently told him as if they had

had any number of earlier conversations, "it's time for you to come to my office and talk to me."

"About what?" Henry asked. "I don't think you understand that . . ."

"Listen, Henry," Irving had interrupted. "*really* think it's time for you and I to get together."

"I'm not sure we . . ."

"Henry, excuse me for interrupting, but please, I know what I'm talking about. We need to sit down together. And soon."

Swept along by the power of Irving's conviction, Henry, without knowing exactly why, had agreed to drive to Beverly Hills.

"No trouble at all," Henry confirmed as he sat down. "Your directions were both clear and accurate."

Before Irving could respond, his office door opened and Fredrica entered the office, carrying an antique butler's table. A tall, fiftyish woman of color, she moved with exceptional grace and dignity, bending from both the waist and knees to place the butler's table between Irving and Henry. She straightened up and smiled down at Henry. "We have chilled mineral water, a freshly brewed pot of coffee, and several kinds of tea, both herbal and regular."

"Pardon me," Irving inserted, looking at Henry. "I did not formally introduce Fredrica Hooks, my administrative assistant, to you." He paused and smiled at her. "I cannot imagine how I would function without Fredrica." He looked back at Henry. "She has both an undergraduate and a master's degree in accounting from UCLA and a doctorate in economics from Columbia." He shook his head, feigning wonder. "Fredrica could write her own ticket anywhere in California and she works with me."

"I work with you," Fredrica said, humor evident in her voice, "because you pay me a great deal of money."

"Money my ass," Irving growled, waving a hand as she left the room to get the mineral water. "When you're as smart as Fredrica Hooks, believe me, money is so far down on the list of priorities that it's not even an issue. Normally she would sit in with us, but she's got to catch a flight to Boston in an hour."

Fredrica returned with a bottle of water and two crystal glasses, which she placed on the butler's table. She extended her hand to Henry. "It was a pleasure meeting you, Henry. I look forward to working with you."

"Be safe," Irving admonished as she left the office. "Call me from the hotel when you get in." He poured a small amount of mineral water in their glasses and, holding his aloft, proposed a toast. "To Henry and, if I may be so bold, to Irving, at that best of times: the beginning of a friendship." He drank his water and sat back in the club chair, a contented smile on his face. "I have been exceptionally fortunate in my life, Henry Spencer, much as you have. And," he crossed his right leg over his left, revealing a small foot encased in a golden brown slip-on of butter soft Italian leather with a wafer-thin sole that did not appear to have ever touched concrete, "I don't mind telling you, I enjoy every minute of it." He smiled and waved his hand, encompassing the entire luxurious office. "None of . . ."

"I assume that you wish to represent me," Henry interrupted.

"To be honest, your assumption is premature." If Henry's interruption annoyed him he did not show it. "For starters, neither one of us knows yet whether you need representation, am I correct?" Without waiting for an answer, Irving continued. "Now, as I was saying, none of this," Irving again waved his arm, "is meant, strictly speaking, to impress you. The furnishings, the antiques, the artwork, the Persian rugs, they're all here solely because I like them. Some people might say that makes me shallow, but then I never worry a great deal about what other people might say. I like nice things. I like the way they make me feel. I mention this because I would like for you to get to know me a little before we talk about you, and, possibly, business." He shifted in his chair, recrossing his legs. "Believe it or not, Henry, you and I have a number of very important things in common. First, we both came from exceedingly humble beginnings. We'll talk about yours in a minute, but, let me tell you, my childhood was nothing to wax sentimental about. Suffice it to say that I've been on my own since I was seventeen, close to the time you attained your own emancipation. I scrambled around, worked in more jobs than you can imagine, even enrolled in, and shortly thereafter dropped out of, a small, second-rate college here in California. Somewhere along the way I discovered that I was possessed of two exceptional abilities: first, a willingness to work harder than anyone else I knew, and second, an extraordinary intuitive sense."

"Intuitive sense?"

"Indeed. A handy thing to have in this business, I don't mind telling you." Irving paused to replenish the water in their glasses. "But in and of itself intuition isn't worth a great deal. To truly exploit such a gift you have to be focused, you have to work hard, pay careful attention to detail, and, this is critical, you must always be better prepared than the other guy. Always. You also have to be aware of your own shortcomings. That's why Fredrica Hooks is here. She interprets the numbers, analyzes the economics that drive every deal. You know the old saying 'Figures lie and liars figure'?" Irving shook his head, a sardonic smile on his face. "Not to Fredrica they don't." He shook his head again. "Now, as to what *I* bring to the party, let me give you a modest example. Like everyone else, I was more than a little impressed this spring and early summer with the young rookie everyone was calling the Soldier. Unlike everyone else, however, I soon realized that there was little likelihood he would finish the season without leaving the team, at least for some period of time."

Henry smiled. "That's easy enough to say now."

Irving got up and walked to the walnut credenza along

the far wall of the office. Taking a thick manila file out of a drawer, he walked back and sat down. "You're right," he said. "It is easy to say now." He opened the file and took out an envelope. Addressed to himself, it had been sent by registered mail. The return addressee was also Irving Le-Clair. He handed it to Henry. "Note the date on both the postmark and the postal registration sticker," he said.

Henry examined the envelope closely. It had been un-opened and was postmarked over two months ago. He looked back at Irving.

"Open it," Irving said.

Henry did. Inside was a sheet of bond paper with a single typewritten line of text:

Henry Spencer will take an unauthorized leave-of-absence from the Oakland A's baseball club before the end of the season.

The note was signed by Irving LeClair and notarized. The notary public's signature was dated the same date as the postmark on the envelope. Henry read it twice and passed it back to Irving.

"At the risk of stealing some of my own thunder, I have to tell you that this prediction," Irving held the note up, "was not as remarkable as it may otherwise seem. In fact, I'd go so far as to say that for anyone willing to look closely enough no other scenario or conclusion was possible." He shrugged. "Don't get me wrong, it wasn't easy, but getting to the heart of something seldom is. For example, the warmly romantic, 'soft focus' image the press has come up with regarding your youth in North Carolina—good kid, nothing special, parents were salt-of-the-earth, blue-collar workers, lots of love, et cetera, et cetera. Sweet, right? But all, not surprisingly given the generally low intellectual level of most journalists, bullshit. We, Henry, you and I, know that your youth was not exactly one of Aunt Bea and little Opie, don't we?"

"No, not exactly," Henry said carefully. He didn't know who Aunt Bea or little Opie was but, given the context, had no trouble understanding what they stood for.

"I particularly loved the story that Warren Mercer, the sportswriter for the *Oakland Tribune,* wrote early in the season. The wire services picked it up and it became the source for all subsequent stories run on the rookie pheenom nicknamed the Soldier." Irving shook his head and laughed. "Too bad almost none of it was true."

"At least Warren got my name right," Henry observed dryly, beginning, for reasons he could not yet put his finger on, to like Irving.

"I'm thinking he even screwed that up." Irving looked carefully at Henry. "I'm curious. Why did you keep Louise and William Spencer's name when they never actually adopted you?"

"You *did* do your homework, didn't you?"

Irving, sensing that Henry's question was rhetorical, merely smiled.

"I have almost no memory of either of them. Louise died when I was barely five and William, to the best of my knowledge, simply drifted away shortly thereafter." Henry shook his head, lost in thought. "I must have been entirely on my own for the better part of a week before anyone noticed. As to the name," Henry shrugged, "it was just what I was always called." The hint of a smile passed across his face. "I was twelve or thirteen before I found out that the state was paying people, husbands and wives, to take care of me. William and Louise Spencer were just the first of my 'salaried' foster parents."

Irving nodded. "And the state didn't exactly over-compensate any of them—one hundred and twelve dollars a month, to be precise. You had the dubious good fortune to be an initial, albeit unwitting, participant in a new state program aimed at moving unwanted foundlings and orphans out of state institutions and into foster families. I'm sure," he added cynically, "that it was merely coincidence that the cost turned out to be a great deal less than that of maintaining state facilities. In any event, after the Spencer household, such as it was, disintegrated, you were shuffled around the county."

"Four different families by the time I finished high school," Henry confirmed. "All nice in varying degrees, but all clearly in need of the money the state paid for my support. To tell you the truth, I don't remember much about any of them."

"I'm not surprised." Irving paused for a second, choosing his words with care. "My information is that you never knew who your biological parents were."

"That's correct. Once, when I was still in the army, I tried to find out, but the state agency I contacted told me that there were no records whatever." Henry shrugged. "They said something about a fire at the county registrar's office in the county where I was born. In any event, I suppose it could have been a lot worse. Growing up, that is. Actually, I don't remember any of it as being either particularly bad or good." He smiled ruefully. "I suppose the good years were those where I got more than a pair of socks and some candy for Christmas. It seems like I was always changing schools, never making close friends or impressing teachers."

"Which is why nobody seemed to remember you when that moron Warren Mercer was checking facts for his story. Of course, like most journalists he looked no further than the superficial. Apparently he couldn't be bothered, assuming the idea even occurred to him, to check out the state or county archives."

"Is that where you got most of your information?"

"No. And, in fact, a fire did destroy many, if not most, of the county registrar's records, just like you were told. It was the logical starting place, however. From there a hell of lot of work remained to be done to get us where we are today."

"And where are we?"

"You tell me."

"Who exactly are you?"

Irving smiled. "I'm the Henry Spencer of the agency business. Much like you I came from nowhere, with nothing and nobody to vouch for me." He pointed at the wall behind Henry's head. "No framed diplomas, no degrees from prestigious universities, no testimonials from grateful clients. Nonetheless, I am quite simply the best at what I do. I never, ever, enter into even a conversation such as we're now having unless and until I know more about the person with whom I'm speaking than they themselves know." He winked at Henry. "Something of an exaggeration, but you get the point." He held up Henry's thick file. "I've got three files much bigger than yours on the Oakland A's and their managing general partner Robert Edgerton. Not only can I tell you how much profit the team actually makes notwithstanding the fact that they report a loss to the league office every year; I can tell you Edgerton's net worth. I can also tell you that he's sleeping with his lawyer—always a bad idea, by the way. In addition, I have a copy not only of your contract but of the contracts of the team's five most highly paid players."

Henry shook his head. "How can you get such information?"

"Believe me, it used to be a lot harder than it is today. Before computers took over the world, I had to enlist the aid of, shall we say, disaffected employees, disappointed bankers, passed over law clerks, unhappy ex- or soon-to-be ex-spouses. Today, though, almost everything you could possibly wish to know about someone, from their bank balance to the results of their most recent EKG, can be had via computer. I have in my employ a young woman, a graduate student in computer science at the University of Washington,

to whom computer databases around the world eagerly disgorge all of their secrets at the merest flick of her mouse. If
I may wax poetic, encryption and security software programs open before her algorithms much like the Red Sea
before Moses and the Israelites." He chuckled, pleased with
the image. "If not as dramatically."

"I had no idea."

"Few people do. You," Irving pointed playfully at Henry,
"however, were more of a challenge than most. Imagine my
annoyance to discover that you did not even own a credit
card, that you paid for everything with cash. Fortunately,
most of what I needed to learn about your childhood was
not dependent on financial records."

"How did you do it?"

Irving shrugged. "The old-fashioned way. I engaged, for
a reasonably large sum of money, a retired FBI agent, a man
characterized by a limited imagination and a bulldog-like
tenacity in ferreting out the truth."

"You've invested a great deal of time and money on the
mere speculation that I may wish to engage your services,"
Henry pointed out.

Irving waved a hand dismissively. "In the first place, I
wouldn't call it 'mere speculation.' At each discrete step in
the process of learning about you I made an evaluation of
what I had learned and where it was likely to lead me before
taking the next step. I believed at each such stage of the
process, and continue to believe as we sit here today, that
we, you and I, will do profitable business together. As for
the money my 'speculative' investigation has cost so far,"
Irving waved his hand again, "well, let's just say that money
spent in obtaining good information is never wasted." He
suddenly sat forward in his chair. "Henry, I represent no
more than eight individuals at any given time. At present I
have six active clients." He handed Henry another piece of
paper from the file in his lap. "Even you, and I don't say
that in a condescending manner, will recognize all six of

these names. Three are professional athletes, two are enter-
tainers, and one is a retired politician. I take 35 percent of
every dollar they earn, a very high percentage, and not once
have I had a client discharge me. Not once. My success
allows me to be extremely discriminating in who I choose
to represent. Frankly, I have found you to be so interesting
that even if we were never to do business together, I will
consider the time and money spent to date a sound and wise
investment." Irving paused for a second to allow Henry to
mull over what had been said. "Lastly, it's important to understand that the bare facts contained in these files, the data
I collect from so many sources, in and of itself is of relatively little use. Its true value lies in the direction it leads
me as I study and evaluate the individuals with whom I plan
to do business. For example, you may be interested to know
that I believe Mr. Edgerton to be an exceptionally weak
individual, a frightened man who uses bluster to cover a
fragile ego. An important key to doing business with anyone
is to recognize what makes them afraid. It has been my
experience that a frightened man can often be a far more
dangerous adversary than a confident one."

"How did you know I would leave the team before the
end of the season?"

Irving smiled. "I knew that the minute I read your contract. Actually, I knew it even before that, but the contract
was a big confirmation for me."

"How so?"

"Well, for one thing, you are far too smart to have signed
for the major-league minimum salary if you had truly made
a commitment to be a professional athlete. No, Henry,
major-league baseball so far has been only a way station for
you, a place to be while you continued your search."

"My search for what?"

"Your search for who you are." Irving reached back into
the file and took out two eight-by-ten glossy black-and-white
photographs. He studied them for a second and then handed

the first to Henry. "This was your mother. Your biological mother."

Henry, stunned, stared at the photograph. A young girl, barely out of her teens, smiled back at him, roundly pregnant and obviously in love. He looked back at Irving. "How . . ."

"And this," Irving interrupted, handing the second photograph to him, "was your father."

TWENTY

★ ★ ★

Needles, California

"Look out there," Benny said, sweeping his arm in an arc that encompassed most of the Mojave Desert.

He and Henry had just come back from a five-and-a-half-hour walkabout and were sitting on the patio of his trailer enjoying gin-and-tonics and fresh cucumber from Sophie's garden. Becky had sliced the crisp, fat cucumber into wafer-thin slices and placed them in a bowl filled with a raspberry vinegar Gunter had made.

"What do you see?"

Henry smiled. In the near distance Sophie Schmidtbauer could be seen, on her hands and knees, working in her garden. She and José, one of her two young employees, had erected canopies of cotton gauze to shield the more delicate plants from the power of the desert sun, and they billowed in the late afternoon breezes coming in from the north and east. He knew she wasn't the answer Benny was seeking, but he nonetheless pointed her out.

"Sophie Schmidtbauer." Benny nodded his head. "Christ Almighty, that woman has the constitution of a mule. I understand she's hired another of Hector's many nephews. Out there in her garden she's the prototypical European peasant woman and, believe me, I don't mean that in a pejorative sense. But, no, she wasn't what I had in mind. It's the light.

It's always changing, being refracted through layers of air with different ambient temperatures, and reflected off a myriad of differing surfaces, some of them almost prismatic in effect. It's extraordinary." He looked back at Sophie, working her way methodically down the rows of her garden. "Did you know that she used to teach high school chemistry back in Germany?"

Henry said nothing and Benny felt suddenly a little chagrined. He knew Henry wanted badly to talk about why he and Ramona had come to Needles, but he, Benny, had carefully deflected all attempts Henry made to start such a conversation.

"You and Ramona have been here, what, four weeks now?"

"Four weeks the day after tomorrow."

"Gunter tells me that you're buying the Airstream."

Henry nodded. "Ramona likes it, and whatever we do we're going to need a place to live. With the baby coming."

"Hard to argue with that." Benny took a sip of his drink. "Are you planning to stay here in Needles?"

"In the long run I don't know. I thought at first we might, but now . . ." He shrugged his shoulders and told Benny a little about his meeting with Irving LeClair. "To be honest, after talking to Mr. LeClair things aren't as clear as I'd hoped they were going to be."

"Things are *never* as clear as we'd like them to be. That's why religions flourish, why the gullible seek refuge in everything from astrology to number theory. You came here because Gunter, acting with the best of intentions, wrote you a letter suggesting that the answer to something that has always troubled you could be found here in the desert. Unfortunately, what you did not know at the time was that in attracting you here, Gunter also had an ulterior motive." Benny delicately snared a cucumber slice with a toothpick and dropped it into his mouth. "The thing you have to understand is that Gunter Schmidtbauer, whatever other positive and wonderful personal attributes he may possess, and there are many, is as mad as a hatter." Benny took another cucumber slice and laughed. "But he makes a hell of a vinegar, not to mention his home-brewed wheat beer. I'll admit to a certain amount of personal prejudice with regard to Gunter's profession. As you probably know, after the war he became an engineer, and all pure scientists, whether physicists, or mathematicians, or biologists, or whatever, tend to view engineers with more than a little disdain, for good reason. Although Gunter is far less so than most, probably as a result of his near-death experiences as a fighter pilot, engineers as a group tend to be exceedingly small-minded and parochial in their outlook. They're technocrats, and all such people, men and women alike, tend to be constitutionally petty if not downright venal. That aside, as I said a minute ago, in certain, let us say, *spiritual* matters Gunter has only the most tenuous of holds on reality. And Al, coming exceedingly late to knowledge and self-awareness as he has, is highly susceptible to suggestion."

Becky stepped out of the trailer carrying a large crockery pot covered with foil.

"What's in there?" Benny asked.

"A *chipotle-tomatillo salsa*," Becky answered. "Al's grilling swordfish for dinner tonight and the *salsa* is both a marinade and an accompaniment."

"Life has gotten a hell of a lot better around here since Al got rid of his laptop and started cooking," Benny said with an almost childish delight.

"It's all thanks to Ramona." Becky looked at Henry. "She told us that the two of you met at her father's restaurant."

"That's right. In fact, she was quite put out that I didn't know what a 'flan' was."

"Then I don't feel so bad asking," Benny asked. "What exactly is a *chipotle*?"

"A kind of smoked *jalapeño*," Henry said. "Ramona uses them a lot in her cooking."

"I know," Becky said. "This *chipotle-tomatillo salsa* is her recipe. Or her father's." She laughed. "Al's not the only one who's learning a lot from Ramona. The first time I saw her preparing something with *tomatillos* I thought they were Brussels sprouts."

"Did you know what *tomatillos* were when you met Ramona?" Henry asked after Becky had left.

"No, I didn't. Tell me about Gunter's problems with reality."

Benny laughed. "Well, Gunter's not the only person in recent memory who left rational thinking behind on a flight of fantasy." Benny described some of his first conversations with Gunter. "Almost immediately he began to think that Needles, and in particular this trailer park, was some sort of spiritual nexus to which we, he and I at first, only later did his thinking expand to include Al, had been drawn."

Henry nodded. "He told me essentially the same thing."

"Well," Benny continued, "Gunter felt that some momentous cosmic event was going to unfold here on the edge of the Mojave, an event he could never clearly define but about which he has never been in doubt. In physics we might call such a momentous event a singularity."

"A singularity is the point at which the derivative of a given function of a complex variable no longer exists."

"Indeed," Benny said dryly, somewhat amused by Henry's textbook definition. "I was using the term in a less literal, less *mathematical* sense." He paused to enjoy a cucumber slice. "I believe the majority of physicists would agree that, for the most part, mathematicians have an unfortunate tendency to be somewhat anal in their thinking."

Henry smiled, understanding for the first time how Preacher Brown must have felt whenever he, Henry, spoke up in the clubhouse. "How did I come to be included in Gunter's singularity?"

"You are best described by a term the military popularized some years ago; a target of opportunity. You see, Al, even as I was, used to be an avid baseball fan. I say 'used to be' because, again, just like me, almost overnight Al entered a new phase of his life, one in which the void that baseball used to fill no longer needed filling. In any event, before he lost the ball-and-chain . . ."

"The 'ball-and-chain'?"

Benny smiled. "His wife. Before Al left her, he followed baseball closely, and anyone following baseball even from a distance this spring and summer heard a great deal about a rookie nicknamed 'Soldier.' He knew I used to be a Red Sox fan, so he kept me up-to-date on your improbable statistics. It's important to keep in mind that at this point, none of this meant anything to Gunter—Al was a nonentity as far as he was concerned. A friendly enough fellow, if a little dull-witted, but definitely a nonentity. I was the only one that fit somehow into his grand scheme of things. However, Al became, strangely enough, fascinated with math and science and, even more startling, the German language. He and Gunter became something of an odd couple, with Gunter tutoring him in both areas. When Al threw the ball-and-chain over for Ruth, Gunter concluded *ipso facto* that Al, too, had been brought here to our so-called nexus in the desert for the same purpose we, Gunter and I, had."

"The singularity."

"Precisely. And it wasn't long before he put two and two together and came up with five."

"Five?"

Benny nodded and tilted his glass in Henry's direction. "You." He chuckled at Henry's confusion. "If none of this makes a great deal of sense, then you're as smart as I think you are." He stood up and stretched, turning his face in the direction of the setting sun. "God, I love these desert evenings. The sun seems to take forever to drop below the Sacramento Mountains, and even then the glow in the sky lasts and lasts."

"The colors are particularly brilliant this evening," Henry pointed out.

Benny nodded, running a hand over his face. "They are. A little too brilliant, as a matter of fact."

"What do you mean?"

"I think a storm must be brewing somewhere to the north and west. Whenever I see colors in a sunset like these, plus, I don't know, just a dicey feeling I've had all day, I think storm. But that aside, I love the way the light lasts so long after the sun drops behind the Sacramentos." He turned back to Henry and sat down again. "In Boston, even in the summer, darkness always seemed to me to arrive rather precipitously at the end of the day, as if the night were in a hurry to cover up something unattractive, something unseemly." He fell silent for several seconds, swirling the ice in his glass. "You are not," he finally said, looking up from his glass, "some sort of reincarnation of Arthur Hodges. Neither Gunter, nor Al, nor I were drawn here to Needles by some strange metaphysical attraction or force related to the death of Arthur Hodges or the presumed reincarnation of his spirit in your body."

"Why would Gunter, an intelligent, educated man, believe such a thing?" Henry asked in a quiet voice.

"Because he's an old man who wants desperately to believe that there is at least a chance that life isn't just the result of a biological crap shoot, a four-billion-year-old game of chance. He wants reassurance and hope, and, next to running across a burning bush in the Mojave Desert, he has convinced himself that you're as close to a sure thing as he's likely to come. And if he can convince Al of it, and, even more importantly, if he can convince you of it, then maybe, just maybe, it's true."

"But Al . . ."

Benny waved a hand dismissively. "Forget Al. Al's a nice guy and it's wonderful to see him becoming so committed to educating himself after a lifetime of watching television, but you need to focus on Gunter. The fact is that this is Gunter's obsession, not Al's. Believe me, Al is just along for the ride."

"It's not just Gunter, though. I know this sounds odd, but ever since I joined the A's in spring training I've had a sense that I'm not who I seem to be. There's a veil over my entire life prior to the A's, and I seem familiar with things, particularly mathematics and physics, far beyond what one would expect from a young baseball player." He tried to smile but didn't quite make it. "And my baseball skills—everyone seems to find them almost beyond belief."

"So?" Benny shrugged. "I don't mean to sound coldly dismissive, but nothing you describe even comes close to being sufficiently . . ." he paused for a second, searching for the appropriate adjective, ". . . sufficiently *momentous* to support even an inference of something as profound as re-incarnation. Take, for example, your uncertainty regarding your childhood or youth. I can think of several possible reasons just off the top of my head. From what you've told me, you had a pretty bad childhood: orphaned at birth, shuttled between several families who took you in primarily for the money they received from the state. I'm not at all surprised at how little you seem to remember from that part of your life. It's common knowledge that people sublimate such memories all the time. It's probably the means by which many people hang onto their sanity. Or, there could be a pathological source—God forbid, you might have a brain lesion of some kind that is affecting your memory, although statistically that's not very likely in a man your age. As to your knowledge of mathematics and physics . . ." Benny shrugged again. "In the past ten or fifteen years there's been an explosion of interest in the physical sciences on the part of the general public—at least that part of the general public that went to college and got undergraduate degrees in one of the liberal arts. I don't know what it is, whether they feel they missed something important while they were laying around smoking marijuana and reading poetry, or what, but it didn't take long for the more articulate of the physicists and mathematicians to realize that there was a great deal of money to be made selling the absurd notion that differential calculus could be, even for aging English majors, fun and easy to learn. So you could have picked up much of your 'knowledge' of these things quite easily in the last couple of years. And, when you speak of things like the calculus, or quantum mechanics, or whatever, in the company of, shall we say, challenged intellects such as comprise the majority of professional baseball players, it suddenly seems 'mysterious.' " Benny remembered something and smiled. "Did you ever read *A Connecticut Yankee in King Arthur's Court?*"

Henry shook his head negatively.

"You should. And as to your thoughts about Arthur Hodges specifically, you could have easily read about him at the time of his death. He was an extremely competent young physicist and mathematician, a man who was known throughout academia and much of industry as well, and his death was noted and commented upon in *Time* magazine and other such popular mass media publications. You undoubtedly read about it but paid no attention to it at the time and so later, when it resurfaced in your consciousness and you had no recollection of having read about it earlier, it became mysterious and troubling to you, particularly in conjunction with the other doubts you've been having. It's a phenomenon that happens all the time and ignorant people, superstitious people," he shook his head, "people who read horoscopes, obsess about it and call it *déjà vu.*"

"And my skills?"

"Oh, hell, Henry, you're just bigger and stronger than even most professional athletes. That's purely and simply the luck of the draw genetically. Believe me, whenever a true prodigy comes along, whether in sports, or music, or science, stupid people always mumble about black magic, or whatever. I'll give you a good example: at the beginning of the nineteenth century, much of the Catholic hierarchy at the Vatican actually believed that Niccolò Paganini had made a pact with the devil—how else to explain the fact that he played the violin like no one before him? It was clearly diabolical in their minds. No," Benny shook his head again, "your talents are no more than one would expect to result periodically as a function of the random distribution of genetic material throughout a very large gene pool." Benny looked at his watch and stood up. "Just enough time to take a shower before dinner."

"Could you be wrong?" Henry asked.

Benny stopped at the door of the trailer and turned back, a smile on his face. "Of course. But we'll never know, will we? At least not in this life."

Henry thought for a second. "Would you tell me about Arthur Hodges sometime—what kind of person he was, what his life was like?"

Benny shook his head. "No, Henry, I don't think so. He's dead now. It's time to let him go."

TWENTY-ONE

★ ★ ★

The storm had been brewing and intensifying for a number of days as it moved slowly south, weather cells slipping back and forth across the Colorado River, sending wild pigs, coyotes, and feral donkeys scrambling out of arroyos and washes from the Turtle Mountains south of Needles all the way up to Reno in the north. The air force and marine fighter pilots out of bases at Nellis and China Lake flew the tops of the storm, looking down into a noonday blackness pierced only by strobes of lightning, returning to their desert bases chastened and humbled by the experience, although none would say so. The steady stream of disgruntled losers fleeing Las Vegas on Interstate 15 saw glimpses of the storm to the south, a vision of something that reminded at least one poorer and none-the-wiser pilgrim of a mailed fist striking a helpless victim, and for reasons most couldn't begin to understand they all sighed with relief when they crested the peaks above Barstow, in California, and began the long descent into the murky and acidic Greater Los Angeles Basin.

"Hey, Doc, what brings you into town?"

Mark Little walked out from one of the bays in the radiator shop, pleased to see Benny.

"The usual," Benny answered. "Becky's at the obstetrician's office for a checkup. After that we'll do some grocery shopping, maybe get an ice-cream cone, and then head back out to the ranch. How's business?"

Mark smiled and pointed at the Proctaid Hemorrhoid Cream thermometer. The large red needle was glued to 112 degrees. "You're kidding, right? I'm working my butt off replacing thermostats and radiators. Christ, some bozo from Chicago with a late model Volvo was parked here this morning waiting for me to open up. He wanted to know didn't we have any used radiators for sale." Mark shook his head, astonished at the very thought. "A used radiator for a $35,000 car for chrissakes. Hey, how about a cold one?"

Benny nodded. "A cold beer on a day like today never hurt anybody that I know of."

They walked into the small, cluttered office adjacent to the repair bays. An ancient air conditioner, held together with duct tape, labored mightily to cool the space but failed by several tens of degrees.

"At least the beer's cold," Mark said, handing Benny a long-necked Corona.

"Feels like we might be in for some bad weather," Benny casually mentioned, leaning against the doorjamb. "Some wild colors in the sunset yesterday, and today's feeling a little unsettled."

"Right on the money," Mark confirmed. "The Doppler radar on the Weather Channel was showing some heavy shit north of here. A big dip in the jet stream sent a mass of frigid air shooting down from the Gulf of Alaska, and a tropical storm from the South Pacific ran right into it. And it's heading this way." He pointed the neck of his Corona out the window toward the northwest. "Not a cloud in the sky right now, but it could be a pisser by this evening." He took a drink of beer and belched delicately. "No kidding, Doc, stay out of the desert this afternoon, you know what I'm saying?"

Doppler radar, Benny thought. *I love it.* "No offense, Mark, but I'm curious, do you know what the Doppler effect is?"

Mark nodded confidently as if being asked to explain nothing more complicated than the workings of an internal combustion engine. "Sure. It has to do with the change in frequency of sound or light of an object moving towards or away from you. Right?"

"Right enough," Benny said, finishing his beer. "Right enough for sure. We'll talk about how the effect was adapted to radar the next time I get into town."

"What'd the doctor say?" Ruth asked. She and Becky and Benny were sitting on the verandah of her trailer, enjoying a cold drink in the late afternoon.

"Everything's fine," Becky confirmed, enjoying the steady, if hot, breeze sweeping through the trailer park.

Benny pointed to the northwest, where the sky was visibly darkening. "Mark Little told me that he had heard that this storm coming in is likely to be a big one."

"I expect we'll get a good blow out of it," Ruth Pierpont allowed. "Once the wind kicks up there'll be so goddamned much sand blowing around you won't be able to see your hand in front of your face."

Becky looked nervously at the quickening sky and shifted her weight in the Adirondack chair. "The weather reporter on the radio said there was probably nothing to worry about," she murmured, trying to convince herself. "She said that the Weather Service in Las Vegas thinks the storm will play itself out before long."

Ruth grunted and lit another Camel. She was already over her two-smoke limit for the day, but she didn't much care. She could sense the barometric pressure dropping even as they sat there, and for one who had lived on the fringes of desolation for as many years as she had it was not a pleasant sensation. "If I hadn't had my ovaries taken out twelve years ago I'd blame the way I was feeling on PMS," she said with little humor. *Can't you feel it?* she wanted to ask the younger woman. *Can't you smell the danger?* "Those idiots up in Vegas wouldn't know a storm in the desert if it bit them on the ass."

"Where's Al?" Benny asked.

Ruth nodded in an easterly direction. "He and Ramona decided on the spur of the moment to drive over to Kingman. They left a couple of hours ago, while you were in Needles." She shook her head in bemused affection. "Ramona knows about a market there that specializes in Mexican herbs and spices and peppers. She said her father even gets things from them that he can't get anywhere else outside of Mexico."

"I hope they don't run into this bad weather," Becky said.

"They can't get into too much trouble in a car on the Interstate," Ruth said confidently.

"I wonder what they're going to bring back for dinner?" Benny wondered. Al, under Ramona's tutelage, had quickly developed into quite a cook, one such that Benny eagerly looked forward to the evening meal.

Before Ruth could answer, Sophie Schmidtbauer walked up to the verandah, obviously distracted.

"I am worried about Gunter," she said as soon as she arrived.

"Worried?" Benny asked. "How so?"

"He and Henry went out into the desert an hour or two ago and they haven't returned yet."

"Out into the desert? What for?"

Although Henry clearly enjoyed the strenuous walkabouts he took with Benny, Gunter had never indicated an interest in walking more than a few hundred meters out past the boundaries of the trailer park.

"Gunter said he wanted the two of them to see this storm," she waved anxiously in the direction of the dark clouds, "up close."

"What?" Ruth couldn't believe her ears. "He may see more than he by-God bargained for." She shook her head. "And I'll tell you something else—I'm sorry now that Al and Ramona decided at the last minute to drive over to Kingman this afternoon. I guarantee you she would have never let him out of the trailer with a storm like this brewing. Mexicans know what weather like this can do."

"I'm worried," Sophie repeated, wringing her sun bonnet nervously between her hands. "Would you go look for them?" she asked Benny.

"Of course," he answered, standing up. "I think I know right where they would have gone. It's a place I've taken Henry several times."

"Are you sure it's safe?" Becky asked nervously. She could deal easily enough with Sophie's uninformed anxiety, but Ruth's obvious concern, given all the years she had lived here, was something to worry about. "Shouldn't we call Hector Gonzalez or something?"

"By the time he could get here, even if he's not tied up with something else, I'll be back with the two of them in tow," Benny said confidently. He squinted at the clouds still forming on the horizon. "That storm's at least four hours away," he added, bending down to kiss Becky on the cheek. "There's nothing to worry about."

Benny rather easily covered in just over an hour what had taken Gunter and Henry almost two-and-a-half hours. He felt certain that they would be going to an area of high ground that was bisected by a deep arroyo that ran from the north, up in the Sacramento Mountains, to the south, petering out into a broad, sandy basin to the west of Needles. Moving directly into the face of the oncoming storm he quickly realized that the four-hour estimate he had confidently given Becky was wildly optimistic, but he felt that by pushing them on the return to the trailer court they could still beat the worst of the weather. Barely. Shortly before he caught sight of Gunter and Henry he saw three wild pigs running crazily along the bottom of the arroyo, just to his left, an adult and two adolescents. Following them at a dead run, not seconds behind, was a coyote, itself trailed by two large, bounding jackrabbits. The arroyo itself was some fifteen to twenty feet wide and six feet deep, with steep, scoured banks. Off to his right he heard, but could not see, what sounded like several donkeys galloping away from the darkening sky.

Just then he saw them, standing on the edge of the arroyo.

"Gunter. Henry." Benny waved his right arm.

"Lieber Gott," Gunter exclaimed, plainly disturbed to see him. "What are you doing out here?"

"I've come to bring you two fools back. It's too dangerous to be out here with this storm coming in."

"No," Gunter said, waving his arms as if to fend Benny off. "This storm is the sign I have been waiting for."

"What the hell are you talking about?"

"Him." Gunter pointed at Henry. "Your friend Arthur Hodges."

"Gunter, this young man is *not* the reincarnation of Arthur Hodges." He turned angrily to Henry. "What the hell is this all about?"

Henry, plainly embarrassed, shrugged. "He said he was going to come out here whether I accompanied him or not. I felt that with the storm coming I had no choice."

A sudden gust of wind sent a cascade of gravel over the edge of the arroyo, startling all three of them.

"Listen to me. Whatever nonsense is going through his head, or yours for that matter, is going to get us all killed if we don't start moving right now. You have no idea how violent this storm is likely to be." He turned back to Gunter as the force of the wind increased noticeably. "Gunter, for God's sake, believe whatever you like, but we've got to return to the trailer park. Sophie is worried sick, as . . ." He paused, thinking he heard something odd on the wind.

"Look at that," Henry interrupted, pointing to the edge of the arroyo. Three large tarantulas were scurrying up and over the bank, their thick, hairy legs driving up and down like miniature pistons.

"They're trying to get to high ground," Benny said, stooping down to get a closer look, even as he fully realized the implication of the spiders' frantic haste. He thought briefly of helping them but knew there was nothing he could think to do that wouldn't likely cause them more harm than good. "As we should be doing." He turned to back Gunter. "This was a bad idea," he said, raising his voice to be heard over the suddenly keening wind. "A *real* bad idea." He pointed to the north and west, the direction from which the arroyo originated. "It's probably raining up in those mountains right now. If it is, and if it's raining as hard as I think it is, a flash flood could come through here and drown us before we even know we're in trouble."

"I think he's right," Henry added, plainly worried. He had had no idea a storm of such power could have come upon them so quickly.

"We have nothing to be worried about," Gunter said calmly, smiling. "I do not believe that I survived the Russian Front in 1943 only to drown in the desert as an old man." He put an arm around Henry's broad shoulders. "He will protect us."

"Have him call me as soon as he checks in, will you?"

Ruth hung up the telephone and stepped back out to the verandah. "That was the dispatcher," she told Becky. "Hector's working a big wreck out on the Interstate, but they're going to have him call me as soon as he's done." She sat down and lit another Camel. "Al and Ramona should be getting back before too much longer," she added hopefully. It had been just over an hour since Benny had trotted off into the desert. "I'm going to wring that goddamn German's neck when they get back here."

Sophie had returned to her Airstream and Ruth felt free to vent her considerable anger.

"I don't think they're going to get back here before the storm hits," Becky said, meaning Benny, Gunter, and Henry. She was frantic with worry.

The words were barely out of her mouth when the sky, as if caught up in a sudden and unexpected total eclipse of the sun, darkened dramatically and twin bolts of lightning, one following the other by mere nanoseconds, reached for the desert floor barely a mile from the trailer park. Crackling, concussive thunder rolled over them, rattling the trailer's snatched windows.

"Sonofabitch," Ruth cursed. "We need to get into the trailer. With your old man and those two other fools wandering around out in the desert you better stay with me until this blows over."

"What about them?" Becky asked, frightened by the sudden darkness of the sky and the palpable violence of the coming storm.

The wind began to howl through the trailer park, tugging at loose corners and rocking the lightly built single-wides scattered about on their concrete pads. Grains of sand and gravel peppered the aluminum sides of the trailer like buckshot. Ruth forcefully grabbed Becky by the arm.

"They're on their own now. Can't nobody do nothin' as long as this wind is blowing like this," she shouted, pushing the nonresistant Becky into the trailer.

Slamming the door behind them, Ruth breathed a sigh of ostensible relief for Becky's sake, although in fact she was quite concerned as to the airworthiness of her metal home. She had no doubt that a strong enough wind would send them flying. "Don't worry about them men," she said, getting out an aptly named hurricane lantern. "Young Henry might be a bit too moony for my taste, and God alone knows what runs through Gunter's mind, but that old man of yours is nobody's fool and you can believe the German's seen a thing or two as well. I expect between the two of them they'll know enough sense to grab Henry and lay low out there until this thing blows through." *If they don't get killed by lightning or swept away and drowned by a flash flood,* she thought but did not say.

Benny turned from the frantically scurrying tarantulas and tried to reason again with Gunter. "We've got to get back to the trailers," he said. "The storm is almost on us and there is absolutely no cover or shelter out here."

"It's too late," Henry replied, his voice loud but calm. He pointed to the onrushing storm clouds that now appeared to be almost directly overhead.

Almost from one second to the next the light fell away and the wind began to howl in a single sustained low note, a sound that none of the three men had ever heard before. Benny saw immediately that Henry was correct and began to cast about for a place close at hand where they could at least crouch out of the wind. Lightning began to surge from the black clouds, striking the earth all around them in an extraordinary display of electrical power and violence. Benny could feel a powerful field of static electricity building around them and he saw a ghostly bluish-green discharge dancing about the top of a tall cactus on the other side of the arroyo.

"St. Elmo's Fire," he said, pointing it out to the others.

"What?"

Benny saw more than heard Henry's question as the roar of the wind sucked his words away.

"St. Elmo's Fire," Benny repeated, yelling now as he

pointed to the frightening display of electrical discharge.

"We have to get into the arroyo," Henry shouted, ducking instinctively as each bolt of lightning strobe lit the stark desert scene around them. "Into the arroyo," he repeated for emphasis, pointing to the dry gully.

"No," Benny yelled desperately, waving his arms back and forth in an unmistakable negative. He put his head close to Henry's to be sure he was understood over the fearsome noise of the storm. "I think a flash flood may be coming soon, and we'll be swept away and drowned if we're any-where nearby when it hits. We've got to get to higher ground, away from the arroyo."

"But the lightning . . ."

"I know, goddamn it," Benny interrupted, pulling Henry away from the edge of the arroyo as he yelled, "but at least we have a chance that the lightning won't strike us. If we're near low ground when the flash flood comes through we'll have no chance at all." Some twenty yards from the arroyo he saw a large boulder and dragged Henry to it. In the strobe of another lightning strike he looked around for Gunter and saw him slowly and deliberately climbing down into the ar-royo. "Shit!" Benny cursed at the top of his lungs. "Wait here," he said to Henry, pointing to the boulder for emphasis. He turned and, fighting the wind, stumbled once again to the edge of the arroyo, yelling Gunter's name as loudly as he could.

Gunter stopped in the middle of the arroyo and turned back towards Benny. He pointed at the ongoing display of St. Elmo's Fire beyond the far bank and started to yell some-thing, words that were snatched away by the storm long before they could reach Benny's ears. Suddenly he stopped and, holding up a hand as if to momentarily forestall further conversation, cocked his head into the wind. Benny, too, heard, or more accurately felt, a new sound, one that he hadn't been aware of until that instant. It seemed to Benny to be more of a rumbling, an earth sound, of such a low frequency that at first it was omnidirectional, and he, as Gunter had done, instinctively cocked and turned his head from one side to the other, trying to pinpoint a source. *My God,* he thought, still trying to understand what he and Gunter both heard, *that can't be an earthquake, can it?* Suddenly the sound coalesced, rose a degree in pitch, and presented itself solely from the north, where the arroyo and the land around it disappeared into the storm's darkness.

"Gunter," Benny screamed, terror overcoming him as he realized what the sound was. He stumbled from the edge of the arroyo, back toward Henry and the boulder, scrabbling with his feet and hands like the spiders they had seen only scant minutes earlier.

Gunter recognized what the sound represented at the same instant Benny did. Oddly enough, a beatific smile played across his face and he turned to face the source straight on, his arms raised parallel to the ground, his feet spread. The malignant darkness in front of him seemed to intensify, as if it were actually attracting and drawing in whatever ambient light existed around its periphery like some sort of terrestrial black hole, so that even the blinding strobes of lightning no longer lit the floor and banks of the arroyo. The deep, guttural sound continued to rise in volume and pitch until it overcame and canceled out the sound of the storm itself, taking on a hatefully shrieking, grinding quality, like the coming together of the molars of an impossibly large, prehistoric ruminant on the skulls of living, sentient creatures. The now palpable darkness at the head of the arroyo seemed strangely to waver, to pull back fractionally, almost delicately, hesitating until with an ineffable and paralyzing crescendo of sound and violence it burst forth in a sheer cataract of black water, fifteen feet high and moving at what might as well have been the speed of light.

TWENTY-TWO

Hector Gonzalez thought wistfully from time to time that it might not be such a bad thing to be a smoker, because he saw the comfort they took in the simple act of lighting a cigarette in times of great stress. He knew, of course, that in reality it was far better not to smoke, but whenever he had to tell someone, a husband or a wife, a brother or a sister, that their loved one was dead, he found himself wishing he had a cigarette to light. A little earlier in the evening he surely envied Ruth her Camel as he told everyone that without a doubt Gunter Schmidtbauer was dead.

"I doubt we'll ever find the body," he confided confidentially to Benny and Al and Henry after the women had gone to sit with Sophie in her trailer. Of all of them he thought the young Chicana, Ramona, had taken the news most stoically. It did not surprise him. "We'll look tomorrow, of course, but . . ." He shrugged eloquently, knowing that few people, particularly those not born to the badlands and the deserts of the American Southwest, could ever appreciate the power contained in the fast-moving storms that occasionally swept from north to south. The one good thing about the sudden influx of water was that for a few days the desert would blossom, and new life would flourish, quickly and efficiently replacing that which had been lost.

"Would you like . . ." Al offered a small plate with what

appeared to be a piece of pie or quiche on it to Hector. "It's *jalapeño* pie I made for breakfast."

Hector took a bite and a pleased smile spread over his face. *"Gracias,"* he murmured, taking another bite, finding it to be better than his own wife could make. He looked at Al, astonished that he had learned to cook Mexican food so well so quickly. "If this is what you are making for breakfast these days please feel free to invite me to supper anytime."

Al beamed and asked if Hector would like another piece.

"No, thank you," Hector replied, wishing he were off duty so he could have a beer. He took a small notebook and the stub of a pencil out of his breast pocket. "Tell me again how it happened," he said to Benny, thinking that perhaps now that the widow, Sophie, had been taken back to her trailer Benny might feel free to provide more details.

Benny sighed and ran a nervous hand across his gleaming bald head. "It was a miscalculation," he said. "Pure and simple."

The violence of the storm, the stupendous amount of energy that it unleashed, completely overwhelmed both Benny's and Henry's senses. They had clung to each other desperately as the earth literally groaned and shook with the combined assault of wind, water, and lightning. Benny knew that Gunter was dead and quickly became convinced that both he and Henry were going to die as well, either swept somehow into the floodwater raging down the arroyo or electrocuted by one of the countless bolts of lightning that continued to slam into the desert floor all around them with trip-hammer rapidity. At the height of the storm, when it became clear that they could not possibly survive such violence, Benny simply stopped thinking and, like all of the other creatures of the desert, waited for the end.

Almost as quickly as the storm had come upon them it passed, racing south to die over the Gulf of California, its howling, almost demonic winds ultimately to be no more than a gentle zephyr skipping playfully across the western edge of Mexico's Sonoran badlands. Benny wasn't at all sure for how long after the storm had actually passed he and Henry continued to huddle in the lee of the boulder. All he could remember was looking around and realizing that the sky was clear and that the continuing rumbles of thunder were now coming from well to the south. As he was trying to clear his head he saw a coyote emerge from behind a clump of sagebrush on the other side of the arroyo. It stumbled several times as if drunk and disappeared behind the tall cactus from which the St. Elmo's Fire had emanated. *I know exactly how you feel,* Benny thought, still too stunned to try to stand himself.

Henry stood up first, looking around as if wondering where he was and how he came to be there. He helped Benny up and for several seconds the two of them looked carefully at the ground, as if afraid it might start moving under their feet. When it didn't, Benny smiled, a broad, toothy grin that made Henry laugh, a short hiccup that in turn started Benny giggling, and suddenly they were both laughing hysterically, holding on to the boulder and each other to keep from falling down. When the hysteria at being so unexpectedly alive finally passed, their laughter slowly wound down and they wiped the tears from their cheeks.

"Gunter."

Henry spoke quietly, yet the sound of Gunter's name was sufficient to wipe the smiles from both of their faces.

"He's gone," Benny said as he walked toward the arroyo. "Swept away. I think he was trying to get over to the other side, to where the St. Elmo's Fire was, when the flash flood caught him."

The arroyo was full of debris, left behind when the wall of water passed through and quickly subsided to a trickle, leaving only isolated puddles, which themselves were rapidly disappearing into the sandy soil.

"Why . . ."

"We really don't have time to talk about this now," Benny interrupted. "We've got to get moving." He gestured at the lengthening shadows all around them. Stars were already visible in the eastern sky. "We're at least an hour away from the trailer park and we've got only half-an-hour or so until it's full dark." He was pretty sure he could navigate the last half hour in the darkness, but he was not a little concerned about the fact that so many feral creatures would be wandering around slightly dazed and in a bad frame of mind because of the storm. "I'd like not to run into a family of wild pigs after dark, or a nest of rattlesnakes stirred up by the weather, if we can avoid it," he said as they started walking.

"Did you see the floodwater take him?" Hector asked gently.

Benny shook his head. "No. We both heard it coming down the arroyo and I was scrambling as fast as I could to get back to the boulder where I had left Henry." He saw no point in engaging in idle speculation as to whether or not Gunter could have escaped the oncoming flood had he been inclined to try.

"You are lucky," Hector said, jotting something in his small notebook. "You are *both* lucky," he amended, broadening his glance to take in Henry, "to be alive. Tell me once more," to Henry, "why the two of you went out into the desert."

Henry caught Benny's discrete warning glance and shrugged. "He said that he wanted to see the approach of the storm. He knew it was going to be an impressive one and he thought . . ." Henry paused for a second and shook his head. "Honestly, I don't know what he thought. I know that both of us felt that the storm would take a good deal longer to get to us than it did. We believed that we could watch it approach and still have sufficient time to return here before it actually struck. Obviously we were wrong. By the time Benny caught up to us it was already too late."

Hector grunted and wrote a few last words in his notebook before closing it and returning it to his breast pocket. Twenty-three years as a deputy sheriff had taught him that most accidental deaths were attributable first and foremost to stupidity, and clearly this one was no exception.

Mark Little and his girlfriend came out for the memorial service, a thoughtful gesture that pleased Benny to no end. Hector and Tranquilina and their children also came, as did his two nephews who worked with Sophie in her garden. The service itself was given by Tranquilina's brother, a Catholic priest from a rural Indian parish between Nogales and Hermosillo who was coincidentally visiting the Gonzalez family at the time of Gunter's death. A strikingly handsome man, he wore his shoulder length black hair braided in the style of his Mimbres Indian parishioners. Accompanied by a dark, young Indian woman, obviously pregnant, he spoke not a word of English, so Ramona gave a simultaneous translation to Sophie during the short service. Benny spoke briefly, as did Becky, both remembering the kindness of spirit of the man who had greeted them and invited them to stay for supper when first they came to Needles. Al also spoke, reminding everyone that it was Gunter who had been so open-minded, so encouraging, when he first began to expand his own horizons. Then, after a final prayer from the priest and a short, piercing chant from his young companion, Al invited everyone to eat and drink.

"*Dios mio,*" Hector mumbled, minutes later, his mouth full of *carnitas,* "I thought I would go crazy during the service with the smell of this food."

In preparing for the post-memorial service feast and celebration Al had cooked for the better part of two full days, utilizing not only the kitchen in Ruth's trailer but Becky's and Ramona's as well. Hector's two oldest children were employed during the actual service to tend the three outdoor grills that were barbecuing and cooking the last of the meat and chicken dishes. The results of Al's labors were talked about in Needles for some years after the feast itself. In addition to three different salsas, a chunky *pico de gallo,* a salsa *cocida de chiles gueros,* and a green chile salsa, there were three kinds of meatless enchiladas: stacked blue corn and red chile *enchiladas* topped with a tangy *queso de cabra;* rancho cheese, onion, and olive *enchiladas*; and *enchiladas en chipotle.* Two chicken dishes were served, *chipotle-tomatillo* chicken breasts and *tamales con pavo y pollo,* the latter served drenched in a stinging California Colorado red chile sauce, and two pork dishes, *carnitas,* a border favorite, and a tenderloin *asada* with apples and pears, and, last, just to prove he could do it, a spectacular blue corn *poblanos rellenos.*

"Whoa, this is some way excellent food, Mr. Bartholomeo," Mark Little said, taking two Coronas out of a huge galvanized tub. He opened them and gave one to his main squeeze, a bottle blonde with a sweet disposition, long, red fingernails, and an exceedingly short skirt. "I don't know where to start." He leaned in next to Al and lowered his voice somewhat. "Man, that Mexican priest is a serious south-of-the-border dude, you know what I'm saying?"

Al hadn't the faintest idea, but he was too busy getting all the food put out on the patio to indulge in idle speculation. "You bet," he agreed. "Listen, Mark, you and your friend . . ."

"Angie," Mark volunteered.

"You and your friend Angie feel free to dig in and," he paused to put down a large bowl of *pico de gallo,* "call me Al."

Benny sat in one of his Adirondack knockoffs drinking a beer and watched with some interest as the priest and the pregnant Indian woman gravitated unerringly towards Henry and Ramona. He got up and walked over to where Hector stood working on his second plate of blue corn *enchiladas* and *chipotle-tomatillo* chicken.

"Your brother-in-law strikes me as a somewhat unconventional Catholic priest," he said dryly.

"Shit," Hector muttered, looking around quickly to make sure Tranquilina couldn't hear him. "Father Carlos. He's an asshole. He claims to be a descendant of Mangas Coloradas, the father-in-law of the Chiricahua Apache chief Cochise, although how he could possibly know such a thing is beyond me. I might as well claim to be a direct descendant of Pancho Villa." He laughed derisively. "He and Tranquilina are only half siblings—same mother, different fathers—but they were raised together as brother and sister and she loves him to death."

"So he's Indian rather than Mexican?"

"*Mestizo,*" Hector grunted. It was not a compliment. "Maybe 40 percent Indian, maybe less, the rest Spanish." He paused for a second, considering his words. "You have to understand," he added with a shrug to show that perhaps he was being a little harsh, "that as on this side of the border with the Anglos and the Indians there is a long history of bitter animosity between the Indians and the Mexicans. There was much killing, much cruelty, on both sides. Carlos was raised by Tranquilina's family, not his father's, and many in her family are uncomfortable now that he has, shall we say, embraced his roots. Or at least what he would like to believe are his roots."

"Who's the young woman?"

Hector laughed again. "His wife. She's a full-blooded Mimbres from his so-called flock. Her name is Yones."

"I had no idea the Catholic Church in Mexico was so liberal as to allow its priests to marry," Benny said with a smile.

"It isn't."

Before Hector could explain, Mark Little and his girlfriend came up carrying a bottle of tequila, several shot glasses, and a plate of quartered limes.

"How about a tequila shooter, dudes?" Mark asked. "Mr. Bartholomeo, Al, asked me to, like, do the bartender thing," he explained.

"Why not?" Benny said, taking two glasses and handing one to Hector.

They both drank the tequila in one swallow, chasing it with the limes. Benny blinked several times, inhaled loudly through his lips, and did a little shuffle-off-to-Buffalo routine with his sandaled feet. Hector laughed with him and got them both cold Coronas from the tub.

"So," Benny said as soon as he and Hector sat down with their beer, "tell me more about your Apache brother-in-law."

Hector smiled, the tequila and beer already starting to mellow his disposition. "Being married is only one of his several problems with the Church. In addition to preaching a particularly virulent brand of revolutionary theology, he's been conducting Mass among his Mimbres parishioners using peyote as the Sacrament, a big no-no with the Diocese." He took a long drink of beer and sighed contentedly. "The Bishop gave him a choice: resign his priesthood immediately or face certain excommunication."

Ruth sat in the small kitchen of her trailer with Becky and Sophie. The two older women drank beer while Becky sipped from a glass of watermelon *agua fresca*.

"I have decided to stay here," Sophie informed them. "Permanently. Gunter was right when he said that we had come here to die in the sun." She smiled sadly. "*Gut is gut und besser ist besser*. He is dead, but my garden lives on and I want to tend it for many years to come."

"I'm so pleased to hear that you're staying," Becky said. She looked at Ruth. "Should we tell her?"

Ruth wiped a tear from the corner of her eye and shrugged. "Why not?"

"Tell me what?" Sophie asked.

*   *   *

"So, Doc, what's this I hear about you buying the trailer park from Miz Pierpont?" Mark Little flopped into a vacant Adirondack next to Benny, not a little intoxicated.

Benny shook his head in wonder and looked at Al.

"Don't look at me," Al said. "I haven't mentioned it to a living soul."

"What are you talking about?" Hector was slurring his words somewhat, but the prodigious amount of food, beer, and tequila he had consumed in the past hour made it rather difficult to tell whether he was stunned by the unexpected news or merely suffering from a lack of blood flow to the brain caused by extraordinary overindulgence.

"I'll be damned if I know how Mark, here, knows," Benny started to say, "but . . ."

"Easy," Mark told everyone. "Angie," his girlfriend, "had to pee and heard Miz Pierpont telling someone about it."

" 'Loose lips sink ships,' " Benny intoned. "We used to laugh like hell at platitudes like that, but the joke's on me." Benny could feel the effects of the several shooters he had consumed, not to mention the beer. He looked from Mark to Hector. "It's true. I'm buying the trailer park from Ruth."

"Why is she selling it?" Hector asked biliously. He seemed to be having a hard time catching his breath.

Benny jerked a thumb in Al's direction. "Al stole her heart."

"Bitchin'," Mark said happily. He, like most young men, longed to believe that love could conquer all, and it seemed to him that if it could move a pair of oldsters like Miz Pierpont and Mr. Bartholomeo, it could surely do anything.

"We're moving to San Luis Obispo," Al clarified. "We're going to get married and open a Mexican restaurant on the coast."

"Married?" Hector was becoming more confused by the minute. He looked around but could see only Al standing there, grinning like a fool. "Who's getting married?"

*   *   *

"Married?" Sophie shrieked. *"Lieber Gott im Himmel."* She jumped up and embraced Ruth. "I am so happy for you."

"Yeah, well, I'm sort of blown away myself, to tell you the truth," Ruth said, embarrassed. "Who would have guessed it?"

It was after midnight by the time Tranquilina got Hector loaded into the back of their station wagon. Since she, too, had overindulged somewhat, their eldest son, fourteen-year-old Ramon, drove them home.

Mark and his girlfriend were both deemed unable to drive and spent the night in the spare bedroom of Sophie's Airstream, where they were awakened at about 2:00 A.M. by the sound of chanting coming from Henry and Ramona's trailer. The wailing, piercing sound woke Angie first.

"Mark, baby," she whispered, tugging at his arm. She could hear Sophie snoring loudly just down the narrow hallway from their Pullman-sized bedroom.

"What?" Mark, never an early riser, came to the surface slowly.

A sliver of moonlight worked its way through the louvered window next to the bed and fell across Angie's firm, young breasts, a sight that stirred Mark to full wakefulness. It took him several seconds to remember where he was, and when he did he started rubbing his semi-turgid member against Angie's bare thigh.

"Quiet," Angie warned, stilling him with a finger to her lips. "We don't want to wake Mrs. Schmidtbauer." She pointed to the small window through which the moonlight was falling. Its louvers were cranked wide open and the light curtain ruffled gently in the breeze. "Listen."

The chanting had grown in volume somewhat as another voice joined in.

"Whoa," Mark said, raising himself up in his elbows so

he could peer out the window. "That's some strange shit." He looked at her in the darkness. "It must be that heavy Mexican dude and his wife. They were going to spend the night with Henry and Ramona."

"What's that other sound?" Angie asked.

"You mean the old German lady snoring down the hall?"

"No, there's something else coming from out there." She nodded her head at the window.

Mark listened for a second and a smile spread across his face. "That's old Miz Pierpont and Al, going at it." He shook his head, unable and unwilling to picture the scene in any detail. "Man, I don't know how anybody gets any sleep out here."

"What is going on out there?" Becky asked sleepily. She could place the chanting, and knew that it came from Henry and Ramona's Airstream, and a little earlier had heard Ruth and Al making love. But now the chanting was joined by another, somewhat more highly pitched, sound. Definitely not Ruth and Al again. She frowned and tugged on Benny's arm.

"What do you think is going on?" Benny asked, a smile on his face as he recognized the sounds of Mark and Angie making love mingled with the atavistic rhythm of the chanting.

He reached out and turned her on her side, snuggling his pelvis into her buttocks. Kissing the back of her neck, he cupped one of her breasts in his hand. Soon Benny's and Becky's voices were carried on the night breeze out beyond the *laagered* trailers to the park's perimeter, where they were heard quite distinctly by a group of coyotes drawn by the lingering smell of Al's cooking. The sounds from the trailer park so delighted them that they added their own voices to the human hymns of joy that accompanied Gunter's spirit on the beginning of its timeless journey towards a hoped-for rebirth.

TWENTY-THREE

"How about a cup of coffee?" Henry asked.

Benny looked up from the magazine he was reading. Four days had gone by since the memorial service and things had gotten back to normal at the trailer park, which is to say that not much was going on. "Are you offering or asking?" he inquired with a smile.

"Asking, actually." Henry gestured in the general direction of Needles. "Ramona went into town to pick up a few things and, well, to tell you the truth . . ." Henry paused, somewhat embarrassed to say that he wasn't sure how much coffee to put into the coffeemaker.

Benny stood up. "As luck would have it, I just brewed a fresh pot. Sit down and I'll get us both a cup."

"Where's Becky?" Henry asked when Benny returned with the coffee.

Benny nodded towards Ruth's trailer. "Helping Ruth and Al do a little last-minute packing. They're taking off in the morning."

"Are you surprised about them getting married and moving to San Luis Obispo?"

Benny shook his head. "I don't know that I am. Gunter always said that this . . ." he spread his arms to encompass all that they could see, "this Mojave Desert, was a special place in the universe. Could be they were drawn here just to be together."

"I thought you didn't believe any of that."

"I said I didn't believe Gunter's notion that you were the reincarnation of Arthur Hodges, not that I didn't believe his feeling that this was somehow a special place. There's a big difference." Benny took a sip of his coffee. "We haven't seen much of you and Ramona since the service. Come to think of it, we haven't seen much of Sophie either."

Henry nodded. "We've been pretty busy with Coyuntura and Yones."

"Coyuntura? I thought his name was Carlos. Father Carlos."

"He's changed his name since leaving the Church. Coyuntura is an Indian name. Anyway, the chanting . . ."

"Oh, yes," Benny interrupted, "I've been wanting to ask you about the chanting."

For three nights after Gunter's memorial service the otherworldly sounds of intermittent chanting had been heard coming from Henry and Ramona's Airstream.

Henry smiled. "You don't think much of things like that, do you?"

"No, not really, although I'm trying to maintain more of an open mind than once I did." He paused for a second and took another sip of coffee. "I think one of the real shortcomings of a scientific education is that it, ironically enough, instills a kind of closed-mindedness in its disciples, so that we find it very difficult to consider alternative ways of thinking. In that sense you and Al, and even Gunter for that matter, are much more able than I to look at new ideas, to be more, I don't know . . ." he shrugged, "creative, I guess. Anyway, you were going to tell me about the chanting."

"Coyuntura and Yones felt an immediate spiritual attraction to both Ramona and me, and wanted to do a blessing ceremony for the baby. They're interesting people, very spiritual, concerned with trying to live their lives in harmony with nature. His decision to leave the Church is for the most part informed by a belief that for him, for the Indian culture he has adopted, the Church and its teachings are unbalanced, do not reflect reality as he and his people know it."

"Did you tell them about . . ." Benny paused, considering how best to ask the question, "about Arthur Hodges?"

Henry shook his head and looked uncomfortable.

"If you'd rather not discuss . . ." Benny started to say.

"No, I would. It's a little awkward for me because I'm aware of your," he smiled, "science-based disbelief, but I think it's important that you know how I feel. In answer to your question, I did not tell them about my feeling concerning Arthur Hodges. As it turned out I didn't have to. Yones immediately sensed what she called a duality of spirits in me, even before we formally met after the memorial service. She was able to see an aura about me that she interpreted as generated by two spirits, two souls, in one body. The first chanting they did was to enable her to commune with the spirits. She took a drug of some sort . . ."

"A drug?"

Henry nodded. "Something like peyote or mescaline."

"Actually," Benny interrupted, "mescaline comes from the peyote cactus. Sorry," he added, suddenly embarrassed. "I didn't mean to sound like a walking encyclopedia."

"It may have been mescaline," Henry continued, unperturbed, "or it may have been some other naturally occurring psychoactive substance. In any event, taking it allowed her to, in some fashion, commune with my spirits."

"And what did she tell you?"

"In one sense, the same thing you did."

Benny raised his eyebrows. "Really?"

"Really. Although the two of you came at it from radically different directions, you both came to essentially the same conclusion: Henry Spencer has to live the life he's been given, not one that may or may not have been lived before."

Benny smiled, genuinely pleased. "As a scientist I've always believed in the wisdom of getting a second opinion."

He took another sip of his coffee and looked at Henry. "Something seems to be troubling you."

"I worry that I was the cause of Gunter's death."

"Nonsense." Benny waved a hand. "I told you some time ago that in my opinion Gunter had become a little unbalanced, a little obsessive, about the whole reincarnation thing. Listen." Benny leaned forward in his chair. "Gunter, despite his keen intellect and education, fell prey to the same atavistic fear of death that has tormented most people since the beginning of time. Simply put, Gunter was afraid of dying. Hell, that's why he left Germany in the first place. He was an old man who had already buried most of his friends and colleagues. He got here to Needles, on the edge of one of the great deserts of the world, and after God knows how many nights of staring up into the Milky Way concluded, completely irrationally of course, that he had found his 'special place.' *Why* it was special he didn't know, as in fact he happily admitted during one of the very first conversations he and I had. What he did know was that he was going to die at some point in the not-too-distant future, and the finality of that death terrified him more and more as time passed. All *you* did was allow him to move from the inchoate to the concrete, insofar as his growing need for a sign of some sort was concerned. You and Al, that is, because of course without Al, Gunter would have never heard of you." Benny chuckled. "So if you want to blame someone for Gunter's death, blame Al." He held up a hand. "Just kidding, of course. But you can see that you were nothing more than a convenient, excuse the expression, lightning rod for Gunter's growing obsession."

"Even so, I can't help but think that I could have kept him from going out into the desert before the storm."

Benny shrugged and sat back in his chair. "Maybe yes, maybe no. Obviously he was determined to put his belief in you to some sort of test. If the storm hadn't come along

when it did something else would have, sooner or later. Furthermore, an additional thing to keep in mind is that storms,
particularly of the magnitude of the one that killed Gunter,
can, and often do, induce almost psychotic behavior in some
individuals. Frankly, I wouldn't lightly dismiss such a possibility in this case. In any event, Gunter came to believe in
his obsession and like all true believers he was bound to be
disappointed when he put you to the test." Benny smiled.
"Wise men and women know that it's best not to ask God
for tangible signs. And remember, too, we'll never know
why he climbed into the arroyo when he did. Although in
fact he may have expected you to somehow save him from
the flash flood, he also simply may have gotten confused or
disoriented by the unexpected power of the storm. The only
thing we'll ever know for certain is that he's dead. As is
Arthur Hodges. You," Benny pointed at Henry, "need to take
that young Indian woman's advice and get about living your
own life. Now, how about a refill on that coffee?" Benny
got up and took the two cups into the trailer. "By the way,"
he called out through the screen door, "now that I'm the
owner of the trailer park, are you and Ramona going to
continue to be my tenants?"

"Yes, we are," Henry answered, taking the full cup from
Benny's hand as he stepped back out onto the patio. "Although we're going to be spending a lot of our time in Mexico, we'd like to consider this," he extended an arm to
include the trailer park, "one of our homes. In fact, although
it may seem a little unusual . . ."

"Nothing about you seems unusual," Benny interrupted
with a smile.

"We, Ramona and I, would like for you and Becky, as
well as Coyuntura and Yones, and Mrs. Schmidtbauer, to be
godparents and spiritual advisors to our daughter when she
is born. In case you hadn't heard, Mrs. Schmidtbauer will
be accompanying us on our first visit to Mexico."

"Sophie?" Benny seemed more than a little surprised.

"Yes. Old people are highly venerated by the Indians, and Yones sensed in Sophie an extremely powerful spirit of growth and regeneration. That's why her garden has done so well. Coyuntura and Yones asked her to travel to Mexico with us to bless their tribal fields, and she has agreed to go."

"Well, I'll be damned," Benny murmured, more to himself than to Henry. He focused again on the young man. "It sounds like you're all done with your baseball career."

Henry shook his head. "Actually no, I'm not. I think baseball has been . . ." he paused for a second, searching for the right words, "an introduction."

"An introduction?"

"It may not be the correct word, but it's the best I can do." Henry smiled and shook his head sheepishly. He took a sip of coffee and looked carefully at Benny. "I found out that my father, my biological father, was a mathematics professor at North Carolina State."

Benny's face registered his surprise. "You told me that . . ."

"That I never knew my parents," Henry said, finishing Benny's sentence for him. "That's true; I never did. I had been told, when I was in the army, that the county registrar's records, records that would have identified them for me, had been destroyed in a fire. But Mr. LeClair's private investigator discovered who they were." Henry sighed. "He even found photographs of them shortly before I was born."

"I'll be damned," Benny murmured. "Are you . . ." He paused, searching for words, "I guess I'm trying to ask if you're . . ." Benny paused again, unable to articulate his concern for Henry. He shrugged. "You know what I'm trying to say, don't you?"

Henry nodded. "Yeah, I know. It took some getting used to. My mother was a student of his." He smiled shyly. "Her name was Veronica. Veronica Mason."

"A good name," Benny said softly.

"I think so. Unfortunately, Mr. LeClair's investigator ran

into a stone wall on any background for her. He thinks she was probably an orphan herself. Apparently she was just a sophomore when she got pregnant and dropped out of her classes. The university archives don't have any of her academic records, her original application, nothing. Obviously, it was a different story with my father."

"I can imagine."

"He was married . . ."

"Any children?"

Henry nodded. "Three. Anyway, the investigator found a faculty colleague of his, retired now, who was willing to tell the whole story. My father . . ."

"What was his name?"

"Randall. Louis Randall. According to the colleague, my father acknowledged paternity and even promised to contribute child support after I was born. Unfortunately, just as my mother was approaching full term he was killed in an automobile accident. She went into early labor, there were complications, I was born, and she died. Meanwhile, Randall's wife had his body cremated and immediately began denying that her husband was my father. In fact, the investigator thinks there's a good possibility that right after his and my mother's deaths she paid someone at the university to have all my mother's records expunged from the university's archives. Whoever it was did a good job, because it's as if she never existed, at least not as a student at North Carolina State." Henry shrugged. "Randall's wife died of cancer about five years ago, and it doesn't appear as if their children have any idea that they have a half sibling."

Benny sat stunned for several seconds. "I've got to tell you Henry, that is, with a doubt, the damnedest story I have ever heard." He looked at his and Henry's empty coffee cups. "I know it's a little early, but I'd say a beer is in order." He got up and brought out two cold Coronas. Handing one to Henry, he took a long drink and sighed. "So you're going to return to the Oakland A's?"

Henry nodded and sipped at his beer. "Mr. LeClair re-negotiated my contract two days ago." He shook his head in honest wonder. "For more money than I could have imagined in my wildest dreams."

"And you're going to live here in the off-season?"

"Here and in Mexico." Henry smiled sheepishly. "You see, I know you don't agree, but I'm not letting go of Arthur Hodges, or perhaps I should say that he's not letting go of me. I believe that Gunter was right, that we, you and Becky, Gunter and Sophie, Al and Ruth," he paused for a second, "Ramona and I, were all brought here for a purpose."

"Only in America," Benny muttered, pleased in spite of himself. "When are you going back to Oakland?"

"In a week. Ramona and I promised to take Sophie down for a quick trip to Mexico first. Then Ramona and I will drive up to Oakland to finish the season."

Benny took another long drink of his Corona. "By the way," he asked casually, curious in spite of himself, "what do you suppose the young Indian woman, Yones, sensed in me?"

The faint beginnings of a smile traced across Henry's face. "Perhaps it would be better if you asked her yourself when she and Coyuntura come up to christen the babies." He paused for a second. "I will divulge, though, that she found you to be exceptionally interesting, to say the least. Perhaps, even," Henry's smile broadened, "a singularity."

The sun seemed loath to disappear behind the Sacramento Mountains, and in the final moments before it succumbed to the immutable Newtonian laws of motion that govern the universe, it flooded the eastern reaches of the Mojave Desert with a remarkable bloodred light. Benny and Becky sat on the patio of what had been Ruth's trailer, Benny with a cold Corona, Becky with ice water. It had been two weeks since

Henry and Ramona, together with Sophie Schmidtbauer, had disappeared into Mexico.

"Any day," Becky assured Benny as she shifted uncomfortably in the Adirondack chair. "This baby's going to be born any day now."

The thought pleased Benny to no end and he was about to say so when they both heard the sound of a pickup truck approaching the trailer. Seconds later it hove into view, a dusty blue Ford of indeterminate age with a battered California license plate. A youngish man debarked and smiled at them.

"Howdy," he said, brushing dust from his jeans. "I'm looking for the Soldier."

"Soldier?" Becky repeated.

"Yes, ma'am. Soldier. At least that's his nickname. Henry Spencer's his real name, but I and the rest of the boys always called him Soldier."

"And who might you be?" Benny asked pleasantly.

"I'm Bobby Clarke, a teammate of his from the A's."

"Have a seat," Benny invited. He held up his sweating bottle of beer in an unmistakable invitation.

"Yes, sir, I'd love a cold one," Bobby said. "I drove down straight through from Oakland." He accepted the proffered beer and sighed, obviously exhausted. "Left before dawn this morning."

"Unfortunately," Becky said, "Henry and Ramona aren't due back until the day after tomorrow. They're still in Mexico."

"Communing with the dead," Benny interjected dryly.

"Hush," Becky chided gently, seeing the look of consternation on Bobby's face. "He's teasing you," she assured the ballplayer.

"Well, dern," Bobby said. "Preacher Brown sent me down to make sure the Soldier got back to Oakland as quick as possible." He thought for a second. "I guess I'll have to call him tomorrow and let him know we won't be back for a couple of days."

Benny took a long drink of his beer. "How've the A's been doing in Henry's absence?"

Bobby shook his head. "Poorly. We've lost a bunch more than we've won, the suits are all hanging around the club-house upsetting everyone, and the team has got to bickering with each other most of the time. It ain't exactly been pretty." He drank half his beer in one long swallow. "I guess I'd sorta hoped my last season would have been . . ." he paused, looking for a word that it quickly became clear he wasn't going to find, "*nicer,* I guess."

"Your last season?" Becky asked.

"Yes, ma'am. Preacher's already told me not to get too settled in Oakland, if you know what I mean. Anyway, I thought after I came over to the A's, and the Soldier was heating up the league like he was, that, you know, I'd be going out a winner." He laughed quietly. "Welcome to the bigs, kid."

"What are your plans?" Becky asked.

Bobby shrugged. "Don't know. I sort of figured this was going to be my last season playing ball anyway, but hell, I've never knowed a ballplayer who could plan much further ahead than the next road trip. Maybe I'll ease on down here to the desert and just sit around for a spell." He laughed again. "If it was good enough for the Soldier, maybe it'll be good enough for me." He finished his beer and looked at Benny. "What's he been doing here, anyway?"

"It's a long story and you've been driving all day. Tell you what we'll do." He pointed to the trailer he and Becky had just moved out of. "That trailer's vacant. And clean. For now, why don't you get a good night's sleep. If nothing else, spending two or three days here on the edge of the Mojave waiting for Henry and Ramona to get back from Mexico will give you a chance to decompress. And believe me," he smiled and winked at Becky, "there's a great deal to be said for decompression. Besides, you'll be my first official tenant. Actually," he amended, "my *only* tenant until Henry and Ramona and Sophie Schmidtbauer get back from Mexico." He pointed to the two Airstreams, their sides reflecting the deepening reds thrown off by the setting sun. "And, since you're a friend of Henry's, if you decide to move back here after the season's over I'll give you the first month's rent free."

Bobby stood up slowly. "I appreciate it," he said, turning toward the trailer that was to be his new home. He paused for a second and looked back at Benny. "You know," he said with a smile of understanding, nodding to himself as if to confirm the truth of his sudden epiphany, "you talk just like the Soldier."

The last of the sun's penumbral glow disappeared behind the Sacramento Mountains and, almost as if turned on by a switch, the vaulted heavens were aglow with the light of countless stars, woven together by the silky, pulsating arms of the Milky Way. An owl hooted from somewhere behind Benny's trailer and in the middle distance a coyote barked, a tentative questioning cry: *Are you there?* Almost immediately she was answered and canine laughter filled the desert air.

Oakland, California

Preacher Brown, sitting at his incongruously small wooden desk in his underwear and shower shoes, lit a cigarette and set about the task of penciling in a lineup for the game. He hunched over the desk as he worked, laboriously printing each letter of every name, much as he had as a schoolboy in Enid, Oklahoma, more years ago than he cared to think about. He paused frequently to sip from a glass of milk, laced with a healthy dollop of scotch, and to run a hand over what little gray stubble remained of his hair. He put his pencil down when he got to the number four position on his lineup card and spiked the glass of milk with another generous shot of Scotch. Narrowing his eyes against the smoke rising from his cigarette, he picked up the pencil, touched the point to his tongue, and slowly, deliberately, printed SPENCER, H. Never a particularly contemplative man, he knew, without even having to be told, that this season was his last as a manager, and he thought briefly of all the lineup cards he had filled out over the years. It was a task he enjoyed and a privilege he jealously guarded. When filling out lineup cards he kept his office door shut, excluding not only other members of his coaching staff but also players, front office personnel, the press, anyone who might happen to wander in and thoughtlessly intrude upon his privacy. Only when the lineup was complete did he open the door and allow kibitzers into his inner sanctum. Today, though, he had other business to attend to. When he completed the lineup card he opened his office door and grabbed the first person who walked by.

"Get into the clubhouse and tell Spencer I want to see him in my office," Preacher ordered Scotty Harrison, the young assistant equipment manager. "Now." Slamming the door in Harrison's face he returned to his desk and his milk-and-Scotch.

"We're back safe and sound, Skipper." Bobby Clarke had called him at home late the night before to report that he and Henry had arrived back in the Bay Area from Needles. "Whoa," he added, somewhat breathlessly, "and guess what?"

"Don't fuck with me," Preacher had warned, his low, threatening tone calling to mind the baring of fangs. He had no idea what sort of surprise Bobby was eager to reveal, but he knew, if Henry Spencer was involved, there was little likelihood it would please him.

"No, no, it's not like that," Bobby had hastened to assure

him. "Henry and Ramona got married three days ago." Pausing for a heartbeat, he added, "In Mexico." Another heartbeat. "By an Indian."

Preacher would not have been particularly surprised had Bobby informed him that the ceremony had been conducted by Martians on the dark side of the moon.

There was a knock on the office door.

"Come in," Preacher bellowed.

"You wanted to see me?" Henry's head appeared in the partially opened door.

"Get in here." Preacher pointed to a wooden chair in front of his desk. "Close the door and sit down." He paused for a second, taking a drink of milk-and-Scotch while Henry sat down. "Are you ready to play ball?" he asked abruptly. No *welcome back,* no *how've you been,* no *hey, it's good to see you.* Just, *Are you ready to play ball?*

Henry smiled. "Yes, sir."

Preacher waited a second to see if Henry would say more and then grunted, a sound meant to convey approval, however meager. "You've always had some damned queer ways, but you never had much to say, leastwise not to me." Preacher looked Henry in the eye. "That's one thing I've always liked about you," he said, his tone of voice implying that there weren't too many others. "You been staying in shape?"

"Yes, sir."

"Good. You're catching today and batting cleanup. Bell's pitching."

Henry nodded but said nothing.

"I understand you're married now."

"Yes, sir. Ramona and I got married in Mexico."

"Did you get your old place back?" meaning the house above the campus of the University of California. Preacher didn't particularly care but felt he had to ask for form's sake.

"No, sir." Henry shook his head. "I took a room in a small boardinghouse in Berkeley, down on the flats. Ramona stayed in Needles to help a friend have her baby. Depending on how things go, she may not get back up here before the end of the season."

"That's fine," Preacher muttered, clearly uninterested. "You ready to play ball?" He had to ask one more time.

Henry stood up, knowing the interview was over. "Yes, sir, I'm ready," he said.

The grass, watered and freshly mown in that checkerboard pattern peculiar to putting greens and major-league infields, glistened in the afternoon sun like a field of emeralds. Bay Area newspapers had trumpeted the return of the Soldier and fans began streaming into the ballpark as soon as the gates were opened, a full hour-and-a-half before game time. As the crowd grew, its energy ebbed and flowed, waxed and waned, its attention seeking a focal point. A critical mass was finally achieved at about the time the National Anthem was sung a *cappella* by a rock star from Seattle, newly released from a Bay Area inpatient substance abuse program. Obviously chemically impaired, she forgot many of the words and slurred most of those she did know, sending an electric charge through forty-two thousand fans who were first embarrassed and then outraged by the appalling performance.

Henry's return to the A's happened to fall on Bobble-head Doll Day, one of the numerous moronic giveaway promotions that the suits in the front office felt were needed to lure fans to the park. Although it had been made clear that only the first 20,000 fans through the turnstiles would receive Bobble-head Dolls, the subsequent 22,000 ticket holders were disappointed in the extreme. The first fistfight over possession of one of the dolls broke out in the left field bleacher seats just before the singing of the National Anthem and, viewed throughout the ballpark as it sprawled down one row and into the aisle before security could break it up, instantly ratcheted up the testosterone level throughout the park. The crowd was diverted shortly thereafter by the sight of the rock star moving unsteadily towards the pitcher's mound to begin her performance. The first Bobble-head Doll flew onto the field midway through the National Anthem, when it became clear that she was attempting to sing while high as a kite. The effect of the first doll, which landed on the third base line, called to mind the ubiquitous demonstration of nuclear fission popular throughout most of the 1950s: a single Ping-Pong ball thrown into a room full of rattraps loaded with other Ping-Pong balls. In less time than it took to say *National Pastime* the air was full of Bobble-head Dolls, all thrown by fans eager to be the first to bounce one off the head of the rock star from Seattle. As the confused singer was hustled off the field by a flying wedge of security personnel, the crowd headed enthusiastically for the beer concession stands, the anger of the nonrecipients of the dolls assuaged somewhat by the obvious patriotic fervor of the recipients.

A roar of approval rose when the starting nine of the A's erupted from the dugout and ran to their positions on the field. The sustained applause rose several decibels when Henry, the last man out of the dugout, walked to home plate and assumed the position of catcher. Dickhead Bell, undone by the noise, walked the first two batters on eight straight pitches. After the eighth pitch, a fastball that went into the dirt a full ten feet in front of the plate, Henry called time and walked out to the mound.

"Jesus, Soldier," was all Dickhead, his eyes darting wildly about the stands, could manage to say.

Henry put his hand on the shaken pitcher's shoulder. "William," Henry was the only person on the team who called Bell by his Christian name, "do you still have the hula dancer tie I gave you before our first road trip?"

"Huh?" Dickhead asked.

"The tie," Henry repeated. "The one with the topless hula dancer painted on it. Do you still have it?"

"Well, yeah," Dickhead responded slowly as he tried to remember what he had done with it. "It's at home." His eyes narrowed in sudden suspicion. "You don't want it back, do you?"

"No," Henry said, turning to return to the plate, "I just wanted to know if you still had it."

Dickhead, unable now to get the tie out of his mind, struck out the next three batters on ten pitches.

When the A's came to bat in the bottom of the first inning the crowd noise rose to a sustained hurricane-like roar. The first two A's struck out, swinging wildly on pitches outside the strike zone. Theo Carter, batting third, ran out a surprise two-out drag bunt, catching the pitcher, first baseman, and catcher completely off guard. Henry walked slowly from the on-deck circle to the plate, and with each step the noise level declined until, as he dug in and readied himself for the pitch, the stadium had become eerily silent. Players from both teams came up onto the steps of their respective dugouts to better view the confrontation. The pitcher took the sign from the catcher and cut his eyes to first, checking on Carter's lead.

Grass, Henry thought, stepping quickly from the batter's box, motioning to the home plate umpire for time. He felt suddenly as if he were dreaming, a dream so vivid and real that he could smell the freshly mown grass, could see and touch the precise geometric shapes delineated by the still-pristine chalk lines. He shook his head and, stepping back into the box, set himself to receive the first pitch. As soon as the ball left the pitcher's hand he picked up the spin, saw the seams rotating around a center axis, the ball beginning to curve through space. In his mind he suddenly saw an Einsteinian relativistic universe, grid lines deformed by gravity, the baseball curving inexorably as it passed through the gravitational deformity. *Spin,* he clearly heard a kindly, paternal voice say, *is one of the fundamental characteristics of subatomic particles.* Henry knew that he could predict the precise curvature of the ball based upon its spin and velocity and he began to swing the bat. *Can you see it, Son?* Henry heard the voice ask as bat and ball intersected at the precise instant in time that he had calculated. *Can you see the beauty of its flight?*

"Yes," he whispered, tears of joy streaking down his face as he rounded the bases. "Yes, Father."